Uncle John's Band

Books by Deborah Grabien

The JP Kinkaid Chronicles

Rock and Roll Never Forgets
While My Guitar Gently Weeps
London Calling
Graceland
Book of Days
Uncle John's Band
Dead Flowers *
Comfortably Numb *
Gimme Shelter *

The Haunted Ballads

The Weaver and the Factory Maid
The Famous Flower of Serving Men
Matty Groves
Cruel Sister
New-Slain Knight
Geordie *

Other Novels

Woman of Fire
Fire Queen
Plainsong
And Then Put Out the Light
Still Life With Devils
Dark's Tale

* *forthcoming*

Uncle John's Band

Book #6 of the JP Kinkaid Chronicles

Deborah Grabien

Plus One Press
San Francisco

Plus One Press

UNCLE JOHN'S BAND. Copyright © 2012 by Deborah Grabien. All rights reserved. Printed in the United States of America. For information, address Plus One Press, 2885 Golden Gate Avenue, San Francisco, California, 94118.

www.plusonepress.com

Book Design by Plus One Press

Publisher's Cataloging-in-Publication Data

Grabien, Deborah.
Uncle john's band : book #6 of the jp kinkaid chronicles / Deborah Grabien.—1st. Plus One Press ed.
  p. cm.
ISBN: 0-9844362-8-6
ISBN: 978-0-9844362-8-6
1. Rock Musicians—Fiction. 2. Musical Fiction. 3. Murder—Fiction.
I. Title. II. Title: Uncle John's Band
PS3557.R1145 U46 2012
813'.54—dc22

                                      2011962369

First Edition: April, 2012

10 9 8 7 6 5 4 3 2 1

*In memory of all those smaller Bay Area
venues, back in the day*

Acknowledgements

I had fewer wip readers on this one, but they were absolutely stellar: Anne Weber, Marty Grabien, Sandra Larkin, Hillevi Wyman, Andrea Lindgren and Alexandra Lynch. And of course, the nifty husband.

Uncle John's Band

Chapter One

For Immediate Release, from the desk of Carla Fanucci:

Guitar Wizard Magazine, in cooperation with Keep the Music Going and Lindyhop Productions, is pleased to announce an evening of music with the Fog City Geezers, on Friday, March 12, 8:00 PM, at the 707 Club, 707 Francisco Boulevard, San Rafael, California. All proceeds will go to Keep the Music Going. Thanks to the staff at 707 for giving their time! Tickets go on sale to the general public Wednesday morning at 9:00 AM, at $50 per head, four ticket limit per order. Tickets are for open floor, no reserved seating. The 707 has an official capacity of 1423, per San Rafael city fire code specifications. For additional information or media credentials for access to the show, please contact Carla Fanucci or Andy Valdon at info@fanuccipros.com.

"John?" Bree sounded wistful, anxious, a bit restless. "Anything going on?"

"Just a press release from Carla, about the 707 gig. Nice to be playing again." I looked up from my email. "Why don't you get something to eat? Instead of pushing that slop round the bowl? You're not going to eat that, and we both know it, yeah?"

Bree made a face at me. She was eating breakfast, if you want to call it that—what she was really doing was, she was pushing a wet mess around in her cereal bowl. She'd done me up some eggs and toast and fresh orange juice, but her own breakfast was flax seed cereal or something equally nasty. She didn't look to be enjoying it much.

But her mum had suggested it, something about it being good for Bree's diabetes or her immune system or whatever, and since her mum's a doctor, Bree'd gone for it. One mouthful had pretty much kicked this particular experiment out of doors. Bree being Bree, though, she was giving it a shot. She took a mouthful, chewed it, and made the sort of face that you get on postcards from Paris: those gargoyles on top of Notre Dame, you know?

She looked up and caught my eye. I was grinning; I could feel it.

"Bree, love, give it up, all right? Spit it out and get something you're actually willing to eat." Something touched me on the leg. I looked down at our Siamese, Farrowen, getting ready to do what she does best, which is be somewhere she's not supposed to be. "Does it really taste that bad?"

"It tastes like ass." She spat it out into a napkin, and headed for the sink and a glass of water. "No, I take it back. It tastes like feet sautéed in ass. I can't believe my mother thinks this stuff is edible. She must be out of her mind. I wouldn't feed it to the cats—Farrowen! Get off the table! John, would you please stop laughing and push that cat off...?"

Bree got busy with a bagel and some sugar-free jam, and I went back to my email. Nice peaceful morning, in San Francisco. There was sun coming through the bay windows, touching Bree's hair, and that gave me a pang, all right. A year ago, less than

2

that, her hair had still been the rich dark auburn I always saw when I closed my eyes and thought of her. I mean, yeah, it had been fading; she's in her late forties, and she'd been going grey at the edges. But still—auburn.

It was nearly white now. She lost all the colour over a few long months in London, helping me get something that looked like my health back after a heart attack and infection had nearly dumped me. It had sucked for me, but way worse for poor Bree. We'd been stuck in a city that had bad associations for her to begin with, in a house she had nothing but reasons to hate. Plus, she'd been blaming herself for my heart attack in the first place.

Not a good winter for either of us. At least the heart attack had waited until the last night of our tour to hit. Even a week earlier would have cost the band a fortune.

But I'll tell you what, I'm alive. I made it back. Hell, I'd even got a sort of bonus out of the whole mess: the fact that they'd stuck an ICD in my chest meant I didn't ever have to deal with the annual MRI again. My first visit with my San Francisco neurologist after we'd got home, she'd practically accused me of giving myself the heart attack just to get out of doing the MRI, and yeah, I really do hate the fucking things that much.

I checked down the rest of my email. More press releases, a nice casual one from the 707 Club staff, one from Guitar Wizard, one from someone named Star Woodley at Lindyhop Productions. None of them were half as good as Carla's—the one from Lindyhop had a subject line that was all upper case letters and about nine exclamation points—but of course, it's not fair comparing anyone to Carla. No one out there does media as well as she does it. She's brilliant.

The toaster popped, and Bree got some decent breakfast, finally. She munched, I deserted my email and read some news sites instead, all three of our cats did the ankle-rub thing they do when they want food, around Bree's ankles instead of mine. Nice peaceful morning, broken up by the ringtone for a hit song I'd written for Blacklight, "Remember Me."

"John?" Bree started to get up. "That's your cell."

She has issues with the song, and that's honestly a damned shame. For her, it's always going to bring back the memory of me on the floor at Wembley, with her mum the surgeon telling her not to touch me, me about to go into ventricular fibrillation and Bree asking me to hold on, don't die, her mum getting ready to shock me back to life. "Remember Me" was what they'd been playing on the Wembley sound system. It's like her own personal soundtrack from Hell.

I don't blame her for not wanting to hear it. I'm not dim and I get why it's tricky for her, but, see, for me it's just the opposite. It's a sort of yell of triumph: *yeah, I beat the odds, still here, you hit me with your best shot and I took it, sod off if you don't like it, mate.* So we've got this weird little silent tussle happening: she wants me to get rid of the ringtone, replace it with anything else in the world, and I'm hanging on to it. What it comes down to is, I jump to answer my cell a lot faster than I used to.

"I'll get it." I'd left it in its charger, in Bree's office alcove, just off the kitchen. "You finish your breakfast."

Her shoulders were hunched tight. I hate seeing that, her being tensed up that way, but at least I knew why, this time. She'd relax as soon as the song stopped, and she did, the moment I clicked the phone open.

"Uncle John?" It was about the last voice in the world I would have expected. "It's Solange."

"Oi! Hello, love." I saw Bree's head jerk up, and grinned to myself. She doesn't get jealous—no reason for it, and she knows it—but I could see her running through the shortlist of people I'd call "love" on the phone. I caught her eye, mouthed *Solange* at her, and watched her go from puzzled to pleased. "Everything all right, then?"

Solange sounded pretty pleased herself. "More than all right, actually. I'm in San Francisco, with Dad; we're at the Fairmont. He's just getting out of the shower. I told him I'd ring you and Aunt Bree."

"You're in San Francisco? Here, hang on a minute, let me get your aunt in on this, yeah?"

I headed back to the table, and hit the speaker button. I could hear voices at the other end, that echoing thing you get over a small speaker, when both ends have it on. I sat down, and settled in next to Bree.

"Solange? Still there? Luke? Oi! What brings you to Fog City, mate?"

"Hey, JP." Luke Hedley, Blacklight's other guitarist and one of my best mates, was sounding about as mellow as I'd ever heard him. "Solange not tell you the news yet, about her getting accepted at the Chef's Academy? Ouch, what was that? You step on one of the cats?"

"Sorry. That was me." Bree had squealed, a high-pitched piercing little noise that sent the cats in all directions. She'd lit up like Regent Street at Christmas, as well. "Solange! You didn't tell me you wanted to be a chef! Last I heard, you had no idea what you wanted to major in. What happened? What made you decide you wanted to cook? And when did you apply to SFCA?"

"It was because of you and Uncle John, actually." She paused, just for a moment. "And because of Karen, of course. I mean, you and my stepmother both having diabetes, and then what happened to Uncle John at Wembley—it focussed my attention, I guess. I just suddenly got it, got what I really wanted to do. So I looked at a few schools, and this was the one I picked."

"You want to cook?" Bree had an odd look in her eye, very intent. "You've really got a pull to do that?"

"Well—it's not so much about cooking to just cook, not really." Solange had obviously thought it out. That didn't surprise me—she's always had a good hard-headed streak. But she wasn't hiding her enthusiasm, either. "It's more about nutrition, about wanting to cook in a way that makes food work for people with nutrition issues. What I really want is to open a restaurant some-day, where anyone with special food circs can walk in, sit down, and put together a five-star meal right off the menu. You know what I mean? Things like a low carb diet, or allergies, or high cholesterol, or diabetes. I've been reading a lot of medical stuff, about all those things. I don't think professional food people think about that enough—I mean, I can't remember ever seeing a top restaurant that had anything like that on the menu. And, well, I *am* thinking about it. So I applied to SFCA and they put me through some hoops and I guess I jumped through them the right way, because I'm in."

"Oh, wow." Bree was smiling, something she doesn't do much, but there were tears in her eyes, too. Solange had made her mist up. It suddenly hit me, just how beautiful Bree really is. She seems to get more gorgeous every year. Blows my mind. "Solange, you know what? You rock."

"Doesn't she?" I could picture Luke, the way he was looking at his daughter just then. "Anyway, we're here getting her a place to live, getting the paperwork signed, doing bank transfer stuff, all that. I was wondering, you two fancy having dinner with us to-night? We've got to go deal with the admissions office today, but we've got all sorts of stuff to talk about…"

We ended up having dinner in Sausalito, just across the Golden Gate Bridge. We've got a favourite spot over there, a great Italian restaurant called Angelino's, right on the water. On clear nights, you get a view of San Francisco that can leave your jaw on the tablecloth, and we got lucky that night; the fog held off until late. We hadn't ever brought Luke or Solange here be-fore, and they were gobsmacked by it.

While we were waiting for plates of food, Solange and Bree got deep into foodie tech talk, and Luke and I had a nice natter of our own. He'd mentioned that they were in town for another week, finding Solange a flat, and something popped into my head.

"I've got a notion." The waiter was hovering, with breadsticks and soft rolls and dipping oil. "You fancy sitting in with us for this gig we're doing Friday night? It's me and the Fog City Geezers, up at the 707 in San Rafael. Benefit show, for Keep the Music Going; Guitar Wizard's got a hand in it, so it'll be well-produced. Me, Tony, Kris Corcoran and Billy Dumont from the Bombardiers, and a harp player we work with, if he's available—bloke called Jack Carter. Nothing major you'd have to get down—we do a lot of old standards and the occasional Bombardier or Blacklight tune."

"I was hoping you were going to ask that." He grinned at me. "You realise, we've got an octopus connection, here? With the gig itself, and with the 707?"

I blinked at him. "Sorry, Luke, not following. What in hell's an octopus connection?"

"A creature with a lot of legs." He let the waiter finish and head off. "Lindyhop Productions is one of the promoters for the show, aren't they? I got an email this morning, from Norfolk Lind—he's the bloke behind Lindyhop. You meet him yet?"

I broke off a chunk of warm bread. It smelled brilliant. I saw Solange's nose twitch, and she grabbed a piece for herself. "Never set eyes on the man. What I can't suss out is why the name's so familiar. Friend of yours?"

"Not him, his son." He nodded at Solange, who looked up and turned bright pink. "And not my friend, my daughter's. Curt Lind is the frontman and guitarist for Mad At Our Dads. They won the Best New Artist Grammy last year, remember?"

I thought about it for a minute, looking back. The *Book of Days* tour had been a monster, nearly two years on the road, and a hell of a lot had gone down.

The double CD had sold over fourteen million copies to date, and was still selling at a scary pace. We'd had three number one singles off it, and we'd locked up the first three Billboard singles slots, first time in history anyone had ever managed that. The tour left us with so much money, we hardly knew what to do with it all. Luke had fallen in love with a sweet woman named Karen McElroy; he'd remarried after eighteen years of being a widower and a single father, and got himself a Type 1 diabetic wife and a handful of a stepdaughter in the process. Bree had been diagnosed with type 2 diabetes. And the band had hired the last man on earth I wanted around on a regular basis to be our head of security, after we'd lost the perfectly good head of security we'd had for twenty years.

The tour had also broken some hearts, not to mention a few necks; we'd had someone stalking the tour and people had died because of it, including members of the band family. Plus, there was my own little tin cupola, the heart attack on the closing night of the tour, back at Wembley Stadium.

So we were talking about more than two years of my life, but it was really more of a highly compressed surreal jumble, sort of a blurry rock and roll *Guernica*, complete with a soundtrack. I keep most of my memories of the tour in nice little individual compartments. So much had happened that putting them in compartments was the only way to access them.

I thought for a moment, and there it was, the memory of the night Blacklight swept the Grammys. I remembered watching the way Solange stared at Curtis Lind on the green room monitors; I remembered thinking she looked as if she'd lost her heart, or at least her inhibitions. Mac had wandered in while Lind was accepting his band's award for Best New Artist, joking that he was glad he and his band had been nominated in one category Blacklight wasn't competing for—I remembered that, nice and clear. Mac had actually teased his goddaughter about having the sense and taste to get the hots for the frontman. And of course, that was the night Bree's mum Miranda had rung me from San Francisco, to tell me Bree was in hospital with pneumonia...

"Right." I lifted one eyebrow at Solange. "You two get together, then, you and Curtis Lind? Nobody told me that."

Solange mumbled something. She was still bright pink, which, by the way, looks really bizarre on a pale blonde. I wondered if maybe she hadn't had to take a bit too much teasing about having a boyfriend. After all, her godfather being Malcolm Sharpe, she'd probably heard it all. Mac's got three claims to fame: fronting Blacklight, activist humanist politics, and being one of the horniest men in rock and roll, or maybe on earth.

Luke was looking amused, but he looked indulgent too. That was a good thing. Solange is our only band baby, and if she'd hooked up with a druggie, or someone who knocked her about, there would have been hell to pay. But it was pretty clear that Luke had no problem with Curtis Lind. "Curt's a good kid. They're local Bay Area, the family is, from Marin. Curt went to Santa Cruz. Plus, his dad's been a promoter for, shit, about twenty years. That's Lindyhop Productions. Supposedly they do a lot of gigs around here, city and South Bay, and some Marin County. You never did business with him, JP, maybe with the Geezers? I was hoping you could tell me a bit about him."

"Never even heard of him. Sorry."

I lifted an eyebrow at the two women; they'd stopped talking about food and were both quiet, listening to us. Solange was still pinkish, she was chewing on her lower lip, and she wasn't meeting anyone's eye. It took me a moment, but I suddenly got it. "What? Dad not quite as cool as his son?"

"That's what I'm trying to sort out." Luke wasn't smiling anymore, and he was looking at his daughter. "Thing is, Curt doesn't like him. They only speak to each other if they have to. And yeah, I know a lot of dads don't get on with their sons. But I still want to know."

9

"So do I. But I'm not dating his father, Dad." Solange's voice was a bit too loud; a couple of heads turned, and then turned right round again. She dropped her voice. "And you like Curt, right? You keep saying you like him."

He dropped a hand over hers. "Yeah, love, I really do. Nice kid, and talented as hell. I'm just trying to get the big picture here, Solange. And this really hasn't got much to do with Curt, it's about business. If we're going to be investing in the same club, there's a lot of money involved. If this bloke's going to be my business partner, I want to know who I'm dealing with. But suppose Curt's dad asked you about me—you think you'd be as negative about me as Curt is about his father? I hope to hell you never feel that way about me."

Solange shook her head. I turned and stared at Luke.

"Hang on a minute. Investing in the same club? What's all that about, then?"

"Didn't you check your email this morning?" He looked surprised. "You were on David Walters' list—I saw your name."

"Not all of it. You rang just as I was getting to it, and I never looked at the rest. It probably came in after I shut down. What's going on, Luke?"

"Well, you know the 707 Club's up for sale, right?"

I already knew where this conversation was going—if David Walters, Blacklight's UK operations manager, had his name on an email, it meant the band's corporate entity was getting involved. David heads up that division of Corporate. And there was only one way I could think of that happening that made any sense. "Yeah, I know. They've been looking for a buyer ever since Paul Morgenstern went to prison. Hadn't thought much about it, though—fundraising by way of gigging's more my thing. That's what the Geezers show on Friday's in aid of. So, Blacklight planning on investing? We want a piece of the 707?"

The food had arrived and our waiter was directing traffic, boss-ing a couple of blokes with trays. They know us there; Bree being a caterer and me being pretty well-known locally, we get the star treatment. Luke picked up a fork.

"Yeah, David's looking for the okay from us—a majority share. Problem is, there's already a bid on the table. Way less than ours, but it was there first, and there's some sort of clause we might not be able to get around. And David rang me up just before you got to our hotel—he says the other party's being pigheaded."

"Right. Let me guess." Local promoter, son dating Luke's daughter, money on the table, one of the last remaining venues in the Bay Area in that size and capacity range. Plus, it was in Marin County, and that made it even more valuable. "Lindy-hop?"

"None other." Luke took a mouthful of wine. "You can see why I want some gen. Oh, and yes, of course, I'd love to sit in with the Geezers. Norfolk Lind will be at the show Friday night. We'll meet him then."

In the three days between dinner in Sausalito and the show that Friday night, we ended up having a busy week. First order of business was showing Luke and Solange all over San Francisco. Luke's actually familiar with the city; he'd spent a full month here, back in 1997. I've got good reasons to remember that visit of his.

When I first got diagnosed with multiple sclerosis, before we managed to get it under some sort of control, there'd been a question of whether I'd be able to carry on with Blacklight. After all, the band is one of the most successful acts in music history, and that means touring. The Beatles found out back in the Sixties that you can't stay on top if you don't tour, and the band and our management learned from that.

I didn't know if I could do it. My hands were numb and tingling, I could hardly stand up for more than a few minutes without myokimia or ataxia kicking in, and carrying a nine-pound

11

Les Paul for two hours per show didn't even seem possible. So there was the question I was asking myself: should I leave the band, let them find someone younger and healthier?

I'd stopped boozing and lost my heroin addiction as much for my mates as for Bree or myself. I'd dedicated half my life to working with Blacklight, but I didn't know if I could keep it up. And there were probably twenty brilliant guitarists out there, queued up and waiting for a shot if I left the band. I wanted to be fair.

Luke wasn't having any of that. Bree and I had barely had time to even accept the diagnosis—we were both still reeling—when Luke rang up from SFO. I've never forgotten that; he sounded flat and calm, the kind of voice you weren't about to argue with, and he told Bree one of us needed to be home to let him in, as soon as he got a cab into the city. Of course Bree and I went down to get him—we were rattled and off-balance but, like I said, there wasn't any arguing with that voice, and anyway, he was already here. He spent the next month at Clay Street, learning damned near every lick I play for Blacklight, basically.

Back in those days, my first wife was still alive; even though I hadn't seen Cilla in fifteen years, I'd never bothered going through a formal divorce, and Bree—right. To say she was insecure about it would be like saying Antarctica gets a bit chilly in the winter. She had this almost obsessive need to stay invisible around Blacklight; she was fine with Tony Mancuso and the rest of the Bombardiers, the local friends, but Blacklight, what she saw as my rock stardom, that was something else entirely.

It took me twenty-five years, and one really bad week where Bree went missing, to understand that, in her head, me not divorcing Cilla meant that I valued Cilla more than I valued her. Sounds insane, because Bree, well, everything in my world that isn't music is all about Bree, and it always had been, from the minute we'd got together. But that's what she thought, believe it or not.

I get a lump at the back of my throat whenever I think about that visit from Luke, what he did, how Bree dealt. All she wanted was invisibility, but she stepped out of the shadows and welcomed him in. She fed him, drove him places, opened up, worked with him. She helped him nag me and bully me, and she left us both alone when we needed to be just me and Luke. The bottom line was simple: Luke wasn't letting me leave Blacklight without a fight, because he believed I belonged with the band. And Bree believed what he believed, because she knew, bone-deep, that I wouldn't bother staying alive without playing, and staying with Blacklight would keep me playing.

So they tag-teamed me, the pair of them. Bree went against every instinct she had to do it, and Luke—a single dad, still grieving for Solange's mum and with a young daughter on his hands—had taken a month out of his life to come help me, because he was my mate and he wasn't willing to let the disease take me down. I wasn't thinking about it at the time, not in those terms, but I'm pretty sure the fact that he'd lost Viv less than a month after the initial diagnosis of ovarian cancer had something to do with him refusing to lose me, as well.

So I kept playing, and I stayed with Blacklight. And yeah, trust me, I know damned well that I'm lucky in the people who love me. I'm a jammy sod, all told. Hard to get luckier.

The day after that dinner at Angelino's, we did the tourist thing. We took pictures of Luke and Solange at the Cannery, at the top of Pacific Heights with the Bay and Alcatraz behind them, out at the Cliff House at Ocean Beach. One of the coolest things about it was watching Solange fall in love with the city; she just *got* it, the way I'd just got it, my first trip in.

Luke knows San Francisco. But Solange didn't know the place at all, really, and taking her around was a particular sort of fun. Bree has this Grand Tour she likes to give people who haven't seen the city properly. What she does is, she stuffs them in the

Jag and drives them to the most amazing views she knows. Since she's a San Francisco native, she knows where all the best spots are, the ones only a native knows to look for.

But this was a tour with a purpose, and that meant Solange had to pick a neighbourhood she felt comfortable living in. She had a list of stuff she told us she needed to think about. For one thing, she wanted to be close to her school; SFCA operates out of what used to be an old warehouse in SOMA, about five minutes' walk from the Bombardiers' rehearsal studio on Freelon Street.

The drive round the SOMA area had her wrinkling her nose. Not where she wanted to be. Fortunately, San Francisco's not London. In terms of size, it's quite small, really, and that meant she could opt for another part of town and still not have to stress over getting back and forth to her school.

We headed over to North Beach next. Right from the moment we came out of the Broadway tunnel, she dug it. You couldn't miss it—she loved the energy and the colour and the noise. We parked, got out of the car, and watched her fall completely in love. It was neon sign levels of obvious.

She zipped up her coat against the weather—March in the Bay Area, we were just getting over some major rains and it was still cold. She spent about a hundred dollars at City Lights, had an Irish coffee at Vesuvio, giggled at the porn shops, flirted with the blokes standing out front of the eateries trying to charm people into coming inside and trying their food or their naked dancers, and made a happy noise when she saw there was an Afghan restaurant right on Broadway.

We followed her from point to point, just digging it, you know? Luke was digging it, as well; it had to be a relief she'd finally chosen a career and a school anyway, because she'd been wandering around the planet looking at schools for a good three years now, and it had driven him nuts. But he really loves his daughter; seeing Solange happy always does it for Luke.

14

It was all looking good, but what really sealed the deal was a shop window. We'd turned up Columbus and were heading toward Grant Avenue, when we passed a shop that sells dishes and whatnots from Tuscany, and that was it, Bob's your uncle, game over. Solange went through the shop door like cat hair getting sucked into a vacuum cleaner. Five minutes of touching hand-painted dinner plates and urns with lions on them, and that was it, done deal. Right round that point, Bree and I grinned at each other, and Solange started asking what the chances were for getting something with parking, because Curt Lind lived over the bridge, in Mill Valley, and unless Luke fancied the idea of her spending a lot of time on the back of Curt's motorbike, she was going to need a car...

We had the next day off from playing local tour guides for the Hedleys, because Luke hooked up with a rental broker. I didn't ask, but I suspect he got the name and number from Carla—the fact that she's four hundred miles from San Francisco wouldn't keep her from knowing the perfect person to talk to for listings in North Beach. She probably knew their phone number, their shoe size and their dead grandmother's favourite song. Hell, the bloke probably owed her a favour.

Wherever Luke got the name from, he and Solange told us they were off the next morning after breakfast with the broker, to look at possibilities in North Beach. Bree got back to some research she said she wanted to do. She'd been into something for the past few weeks, from right around the time I'd told her that if I didn't start playing live again, maybe some small local gigs with the Geezers, I was going to go totally off my nut. I mean, yeah, I know a heart attack takes time to recover from, but this sitting on my hands and doing nothing was driving me fruit.

I'd expected her to argue with me. After all, Bree's spent thirty years worrying that I was going to keel over and die on her, and this last time, she'd come way the hell too close to being right.

But she didn't argue, she stayed quiet, and I could tell she was thinking. Bit surprising, that was, but I figured she's sussed that I was serious, about not playing being worse for my health than a few hours of making some live music with my mates. Besides, it was exercise, you know?

It was right after that she'd started wandering all over the internet, writing things down in one of the notebooks she keeps stashed all over the house. I had no clue what that was about—she was being very mysterious about it, but she'd tell me when she wanted me to know. My guess was, she was going to present me with a list. I couldn't imagine of what, though.

In the meantime, I rang up Tony Mancuso and the rest of my mates in the Fog City Geezers, and told them about Luke being in town and wanting to sit in for the show on Friday night. That led to what that kind of conversation always seems to lead to: half the local music community wandering in through our front door, and Bree stopping whatever she's doing so that she can feed them.

The thing about the Fog City Geezers is, it's my band. Blacklight had already been a successful four-piece combo for a few years, when they asked me to join. The first major tour I did with them, we were actually supporting their fifth album. Blacklight is Mac and Luke's band—they founded it, and until *Book of Days*, they'd written pretty much every song. I'd shocked myself, not to mention Tony, during that last tour, when I finally realised something I'd never even looked at before: I've never seen myself as a full member of Blacklight. That's totally my own thing. The rest of the band doesn't agree, but it seems to be how I feel about it. In my own head, I'll always be the new kid, the add-on.

The Geezers, though—that's different. That's my band, and there's no question about it, none at all. I put the Geezers together, I handle the bookings, I talk to the crowd. I'm the only guitar up there, unless we've got someone sitting in. I even sing

16

some lead vocals, something that'll never happen with Blacklight, not even for the songs I write. With the Fog City Geezers, I'm the frontman.

So when Jeff Kintera, the interim manager from the 707, rang me to ask if we'd consider playing a benefit up there, I said yes, straight off. It wasn't a risk, committing the band to doing the gig, not with everyone else in the Geezers except our occasional harp player being members of the Bombardiers. They were home at the moment, not in the studio or touring. And hell, they'd all come to see me after Bree and I'd got back from my recuperation period in London, and all of them wanted to know if the Geezers were still on as a band. I told them, fuck yeah, we're still a band, and soon as something comes up and I'm a little steadier on my pins, we'll go rock the house. Bree was glaring at me at the time, but I'd meant it.

Everyone showed up within a few minutes of each other, and Kris and Tony brought their wives with them. That made things easier for Bree, because Katia Mancuso and Kris Corcoran's wife Sandra are about her tightest friends—she'd actually got very close to Karen Hedley, as well, but Karen can't exactly pop in for a cuppa and a natter, not from the Hedley farm in the UK. Bree closed down her computer, went into serious bustle mode in the kitchen, and put together a table full of food. Really good food, too. She never brings anything else to the table.

"Bree, that was great. I'll never understand why JP doesn't weigh four hundred pounds." Billy Dumont had finished eating, and was doing an interesting tap-tap thing on the table with his fingers, a tricky little timing pattern. It's as if he's holding drumsticks 24/7. "JP, do we have a set list for Friday night? We adding or changing anything, or is Luke going to be okay with whatever? Either way, I'm thinking we ought to rehearse a set, give it a runthrough. And man, I have to say, you're looking a lot better than you were last time I was here."

"What Billy said." Kris was nodding. "When was the last time we were over here—like, a month ago? Shit, you look about a thousand times better. Bree's doing something right."

"Yeah, well, Bree does a lot of things right." She was sitting next to me, and I slid one hand under the table, and patted her thigh. I watched a small smile tremble up and then fade out; she was nice and pale, which was her way of blushing. "I'm good, you know? Ready to get off my arse and blast the paint off the walls somewhere. I'm thinking we could lean the set toward some good crunchy bluesy rock—don't know if Luke has a guitar with him, but I've got a pair of PRS axes upstairs he can use…"

We headed down to my studio. Yeah, I know, it sounds like some stupid bullshit sitcom, total stereotype, letting the women do the washing up while the blokes go off and work, but the truth is, Bree really gets narked with people mucking about in her kitchen. She probably let Katia and Sandra help her carry things, but beyond that, she'd have made it clear that she wanted them to sit down, stay out of her way, and let her get on with it. It's her turf, no interference welcomed.

We got about an hour of solid playing in, blowing the dust off our chops as a functional band, and we needed it. After all, we hadn't gigged together for two years, and even though a musician doesn't forget how to play, the trick of synching up to other musicians is something else entirely. Once we got hooked in, though, it started coming faster and easier, and by the time the basement door opened and Luke walked in, I was feeling a lot less worried about sounding like a garage band at the 707 Friday night.

"Oi!" Luke waved at everyone, and grinned at Tony. They'd got to be good friends during the *Book of Days* tour. "Haven't seen you since Wembley—I just gave your wife a hug, so don't tell Karen. Sorry I wasn't here earlier, but my daughter's now officially a student at the San Francisco Chef's Academy, and I've

18

just signed a shitload of papers to get her a place to live and something to drive for the next three years. Remind me to check my bank balance when I get home—this city's bloody expensive to live in. Or is that just North Beach? Because the one-bedroom condo I just co-signed for is going to run her about four thousand dollars a month."

"Must be one of the ones at the top of Telegraph Hill." Bree had poked her head in; she was holding a cell phone. "John? Sorry to interrupt, but can I talk to you a minute?"

I raised an eyebrow at her, our usual signal: *you planning on telling me who it is?* But she shook her head at me, just a tiny movement. That's the other half of that same signal, that no one else in the room needed to share, or that she felt off about it for some reason.

"Right. Luke, I'll get a PRS from upstairs, unless you fancy thrashing away on one of my chambered Pauls. Be back in a minute, yeah?"

I followed Bree out, and up the stairs. My cell gets crap reception downstairs, anyway. Up in the kitchen, Bree turned and set the phone down.

"Sorry—I just didn't feel like sharing this one with anyone but you. That was Patrick Ormand. He already hung up."

She didn't look worried, and I relaxed. It takes me a minute these days to remember that Patrick doesn't work for the police anymore—he works for Blacklight. Actually, she looked more amused than anything else.

"Right. What's he after this time?"

She grinned, a full grin. "You're going to love this. He's apparently opening his own detective agency, and he wants to hire me to cater the kick-off party."

Chapter Two

For Immediate Release, from the desk of Carla Fanucci:

Blacklight Ltd. UK, acting in conjunction with Keep The Music Going, today announced the acquisition of a majority ownership share in the 707 Club in San Rafael, California. There will be no interruption of the club's day-to-day operations.

The deal includes full funding for a state of the art upgrade of the facility and equipment, over a two-month period. It also formalizes the appointment of interim club manager Jeffrey Kintera to permanent status. Blacklight Ltd. will work closely with the consortium of minority owners to ensure that Marin County continues its tradition of providing affordable world-class music in an intimate venue...

"Good evening, and welcome to the 707! I'm Jeff Kintera and I want to thank everyone for coming out tonight. We've got an incredible show for you, just waiting to happen: JP Kinkaid and the Fog City

Geezers, with special guest guitarist Luke Hedley of Blacklight. Are you all ready to rock and roll?"

"Full house out there." Luke handed his Strat to Doug, one of the two Bombardier roadies who come out and work every Geezers show, and watched Doug head out with it. The crowd was going nuts—I could feel the floor in the band room move under me, from all the foot-stomping going on out there, front of house. "I always forget how noisy and cheerful your local crowds get. Really great energy. The place sounds packed."

I was tuning my favourite stage axe, Little Queenie. Bruno Baines, the brilliant luthier who'd built her to Bree's specs as her wedding present to me, was actually in the house tonight. He'd stuck his head backstage, hung out for a few minutes, and disappeared out into the house. He'd told me he just wanted to say hello, but that was rubbish—he wanted to make sure I was taking proper care of the guitar.

"Yeah, it sold out pretty much the minute the tickets went on sale. Anyone meet the other new owners yet?"

"Well, you've met me." Tony was grinning. He'd bought in to the 707 himself—good job, too, since I was the only local member of Blacklight, and I had quite a long list of things I'd rather do than dealing with business and finance, like watching paint dry, or eating my own head. "But not the Lindyhop people. Are they here tonight?"

"No clue." Luke flexed his wrists, stretched his legs and rotated his ankles; I heard them crack. "Crikey, I'm getting too old to keep up with my kid. Be glad to get home to Draycote and Karen. If the Lindyhop people are here, I haven't been introduced, but I wouldn't know them if I fell over them. When Solange and Curt get here, you can check with them. My daughter and her boyfriend are fashionably late."

"We are *not*." Of course, Solange had been pushing the door open just in time to hear that last bit. "Right, okay, I'm late. I'm

21

not used to traffic on the bridge at rush hour—it doesn't actually move, does it? And then I had to find a place to put Duke. Cut me a bit of slack, Daddy, will you please? Tony! Hi! Is Katia here? And where's Aunt Bree?"

"Table, right out front, just inside the backstage area." I strapped Little Queenie on over my shoulder. "Surprised you didn't see them on your way in. Who's Duke? I thought your sweetie was called Curt?"

"He is. I mean, I am."

He'd come in behind her, and no one had noticed. Now, that was interesting, from a frontman—knowing how to be invisible when it's someone else's turn in the spotlight. He was really easy with it, the kind of mellow I've come to associate with Marin natives over the years.

"Duke is that hybrid truck of hers, the Lexus. It's a practical music pun: Duke, duke, duke, Duke of Oil, oil, oil. Hi, Luke— wow, will you be really nice and introduce me? We've got one of my seminal influences in here right now, and I'm feeling shy."

Right, I thought, *last time you were shy, you were in nappies.* Four seconds through the door, and you knew what you were looking at: a born frontman. I can suss one of them mile away—not surprising, seeing as how I've spent thirty years onstage with Malcolm Sharpe. The vibe was there, with this kid.

It's a thing I can't describe, not properly—it's not ego or conceit, and yeah, those are two different things. It's not exhibitionism, either. There's some of all those things in the mix, but there's other stuff, as well. Maybe it's that a born frontman has a sort of mystical comfort zone, that not only keeps him comfortable, it pulls an audience in as well, seduces them, keeps them warm and right there with him. Kind of personal room to expand, you know? A real frontman can expand halfway into infinity. The trick is to not get lost in there himself.

Anyway, whatever it is, Curt Lind had it, in spades. And he

22

didn't even much look like a frontman—a skinny kid with a dark curly mop and glasses. But he had the vibe. The fact that he had the Marin County easiness thing to go along with the rest sealed the deal. And more than that: from what I'd heard of his band, the kid could play.

"Like hell you're feeling shy." Luke was grinning. So was Tony, and so were the rest of us. You couldn't not grin; there was just something about Curtis Lind that left you knowing that, by the time you'd spent a few minutes hanging out with the bloke, you were going to be in a good mood. But it was pretty obvious that Luke already knew everything I'd just sussed out. Not surprising, all things considered. He had to have been looking at Curt pretty damned carefully.

"No, I mean it, Luke. I feel like a blushing baby." Curt had been staring at me, not hiding it; now grabbed a fast kiss off Solange as she headed out in search of Bree and Katia. "Hey, babe—save me a chair?"

"So put your hands together and give it up..."

Luke was on his feet; the band was lining up behind me. "And, we're on. Go keep my daughter from getting too bored. I'll introduce you properly at the break."

"...the Fog City Geezers!"

Right. Showtime.

It was a really good show. Luke and I have been playing together so many years, we fall straight into each other's rhythms, and of course he was just as familiar with Tony, now. The *Book of Days* tour had created that musical tie.

And the rhythm section, Billy and Kris, are always rock-solid. Jack Carter's an intuitive harp player, a huge Sonny Boy Williamson fan, and that made him a Mac Sharpe fan, which meant he was as familiar with Luke's work as he was with mine.

We'd settled for a blues-rock tilt that night, with a hard edge to it. That fit my mood and Tony's as well; he'd been into a major barrelhouse headspace recently, and we were into feeding that. The bluesy thing also worked with Luke's Strat—it turned out that he'd brought that one along for the trip, because like me, he never goes anywhere for more than a few hours without a guitar. We did a couple of country-blues things as well, and he let the Strat do what it's supposed to do: all Strats do that honking quacking thing, but Luke had a '57 vintage with him, three single coil pickups. He could have been backing up Johnny Cash or Hank Williams or Patsy Cline with that axe—it's got a brilliant voice for country music.

We ended the first set nice and strong with a cooker, Bill Monroe's "Rocky Road Blues." Every time we play that one, I ask myself why we don't do it more often, because every version has been shit-hot, just burning down the house with it. We've never done a weak version of it, ever. We nail it every time. It did the same thing tonight that it always does: left the crowd yelling and psyched and shouting for more.

I got Little Queenie off from around my neck, handed it to one of the roadies, and stepped up to the mic. I'd had Bree at the edge of my vision the whole set—that's automatic with me, if she's at the gig, I have to know where she is—and she'd been dancing up a storm. But she's been to enough Geezer gigs over the years to know when we've hit the set closer, and she'd already headed backstage.

"We're going to take a short break." The rest of the band was already offstage, and the crowd was noisy, hooting and yelling. I raised my voice. "Right, calm down, we'll be back in a bit. And thanks for coming tonight—you're a great audience, and it's a pleasure to play for you. See you in about twenty, all right?"

The band room was a lot more crowded than it had been when we'd gone on. That always happens, but tonight it was seriously cramped in there, crowded enough that I had to edge my way through the spillover out in the passage. The 707 band room's not much bigger than our kitchen, and right now, it had the band, our families, and friends. Bruno was there; Jeff Kintera was backstage as well, talking to a man and woman I'd never seen before. He looked edgy, for some reason. Solange and Curt were backstage, opposite corner of the room, hanging out with Bree. They were talking to some bloke, with his back to the room.

Bree saw me, and waved. The bloke with his back to me turned round, saw me, and waved as well.

Oh, bloody hell. Yeah, now, why was I surprised to see Patrick Ormand...?

"JP? Hey, can I bug you for a minute?"

I turned back the way I'd come. It was Jeff Kintera, with the couple I didn't know. They both looked expectant; Jeff just looked nervous.

I'd dealt with Jeff a few times, and quite liked him—he knew what he was doing, he did it well, and he was easy to deal with. A lot of club managers are pushy prats who can't tell the difference between getting something done and power-tripping while they shit all over the rest of the staff, but I hadn't got even a whiff of that off Jeff. His staff seemed to like him, as well, and that's always a good way to tell.

"Yeah, sure," I told him. "Nice job out there tonight, mate. Good opening intro, and we ought to raise a nice chunk of dosh. What can I do for you?"

"I'd like to introduce you to Folkie and Star. Guys, this is JP Kinkaid. I know you have some things to talk about. I'll catch you later."

He edged his way through the crush. Off in corner, Bree was waiting for me. I nodded at her, and mouthed *two minutes, right there*. She nodded back, and I turned round to face the couple again. I offered a hand to the bloke; this had to be Folkie, but bloody hell, the poor sod must have had hippie parents, because what the fuck kind of name was that?

"Hey, cool, JP Kinkaid! Nice to meet you, finally. Did you get our press release about the gig tonight? I told her to send it, but I never heard back."

The bloke jerked his head at the woman behind him, pretty much the way you might expect him to nod at his dog. I was half-expecting her to step out in front of him and deck him—I mean, someone used that tone of voice on me, that dismissive, he'd be spitting teeth.

We were eye to eye. He was just about my age and just about my height, a skinny little bloke with a head of curly hair that probably used to be dark; his hair reminded me of someone else's, I couldn't quite place who. I got distracted by his eyes, anyway—he had the same sort of pale eyes Patrick Ormand has, just not nearly as scary.

The woman just stood there, not quite making eye contact with me. It was weird, you know? There was this tall faded brunette woman, normal-looking enough. There was nothing memorable about her at all, she could have been anybody and you wouldn't pick her in a crowd, but she had these restless eyes. It was as if she couldn't stand the idea of someone making her have to look at someone else too long or too deep. I suddenly remembered an email from someone called Star, at Lindyhop Productions, and I got who they had to be.

"Right. Yeah, I got it." I wasn't about to tell him that I hadn't answered the press release because who the hell answers press releases? Besides, that particular release had looked more like one of those spam things that want to sell me viagra or something, everything upper case and emphasised, as if she didn't trust people to figure it out on their own. "Norfolk Lind and—sorry, I don't remember your last name."

"Everyone just calls her Star." Crikey, maybe she really was his dog, letting him speak for her. Or maybe she was mute? "So, I was really hoping to sit down and maybe get a dialogue going, about what our joint expectations are for the 707."

I stood there, middle of a crammed band room, ten minutes before I had to get back onstage and I still needed a mouthful of food, just blinking at this bloke. He sounded like some sort of motivational seminar speaking, or something. I mean, get a dialogue going? Joint expectations? I hadn't got a clue what he was on about.

Bree saved me, of course. One second she was across the room, the next she was right there, at my shoulder.

"John? Have you had some food?" She nodded at Folkie Lind, turned, and was eye to eye with Star Woodley.

Her whole body went rigid, just for a moment. She does this turtle thing when she's tense, her shoulders hunching up—right that moment, and just for a blink's worth of time, you would have needed a diamond drill to carve your name into those shoulders, she was so tense.

Something passed between them. I know, sounds bizarre, but I could feel it, sort of a crackling little recognition thing. I could see it, too, because this Star bird, her eyes were flitting all over the place, but just for a second, Bree had her locked up.

I saw Star Woodley stiffen up. Then she relaxed, her eyes moving off again. But Bree didn't relax.

"Excuse us, please." Oh, bloody hell. Yeah, something was going on. Whatever it was, it wasn't friendly, and neither was my wife's voice. "John has to go back onstage in a few minutes and he hasn't eaten yet."

About half a second later, we were halfway across the room. Bree cut through the crush of people, with me in tow, and no one stopped her, or got in her way, either. She wasn't saying a word, and neither was I, but I managed to turn round and wave back at the Lindyhop people.

"Here. I got a plate of food together for you." She was shaking. What in hell was all this about? "Sit down and eat something, will you?"

All the chairs were full, but Patrick got up and gave me his. I ate, listening to conversations going on around me. Solange and Curt were making plans for a day trip up to the Wine Country, Napa and Sonoma, and Luke was coming up with ways to suggest that they take Solange's truck instead of Curt's bike. Sandra Corcoran and Katia Mancuso got into it as well, everyone tossing favourite places to eat, wineries, where to buy the best olive oil, back and forth. Even Patrick had an opinion.

It was just the kind of conversation Bree should have been right in the middle of, but she wasn't. She wasn't saying a word. What she was doing was staring across the room, catching herself staring, jerking her head, making herself not stare, staring...

She was dead silent, not a word, nothing. She might as well have not even been there: no one was trying to get her involved, no one seemed to be noticing that she wasn't with them. Invisible, you know? Just like old times. I didn't know what had brought that on, but I was damned if I was having it.

"Oi! Bree! Come back, will you please?" I reached out and gave her hair a light pull. "No hiding, lady. What's all this?"

"Nothing." She caught my eye, and went dead pale. "Sorry. Not a good moment. I'll tell you later, John, okay?"

I opened my mouth, to tell her *no, you being invisible again is seriously not okay and what the fuck is all this*, but I didn't get the chance. The lights flickered twice, and Jeff Kintera's voice echoed in from out onstage.

"Okay, everyone, here we go, welcome back to the second set..."

I shovelled the rest of the food down, and we headed back out. I pushed the weirdness at the break out of my mind for an hour, and we kicked the blues into a higher gear with a rougher, sharper rock edge. We got deep into it, taking the crowd with us. Once, looking up to make sure Bree was where I'd left her, I caught a glimpse of Curt Lind, watching what my hands were doing, and I remembered, Curt wasn't just the singer for Mad

At Our Dads, he was the guitarist as well. There was no sign of his father, at least not anywhere near our table, but I thought I caught a glimpse of Star Woodley—there was no sodding way I was believing that was her real name—flitting around next to Bree's table.

We finished it out at right round half past eleven, with a bone-crunching encore version of the Stones' "Satisfaction", complete with vicious little trade-off leads: Luke handling that world-famous lead riff, me coming in under it and ramming it home with Little Queenie, Jack Carter wailing away on harp, and Tony giving it the sort of piano the original hadn't had going for it, back in 1964 or whenever it first came out.

Up to the mic, thank everyone for coming. Offstage and into the band room, house lights up and some canned music playing. Doesn't matter what the venue is, you could be playing a stadium in Capetown or a folk club in East London. Those signals are the same everywhere: *show's over, drive safe, goodnight.*

The crowd in the band room was a lot thinner than it was at the break. Curt and Solange had already left; Solange had some sort of orientation or interview or something at her school, early in the morning. She hadn't ever driven the Golden Gate Bridge at night before, and she was dropping Curt off in Mill Valley, where he lived. Patrick had split, as well. Folkie Lind and his Human Shadow were gone, or at least they weren't in the band room. All the people I hadn't recognised at the break seemed to be gone, as well—all business as usual.

We waited for the 707 to empty out, for enough space for Bree to bring our car round to the dressing room door. And whether she knew it or not, we had a conversation coming up, sometime between now and sleep.

Two in the morning's probably not when most couples have the big conversations. And I'd bet money on two minutes after finishing up a really intense half-hour's worth of belly-bump not being most blokes' idea of good timing, either.

Yeah, well, I'm not most blokes, and me and Bree, we're not most couples, either. We seem to have most of the Big Talks in bed, and we always have done. Might be something about our bed being Bree's home turf; she has a thing about that.

So I was good with asking her about what had gone down with Folkie Lind's Human Dog, even though she was naked and still pinned under me. I hadn't bothered rolling over yet; since the heart attack, she wanted that skin to skin contact, as much of it as she could get, and for longer than she used to want it. I'm not talking about sex. I'm talking about afterward.

That whole thing, sex after the heart attack, that actually had a funny side to it. I didn't realise it right off—I was too busy learning to cope with having this bizarre little tickybox thing tucked into my chest—but Bree'd got clingy. That took some coping with, because she'd always been the one who fell asleep after a dozen orgasms or so, and I'd been the one who'd stayed awake and wanted to cuddle.

But we'd got back to sex, after a visit to the cardiologist together that left me laughing like an idiot and Bree pale as she could get, and I'd noticed the difference straight off. The sex was as good as it ever was. Hell, it was better, because she'd stopped worrying that I was going to suddenly conk out and die on her. And once she'd got that, once she accepted that the ICD took the worry out it, the sex got punched up a notch or ten. She got really intense about it; I hadn't realised quite how much she'd been missing it.

The change I noticed first was, she seemed to want my weight. It wasn't new, she'd always liked me up there for a minute or two afterward, but it used to be that, when I rolled over and off, she'd let me. Not anymore, though. Since the ICD surgery, didn't matter if she'd got where I wanted to take her or not—she'd have both arms round me, not letting me go, and legs as well, if she thought it would hold me there with her.

It couldn't have been comfortable, especially since she knew to be careful with that square bulge just under my left collarbone, but there you go. Since that first coming together after the heart attack, the sex might not have been as often as it had before, but it had got even more intense. And I'll tell you what, I didn't mind. The only thing in my world that comes close to being belly to belly against my wife with nothing in the way is making music.

"Nice gig tonight." I had my fingers laced through Bree's. That's a nice feeling, feeling her wedding ring against me, and knowing she was feeling mine on the other side. "Some new faces in the crowd to think about, though. What was all that with you and that Star bird, then? You know her from somewhere?"

Nothing, not a word. She tensed up under me, realised that I'd felt her do it, and tried to relax. It didn't work. I could feel every muscle in her body trying to not give away how stiff she'd gone.

I eased off her, and rolled onto my side, and she didn't try stopping me. I got one arm across her, and turned her to face me. There was some moonlight, coming through the bay window, just enough to make her look like mother of pearl.

"Okay. Bree, baby, what the bleeding hell is all this? You want to talk to me, please?"

"Fuck." She sounded miserable. "No. I really don't."

I let go of her, and sat up. I could feel one eyebrow climbing up toward my hairline.

"No?" The other eyebrow had gone up, as well. "Not an answer I think I can live with, Bree. Look at me, please."

Nothing, not a word. She wasn't meeting my eye, either; she was looking anywhere but at me. It reminded me of Star Woodley, the way her eyes didn't seem comfortable meeting anyone else's.

We've got plenty of landmines out there, me and Bree. Most of them had to do with Cilla, my first wife. But there are other ones,

31

just lying about, waiting to blow up in our faces. Thing is, a lot of those are still there and still dangerous because Bree got into the habit of hiding things, over the years. She hid herself from the world, but she hid things from me, as well. It was part of her invisibility thing, maybe the only thing that gave her any sense of control during the Cilla days.

Whatever was going on here, it was something major, at least for Bree. And I was damned if I was having anything blow up in my face or hers either, not if I could avoid it.

"Bree." I pulled her up next to me, and got her face between my hands. She had her teeth all the way into her lower lip. "Okay. Look, love, it's pretty obvious that some serious shit went down somewhere, between you and her. I don't know where it was, or when, or what, but if I've got to deal with this chick, I need to know exactly what I might be stepping in. So you need to talk to me, and I don't want to argue about it, either. What the hell happened, between you and Star Woodley?"

She started to cry.

I felt my heart want to do a little jittery thing, because sitting there with my hands cupped round her face, naked in the moonlight with her hair messed and tumbled from where I'd run my hands through it, she looked like a teenager again, or maybe a ghost. She wasn't shaking or sobbing or anything like that. There were just these two small lines of tears, running down her cheeks, splashing against my wrists.

"I hate this." Her voice was flat, remote, as if the only way she was going to get this out was by putting some distance between what she remembered and having to remember at all, never mind talk about it. Yeah, this looked to be one huge sodding landmine, all right. "I thought I'd never have to think about it or remember it again. I don't want to tell you. I hate this, I just hate it. I should have known there was no way I wouldn't run into Esther Woodley again. Fuck!"

"Breathe." I kissed her, and dropped one arm round her shoulders. I was filing that "Esther" away at the back of my mind. "Just let it out, love. Dish. It must have been bad, but I'm right here, yeah? Who is this bird, anyway? And what did she do to you?"

The story came out. With every word she said, I found myself more thankful for the regulator in my chest, because my heart would have been doing an Irish jig without it.

"It was when I was volunteering at Mission Bells Clinic, back in 1979." She was dragging every word. "There were some occasional volunteers, but really just three regulars, me and two other students. One of them was a guy in my class at school, Kevin something, I don't remember his last name. I don't know what happened to him—I lost touch with him, after they stopped letting me volunteer at the clinic. The other one was this girl, a college student named Esther Woodley."

She stopped. I wasn't saying anything, not yet. Just the mention of the free clinic her mum used to run in the Haight-Ashbury had been enough to get my alarm bells ringing. There's some serious history there, for both of us. Bree was looking back into the past, and whatever she was seeing wasn't anything she wanted to look at. Her face was bleak.

"Esther—Star, she called herself—she hated my guts. Just *hated* me. Man, she'd have loved to see me beamed right off the planet. But no way would she ever actually have the honesty to say so— she was a total hypocrite. She'd suck up, be friendly, and then you'd find out she'd done something horrible behind your back. She was…I don't know if I can explain her to you, John. She's a type. She was one of those women with no sense of self-worth, so she'd get her sense of control by trying to manipulate everyone and everything around her so that she can claim to be a part of it. She wanted to be some local Rock Queen or something, everyone's personal confidante or BFF or some bullshit. Everything she said, she tried making it sound like it was something she'd discussed with some Very Important Whatever just before she got there. She was always talking about the sixties like she'd helped manage the stage crew at every gig, but she was just a couple of years older than me. She was maybe nine years old or something during the Monterey Festival, but listening to her talk, you'd think she was partying with Hendrix after the show, or something."

"Yeah, I've met some of those." I could hear foghorns, out over the Golden Gate; there wasn't going to be any light in the room at all, pretty soon, not if the fog was rolling in off the ocean. "It's okay, love. I'm right here. What happened?"

"I didn't know why she couldn't stand me, not back then. Now I think it was because my mom was in charge, that I was the one who got to go to all the gigs as part of the clinic support staff. Nepotism, or something—if mom needed a volunteer she trusted to work backstage at a local gig, I was the one she took with her. But it wasn't because I was her kid, John. It was because I was reliable."

"Yeah, you were." I was remembering Bree, that first time I'd seen her, taking care of a stoner who'd fallen on her head during the hurricane relief benefit we'd played, my first trip into San Francisco. "Competent, too. And Star wasn't?"

"Star was—oh, man." She swallowed, hard. "She used to say shit to me about Kevin, little things, *Kevin said blah blah*, and none of it was true, and then she'd turn around and tell Kevin I'd said it about him. She was pathetic. She could have discovered the cure for cancer and she'd still be not quite meeting anyone's eye and despising herself, and trying to fuck over everyone around her just to make herself feel important. But she was toxic, too. She was like this little black cloud, just dripping poison, her fingers all covered with poison and stuck in everyone's business."

"Wow." I held on. There was something coming; I could tell from her voice, from the way her shoulders had tightened up. "Yeah, she sounds a total slag."

34

"She was a fucking evil bitch. I'm betting she still is."

I jumped. She met my eye, finally, and the tickybox seemed to move under my skin, regulating my heart back down from the sudden stampede it wanted to do. That pure hate, that didn't sound like my wife. She usually bends over so far backward to be fair to people, she's in constant danger of hurting herself, and it doesn't matter whether they deserve it or not. Her nickname, one her mum and I both use sometimes, is Bree of Arc, or Saint Bree. Hell, she'd nearly gone to jail for ten years trying to be fair to Cilla...

We looked at each other in the dark, and she let it out.

"Ah, screw it. I'll give you the short version. The night you OD'd? The night I helped myself to that glassine envelope with the snowball in it and brought it over to you at the Saturn Hotel? Star Woodley was the one who told the cops about it. She was the one who called my mother to tell her that her daughter had proved unworthy of her trust."

I swallowed hard, and held on. Nothing to say, not yet. She wasn't done, not with this particular bit of her personal hell.

"I wasn't there to hear her put the knife in—I was downtown, being given the third degree about you and the missing dope—but I can imagine it. She must have wet herself when she realised what was happening, that she had a clear shot at getting rid of the boss's daughter and the biggest risk was maybe breaking a fucking nail making the phone calls. And hey, bonus! She could break my mother's heart, too. And tonight—*tonight*—she actually had the stones to come over during the gig, and try to sit down at my table and chatter, like we were old friends, like nothing had ever happened."

I'm not a visual bloke, and I've got virtually no memory of that night anyway, but I could see the picture in my head. Bree, the fierce passionate teenager I remembered, me with the withdrawal horrors, ringing up the clinic, getting her on the phone, babbling and incoherent. I'd told her that night that I would die without some snowball.

And Bree—she'd met me once, for two minutes, and I was married to someone else—Bree had risked jail without thinking twice, trying to help me. As it was, I'd OD'd, my heart had stopped, she'd done some CPR and got me started again, but everything that happened that night was still echoing down over thirty years, and here was another miserable little piece of the puzzle. The past, the bloody past—it never lets go.

"You sure about that, love? That she played copper's nark?"

Her face was twisted up, and I suddenly realised something. That landmine I'd been worried about, she'd stepped on that one all by herself. "Oh, hell yes, I'm sure. I'm not a moron, John. The cops wouldn't tell me anything, not about you or anything else. I was underage and things were really fucked up. But I asked my mother, after she took the blame for what I did. Star was in the clinic that night, doing some filing. She watched me break that damned locker open, and she didn't say a word, or try to stop me. She didn't even let me see she was watching me. She just waited until I was gone, and then she called the cops. And my mother. And now you know. This fucking local incestuous music scene, of course she'd show up. Just my luck. Why, why, why does she have to still be around!"

"Bloody hell."

I had both arms round her. Here it was, one more reason she'd stayed hidden so long; the local music scene is small and tight. No wonder she'd always been fine with having people over, but not with hanging out in dressing rooms. No wonder she was so fierce about her home court advantage. "Baby, I'm sorry this came up. Don't let her make you crazy, all right? Just because I might have to deal with her, that doesn't mean you have to. I'm not having her or anyone else make you crazy. That's my job, yeah?"

She was slumping now, a lot of the tension going out of her shoulders. Telling me about it might not have been pleasant, but it looked to have done her some good.

"Besides, there's one thing you haven't thought about." I knuckled her under the chin, and got her to look at me. Good job, since I was grinning. "You think you didn't enjoy meeting her again, imagine how she must have felt about it. I mean, if she was pissy over you getting to go to shows back in the day—well, you married a rock star. So who's got the advantage now? She probably crapped herself when she realised who you were there with."

That surprised a crack of laughter out of her, so loud it probably scared the cats, locked downstairs for the night. I slid down under the covers, pulling her with me, and we snuggled up. It had been a long day, and I was ready for some serious kip. I was definitely done for the night.

"John?" I was right at the edge of sleep, just far enough down so that her voice, very quiet and coming from just behind my shoulder, couldn't quite pull me awake again. "I'm really sorry."

"Mmmm." I made a mental note, to ask her in the morning just what she thought she had to apologise for. But sleep was hitting me head-on, and the night meds I'd taken just before we'd gone to bed had been waiting for me to let them kick in. "No worries. 'night, love."

I felt soft lips against my shoulder, just a goodnight kiss. One more landmine, exploded and out of the way. Someday, maybe we'd be done with the rest of them.

Chapter Three

I got a good long look at Star Woodley—as well as a look at everyone else with an ownership stake in the 707 Club—two days later, when I got dragged off to a meeting in San Rafael. That two-day lag was lucky, because before I got my first real look at Norfolk Lind, I got to really meet his son.

The morning after that conversation with Bree, I made sure she didn't need me helping with the washing up after breakfast, and headed downstairs to the basement studio. There was a song circling round in my head, or the beginning of one: twelve bars, a break, twelve more bars, very rhythmic and sharp. I'd woken up with it making noise in my head and in the pit of my stomach, demanding to be worked on. When it got to the point where my fingers were tingling, I gave in, let Bree know I had to go scratch a serious musical itch, and went for it.

It was music this time, not words, something deep and crunchy and with a sharp bite to it that felt more like politics than sex; it was outrage-pissy, not sex-edgy. I had the feeling that lyrics for whatever it ended up being were going to take some doing.

I don't generally write angry music. Not sure why, but it's probably got something to do with my blues background. My feel for blues has a lot to do with deeper stuff that's not based in anger. Not sure what it is: acceptance, maybe, or resignation.

This one felt angry, though. Music has a way of telling you what it wants you to do with it, if you've got the ears and you listen. If you argue with it, try to drag it down the wrong road, you end up with shite. I learned that a long time ago, to let the music I do write have its own way. That wasn't a luxury, back when I was a sessions bloke.

I plugged in my Zemaitis, Big Mama Pearl, and started noodling with the run. I've got a sizeable collection of guitars, acoustic and electric. I'm a spokesman for Gibson—there's a line of Les Pauls they put out recently, chambered down to half their original weight, that's named for me. I've even got a few guitars sent on spec, not Gibsons, that I don't play. I dig all of them, and Little Queenie most of all, but the truth is, Big Mama Pearl has the most range of audio attitude of any of them.

This particular run I was working on seemed to want noise and grit and a lot of interesting sustain at both ends of the range: a high snarly growl at the high end, and something like a lion waiting in the tall grass in the jungle, a deep vicious roar on the bass E and A strings. I wasn't sure if I was playing rage or outrage, or maybe both.

I'd been down there the best part of two hours, with the Korg recording every note I'd played, when Bree stuck her head round the door, with my cell phone in one hand. I glanced up and hit the standby switch.

"Oi, love. Sorry—lost track of time. Is that for me?"

I stood up, stopped, and swore under my breath. Hip to ankle, both legs, I was shaking, and shaking badly.

I could have kicked myself. This was just the kind of thing that makes Bree nuts. Yeah, the little tickybox might get most of my attention these days, but that doesn't make forgetting about my multiple sclerosis the smartest thing I could do. There were little electric tingles sliding up both legs, and the balls of my feet were on fire. I sat back down, fast enough to rock the stool I was using.

"John?" She was right there. "What is it—the MS?"

"Yeah, a bit. Legs and feet. Half a sec, all right?"

I stretched, one leg and then the other, rotating the ankles, rubbing both thighs while I was doing it; everything hurt like hell. Yeah, I'd been sitting, but I'd had a guitar on my lap, and the Zemaitis is a damned heavy axe—up around eleven pounds. I'd been so into playing with the song structure, I'd forgotten about getting up and stretching. And of course Bree would know that—she knows how into the music I get. I'd be lucky if she didn't rip me a new one.

I started to get up, talking to my legs and feet the whole time, in my head: *right, okay, no shakes, we don't want to worry Bree and I can't do with her flipping her shit right now, come on legs, hold me up, good, keep it going...* "Okay. Better. Let's try this again. Who's the poor sod on hold?"

"Andy Valdon, down in Carla's office. And he can damned well wait." Bree had an arm under mine. Good—she wasn't going to give me hell, at least not at the moment. "Garden? Do you want help?"

She got me out the back door, and over to the nearest piece of lawn furniture. It's closer than the upstairs, and I couldn't take the call in the studio—there's no reception at all, thanks to all the soundproofing I'd put in to keep our Pacific Heights neighbours from organising a lynch mob. I didn't think my feet were quite up to going up and down the stairs anyway. Lucky for me, it wasn't pouring outside.

"Here." She handed me the phone, and kissed me. "I need to head back upstairs. Ring my cell if you need help?"

"Yeah, I will." I sat myself down on the glider, trying to keep the weight off my feet. "Andy? This is JP."

"Hi, Mr. Kinkaid—yes, this is Andy Valdon."

He'd been working for Carla for just a month or so. He sounded about twelve years old, though that might have been him calling me "Mr. Kinkaid." I hadn't met him yet, but if he really was twelve years old, he had to be a prodigy, because I couldn't see Carla hiring an assistant who wouldn't be able to handle the high-powered shit she'd be throwing at him 24/7.

"What can I do for you?"

"I was calling to follow up on an email I sent out this morning, to make sure you have all the details, about the owners meeting at the 707 tomorrow. The chauffeur is due to arrive at your house at one o'clock. Is that all right?"

"Hang on a minute—what's all this? I've been down in the studio, the past couple of hours. Haven't seen any emails. What are you talking about?"

"The ownership meeting for the new owners of the 707 Club." He sounded surprised. "I'm sorry, Mr. Kinkaid, I thought you knew about it, from David Walters. The email was confirmation."

"Gordon *Bennett!*" I thought about it for five seconds, and decided, *right, let's just nip this in the bud.* I don't like people making plans for me without checking with me first, you know? I get enough of that when Blacklight's on tour. "Sorry, mate, but this is a big hell-no. For one thing, this is the first I've heard about it. I don't do any of the Blacklight business stuff—bores me blind. I've always let Corporate handle money stuff, and I don't plan on changing that."

41

"But -" He sounded seriously rattled now. "But Mr. Kinkaid, Carla told me you were the obvious person to represent Blacklight's interest in the club. She said you were local -"

"Yeah, the 707's local to me, and yeah, I play there occasionally." I was seriously narked now. Carla must have gone off her nut. "That doesn't mean I want to play at being Donald Trump and hang out talking about money. Not my thing. Also, I live in San Francisco and the 707 is up in central Marin. I don't drive a car, and I'm not really up for making my poor wife drive me up and back again. She's got a life. Yeah, I know, you said something about a chauffeur. That's just for tomorrow, and there'd be days it wouldn't work with my schedule anyway. Carla knows that, and if David doesn't, she ought to have bleedin' well told him. Who in hell came up with this?"

That got him stammering, which would have been fine if that's what I'd been trying to do. Thing is, it wasn't. I was just trying to make damned sure no one got any brilliant ideas about me going and hanging out at business meetings, at the 707 Club or anywhere else. I've spent thirty-plus years trying to stay awake at Blacklight Corporate functions, and I was damned if I was going to let myself get guilt-tripped into having to cope with more business stuff. Bree handles all that at our house, anyway.

"I'm really sorry, Mr. Kinkaid." He sounded as if he might break down and start bawling any moment. "Carla told me that David Walters asked us to include you. I would never want to inconvenience you, or Mrs. Kinkaid, either. Of course I'll let David and Carla know that you won't be going. We'll cancel the car and chauffeur..."

Nice kid, sounded twelve, on the verge of tears and it was my fault. So, yeah, of course I ended up saying I'd go to the fucking meeting. Andy nearly fell over himself thanking me.

"I'll just confirm with the chauffeur, then? One o'clock, yes— he'll be picking up Mr. Mancuso too, on the way to your house.

Thank you, Mr. Kinkaid, and I hope the meeting won't be too boring..."

Oh, bloody hell. Last thing in the world I wanted to do. I was quite cross with myself, and the suspicion that I'd just been manipulated into it by the hand of a master didn't help. Between that, the MS playing me up and the fact that being interrupted mid-stream on the new song took me just enough out of it to shut it down for the time being, I was seriously pissy when I headed upstairs.

Thanks to the crampy shakes in both legs, I was moving slowly. I got up to the hall just in time to hear Bree open the front door, and from the sound of it, she was making the kind of noises she makes at unexpected company. Visitors were so not what I wanted right then that I had to bite back a groan. When I saw who it was, though, I dropped the bad mood and headed for the door.

Luke and Solange were just walking in. Curtis Lind was right behind them, and he had a guitar case in one hand.

Luke kissed my wife on the cheek, a nice hearty kiss. She let him, too—not only that, she kissed him right back. That was mind-blowing in a very good way, because even a year ago, she'd have let him, but her shoulders would have bunched up. She was definitely a part of the Blacklight family now; the two-year tour, my heart attack, I didn't know what had finally given her that comfort zone. I was just damned glad that something had done the trick.

Luke let go of her and caught sight of me, heading down the hall. "Hey, Bree. Oi! JP!"

"Mind the cats." I watched Bree getting everyone indoors and nudging the front door closed before Simon, the youngest cat, decided that a nice wander out in the afternoon fog was a good idea. Farrowen, Bree's Siamese, is no problem—she's smart enough to know how good she's got it indoors. And Wolfling, our oldest, is elderly; he spends most of his days curled up asleep on a soft surface. Simon, though, he's not only the youngest, he's a bit dim. "What brings you people out to the wilds of Pacific Heights? Solange, what, you bored with North Beach already?"

"Not a chance." Solange was hugging Bree, good and hard. It was funny, but she seemed to feel a whole lot closer to Bree than she did to her stepmother. That was peculiar, because okay, Bree'd been there with some sensible hard-headed advice when Solange really needed it, but still, she hardly knows Bree, you know? "Curt just bought a new guitar, and Dad and I thought Uncle John might like a peek at it."

"Sure." Curtis and I were eyeing each other. "Always up for looking at an axe."

That vibe I'd got off him, back at the 707 gig, that he was a born frontman who would usually leave you feeling good just because he could? Still there. There was more, though. It was a recognition, me and him, each of us seeing who the other one was, and what we were, were players. And it hit me suddenly: Luke had tapped that in his daughter's boyfriend, as well.

"Let's take that back to the kitchen. The island's big enough to hold the case, and we can keep the cats away from it." Bree sounded amused, pleased, and I glanced at her for a second. She smiled at me, a real smile, and this one stayed there a few moments. She'd seen it, that back and forth, that recognition; last time she'd seen that happen had been the day I'd got to meet the man who'd got me wanting to play guitar in the first place. And she loved seeing that happen.

"Great! I'm dying to show off this puppy." Curtis was watching us. I suddenly got the feeling that he'd seen it, her being happy for me. Not only that, I had the feeling he got why. The kid was about as sharp as they come, but sharp in a way I rather like. "Thanks, Mrs. Kinkaid. Lead on!"

She was heading down the hall, but she stopped and looked back at him. I got another jolt, because she'd read him, cover to cover. I could see it, right there in her face; she knew him, you know? And the only way she could have got him that fast, and that well, was if she saw another me.

"Call me Bree." She caught my eye for a moment, and pushed open the kitchen door. Luke, all the way at the back, held it open for the rest of us, and followed us in. "As much as I love being called Mrs. Kinkaid, it sounds kind of formal for my own kitchen. Besides, I'm damned if I'm calling you Mr. Lind. What are you, half my age?"

"I doubt it." Curtis hoisted the case up on our big maple block, face up, and I saw the "PRS" lettering stamped into it. I'd already sussed it had to be a PRS—they aren't my thing, but they're gorgeous axes, and Luke loves his. I was curious to see if Curtis Lind's new baby was in the same class as the blue waterfall Private Stock Mac had given Luke for a birthday prezzie. That would be a pretty good indication of just how well Mad At Our Dads was doing commercially.

"Here he is." Curt popped the case open. "This is Slim. Isn't he a honey?"

We all clustered round the guitar, sitting there on Bree's prep centre. I looked down at it and thought, right, there's a couple of questions answered. No, it wasn't in the same class as Luke's axe, nowhere near. But yeah, Mad At Our Dad was doing quite well for themselves. A PRS hollowbody doesn't come cheap.

"Mind if I check it out?" The question was just for manners; I was already reaching into the case. It was pretty obvious Curt wanted me to, because otherwise, he wouldn't have got Luke to bring him to meet us, you know? "I'm not a PRS bloke, but they're gorgeous guitars. I like the finish—hard to beat a good tobacco sunburst."

"I couldn't agree more. And the McCarty finish is the bomb." He reached out a hand and just touched the flame maple top. "Take a look at the back. The pattern's a wraparound."

"Nice." I slung it over my shoulder—he'd already put a strap on it. It had the usual PRS neck, a bit wide and fat. I ran the riff I'd been playing with, before the phone rang, and I saw both Luke's and Curt's heads jerk up and over, watching my fingers. "The blokes at PRS know how to do a properly gorgeous top. I like the way the curves echo the F-holes. And it's not heavy at all, really. I wouldn't mind hearing it plugged in. Anyone want to go downstairs for a few minutes? I've got my rig down there, and it's nice and warm. I was working on a new thing when I got called about this meeting tomorrow."

We headed downstairs, all of us, Bree and Solange as well. So I got to see the look that went between the two women when I turned the overhead lights back on, and Curt Lind saw Big Mama Pearl on her stand.

"Oh, holy mother of GOD." He sounded reverent. "Is that a genuine vintage Zemaitis?"

"Yeah, this is Big Mama Pearl. Wedding present from my lead singer, when me and Bree got married." Bree and Solange shot each other that look again: amused, sort of conspiratorial. Very female, you know? "Here, let's plug in. You want to try out the Zemaitis? She weighs a metric fuckload, but give it a pop. Luke, you want an axe, mate? Queenie's in the case."

What happened next—right. Not sure anyone who isn't a musician would get it, or believe it, but you'll have to take my word for it. Three guitar players, one small space, one piece of music I'd only just started even thinking about and feeling.

Sometimes, magic just happens. And that's about as much explanation as I've got for that, yeah? Except to say, thank God for it.

Five minutes of music. Luke was getting bitchy little slaps out of Little Queenie, and the guitar seemed to be digging it. And Curt looked like a bloke who'd died and gone to Guitar Paradise. The Zemaitis is a hundred-thousand-dollar guitar, one of the only ones ever customised after it was built; Tony Zemaitis did the work himself, before he died. It's got enough switches and toggles to pilot a fucking 747 jumbo jet.

Curtis Lind found every last one of them, and knew straight off what they'd do. I was right. This bloke wasn't just a frontman. He was a musician, bred in the bone.

Five minutes of music, the three of us jamming, and I was short of breath. Nothing to do with the tickybox, either; it was adrenaline or endorphins, or something, the rush I only get from sex or music. Some days, it's hard to tell those two apart...

"Wow." Curt was stoned. Seriously, he was high—he'd got the sort of buzz from that five minutes of music that I used to get from snorting eight or ten lines of snowball, before I went clean. He looked moony, totally blissed. "Does this have lyrics? Please say no."

"You got it, mate. No lyrics." I was watching him; we all were. The look on Solange's face reminded me of something, a kind of stab in the heart, and I suddenly got it: she was looking at him the way Bree looked at me, the way she'd always looked at me. One difference, though—Solange was happy. No shadows there, no baggage, no ghosts. "Why? Want to write some?"

"Yes please." He was dead serious, but there was something in his face, a kind of burn. "You don't mind?"

"Mind?" I flipped the amp to standby, and leaned back on my stool. Luke was watching us, Solange was watching us; Bree'd slipped out, probably heading upstairs to get my afternoon meds and a glass of water. "Have at it, mate. You're on."

You'd think, after that intense five minutes of guitar alchemy between the three of us, I'd be past being surprised by anything Curtis Lind pulled off in the way of music, wouldn't you? Yeah, well, I must be dim, because he wrote the lyric in eight minutes, and that surprised me.

Bree came back downstairs after just a couple of minutes.

Turned out she'd gone up not only for my meds, but also for one of the little hard-cover notebooks she keeps all over the house. I wondered if she was still working on whatever the Big Secret Mystery Project was, if having the Hedley contingent pop round unexpectedly had messed with whatever she was doing...

"Here you go." She handed me my pills and water, and handed Curt a notebook and a pencil. "Something to write on, unless you're one of those 'paper, how medieval, my Treo is hardwired to my gall bladder' kids.'"

"I love paper." He grinned at her, but the burn was still there, moving in his eyes and the way his face wanted to work. "Thank you very much. Aren't the pills for me too?"

"Cheeky bugger." I'd caught the shadow of a smile on Bree's face, but I was grinning outright. "You look stoned enough, lad. No drugs for you. You need me to run that riff while you're working the words?"

"Yes please. Luke? Can you play it a step down, sort of to the bass side? Or does anyone here play piano? Because you could do the bass run on that nice little Bechstein over there..."

Solange had grabbed one of the chairs I keep behind the Korg recording console. She was straddling it backwards, her chin on her arms, watching us: dad, uncle, boyfriend, about to saddle up, ride the music and come up with a halfway-decent song at the end of it, hopefully.

I headed over to the Korg—I'd turned it off when Bree'd come down with Andy's phone call. "Hang on a second. Solange, shove over, love—no, just for a moment. Ta."

I fired up the board's recording function, and got back to my own stool; my legs were still wobbly. Luke had grabbed Curt's PRS, and I grabbed Big Mama Pearl back again. He likes playing PRS axes, and I'd started the song out on the Zemaitis, so it was all good, you know?

In the meantime, Curt had pushed his glasses all the way on the bridge of his nose, and started off writing. I mean, his fingers were flying. He was completely concentrated on what he was doing; either that, or he was possessed. There's not much difference, now I think about it.

"Okay." He looked up, first at me, then at Luke. He looked to have forgotten that Solange was still in the room, or maybe even on the planet. I slipped a look over at her, and saw her watching him, just digging it, not minding: musician's daughter, and she knows how it works. "Can one of you give me that first twelve-bar run, with that nifty little extended beat at the end? Do it once, give me a second, then do it again?"

I ran it through, letting the Zemaitis bite and scratch: one run, stop. Luke had the PRS ready in his lap. Curt nodded at us, a nice clear signal—*play it again.* Luke caught my eye, nodded, and we came in together. Curt opened his mouth and sang.

"Boy's got his shoes off, eyes closed, feet crossed, lying in a public park, pretending it's a beach/Boy's just a dreamer, no job, no home can't even count the things that are out of his reach."

I hit the run again. There was something going on under my ribs, a big glorious noise, nice and happy. That feeling, the whole *nailed it, nailed it, got it, keep it going* thing, was just yelling. I remembered being down here with Mac and the Bombardiers, the first time we ever played "Liplock." That had felt just like this, and that time, we'd damned near melted the walls of the studio the first try. Luke hadn't been here for that one, but he was right there with me now. I could see it.

"Boy's got an iPod, no smokes, no hope, Panhandles cigarettes, maybe someone buy him a beer Cop says 'yo, son, pick it up and move along,' wherever he's going, he can't get there from here."

"Bloody hell." It was just a whisper, but Luke was grinning like an idiot. After forty years of writing music with Malcolm Sharpe, he knows when a song is coming together in a way you can't define, you know? "JP, play the break, will you?"

"You got it." I hit the break, a sharp little syncopation that sounded like ground glass on the Zemaitis. "Curt? What have you got, man?"

"*No place to go, nowhere to be.*" His face was smooth, tight, nothing showing except the blaze underneath, the one that comes with getting it down, getting it out, getting it right. "*The gutter or the morgue or the Arabian Sea, Just when you think you got it under control you're looking at the sky from the bottom of a deep dark hole.*"

Playing, synched up with Luke, I had a sudden memory, nice and clear: my first meeting with Bulldog Moody, a session giant most of the world had never even known about, looking at me and me knowing what was there in his head and in his heart, when he saw me pick up his Byrdland and play: *family*. This kid, Curtis Lind, was family, blood and bone.

"JP?" The newest member of the family was looking straight at me, bouncing on the balls of his feet, just the way Mac does when he's working out a lyric. "That little punchy thing you played before—can you play it again?"

"Right." I hit the strings, and stepped on my stomp box, a nice old Ibanez tube screamer. There was stuff going up and down my back, cold and fire. How the fuck had he nailed this so fast? "Here you go."

"'*cause it's Americaland.*" His voice had grit in it, and resignation, and some serious power. "*It's Americaland.*"

Bree came back downstairs after awhile. I felt a bit guilty about not realising she'd gone up, but she's been with me thirty years, and she knows how I get when I'm playing; it's not just daughters of musicians who get it. It turned out she'd been throwing together a scratch meal, and had come down to let us know it was there, whenever we wanted it. She'd made a nice basic pasta sauce and salad, and that meant the sauce could sit there simmering on the big Viking range until we were good and ready to eat it.

"So how's the song coming?" She took a look at my face, and

50

smiled. "Wow, okay, stupid question. How far along is it? And what's it about?"

"It seems to be about interstices. About how there aren't any places for people to just sit and *be*, anymore. About how we all have to keep moving, or else we have to do whatever the space we're in was designed for. No sitting in a parked car—you have to drive. No sitting on the beach—move along. And I think it's done." Curt turned round, saw Solange watching him, and went over for a good hard kiss. She tilted her head back, one hand slipping up behind his neck.

I looked over at Luke—reflex, that was, couldn't help it—and he rolled his eyes. But he was smiling. It looked like Solange had the full family approval for her sweetie. Just as well, because it didn't look to me as if Solange was planning on letting Curt go anytime soon. The girl was besotted with him.

"Done?" Bree was gaping at him. "You mean, you finished the lyrics? Damn, that was fast! Can I hear it? Did you record the first run-through?"

"We haven't had the last verses yet—at least I don't think so." Luke cracked his knuckles. "What we heard was the first half, I'd say. You have more, Curt, right?"

"I sure do." He ran one hand through his hair. It was almost as if the electricity in the process itself had made its way up to his hair; it looked like he'd licked an amp socket, or something. The curls had gone nonlinear on him. "Want to play it? Two verses, break, Americaland, repeat the same structure. We'll see if it's enough. It might need one more verse."

Bree pulled a chair over next to Solange. I looked at Luke.

"On three," I told him, and counted off. "One, two...."

...Boy's got his shoes off, eyes closed, feet crossed, Lying in a public park, pretending it's a beach/Boy's just a dreamer, no job, no home can't even count the things that are out of his reach...

Curt was planted. He had both feet anchoring him, and his

eyes were closed; it looked like he'd already memorised the lyric. He seemed to have forgotten about the reading glasses, because he'd pushed them up onto to the top of his head.

...Boy's got an iPod, no smokes, no hope, panhandles cigarettes, maybe someone buy him a beer/Cops say yo, son, pick it up and move along; wherever he's going, he can't get there from here...

I was locked up with Luke, the PRS and Big Mama Pearl holding it down. We'd been doing this behind a different frontman for a good long time now.

...No place to go, nowhere to be, the gutter or the morgue or the Arabian Sea/Just when you think you got it under control you're looking at the sky from the bottom of a deep dark hole...

Solange was watching us. There were all kinds of cool things going on in her face, watching us play. I had a sudden flash, a memory so close I could damn near touch it: Solange's mum Viv, years before Solange was born, hanging out at Draycote, watching Luke and me play. I'd been married to Cilla then, but I'd left her, headed for Luke and Viv's place to hide, left Cilla back in London with her dope and her addiction and her long slow spiral down. Still married, but over; I'd met Bree by then, cleaned up. In my head, I was gone.

'cause it's Americaland, it's Americaland.

Something moving caught my eye: Bree, reaching out and putting one hand over Solange's hand. Solange smiled at her, a gorgeous smile. She looks so much like her mum, it's scary.

...Boy keeps moving, hits the park after dark, hooks up with some kids, they got a campfire ready to go/Stories shared, so scared, the future's got its teeth bared, when nothing's all you've got, you figure you're the first to know...

Luke leaned in on the A, bending it, making the PRS talk. Curt opened his eyes, just for a moment, and grinned. Then he closed them again, looking for the song in his head.

...Do-rag, sleeping bag, try to keep the cold away, sticks and stones

52

and slugs, he can feel them on the ground below/Cops come, yo, son, no bed for you or anyone, pack it in, pack it up, you better pack your stuff and go...

He was singing it with piss and vinegar in his voice, matching the anger both guitars were putting out. Swaying on his feet, yeah, but never in any danger of toppling over, you know? He reminded me of Mac, that way. Both of them are as sure on their feet as a couple of cats. You need that, when you spend your working life prowling a stage.

...No place for you, no place for me, we're all running scared, from sea to shining sea/Just when you think you see the light of day the men in charge take the rest of your world away

'cause it's Americaland. This is Americaland.

He stopped, and opened his eyes.

"JP?" He nodded at me, and the glasses slipped off the top of his head and snapped back down across the bridge of his nose. "Does this work with the music? Is it what you heard in your head, when you were writing it?"

"Hell yeah." My fingers kept wanting to noodle that last little snap: *This is Americaland.* "Stone fucking perfect. Cheers, mate! But it's not done, you know? It needs another verse, something that ties it up and slaps the audience straight in the face with it."

"I'm on it." He wasn't writing anything down; whatever he was doing, wherever he was finding this song about the lost places where people used to be able to just sit and breathe and couldn't anymore, it was in his head. "Okay. How about this? Run one verse and one Americaland, as a tail—ready? Great."

...We've got the gloves off, pick your fight survive the night, think of what we used to have, and how it used to be/things are different now, dreams lost, what's the cost, how are we supposed to beat what we refuse to see...

In Americaland.

53

Chapter Four

As much fun as we'd had working out "Americaland" down in my studio, I wasn't dim enough to think the business meeting the next day would be anything other than a stone drag.

The hired car showed up right on time, with Tony and Luke in the back. Luke being there, that surprised me—I'd mentioned the meeting yesterday, and he hadn't said a word about planning on being there. I climbed into the car, waved to Bree on our doorstep, let the chauffeur close the door behind me, and lifted one eyebrow at Luke.

"Didn't know you were coming along for this. What, you get your strings pulled by Carla's wonder boy too? He's good at that, is Andy."

"No. Well—yes and no." Luke stretched his legs out; lots of room in the back of the car, fortunately. "I got an email yesterday, from this kid in Carla's office—Andy, is it? Damned thing confirmed me going to this do today. Problem is, I never said I'd do anything of the kind. First I heard about it was that email, and I didn't get that until late last night. I was going to tell him no, and by the way you might want to not schedule my time without my permission, but Solange asked me to go. She wants some feedback on Curt's dad that doesn't come from Curt. I was just telling Tony about it."

"I'm curious to meet Lind Senior. I like Curt." Tony settled back in his seat. "I like this car, too. Really comfy."

"So buy one." It was very weird; Tony'd had three years to get used to things like hire cars with liveried drivers, and five-star hotels. He'd done Blacklight's *Book of Days* tour as our guest keyboard player; suites at the Four Seasons, private planes, the lot. Blacklight's got no reason to do stuff on the cheap, you know? Not with the money we've accumulated over thirty years. And *Book of Days* is sitting square in the top five best-selling albums ever.

Tony had seen the same share of the tour revenues as the rest of us, for the CD and for the tour and merchandising as well. That meant he'd taken in over sixty million dollars.

The rest of the Bombardiers hadn't stopped teasing him, either, not since the day they'd found out what the numbers looked like. If Kris or Billy wanted to poke him, it was "Hey, look, here comes Bankcuso!" Their lead singer, Pete Resnick, had started calling him Elton. Tom Johannsen, their guitar player, tried hanging "Liberace" on him, but that one was mercifully short-lived. Tony lives in jeans and tee-shirts, no spangles or spandex in sight. I was still waiting for Tony to get them back; after all, since "Liplock" had been a massive seller, they'd all seen co-authoring royalties. It wasn't sixty million dollars, but it was still quite a nice little bundle. He could point that out to them any time.

Somehow, though, it still didn't seem to have sunk into Tony's head yet that, whatever else he might need to worry about from here to eternity, it wasn't going to be money. I caught myself wondering if maybe that was because his wife, Katia, handles all his finances, same way Bree does for me. Bree staying on top of all that means I don't even have to think about it. I can keep my head where it ought to be, on the stuff I care about, the music.

Of course, now I think about it, Tony's not even actually allowed to think about money. Katia's a complete shark; she knows where every penny is, every minute of the day, and the last thing she wants is Tony putting a hand in. She got really good at dealing with the money, because the Bombardiers are a very long-lived band and a damned good one, but they've never had the kind of drawing power Blacklight has, and they've never had a sniff at the kind of dosh Blacklight brings in. One gig on that last stadium leg for *Book of Days* had probably put more in Tony's bank account than an entire ten-month tour with the Bombardiers had ever done.

"Nah, I'll stick with my Range Rover. Limos and things are only cool if you've got someone else driving them." He was looking curious. "Someone fill me in on the deal with Curtis Lind's father. First of all, who the hell names their kid Norfolk? Are they from Virginia, or is this some weirdass Navy deal? Does he have a twin brother named Annapolis?"

"His brother's named Coronado. No idea if they're twins, though." There was no humour at all in Luke's voice. I started wondering just what Curt had said about his dad, for Luke to be this straight-faced. I mean, bloody hell, *Coronado*? "Curt's granddad was a Navy bloke. Curt hasn't mentioned him much, but the phrase *needed a fulltime assistant just to help him pull the stick out of his ass* came up a couple of times. Doesn't seem to be much love lost between the men in that family."

"Crikey!" I filed that one away. How Curt had turned out so

loose and funny might be one of those questions that never get answered, unless he'd got it from his mum. Genetics are really strange.

"So yeah, Norfolk's his real name." Luke yawned. "Can't really blame him for wanting to shorten that, personally, but don't ask me why he picked 'Folkie' for a nickname. Makes him sound a right ponce, doesn't it?"

"Yeah, well, if we're talking about why these people chose their nicknames, let's not forget about this Star chick. Bree remembers her from back in the day. Turns out her real name is Esther and she's got self-worth issues and copes with them by being the sort of hanger-on arranger hand-in-every-deal type. Sort of the 'I need everyone to know who I am and what I can do' thing. I'd be surprised if she doesn't really do much of anything—well, anything of any use, that is. Seems what she mostly does is cause damage."

I heard the bite in my own voice, just as Tony and Luke both turned to stare at me, and stopped. I couldn't help it—I was remembering those two lines of tears rolling down Bree's face, the way her voice had deadened out when she talked about what Esther Woodley had done. "Wow. Sorry. Bree's got some bad history with this woman, so yeah, I'm pretty biased. Not about to trust Star Woodley, not on the basis of what my wife told me. Right, I'll just shut up now."

"Whoa." We were crossing the bridge, heading north. There were a few boats out on the water, a long way down. I didn't envy them, not the way they were bouncing about. Tony's eyebrows were all the way up. "This chick tried pulling shit on Bree? That's seriously fucked up. Thanks for the heads-up, JP."

"Right." I was hoping they wouldn't ask me for details, because there was no way I was telling them. It wasn't my story to tell, you know? Seemed like a good moment to change the subject. "So who's going to be at this thing, anyway? Anyone seen a complete guest list?"

"God knows. I'd say the three of us, Lind and his whatever-she-is, probably the club manager—what's his name? Jeff Kintera, right. Maybe a 707 staffer or two—they aren't owners, but they're certainly affected by whatever happens." Luke thought for a second. "Oh, right, and maybe someone from Guitar Wizard. They bought a minority share, didn't they? I haven't seen any of the official paperwork, but that's what Carla's press release seemed to be hinting at. I don't know if any of the minority holders in this went out for venture capital—if they did, there may be a banker or two showing up today, as if the idea of this meeting wasn't already irritating enough. Tony? Any idea?"

He grinned. "Nope. The only small fry I know the details for is me. And all I did was talk it over with Katia, and she wrote the numbers on the pretty pieces of paper. She knows the details. For me, I could give a shit. I let my old lady handle the money at our place. But I couldn't resist having a piece of the 707. I've got a lot of history with that place, and I'm damned if I want to see it go down the crapper along with the rest of the venues around here, just because Paul Morgenstern turned out to be a crook. I love playing there."

We'd gone through the Rainbow Tunnel, heading north through Southern Marin on 101. One nice thing about never being the driver is, I get to look at the views. Thirty years of living here, and I never get tired of them. From the top of the Waldo Grade, you could see the Bay, the East Bay Hills and the San Francisco skyline, stretching out like something designed for the most perfect place on earth.

So yeah, there are definite perqs to not being behind the wheel. The Bay Area's got some serious geography; no matter what else is going on or going wrong, the views are always there. There's something comforting about that.

The rest of the ride to San Rafael, we didn't talk about the

meeting or the Lind family. We talked about music, about Solange settling in and becoming a San Franciscan; she was due to
begin at school for the summer session in about three months, a
lot of time to really figure out if she liked it here. It also gave her
and Curt some space to see how they were going to work as a
real couple. That was something they needed to find out fast,
too, because the circs were about to dump them into a situation:
Mad At Our Dads had just finished mixing down their new CD,
at the Plant in Sausalito, and they were going on tour, their first
time headlining, to support it. The CD's release date was July
and the tour was scheduled to start in September and run
through Christmas, right in the middle of Solange's first semester.
That meant she wouldn't be going.

"Wow." I was remembering back to those tours, the first few
years after me and Bree'd got together. "First major tour since
they got together, and she's stuck at home? Not easy on her."

"It'll be okay." Luke didn't seem worried. The car was pulling
off the highway, making the turn for the 707. "If anyone under-
stands the reality behind a touring band, it's my daughter. Solange knows about touring, and she knows about not being able
to go because she's in school—crikey, JP, how many tours did we
do when she was a kid? Four? Besides—well. You know who they
remind me of, those two? You and Bree. No, don't look at me like
that, I'm serious. Curt is Solange's first love, and yeah, my daughter's young, but she's got this depth to her. Reminds me of Bree,
the way she was back in the day: Completely focused. I think
Solange may have found the real thing, first time out."

I kept my mouth shut, and he sighed. "What the hell, I hope
so. I did, you know? With her mum."

I wasn't saying a word, not yet; I couldn't think of a damned
thing to say, because part of me hoped he was wrong.

I like Solange. She's a great kid. And one thing Luke didn't
know, couldn't know, was just how unhappy Bree'd been, most of

the time. I'd never understood that myself, not back then when I might actually have done something about it.

Luke didn't know about Bree's miscarriage. She'd kept it secret for twenty-five years. No one knew but Bree and her mum; I'd only found out because Miranda let it slip, and I finally got the story out of Bree. He didn't know she'd tried to do for herself with an entire bottle of my pain pills. He hadn't been there to see her, barely nineteen, having to toughen up because I was shivering on my knees with my head in her lap, crying like a baby because the need for a drink was so huge, I couldn't see or even feel anything else. He didn't know that she still talked in her sleep, still woke up sobbing from nightmares about me leaving and not coming back, still probably had a huge steaming mass of unresolved shit she'd never even mentioned to me, because she was all about protecting me, making my life easier.

He didn't know about the landmines. All he knew about was the love.

The chauffeur pulled into the parking lot, right near the stage door. There were quite a few other cars there; people had got here before us. I found myself wondering where they were going to put everyone, because if the band room at the 707 wasn't much larger than our kitchen, the manager's office, which was upstairs in the gallery, made the band room look like Oracle Arena.

I'd been up there once or twice before, after Paul Morgenstern had been sent off to prison. If my memory was working, the office held three people, providing none of them felt like moving or even breathing too deep. If you turned sideways, you risked bruising someone—that's how small the place was. Besides, unless someone had done a major reorganisation in there, the room was thick with piles of papers, old records no one had got round to sorting out yet.

"I wonder where they set up for this?" Tony was thinking the same thing I was, apparently. "I've been in that upstairs office. I've seen bigger linen closets."

"Only one way to find out." The chauffeur had the door open, and Luke had uncoiled himself out into the parking lot. He's a tall bloke, Luke is. "Thanks—we should be out in about an hour, unless we're all dead of boredom. Isn't that Jeff Kintera? Good. Ready?"

The question of where they'd decided to hold this little do was answered when we walked through the backstage entrance. Jeff didn't stop; he led us down the narrow hallway, past the band room and straight out onstage. They'd set up a conference table right there, centre stage, and they had a couple of carts, things that looked like old recycled equipment racks, stocked with ice water and beer and a coffee machine. Someone had gone out and collected a bunch of nice plush wheeled chairs, the kind you find in a bank; rented them, probably.

"I think everyone's here." Jeff was looking around the table, doing a headcount from the looks of it. I could see his lips move: *seven chairs, seven people, good to go.* "Would anyone like some ice water, or something else to drink? JP, we got you a couple of bottles of Volvic—that's your usual, right? Great. So, if everyone's ready, let's get started."

I honestly couldn't tell you much about what got discussed for most of that meeting. I wasn't paying much attention to what was actually getting talked about, mostly because money stuff makes my eyes glaze over. I spent most of the hour we sat there trying to sort out what everyone's trip was.

I knew why Tony was there. His mates in the Bombardiers can call him Bankcuso and Elton, but if he said he wanted a hand in what happened to the 707 because he loved the place, that was the simple truth. Same for Luke; curiosity about Norfolk Lind, and because Solange had asked him to come.

We had one complete stranger at the meeting, a woman from

Guitar Wizard. I'd never met her before, which was surprising, because I do a lot with Guitar Wizard, at least on the actual magazine end, where they keep the journalists. They've interviewed me, asked me for quotes for particular stories, and run ads of me endorsing Gibson's JP Kinkaid signature chambered Les Paul guitar line. But this woman was new to me.

Jeff Kintera had got the chair at the head of the table. That was interesting, since if I understood properly, he didn't actually have an ownership stake in the club—he was an employee. Of course, he knew more about what went on with the club's business than anyone else there, so it made sense, really.

"Before we get down to business, I don't think anyone here has met Heather Speirs. Heather's the new CFO at Guitar Wizard— they're one of the 707 minority owners. I'm really glad you could get up here today, Heather."

"I'm pleased to be here, Jeff. Thanks." She seemed pleasant enough, maybe a bit guarded; financial types tend to sound like that. I saw Star Woodley's head jerk as she turned to check Heather out. I kept my eye on her—I had a bet going on inside, about what was going to happen next.

Heather was busy smiling round the table, making eye contact with everyone. She had the vibe I associate with people who really dig doing the business thing. The rest of us, being rocker types, were making the polite noises people make when someone's been introduced to a group of people at once, you know? And of course, as soon as she tried to lock on to Star, Star's head jerked and her eyes went elsewhere.

So I won the bet with myself on that one. It wasn't just people she'd damaged that Star Woodley couldn't make or keep eye contact with. She couldn't do it with anyone.

"Nice to meet you." Norfolk Lind sounded bored, and impatient with it. He looked down at his watch. "Look, can we get started? I've got a show tonight, up in Rohnert Park, and I need to get to the theatre early. I've been too many years in this business to leave the details to the hired help. They can't even scratch their asses without someone to tell them how."

"Sure." The look Jeff Kintera gave him only lasted about half a second, but that was long enough. I found myself wondering if Norfolk Lind just said whatever the hell came into his head, whenever it got there; he'd just insulted the fuck out of the 707's manager, and I couldn't tell whether he didn't know or just didn't give a rat's arse. The look Jeff had given him wasn't exactly loving.

"You're playing in Rohnert Park tonight?" Luke sounded as if he actually meant the question, and I bit my lip. Cheeky sod. "I didn't know you were a musician."

"I'm a promoter. And a producer." Not much love in the look Folkie shot Luke. "Aren't you pretty tight with my son? He could have told you that."

"Not as tight with him as my daughter is. But I didn't ask him, as it happens. You weren't discussed."

Gordon *Bennett*. I'd forgotten Luke could look like that, never mind sound like that. It was about as *fuck off you useless prat* as he ever gets; last time I'd seen him pull that one out and use it, he'd been telling a New York homicide detective named Maria Genovese that she wouldn't be interviewing Solange or her stepsister Suzanne without both parents there. He didn't pull that vibe out often, but when he did, anyone with half a brain backed off. There was steel in his eye.

"So, what? My kid didn't bother to mention that I put on more shows between San Rafael and Santa Clara over the past five years than any of the local talent combined?" Lind's face had gone bright red, and I could see a vein bulging and thumping, just above his left eye. "The little asshole didn't think that was worth mentioning?"

It was unreal. One second he'd been sitting there, rude and a bit boastful, but perfectly normal; one passing comment later, and he was about to flip his shit, lose it, start a punch-up. His shoulders had pushed all the way up, his jaw was all the way out, and his hands had balled up into fists. I found myself tensing up, getting ready: *bloody hell, the bloke's a nutter, he's going to go for Luke...*

Luke had seen it, as well; both brows were all the way up. He had a very *what, are you fucking joking me?* vibe happening. "Curt didn't tell me anything at all about you. I think I said that your name hasn't really come up. And you know, I'm not a local—I live in the UK. I have no idea what the local music scene looks like, and don't care much. Frankly, I don't even know where Rohnert Park is—Blacklight's never played there. I'm not sure I get why you're narked about it. You want to calm down now, and get on with this meeting, so you can do what you said you wanted to do?"

It hung there for a moment, Lind looking like a wild man trying to decide how to react, pretty much everyone else just blinking in disbelief, not knowing what in hell was going on. Star Woodley glanced at Luke, saw me watching her, and glanced away again. I wondered if Lind pulled this shit on her, as well.

"Um—right, yes, let's get back to the reason for this meeting, shall we?" Jeff Kintera was nervous as hell. He must have dealt with Folkie Lind and his psycho temper before. "I've made copies of the financial breakdowns for everyone, including the percentage packages and the various allotments for the club's upgrades—Heather, would you be kind enough to pass these down the table...?"

So yeah, that's what I really remember about that meeting: Norfolk Lind flipping his shit, and people rabbiting on about money, going over who'd invested how much and what they expected for their bit of dosh, how much of which whose dosh was supposed to go where. They went on about minority shares,

64

about day-to-day operations of the club itself, about who'd be talking to whom. Boring stuff, at least to me. Not my thing, and anyway, I was watching the people, sorting out reactions.

Truth is, I never used to notice much of what was going on around me, not unless something happened that got up in my face and forced me to notice; my old lady being a murder suspect, for instance, that got my attention. These past few years, though, I've got better at it—it's become a lot more natural, that whole paying attention thing. I've found the best way to get a handle on a situation is to look at the people involved, and see if I can suss out who's doing what, or whom.

Luke was irritated, I could see that much. Tony was being cautious, mostly listening, answering in the yea-or-nay parts of the conversation. Heather Speirs took notes on a Blackberry or an iPhone or whatever those computer phone things are called. She looked to be in her early forties, but she was as quick with her thumbs as Solange was. Jeff Kintera was edgy; not exactly a surprise, not if he had experience with Norfolk Lind's temper, and thought there was a brawl in the works. He chilled out toward the end, when he asked whether we wanted him to stay on as manager. We all did, unanimous; even Lind lifted a hand.

Folkie Lind was the one puzzling me. I couldn't sort him out at all. Two minutes after that whole nutter moment, of being about to foam at the mouth and jump the table to mix it up with Luke, he looked to have completely forgotten about it. I couldn't make sense of that, because he'd been right at the edge of it, and now you'd think it never happened...

"...about wraps it up."

Jeff was closing it out, finally, and thank God for it, because my legs were talking to me. It was time for my afternoon meds, and for some reason, I wasn't comfortable taking them at the table. That reaction or instinct or whatever it was, that was something I was going to have to look at later on. I'm not shy about my MS.

I'm not ashamed of it, and I don't try to hide that I've got it. But there was something about that meeting that left me not wanting to expose any weakness, and stopping in the middle to dig out my meds would have left me feeling weak. I was going to have to take them soon, though. My legs were trembling.

"Great. Thanks, Jeff, I'll go over all this with the bank." Tony had pushed back his chair, but he caught the grin I shot him. He must have thought I was going to mouth *Bankcuso* or *Elton* at him, because he grinned back at me. "And with my wife. Hell, she's the one who should have come up today—she handles it, not me. Next time you guys want to have a meeting, I'll send Katia instead. Of course, if I do, you all better look out…"

We all did the usual after-meeting thing, milling about, making conversation about nothing much, waiting for cars to be brought round. I grabbed an unopened bottle of Volvic and took my pills, finally.

"So—are you really married to Bree Godwin?"

I jumped a mile. I hadn't been paying attention to Star Woodley, and Lind had been the first to disappear out the back door and into a car. I was already so used to the idea of her being glued to his hip, I hadn't registered the fact that she was still here.

"Yeah, Bree's my wife." Her eyes were all over the place. We were face to face, she was talking to me, I was talking back to her, and she was watching the wall just over my left shoulder. This was one seriously creepy woman. The question was harmless, and of course I'd married Bree and everyone knew it, so why did I suddenly feel like telling her to get her nose out of my business? "We've been together thirty years."

"It was nice seeing her again." Her eyes were all over the place, darting about like a hummingbird who'd been fed speed: over my right shoulder, up at the ceiling, on my face for a second, away again. It was beginning to get on my nerves. "We used to work together. Did she tell you I'd probably be here today? With Folkie?"

Right about then, I got the feeling that Star Woodley was as big a nutter as her whatever-he-was. She knew Bree and I were married. Bree'd snubbed her a couple of nights ago. So unless she was living in some weird bullshit fairyland, she had to know there was a good chance Bree'd told me the whole miserable story, about what Star had done to her.

So what was all this 'we used to work together' rubbish, then? And how was I supposed to answer her? *Yeah, Bree told me you were a vicious jealous cow who put the knife in with the cops and her mum?*

Ah, sod it. Open the mouth, mate, see what comes out...

"She told me you were part of the hired help at the clinic my mother-in-law ran, yeah." Oh, bloody hell. "That what you mean? That you used to volunteer there?"

"Are you going to be at these meetings?" Not a blink, not a blush, nothing. She ignored what I'd just said. "On behalf of the majority owners? Blacklight's the majority owner. Right?"

This dollybird was barmy. She had to be—just ignoring what she didn't like and asking whatever she wanted. Sod it, if she wanted to play it that way, I could do the same.

"Yeah, we are. Not too clear on what you're doing here, though—business isn't my thing, but I didn't see your name on the papers. Didn't see your signature anywhere, either. You Folkie Lind's girlfriend, or his secretary, or something? Or what?"

That got her attention. Not for long, but there we were, finally, her meeting my eye. Her own were too narrow, and too pale. She was squinting.

"I'm not his girlfriend. Or his secretary." Her voice was a little too loud; I saw Jeff Kintera turn and stare at her for a second. "I'm his business partner. I'm an investor. Didn't Curtis tell you who I was? Didn't he tell you what I do? I'm Folkie's partner at Lindyhop. Everybody knows that."

Luke had stuck his head through the backstage door; he was waving at me. "Yeah, well, I didn't. Thanks for the heads-up."

"I've been Folkie's partner for ten years." Star Woodley was still standing there. She was creeping me out, and I suddenly got why: her expression never seemed to change. She'd had that same not quite blank thing with the shifty eyes going since I'd first seen her. "Curtis should have told you."

I opened my mouth to say *your name didn't even come up with Curt, believe it or not,* but I didn't get the chance. She went past Jeff, past Luke, and out the door, heading for God knows where.

I caught up with Luke in the parking lot. He was watching her car pull out of the lot and merge into the afternoon traffic on Francisco Boulevard. "Well. Mission accomplished. I'd say I've got a few impressions about Curt's dad to share with my daughter."

There wasn't much conversation on the drive back into the city. Not that there wasn't stuff to talk about, but I think we were all still processing it. If the driver had been soaking up all the gossipy tidbits on the way north and was hoping for more on the way back into the city, he must have been disappointed. Nearest we got to it was Luke offering to write up his take on the whole thing for David Walter at Blacklight Corporate, and me telling him, right, go for it and cheers, mate, because I was damned if I was going to do it.

"Cool, I'll send you a copy, and one to Carla, as well. You might want to send her a note on your own, though—let her know you've got better things to do with your time than sit at the same table as Folkie Lind and that lot."

We'd pulled up at Clay Street. Luke waved the chauffeur back to his seat and got out of the limo for a fast word before they headed downtown. "JP, look, can I take you and Bree out to dinner? Maybe bring Solange and Curt along? Turns out I'm going to be here another week, so any time between now and then works for me."

"Yeah, sounds good. I'll check with Bree, see what her timing looks like." I raised an eyebrow at him. "I'm glad to hear you're staying on longer—I was thinking of getting Curt and Tony into the studio, cutting a live demo of 'Americaland.' You up for that?"

"Definitely." He'd caught that eyebrow. "Don't look so worried, there's no problem. Karen suggested I hang out longer, get some quality alone-time with Solange. Suzanne's at home at the moment, and I think Karen's loving having her daughter all to herself—well, not all to herself. Suzanne's using the mobile and Draycote's full of people—Stu and Cal are both there. But she gets Su to herself at the end of the day."

I blinked at him. "Hang on a minute, Luke—what do you mean, Suzanne's using the mobile? The mobile studio? Using it for what? What are the Bunker Brothers doing there?"

"Damn, that's right, not supposed to let it out yet." He grinned suddenly. "Look, I'll ring you when he drops me off at the hotel. The news is about to come out anyway, so you get to be first to know: Suzanne's going on tour with Bergen Sandoval. She's the backup singer on his new CD—he's signed with Fluorescent."

"What!" I saw Tony edging toward the limo door, tapping his watch. "Gordon bleedin *Bennett*, Luke—yeah, ring me soon as you get back. Tony, don't twist your knickers—later."

I let myself into the house. This time of day, if I'm getting home from somewhere, I'll stop just inside the hall and take a good long breath of whatever Bree's got on the stove for supper. It's pretty rare to get home and have the house not smell brilliant, unless we're heading out for a meal. Not tonight, though— no smell of cooking at all.

"Hello? Bree?" I closed the door behind me. I thought I heard voices, back of the house, in the kitchen. Right, so someone had dropped by. I hadn't noticed a car in the driveway, though. "Bree? Oi!"

"John!" She stuck her head out of the kitchen door, a good forty feet away. "Hey babe—we're back here. I was waiting to start dinner. We're almost done, but I need you."

"Company here, then?" I headed towards the kitchen. She had her glasses on, the little drugstore readers she uses for close-up work. That meant she'd been working, taking notes or something, probably that big secret project she was on.

Those glasses—right. They make her look like a librarian. Her wearing them, that used to make me clutch up around the heart, having to admit that she wasn't immortal or invincible, that she could get older and have things go wrong. That changed after I nearly died, though. These days, I think the glasses make her look sexy as hell.

I turned the corner and looked round the swinging doors into the kitchen. Patrick Ormand was sitting at the table.

He had a glass of wine in front of him, half-full, so he looked to have been there awhile. Ridiculous, that I still can't stand the idea of him alone with Bree. There's no real reason for it, except the fact that, from the day I confronted him with it, he's been denying he's hot for her, and that's bullshit.

He got up and offered a hand, and of course I took it. Not much choice, yeah? Besides, he actually works for me now—we'd hired him as Blacklight's security chief during the last tour. He still hits most of my buttons, though, just by breathing.

A lot more of it has to do with the kind of history we've had. We'd got off on the wrong foot, with him working homicide in New York and picking my old lady as his prime candidate for prison gear. He'd jerked our chain, hid what he knew, and generally been an evil wanker. Right about the time I thought we were hosed, though, he'd turned round and done something human.

So he's hard to like, hard to dislike, and impossible to read, generally. And of course, there's the fact that I'm pretty damned sure he fancies my wife.

"Hey, JP. Am I in your chair? I can move."

"Not to worry. Hey, Bree." I snatched a fast hard kiss off my wife, and sat beside her. She had one of her notebooks open; the page in front of her was covered in notes, what I could have told from across the room was her catering shorthand. "What's going on, then?"

"Patrick's been trying to hire me to cater his agency opener. We've been discussing it."

"Right." I lifted an eyebrow at my wife, and then at Patrick. "*Trying* to hire you? What's that about, then?"

"Don't ask me, JP. I'm as much in the dark as you are." Patrick sounded mild enough, maybe a bit amused. "Bree's been telling me that she's not the most economical choice I could make. She told me she has a better idea, but she wouldn't tell me anything about it until you got here. I think this is the first time I've ever tried to give someone a lot of money and had them try and talk me out of it."

"Yeah, well, I'm here now." I thought about bashing him, just for a moment; he'd given Bree the kind of look that makes me sure he's into her. "Bree?"

She had an idea, all right. As she explained it, just the bare bones of the plan at first, I felt myself wanting to grin. Not just me, either; Patrick was right there digging it, at least at first. Whether he was buying it or not, though, I couldn't tell.

I leaned back; there was a cat under my feet, wanting on to my lap, and I made room. Simon jumped up, sharpened his claws, settled and purred. "Okay, wait, hang on a minute, all right? You want to have Patrick's agency opener be a Geezer gig at the 707? And you want to get Solange Hedley to do the catering? That where you're going with this, love?"

"No, Solange wouldn't do the catering. I'd supervise." Bree was

71

ready to argue it, I could tell, and that meant this was something she was ready to fight for. I couldn't suss out why, though—it was just a party. "I'd have to be the primary, because Solange isn't a licensed caterer. I'd get her in as my sous chef and all-around helper, if she wants to do it. Give her some practical experience, see how she does under pressure. That would keep Patrick's costs down, at least on the catering end."

Patrick was watching her. There was no way to read his face— all I could really tell was that he was interested, and listening. That's one of the things I dislike most about him, those moments when he reminds me that he used to be a homicide cop. "Okay, but why a live show, Bree? I love the idea, of course—who wouldn't? But I'm not sure it would save me money. I don't imagine the club rental comes cheap. And then of course I'd have to pay the band." He caught my grin, and grinned back. "I'm betting your husband doesn't hire out cheap, either."

I snorted. Bree shot me a look, and bit back a smile. It was gone a moment later, and she was back to being intense.

"Patrick, look. Let's recap, and I'll see if I can't convince you. How many people were you thinking of inviting to this thing?"

"About seventy five, give or take half a dozen." He had an eyebrow of his own up, now. "Why?"

"And your idea was to throw the kick-off bash at your new office, which is how big?"

"About nine hundred square feet. Bree, would you mind -"

"It won't work." She shook her head at him. She's gorgeous when she focuses, Bree is, at least to me; she gets fierce, and Bree being fierce is one of my big turn-ons. It's right there with the effect her naked back has on me: all the blood heads south. It's pure porn. "Do the math, Patrick. You can't fit that many people into that small a space without violating every health and safety code on the books. The City's really tough on those. But okay, let's say you pulled some strings down at City Hall and got around that. Even if you stacked people three deep, there'd be nowhere to put the catering tables, or the bar. And of course, there's the question of some of your guests maybe wanting to sit down, so where were you planning to put things like chairs?"

"Okay, okay, I get it." He wasn't smiling anymore. "You're right. So, my options are, what? Smaller crowd or bigger venue? But why do I need a club, for my tiny little invite list? Doesn't the 707 seat about twelve hundred people? That sounds like you're going to the other extreme."

Bree explained. It was obvious she'd given it a lot of thought. As she fleshed out the idea, I found myself wondering if she knew just how damned perfect it was.

"The 707's being tricked out, right? No, John, please put the eyebrow down—Katia called, and we were talking about it. Since Blacklight and Tony together have about eighty percent of the ownership interest, she seems to think it may become home base for both the Geezers and the Bombardiers. She emailed me with the list of upgrades to the sound system; she got it in email herself, from Carla's office. I checked the projected completion date, and it's just about a month from today."

"And…?" I'd dropped my right arm around her waist. "Dish, love. What's the grand plan?"

"Why not celebrate Patrick's agency opening and the official upgrade to the 707 at the same party? You could play, either band or solo. It can be a private show, invite only, with Patrick's guest list and another guest list for the club. I'll cater it, and rope in Solange."

She was getting fiercer and more persuasive by the moment, and I was getting turned on. She knew it, too. She slid her hand under the table, and rested it just inside my right thigh.

"If Patrick's okay with that, I'd do the work gratis, for just the cost of the food. The bar at the club can provide the liquid." She squeezed my thigh. It was a signal—*go with me on this one, please*—and of course I did. What I really wanted was to get up, turf Patrick out, and bend her backwards over the kitchen table with her skirt around her ears. Not only was she sounding fierce, she'd squeezed pretty high up on my thigh…

"I think the Geezers could waive a fee for that one." My breath wanted to do some interesting things; she'd slid her hand up as far as it could go, and her eyes had gone bright green, and that meant she was ready as I was. *Right,* I thought, *give Bree anything she asks for, whatever it takes to get Patrick out the door, and me and her upstairs into bed.* "Probably waive the club rental fee as well. But I need to talk to everyone else first. Patrick, you all right with the basic idea? Right, good, I'll talk to everyone and get back to you tomorrow, yeah…?"

I don't know whether Patrick had sussed out why I was in such a hurry to get him out of there. Probably—he's got good eyes, has Patrick Ormand. I didn't really care whether he had or not. All I wanted, right that moment, was to get him out, and get Bree out of her knickers and onto her back. Whether he knew why or not, he said goodbye, and went.

The quack had been right about the tickybox making the sex a lot less stressy. Before Wembley and the implant, a good slap and tickle with Bree'd usually left me panting for breath, and feeling my heart slamming and stuttering. The tickybox had sorted all that out for me.

Half an hour after I'd locked the door behind Patrick, I looked down at Bree, still spasming along under me. That had been half an hour's worth of serious belly-bump, and she hadn't got her balance back. I stayed where I was, flesh to flesh. Not much choice, since she had her legs wrapped round me, and wasn't showing any signs that she was planning to unwrap them. It's like I said, she seems to want my weight on her these days.

"Hello, darling." I touched the tip of my tongue to the hollow of her throat. "You've gone all salty."

She stretched her neck, and kissed me. "Mmmmm. Are you okay, John?"

"Brilliant, ta." She'd never asked me that until Wembley, but she'd asked me every time since. It was annoying, but I could live with it. There's altogether too much stuff between us for me to get pissy over providing reassurance about my health, if she needs to hear it. "So, you want to tell me what's really going on with this party at the 707 thing? Don't fancy I see you getting that fierce over Patrick's devilled eggs."

"Mmmm." She reached one hand behind my head, and pulled me down. Her eyes were still pretty unfocused, and pretty green. "In a minute. Maybe five minutes."

She bit me, very light, just a nip. Right.

"Hello, darling." It was more like fifteen minutes than one or five, which was fine with me. She was absolutely glazed with sweat, sweet and salty all over. "Bree, love, can I have my legs back, please? I need to shift—the tickybox, you know?"

"Oh my God, I'm sorry!" She unwrapped in a hurry. "I'm sorry, I didn't mean -"

I turned over, face to face. "No, it's fine. It just gets heavy after a bit—I mean, I'm more aware of it. Nature's way of telling me to move, that's all. Now, lady. What's the story with this party? Or maybe I can guess."

"Guess?" Yeah, there it was; she'd gone pale. No surprise, not really. I know my old lady reasonably well after thirty years together, and when she digs her heels in, it's because something's got hold of her, and whatever it is, it matters. The only question is why.

I grinned at her. I had one arm draped over her, stroking as much of her back as I could without moving too much.

"Yeah, I said guess. I'll have a go. Not about Patrick, and you don't give a toss for the 707. That leaves me or Solange, or both. Did I get it?"

75

"Curtain number three." She sighed. "Both, yes. Solange—John, listen. This is something I don't talk about much, cooking and food and how it all comes together. But that doesn't mean cooking isn't just as major for me as being a musician is for you. Cooking isn't just what I do, it's part of what I am. I was born a cook—I didn't just make myself one."

"I know that." I wasn't having her on, either. I did know. There were too many memories of her retreating into cookery, when I'd hurt her or let her down, for me to not get that. "Why do you think I don't get in your way when you're working? It's your recording studio and your stage. I do get it, Bree. What I don't get is what that has to do with Solange."

"I want to know about her. I want to know if she's born, or if she's just expecting to be made."

I thought about that a moment. Odd way to put it, but it made sense. She stayed quiet, waiting to see if I was going to say something. When I just nodded, she went on.

"I want to know if she's for real. She's got more money than the U.S. Mint to play with. She could sit on her ass and just be Curt's old lady forever. She doesn't have to do a damned thing. She spent, what, four years, trying to figure out what she wanted to study. It took her father falling in love with a Type One diabetic and marrying her, and the pair of us getting sick and you nearly dying on the tour, to make her see that what she wants to do is cook. That's pretty damned late to figure out that you have a passion for something."

"What, you think she might be wrong about it?" I pushed her hair back off her face. "She seems pretty focused, Bree."

"I don't know. Maybe. But if she's not, this will give her a shot at finding out before she commits. Cooking school is a grind. If you don't have the stuff, it can break your heart."

There was something in her voice as she said that, an edge I couldn't pin down. Another landmine, I thought, one more thing

I either hadn't been there for or just hadn't noticed…

"And then there's you."

That got my attention, all right. She reached out a hand, and rested it on my cheek.

"You need to play, John." She sounded absolutely calm, and absolutely certain. "I hated the idea, I know I was a pain in the ass about it, but I can say it now: I was scared shitless you'd overdo it, keel over and die onstage. I've been almost scared to let you out of my sight, since what happened at Wembley. But the truth is, I've been missing working. I love taking care of you, but I miss cooking for people. And you know what? You need to play. So I need to back off and let you. You're a musician."

"Born, not made." God, she was beautiful. "Crikey, Bree, I love you, you know that? So the idea is, I get to be what I am and do my job, you get to be what you are and keep an eye on me while you do your job, and we get to sort out whether Solange has got the right stuff for being a chef?"

She leaned forward, and planted a nice light kiss on the ticky-box. "And we save Patrick a few bucks. Win-win."

"Yeah, it does sound that way. I'll ring everyone up later and get us together about it. Fog City Geezers, Noshing But The Best Catering, and Big Bad Wolf Investigations, or whatever the hell Patrick's calling his new toy." I reached out and got hold of her. "Works for me. Let's call it booked."

Chapter Five

For Immediate Release, from the desk of Carla Fanucci, for at-tached list only:

As many of the principals of the 707 Club already know, a plan and timeline have been proposed, detailing an extensive expansion of the club's physical structure. While the short-term repairs to the exist-ing building require no architectural changes, any expansion would require submission and approval of full architectural plans to, and by, the city of San Rafael's Planning Commission.

An ownership meeting to discuss this issue is therefore necessary. As the club is at present undergoing the above-mentioned interim up-grade, suggestions as to possible venues for this meeting, as well as a range of dates that will work with a majority of schedules, are being solicited. Please email Andy Valdon at info@fanuccipros.com...

"Oh, bloody hell!" Emails from David Walter's secretary in

London, from Tony, from Heather Speirs at Guitar Wizard. Of course there was one from Lindyhop, in their usual screaming upper case letters and exclamation points. They all had subject lines on the same damned theme: *meeting* this and *meeting* that. There was also one from Mac, no subject listed.

"Uh-oh." Bree looked up at me over her glasses. "What's going on? Problem?"

"You could call it that, yeah. Bree, refresh my memory, since I seem to be getting old and feeble, all right?" I was a bit surprised at just how narked I was. "Did I tell Andy Valdon that I had better things to do with my time than go handle this 707 bullshit?"

She was staring at me. "Yes. At least, that's what you told me. Why? What's he up to?"

"The annoying little ponce seems to have decided to ignore what I told him." I turned my laptop screen toward her. "Here, have a butchers. I'm really close to ringing Carla and telling her that she needs to train her Mother's Little Helper before one of us breaks his neck. I'll be buggered if I'm going to be jerked into—oh shit, yeah, I hear it, hang on."

I got to my phone and clicked it open without looking at the caller ID. Bree's shoulders were small boulders, basically. And even though I might not be ready to get "Remember Me" out as my ringtone and replace it with something else, I didn't need to rub her nose—or ears—in it, either.

"Johnny?"

I nearly dropped the phone. My head had been deep into being pissy and shirty over Andy Valdon. Malcolm Sharpe's voice was about the last one I'd been expecting to hear.

"Oi! Johnny? Are you there?"

"Yeah, I'm here. What's going on, Mac? Everything all right, then?"

I saw Bree's head jerk towards me; I put the phone's speaker on, and set it on the kitchen table. There was an echo in the line that meant he was probably ringing from London, or somewhere a good distance away.

"Everything's fine." He sounded surprised. "Just ringing to ask you when we needed to book flights out there. It's about this ownership meeting; the bright boy in Carla's office didn't seem to have a date set for—sorry, did you say something?"

"I swore," I told him. "And I'm about to damned well do it again. Mac, what is all this? Why are you dragging your bum halfway across the planet to go to a meeting?"

"Well—it seemed like the obvious thing." He didn't sound narked at all. "David Walter's secretary rang me up. David was going to do the honours and charge off to California to protect our interests, but he's in hospital with gallstones, poor sod, and he wanted someone who knows something about the club to cover for him. You'd already told Carla's little sock puppet— Andy?—that you weren't interested in the business angle, and Luke's only just got home from the States. Someone ought to be there, and I've played the club, remember. Besides, it sounds like fun. Domitra's already asking me to find out if her chewtoy from our last visit is still around. That Bombardier roadie, I mean— what's his name? Doug?"

I took a deep breath, and let it out again. It all sounded nice and organic, but I'll tell you what, I just didn't believe it, some-how. I had no idea what Andy Valdon actually looked like, but I had a sudden picture of a skinny kid in LA with a voodoo doll of Blacklight's London ops manager, drawing a circle round where he thought a gall bladder ought to be and sticking pins in it, just to get up my nose and take the piss out of me. Too bloody con-venient by half, that was.

"Okay." I was doing my best to keep my voice even. No point in letting Bree hear my teeth grinding. "So David Walter's in hospital getting his gall bladder repossessed. You've got an inter-est in what happens to the 707, and your bodyguard wants a go

80

at the kind of exercise that doesn't involve maiming anyone. That it, then?"

"To a tee." Definitely amused—you couldn't miss it. "Who knows, maybe I'll see about some of that nice non-maiming-type exercise myself, while I'm out there. There are some lovelies out in your neck of the woods. Seriously, Johnny, you sound livid. Why...?"

"I got the damned press release as well, that's why. It seems to assume I'm going to be there. I was just going to ring up Andy Valdon in LA and maybe do a bit of organ removal myself. Carla's definitely going to hear it, as well. But you want to tell me what's so damned important about this meeting, that David was ready to cross the Atlantic and the US to be here?"

"Crikey, Johnny, calm down! I didn't know anything was going on until I asked David's secretary. Turns out the building was built sixty or seventy years ago, a good long time, anyway. This is the first time it's changed hands since Chuck Berry was in nappies, or something."

I waited. I'd caught a change in Mac's voice; subtle, but the change was there. It was a crispness that only seemed to get in there when he was talking about business.

Our late manager, Chris Fallow, had been a brilliant bloke with some very good ideas. He'd got one of the best ideas of his life, when Blacklight had first shown they were going to be huge: he'd understood that people making mistakes with money was likely the main thing that tore bands apart. The result was that, as soon as there'd been any money to understand, he'd insisted on Mac and Luke taking courses in business management and finance. It had paid off, for all of us.

Mac was still talking, and the tone was still there. "...something in your state code about how when a property changes hands, the changeover requires a full inspection. Or maybe a county code—I honestly don't remember. Anyway, a

81

chunk of dosh from our part of the sale money is earmarked for a major set of improvements to the club—that was a condition of transfer, when the solicitors handling Paul Morgenstern's end of the deal from prison first put the word out that he was selling it."

"Yeah, okay. I wasn't paying much attention when all that went down, Mac—heart attack and getting home again, you know?"

He sounded gentle, all of a sudden, and not amused at all. "I wasn't poking at you, Johnny. None of us paid much attention to the sale. Why do you think we're still scrabbling about the details? We were all there at Wembley, remember? Most of us split the next few months between decompressing from the tour, and not knowing whether Bree would rip our heads off if any of us offered to help her. There was fuck-all we could do except hope, and watch your old lady go grey nursing you back to health. You scared the shit out of us. Got it? Clear now?"

"Yeah." That was all I could say, pretty much; there was a lump at the back of my throat. Bree had her teeth sunk into her lower lip, and her eyes were wet. "Got it."

"Good. So, Carla gave Corporate the heads-up that the city would want to inspect the place anyway, to see what codes have to be met. The idea is to get one big inspection done, to cover both the sale and the fixes."

"Right. So?"

"So, we've got to get everyone's input on the upgrades and improvements, and everyone's signature on the documents that get handed to the local planning people." Mac sounded surprised that I hadn't got it. "If you want to rep Corporate at this thing, say so, but be warned, I'll probably come out anyway. I'm bored half out of my mind and I think my bodyguard is in the mood to get dressed up in tight clothes with little Dougie and pretend they're both Klingons, or something. The girl does seem to get an indecently high percentage of her jollies whacking away at something with a big stick."

82

That got a laugh out of me. "Yeah, I remember she and Doug had something going on. And no worries, I've got no interest in the business side, but you know what, I have the feeling this is going to keep happening. In fact, I can't see any way it won't."

"Andy and his puppetmaster act, you mean?" Mac didn't sound at all surprised. "What, Johnny, you think he's trying to jerk your strings into getting involved?"

"Bloody hell, Mac, of course he is. This is ongoing, this whole 707 thing. That means more meetings and whatnot. It's not as if you can fly out every time, you know?"

"True."

I was sorting it out, and getting shirtier about it every moment. "Which leaves me, basically, unless I tell both Andy and Carla to fuck off, I'm not having it. And you know what, that's what I'm going to do."

"Well, make certain you're convincing." There was amusement in Mac's voice. "In the meantime, though, what are the dates? Any ideas....?"

Of course, I had no clue what to tell him, and that just made it worse. By the time I got off the phone, I was right at the edge of sputtering, I was that pissy. It must have shown—not that Bree would have needed much of a clue, knowing me as long as she has.

She made me a cup of tea. She asked me a couple of leading questions. Right about the time I'd talked myself out and begun to calm down, she floored me.

"Why don't we have the meeting here?" She'd parked herself across the table, watching me. "That would give us some home court advantage, wouldn't it?"

I got control of my jaw, which had dropped. "What, host the damned thing? You're joking, yeah?"

She wasn't smiling. "Not really. Think about it, John. If we had it here, we'd have total control over it. We'd get to say when and how long, and we'd get to boot everyone out if we wanted to. Besides, there's a subliminal thing, kind of—I mean, you and Mac and Tony, it's sort of one big Blacklight-centric voting bloc, or whatever it's called. I know, I know, Tony bought his share separate from Blacklight, but it won't look that way. I mean, he's really Blacklight family. Don't you think having it under our roof and weighting it with our people would maybe keep the Lindy-hops reasonably quiet? I do. I'll even cook for it, if you want. What are you smiling about?"

"You. Wow. You just made my day, you know?"

"Why?" She blinked at me. "For offering to cook? I'll cook for you any time of the day or night, and you know it."

"No." I leaned over and kissed her, long and deep. "For all the we-us stuff. Thirty years, and you know what, this is the first time I've ever heard you admit thinking of yourself as part of the Blacklight family. Yeah, it's a brilliant idea, if you don't mind having Star Woodley sitting at your table. Tell you the truth, Bree, I've taken a total scunner on the woman, myself."

"Yes, well, that's because she's nuts. A total frycake." Bree got up, and stretched, rotating joints around, hearing them settle back into place. "To hell with her, anyway. That's the nice thing about home court advantage: If she misbehaves under my roof, I can kick her ass. When does this meeting have to be set by? We'll need to leave Mac and Dom time to get flights. And by the way, were you going to call Carla…?"

That conversation with Carla had a definite edge to it. I asked Bree to stay in the kitchen with me, and put it on the speaker.

Carla got it on the first ring. "JP? Hey there—I was going to call you. What's going on?"

"A couple of things. Club business first, yeah? I've got Bree with me, and the speaker's on, so you can hear each other."

I let Bree offer to host the meeting at our place. Of course, Carla thought that was brilliant.

"Bree, that's a fantastic idea! Are you sure you're okay with it? It may go on for awhile—there's a lot of paperwork and I'd be willing to bet the Lindyhop people will bitch about every possible detail. Norfolk Lind is a pain in the ass—oh, God, tell me Solange isn't there....?"

"No Solange," I told her. "Wouldn't matter if she was here, though—she's not nuts about him either. He's a nutter and his partner's a fruitbat. Look, Carla, I'm leaving it to you to deal with herding everyone into a date that works. Just let us know, all right? Bree? Great."

"I'm on it." I heard a door open and close at the other end of the line. "You said there was something else?"

"Yeah, there is. Two questions: you alone in your office, and is your phone speaker off? Because this is just between you and me, all right?"

"Yes to both." No surprise in her voice at all. Have I mentioned that Carla's not dim? She must have had a pretty good idea what I wanted to talk about. "This particular conversation is purely one on one, JP—well, one on two, if Bree's still there. What's on your mind?"

It was a shock, realising just how narked I was about her hired help acting like the band were his personal chess pieces. But when I opened my mouth, I heard myself sounding as tight and shirty as I ever get. I let it go, just dumped it straight onto Carla.

"...don't know where he, or you, got the idea that it was okay to act like a damned nanny, scheduling us for play dates or some rubbish." I was finally running out of steam; Bree was watching me with both eyebrows up. "It needs to stop, Carla. Not speaking for anyone but myself, but you might want to ask Luke and Mac how they feel about it. Speaking just for me, it needs to stop. Not having my strings jerked, you know? Not by your assistant or anyone else."

She didn't sound bothered. "I'll talk to him. I should have realised Andy's particular style would drive you guys nuts. Don't worry, though—you won't be dealing with him. The client base I'm grooming him to handle won't include Blacklight. You guys are all mine. He's just getting the training. In the meantime, I'll tell him to chill, and tell him why. But you do have to deal with him for awhile longer. I'm keeping him on this club thing, because his background is perfect for handling it."

"Why?" Bree was on her second cup of tea, warming her hands around the mug. It's one of those little things that spooks me; she's always had rotten circulation, but it's got really major with the diabetes. She saw me watching, and set the mug down. "What did he do before you hired him?"

"Money man for Silver Streak."

Right then, the penny dropped. Not for Bree—she was still in the dark—but for me. I mouthed at her—*tell you later*—and she nodded, and reached for her tea again.

When we rang off, I got behind Bree and began rubbing her shoulders. Tense as hell, and chilly too. It used to be Bree being the one to offer all the rubdowns; these days, though, I do a fair bit of massaging, myself. As she relaxed back into it, I filled her in on why Andy Valdon was going to be annoying me awhile longer.

"Silver Streak's a producer and club bloke, down in LA." I'd got my thumbs into the crook of her neck, where it meets her shoulders. "His name's something like Darrin or Derek or something, but his last name's Silver. He owns ALS Studio, down in West Hollywood, and a couple of nightclubs as well. Been a player down there for donkeys years—I think he had a few places competing with the Troubador, back in the day. You actually met him once, love, first time I took the Geezers down the coast to play. Remember? Tall bloke, skinny, looked like a mop handle with long wavy silver hair?"

She stretched her shoulders, and tossed her neck. "Oh, that guy? I do remember him, vaguely—must be the hair I'm remembering, I guess. So Carla's new AA knows his way around the club scene?"

"Looks like it. What the hell, I don't mind, unless he tries jerking my chain around again. I'm betting he won't, though. When Carla talks to her staff, they listen." I thought about it for a moment. "Shit, so does the King of Norway. And Interpol. It'll be fine. Right now, I'm more concerned with this little catered gathering of the ownership we look to be having. Hell of a guest list. You sure about this, Bree?"

"Absolutely." She was on her feet, hunting for her own cell phone. "Actually, I have an idea of my own, just something to cut the workload down."

She flipped her phone open, and punched in a single digit.

"Solange? Hey, honey, it's Bree. Listen, how would you feel about helping me put together a little dinner...?"

I've said it before, Bree's really good at parties. She's got a magic touch handling social events; odd, considering how many years she did her best to stay invisible. But we should have known it was going to take more than magic to keep that 707 meeting from getting completely out of hand.

I shouldn't have been surprised, but as soon as Carla sent out the email letting everyone know we were hosting it, all the pissing and moaning about a date magically sorted itself out. Carla rang Bree, let her know that everyone including Mac and Dom were good for the following Monday, and was Bree sure that gave her enough lead time? Bree said no problem, four days was more than enough, and was Carla coming up for it? Turned out that yeah, she was, and she asked if it was all right to bring Andy Valdon with her.

Bree clicked her cell off, and stared at me. I could see the wheels turning in her head. She got up and headed into our dining room, me right behind her. She was counting under her breath. "...and Jeff Kintera....I make it a headcount of eleven people. We're going to want the table for the whole paperwork thing, right?"

"Yeah, probably." I was trying not to grin. She'd already gone from hostess to caterer mode; you couldn't miss it. "Where are you getting eleven from, though? Because I'm counting thirteen."

She ticked the list off on her fingers. "You and me. Tony and Katia. Mac and Dom. Lind and his sidekick. Carla and her sidekick. Jeff Kintera. Isn't that eleven?"

"You forgot Solange—does the help get to sit and eat? And then there's the Guitar Wizard rep—Heather, her name is. Thirteen. Not a lucky number for a dinner party, is it?"

"Damn. No, it's not." She shook herself a little. She says she's not superstitious about anything, but that's bollocks. Of course she's superstitious; we both are. "Anyway, the main thing is that our table seats twelve for dinner, and we've got at least thirteen, unless someone cancels. I think we'll do a buffet off the sideboard, and leave the table clear. Lots of nice finger food and chafing dish stuff..."

We actually ended up with fourteen people. Solange showed up the next day for a cookery lesson, and asked if she could invite Curtis to the meeting.

I'd been heading for the basement studio when she dropped that one, and I turned around. Bree'd got her own apron on, and handed Solange a spare; they'd both pulled their hair back, and washed their hands. Bree had her work island rolled out in the middle of the kitchen, so that they both had room to get at things. She'd set out all sorts of food prep stuff: whole cloves of garlic, eggs in a glass bowl, toasted panko crumbs, a colander full of mushrooms, chopped herbs, things like that. I had no clue what she was going to do with most of it, but however it ended up, I'd have bet a year's royalties on it tasting brilliant.

"Curt wants to come?" Bree dried one of her good chef's

knives, and handed it to Solange. "Here, test this for weight. The Henckels work for me, but they might be the wrong balance for you. Curt knows his father's going to be here, right? I thought they didn't get along?"

Solange hefted the knife. There was something in the way she held it, the way the muscles in her forearm were working, that reminded me of Bree. Born or made, the girl looked to have some good instincts. "They don't. I don't think Curt cares about the 707—he's not invested. I just think he wants to watch me dish out food I helped cook. Bree, can you show me things without too much salt? Is it even possible to make things that actually taste of something, if you don't use salt?"

"Absolutely." If Bree'd been able to do the 'one eyebrow up' thing, she'd have done it. "I hardly ever use more than a dash of salt anyway; I go for garlic, and specific herbs and spices, depending on the recipe. Why? Don't you like salt?"

"It's not me, it's Curt. He's got high blood pressure—he has to take meds for it, and everything. Everyone in his family has it. His grandfather had a stroke, his older sister's got it, and so does his father." She turned the Henckel over in her hand. "Wow, this is a fantastic knife. I do like the way it balances, actually. Is it pricey?"

"The eight-inch chef? About a hundred bucks, one-twenty, something like that." The two women seemed to have forgotten that I was still there; Bree was talking exclusively to Solange, and Solange had her back to me. "We'll go shopping for a basic work kit for you, when we get this meeting over with. I'm a licensed caterer, so I get a fifteen percent discount at Sur La Table. So, is Curt's high blood pressure the real reason you want to be a cook?"

It was a damned good thing Solange wasn't looking at me, because my jaw unhinged. Bree just slipped that question in there, nice and smooth, and Solange never saw it coming. For one really unpleasant moment, my wife had reminded me of Patrick Ormand, back in his homicide cop days.

"No." If my jaw could have dropped any lower, it would have, because Solange knew exactly what Bree was doing, and why. She was giving my wife back stare for stare. "I know what you're thinking. That's okay, it's the same thing everyone's thinking. You're all thinking, hell, she took so long deciding what she wanted to do with herself, she's probably not serious. You're all convinced I'll get bored and flutter off like a butterfly and decide I want to do something else next week. I know everyone thinks I decided to do this because of Curt. I didn't. He was a deciding factor, not the deciding factor."

Bree's voice was completely non-committal. Unusual for her. "Good. So what did decide it for you?"

"Going into a five-star restaurant in London, with my dad and Karen, and realising the superstar chef had fuck-all on the menu that my stepmother could eat." Bloody hell, she was absolutely furious. Or maybe it wasn't anger—it was something, though, colouring her voice. "Watching you wrapping up in layers in Europe, because you couldn't get warm. Knowing you and Karen would mostly stick to what the Blacklight chef cooked, because that was the only way you'd have any control over what you ate. And I watched Uncle John flatline at Wembley, and yes, I know his heart attack wasn't because of what he eats, but damn it, too many people have heart trouble and I hate it, I just hate it."

I watched her from behind. All I could see was her back, but it's pretty hard to mistake when someone's trying not to cry. Her shoulders were shaking, and her voice wasn't nearly as steady as it had been. It was plenty passionate, though. What was it Luke had said: that Solange, with her fierceness and focus, reminded him of the younger Bree...?

"I sat in that restaurant in London, with Karen and Dad and Suzanne. It was Su's birthday dinner. The three of us ordered whatever we wanted, but Karen had a salad because every damned thing on the menu was stuff she'd been told by her doctor to avoid until they could get her blood sugar stabilised. Dad ordered a *foie gras* appetiser, and he made a joke, about it having enough fat and cholesterol in it to kill off half the population of an emerging nation somewhere. You know what, Bree? I was the only one who wasn't laughing. It wasn't funny. Because all of a sudden, I had this picture in my head, Uncle John on the floor at Wembley, and the paddles, and the look on your face. And I lost my appetite. I couldn't eat. They all kept asking me why and I wouldn't tell them."

Her voice broke. "And now there's Curt, and he's got this little vein over his left eye, and I end up just staring at it, because sometimes it seems to sort of stick out and I wonder, oh God is he having a stroke, is there anything I can do? And I don't know. But how am I supposed to not try? So can you please show me how to cook without any fucking salt!"

I watched her shoulders sag, and her hands move to cover her face. I took a step forward, but my wife got there first.

"Jesus." Bree got both arms round her, and held on tight. Not sure where her usual matter-of-fact thing had got itself off to, but she was crooning, the way you might to a small child. "Okay, sweetie. It's okay. Long breaths. Come on, Solange, long deep breaths…"

I stayed where I was, just long enough to make sure Bree wasn't going to need backup. We're not responsible for Solange, she's an adult and she's not our kid, but she's the band's baby, in a way. Besides, I'm quite fond of the girl, and from the looks of it, she was hyperventilating.

"Okay." Bree kept one arm around her, but got the other hand free and found some paper towels. "Here. Your face is a mess. You need to not cry into the food, especially if you're worried about salt—what do you think tears are made of? Ha, made you smile.

If you're okay now, let's get started. There's a very simple trick to chopping garlic, but first let's discuss basic knife handling techniques..."

So Solange got her first lesson. She had another one between the first one and the meeting on Monday, and a shopping trip as well, outfitting a chef's portable kit for her.

Carla's press release told people to show up at half past five. Monday's my shot night, the weekly interferon I take to keep my MS under control. That meant Bree would want to kick everyone out by ten, so the idea was, show up and grab some nosh, gather round the table and go over the documents and whatever else we were supposed to be doing, sign whatever wanted signing, out and done with. It was a little extra control over the circs, you know?

If I said I wasn't curious about how Bree would handle having Star Woodley under her roof, I'd be lying. I wasn't worried—she'd said it herself, this was her home turf and she had the advantage. And of course, having Mac and Carla along seriously weighted things our way. But it could easily get tricky, as well.

Solange got there late Monday morning, with her brand new chef's kit bag in one hand. She'd arranged that with Bree, to get here no later than noon, and she got there twenty minutes early. That was a huge point in her favour. Bree has a thing about people who show up late for things—she doesn't like having her time taken for granted. What I wasn't expecting was that Solange would have Curtis Lind with her, complete with his PRS case.

"Hi, Uncle John." She breezed into the hall, Curt at her heels. "Is it all right that I parked Duke in the driveway? I can move it if you need to go out."

"You're asking the wrong member of the family, love. Any going out that involves driving, you want to talk to Bree. I don't drive, remember?" I nodded at Curt. "Oi, Curt. You going to pull up a stool and watch the experts cook, then? Maybe serenade them?"

"I wouldn't dare. Solange offered to gut me like a bluefish if I made her nervous. I was hoping we could maybe work on 'Americaland'—I actually want to ask you about something, an idea I've been rolling around. Ooh! Cat!" He set the guitar case down, as I pushed the front door closed. "Hey kitty, handsome guy—which one is this?"

"That's Wolfling." He was sniffing the case, probably wondering why it didn't smell like mine. I ran one finger down his spine, and he arched his back, and purred. "Oi, mate. You're getting quite an honour here—he doesn't climb out of his basket to talk to people much anymore. He's getting on a bit, you know? Sixteen or thereabouts—geezer, just like me. Sleeps a lot more than he used to. Bree! Your sous-chef has arrived."

We headed down the hall, Wolfling getting under our feet. I was right at the edge of being narked with young Curtis; if he was here to get in Bree's way, that would be her thing to deal with. But he'd brought his PRS with him, and that meant he'd taken it for granted that I had nothing else on my plate, or that, if I did, I'd drop it to play with him. Wrong side of complete arrogance, you know? I don't like having my time pissed on, any more than Bree does.

Bree'd come out of the kitchen, tying her apron. Thank God for marital synchronicity; she shot me a quick look, read exactly what was going on in my head, and promptly handled it. "Hey, Curt. Solange didn't say you were coming this early—I thought you were coming tonight. Were you planning on playing with John? John, why didn't you didn't tell me Curt was coming?"

"Can't tell you what I don't know, can I?" Perfect. I lifted an eyebrow at Curt. He'd gone very pink round the edges. Both women had stopped, a few feet down the hall. They were both listening, Bree not quite nodding, Solange looking like someone hearing the penny drop; there was a definite *oh shit* thing going on in her face. "It's your lucky day, mate—I've got nothing on except staying out of my wife's way and helping set things up if she needs an extra pair of hands. Next time, though, ring me up first, or email me, yeah?"

He was bright pink now. "Oh, crap. Oh, man. Could I have done anything ruder? Way to go, Curt, you total douche. Please kick me in the ass and out the door as needed—I've got it coming. Should I go sit in the truck? I feel as if I ought to. Or maybe just go out in the garden and eat worms?"

"Yeah, well, you said you wanted to ask me about something, so we can do that in the garden." No need to pile-drive it, you know? He'd got the point. That apology was genuine, and yeah, I can tell the difference; I've spent thirty years hanging out with Malcolm Sharpe. Curt Lind had a long way to go to catch up to Mac's level. "Bree, any chance of a cup of tea, and maybe a snack? Tell you the truth, I don't fancy worms."

We ended up watching the women do their thing for a few minutes, after all. Nothing too complicated, just some oversized shellfish and a bowl of greens; Bree showed Solange how to butterfly the prawns and explained about cooking them fast, and showed her how to use her favourite kitchen slicer—it's called a mandolin, of all things—to make skinny strips of a bunch of different veggies. *Julienne*, she calls that style.

"No salt?" Curt was watching Solange, and his voice was the same as usual, but there was something in his face that gave him away. I hadn't realised it before, but there it was: the boy was off his nut for her. "Just a little?"

"No salt."

I jumped. He'd been talking to Solange, but Bree looked up from crushing roasted garlic into a glass dish, and locked eyes with him, very steady.

"That's a remarkably stupid question, Curtis. You have high blood pressure, don't you? I can see that little pulse over your right eye from here. No salt, and please don't try and guilt the woman who's cooking for you into helping you kill yourself, not under my roof. That kind of passive-aggressive manipulation is a shitty way to say thank you for a good meal."

Oh, bloody hell. Curt went crimson, Solange sounded as if she'd just swallowed her own tonsils, and Bree just stood there waiting for an answer, holding a ten-inch Santoku knife like a fucking Samurai warrior. Her voice had been absolutely deadly.

Right. Time to take a hand.

"Might want to listen to Bree, mate." Sounding as if I thought it was amusing might have got me my head handed to me right then, my wife being in the mood she was in. "She's a doctor's daughter and she knows her stuff. I'm not a foodie, so Bree's wasted on me, but I've eaten crap food often enough on the road to know how good I've got it at home. Besides, cooking's not just something people do, Curt. You're a musician, so you ought to get it: a cook's what someone is. And you ought to know when you've got it good."

"I'm sorry." He was still scarlet; nice to know there was some genuine feeling under all that surface charm. "I really am. I didn't mean it that way—shit, maybe I did, but I didn't want to upset anyone—I wasn't—I mean—oh, hell!"

Solange leaned forward suddenly, and kissed him. "It's okay. Yes, you're being an ass today, but I love you anyway. You're cute. But I'm not putting salt in your food. Now go sit in the garden with Uncle John and let us get on with it, okay?"

We left the women getting the buffet stuff started, and settled ourselves out in the garden with a big bowl full of warm butter-flied prawns, strips of raw veggies, and salt-free dip. I let Curtis get a mouthful down, and waited for him to bring up what he wanted to ask me about. Turned out that what he wanted was to be allowed to sit in with the Fog City Geezers—as frontman and backup guitar—at the 707 gig we were planning for Patrick's party. The more I thought about it, the better it sounded.

95

"I tell you what, mate, I like it. Brilliant idea. Were you thinking we'd cover 'Americaland'? I'd need to run it by everyone else, and we'd need to get it down. The Geezers may feel like a pickup band, and we do a lot of improv onstage, but we're actually pretty tight. If everyone else is up for it, though, you're on. Pity Luke's not here—but who knows, nice big party that's supposed to be the 707 kick-off, he may just fly out for that. Feel like heading inside for some work on the song? We've got a couple of hours to kill before people start arriving, and trust me, we need to spend it out of Bree and Solange's way."

Chapter Six

We'd told people to show up at half-past five. So, of course, the Lindyhop people showed up at six.

Not sure whether they wanted to make an entrance, or were just being flaky, or whatever—all I know is, they were late. By the time they got there, everyone had eaten, gone back for seconds, had a sweet, and stacked their plates in the sink.

Tony and Katia got there first, with Heather Speirs and Jeff Kintera right behind. Between them and the time the Blacklight crew arrived a few minutes later, Bree and Solange had lost the aprons and the ponytails, and got dressed. Solange was explaining every dish to everyone, and Curt was watching her, looking lovesick. I caught up with Bree in the kitchen, took one look at what she was wearing, and this time, both eyebrows went up.

"John? What?" She'd been loading glasses on a tray, but she caught my look, and her shoulders turtled up. "Why the look?"

"Just checking out your gear."

Bree's got a closet full of serious stuff she wears for gigs; when I'm playing and she's doing her job as the woman on the rocker's arm, she dresses the part, mostly vintage and designer gear. The rest of the time, it's whatever feels comfy.

Tonight, she had on a bizarre mix: jeans on the bottom half, vintage velvet on top, and the gaudiest, silliest high heels in her closet. You'd have thought she couldn't make up her mind whether she needed to dress for rocker-chick or casual hostess, and had got stuck somewhere in between.

"John?" She was biting her lip. I'd waited too long to say anything, apparently. "Doesn't it work? Damn! I knew it was all wrong. Shit, shit, shit! Okay, look, I'm going upstairs to change, do me a favour and listen for the doorbell -"

"Oi!" Right. If she was this close to flipping her shit, it was time to be a good husband, and lie. "You look brilliant. I was just wondering about those shoes. Can you really deal?"

"My Loboutins?" She glanced down at her feet. It was ridiculous; in those shoes, she was five inches taller than I was, maybe even more. "Of course I can. I wore them to the Geezers gig at the Fillmore, and danced the night away, remember? Are they too much? Is my outfit really okay? I don't want to look pathetic."

I slid a hand behind her, and patted her bottom. I may not be the brightest bulb out there, but I wasn't dim enough to ask her why she cared what Star Woodley thought of her outfit, either. "I don't fancy you looking pathetic anytime in this life, lady. You're fine. Relax, Bree. Don't get your knickers in a twist, yeah? You've got home court advantage. Do you need me to carry that tray? Where do you want it...?"

Getting people settled with food, helping Bree get the party started, meant I couldn't really spend any time with anyone in particular—getting it going, you have to keep moving about. That meant I couldn't do more than nod at Andy Valdon when he and Carla came in, and I was curious about him. I didn't know what to expect. All I knew was a voice on the phone, and his emails. He'd sounded very young, and he'd pissed me off.

After Carla had dropped that tidbit, about Andy's job before he got to Fanucci Productions, every idea I had about this bloke went out the window. If he'd handled money for Silver Streak, there was no way he was naive or timid or young, or anything except hard as a diamond drill bit and up to every trick in the game. Thinking about it, I ought to have known that he was no newbie. Carla didn't usually pick annoying children to work with. She didn't much fancy housebreaking them, either.

So I got one quick look, letting them in, and we shook hands. Supposedly, you can learn a lot about someone by the way they shake hands, but I don't. Maybe it's the guitar callouses. All I saw was a bouncy little bloke, right round my size and nearly as skinny, maybe twenty years younger than me. There was something familiar about him that I couldn't pin down until I thought about it later: he had Patrick Ormand's hair, colour, cut, hairline, the lot. Very weird, that was.

By five minutes of six, Bree was completely distracted and tighter than an over-wound guitar string. It was nuts; her shoulders were hunched, she kept glancing at the door, and she couldn't stay out of the hall. Conversations about everything from real estate to compilation CDs to Homeland Security were floating all over the place, and Bree couldn't keep her attention on anything but the doorbell that hadn't rung, and wasn't ringing.

Just about the time she was being forced into remembering she was the hostess for this little do—people had finished their food and were looking for a place to stack dishes—the bell finally rang. Bree took a step, and was promptly grabbed by Heather Speirs, who wanted to ask her something.

I got the door. As much as I got her wanting to be the lady of the house, opening the door to the invited guests, this party had been her suggestion. She was the hostess; the kitchen and the food were her territory. Not just the food either—handling the guests who were already there was her gig, not mine.

So I answered the bell, and she and Solange got to show everyone else where to set their empty wineglasses. Bree shot me one *are you fucking kidding me I don't believe this* look, remembered her job as hostess, and led Heather into the kitchen.

"Are we late? I don't know what time it is, but I bet we're late." It was Folkie Lind, doing the talking as usual, with Star Woodley right behind him. "Star wasn't ready when I got there, so blame her, not me."

"Not blaming anyone, but yeah, everyone's already eaten. Come in, please, and let me shut that door. Straight down the hall—kitchen's at the back. No, not that door, that leads upstairs, and it needs to stay shut. We've got the cats locked upstairs for the evening. You need a loo, use this one."

They headed down the hall, me behind them. Looking at Star, I found myself wondering what she'd been taking time over. Whatever it was, it hadn't been getting dressed; she looked like an ageing hippie chick, wearing something shapeless with flowers on it, tights, and the same clogs Bree uses when she's working in the garden.

They followed the chatter into the kitchen, and of course, Folkie Lind turned the corner and walked straight into Curt. Literally, I mean; they basically banged foreheads.

Looking back, I think the only thing that kept it from being an even bigger clusterfuck than it was, was that the room was so full of people. It's a big kitchen, but fourteen people is a lot of people for one room, and it was very crowded.

"Oh. Dad." Curtis had stepped backwards, and was adjusting his glasses; they'd got bumped halfway off his nose. "Hi, how are you? Oh—hello, Star. Excuse me, I was just leaving."

Gordon *Bennett*. If I'd been wondering how Curt's band had got its name, here was the answer. His voice was so distant and so damned parky, he damned near left icicles in the air. Made me glad I've got no kids to dislike me that much.

"Hi Curt." Star smiled at him, at least I think it was a smile; it came and went too fast to be sure. "How are you? A little bird told me you're getting ready to go on the road. Too bad you can't take your girlfriend with you. Has to suck for her, sitting at home wondering what you're doing." She did that little not-quite smile again. "Or who you're doing."

It was beyond bizarre. I couldn't suss whether she was deliberately trying to stir up shit, or whether she was missing some sort of filter that might let her function with actual thinking human beings. Either way, she'd stirred it up; Curt was ashy with rage, and Solange was bright red.

"That's a really poisonous thing to say."

If I'd thought Curt sounded parky, he had nothing on Bree. She'd taken a step toward Solange and Curt—solidarity, I'd say—and she was looking at Star Woodley with the sort of hate I hadn't seen in her face for a long time. "It's also inaccurate. Just because you don't know how to spell the word 'loyalty,' that doesn't mean other people are as impaired as you are. So you might want to tell that invisible little bird of yours to schedule a visit with the Clue Fairy, or the Mind Your Own Damned Business For A Change Fairy, or maybe even the Shut The Fuck Up Fairy. But of course, you never were much for minding your own damned business, were you, *Esther?*"

Oh, bloody hell. Everyone was staring, and no surprise; if Bree was angry enough to forget that this toxic woman was a guest under our roof, she was right at the edge of losing it. Mac was watching the byplay, and I saw his lips wanting to purse up; Jeff Kintera backed up a step and Domitra was in battle stance, waiting for something to blow so that she could kill it.

"I wasn't trying to offend anyone, just saying what I think." Star sounded mild, and uninterested, and unaware of anything in the way of undercurrents. "Nice kitchen."

I was thankful for my tickybox right about then, because Star Woodley was making my skin move on my bones. She was looking anywhere but at Bree; her stare was moving all over the room, and this time, I could see what she was doing. She was scoping out everything in Bree's kitchen: the custom-made island, the All-Clad hanging off the ceiling racks, the crystal wineglasses, all the granite and stainless steel, the huge Sub-Zero fridge. You could practically see the dollar signs over her head, or maybe it was something else. Envy, or resentment, or maybe just squirreling info away to use later.

Even back in the days when I was still married to Cilla, back when Bree felt she had no right to spend my money unless it was going to be used on me, our kitchen was something Bree never argued with me about spending money on. Our only row had been over the fridge; I wanted to buy it for her as a prezzie but she'd insisted on paying for it, because I'm not a foodie and it was an extravagance. The kitchen's her workspace, her office, and the place where she feels safest.

So yeah, it's had a lot of dosh spent on it, and that shows. And Star Woodley, having just insulted a couple of guests and been insulted straight back by her hostess, was standing there as if everything was normal, looking around and mentally pricing the cookware.

"Bree, JP, thanks for a nice afternoon." Curt was still narked—you couldn't miss it—but Bree having issued the smackdown seemed to have freed him up to just let it go, and leave. "Solange, babe, I need to take off. Can I get a ride?"

Solange hadn't even glanced Star's way. "Of course. Bree, can you spare me for half an hour? Curt's bike is parked at my place—I'll just drop him off, and come straight back to help with the cleanup. All right?"

"Sure."

She stalked out of the kitchen, Curt and Solange right behind her. Tony and Katia both looked freaked; they've been coming over here on a regular basis for thirty years, and I don't think they'd ever seen Bree be rude to a guest before. Me, I was thinking it was lucky my wife wasn't planning to sit in on the meeting. She was ready to kill something.

"That's my kid for you. Isn't he something?"

However I'd have thought Folkie Lind would sound after that brush-off by Curt, it wasn't what I heard. He sounded, I don't know, proud, or indulgent, or admiring. Personally, I'd have been mortified.

"That was your son?" Andy Valdon was watching Folkie and Star, pretty much to the exclusion of everyone else. I caught his eye, just for a moment, and found myself tightening up, muscles and nerves and the tickybox too. He had more in common with Patrick Ormand than just the hair; the eyes looked to have been chipped out of the same block of dirty ice as Patrick's. "He seems pretty pissed off at you. What's up with that?"

That answered every question I had about Andy Valdon, and his tactics. Folkie Lind had just got the snub royale from his own son, in front of the last group of people on earth he'd want to see that. Everyone else in the room was being tactful, not mentioning it, not even making eye contact. Everyone else was letting it go.

But Andy, ice-dirt eyes and a voice like a twelve-year-old, stated what everyone else in the room was doing their best to avoid, and damned if he didn't get his answer. This bloke wasn't naive; he hadn't been naive since he'd stopped wearing nappies. He was a damned laser beam, is what he was.

"Yeah, Curt and I don't get along. Old news. I get on his last nerve. I'm proud of him, though—he's a good kid." Folkie looked out at the dining room, through the swinging doors, and saw the chafing dishes and trays. Bree was going to leave them there until after the meeting, apparently. "Okay if I get myself something to eat?"

"That's what it's there for, mate." I glanced down the hall. No sign of Bree; she'd probably gone out to talk to Curt and Solange. "We ought to get this meeting started soon, unless we're planning on a late night."

We ended up being eleven people at the dining room table, so that worked out. I basically dozed through most of that meeting; dinner had caught up to me, the house was nice and warm, and the business stuff was mostly going straight over my head. Besides, I wasn't actually needed, not beyond being the other half of Bree's hosting deal, and nodding at whatever our people said. Carla and Andy knew every detail, and Mac probably wasn't far behind. Besides, from what I'd been hearing, it was basic stuff, paperwork and permit signoffs and all that.

Folkie and Star gulped their food, and everyone settled down with a glass of something. Bree stayed in the kitchen, loading the dishwasher and doing the pots, leaving the hand-drying and the wineglasses for Solange. I wasn't expecting any surprises. If there were any, it wasn't my problem or my job to cope: that was why Carla and Andy were here.

Carla introduced Andy, and made it clear he'd be handling anything to do with Blacklight's participation in the 707. She mentioned his credentials with Silver Streak—that gave everyone a good reason to check him out, but I already had. I was planning on having a quiet word with him about his tactics before the night was over, but I'd sussed him out.

Tony wasn't dozing off, but he was letting Katia do what she does best, which is handle his stuff. She'd done her homework, and had a list of questions, from equipment upgrades to fee breakdowns for the individual shareholders. I closed my eyes, just resting them, listening to my MS ramp up, reminding myself to get my interferon out of the fridge, because shooting yourself up with cold medicine is no fun at all. The meeting went on, people talking, asking questions. I could hear Bree moving about in the other room, and a murmur of voices. Solange must have come back in while I was dozing...

"...last set of papers is the city and county inspection agreements." Carla'd been talking, rustling papers. "Andy has the master copies. We'll pass them around, get your signatures, and send you copies. If anyone has any questions, this would be the time to ask them."

"I do." It was Folkie. Now I thought about it, he and Star had been quiet the entire meeting. "What exactly are we giving them permission to inspect? What would they be looking for?"

That got my eyes open and focussed. One chair was empty—Star wasn't at the table.

Andy turned in his chair. "Code violations, mostly. Things like structural integrity. Parking and handicapped access. Foundations, electrical, fire, earthquake strapping. The usual. They also get copies of the full financial disclosures—access to see who's in for how much, and where the money's coming from. Why?"

Lind was holding his pen. "No particular reason. Pass them on down here. Hello, where'd you come from?"

For a moment, I couldn't figure out what he was on about. Then he leaned over the side of his chair, and I heard a high complaining cat voice. Farrowen's a Siamese, and they're talkative buggers. What in hell was she doing down here? We'd locked the cats upstairs. For some reason, I had alarm bells going off along my nervous system.

"Excuse me a minute—be right back." I got up and headed for the kitchen. "Bree?"

She wasn't there. I stepped out into the hall. The door to the guest loo was open, no one inside, but the door leading upstairs was shut.

I opened the door and headed upstairs. Halfway up, I heard voices, and stopped where I was.

"...goddamned fucking gall!" It was Bree, sounding as if she was about to not give a damn who heard her. "Who the hell do you think you are, you sleazy bitch..."

I took the rest of the stairs two at a time. It's a nice wide stair, with a curve in it, and taking it fast always leaves me out of breath and shaky. Tonight, I barely noticed.

"I was just looking for -"

"I don't give a shit what you were looking for." Christ, Bree was about to kill her. It was there, in her voice. I had a serious stitch in one side, but I didn't slow down. They weren't out in the hall—the master bedroom door was open, and the voices were coming from there. "You're a guest under our roof, *Esther*. How dare you abuse our hospitality? How dare you sneak around my house and look through my stuff?"

"Bree?" I'd got there, finally, but the tickybox was practically humming and I had no spare air. "What in hell...?"

They were in the master suite bathroom. Rather, Star was inside—Bree was in the doorway, in full outraged Valkyrie mode, and she wasn't letting Star out. From the set of her shoulders, it was a damned good thing I use an electric razor and not blades or a straight-edge, because my wife was angry enough to do something she couldn't take back or explain later.

"Bree? What's going on here?"

She swung her head towards me. Both her hands were clenched into fists. "I was washing dishes and Wolfling came in and banged my ankles. I found the upstairs door wide open, so I came upstairs. And look what I found: Esther, here, in our bathroom, going through our medicine chest."

"I was just -"

"You were snooping." Oh Christ. Bree had her right arm pulled back and her head cocked. She was going to deck the woman. "You were doing what you always do, what you used to do, getting your rocks off spying around on other people, storing it up like some kind of blackmailer. You think that gives you some kind of power? Cred, maybe? You're a pathetic little loser and a vicious bitch. You always have been, and you haven't changed."

"Okay." I got between them. "Bree, take a breath. Star? Out. You've overstayed your welcome here."

"I was just looking for the bathroom." Her expression hadn't changed, and neither had her voice. "I couldn't find the one downstairs."

"Bollocks to that. I pointed it out to you on the way in." The woman was nuts. "And you're leaving. Let's go. I can't speak for my wife, but I don't want you in my house, not after this. Bree, love, can I get you to move, please? I'm going to see Star off the premises."

"Good evening! I'm Jeff Kintera, and welcome to the 707 Club. On behalf of the ownership and staff, a big thank-you to everyone who RSVP'd for this party tonight."

"Whoa, the new PA sounds great." Billy Dumont, off to one side of me, looked out at the line arrays. "It'll be interesting seeing what the differences are, between this and the old stuff, once we start playing. Damon's practically drooling on the new soundboard computer. He loves his high-tech toys."

He craned his neck around me, and grinned at Tony, who grinned back and flipped him off. He probably knew what was coming. "Nice to see Bankcuso's money going to a good cause."

"As everyone knows, tonight is purely a private affair, guest list only. The band will be on in a moment, but first I've been asked to acknowledge the new ownership of the 707, everyone involved in the revamping of our sound system…"

"Yeah, it's good high-end gear. The house techs seem to be happy with it, as well." I glanced at the stage, made sure the roadies had remembered my usual stool.

We were waiting just offstage. The place was only about a quarter full, but that was fine; this was a private party, no gate receipts to be counted. Patrick had seventy or so guests here, and the rest were friends of the band, friends or clients of the various ownership people, and some local media, probably invited by Guitar Wizard and Jeff himself. "Everyone comfortable with 'Americaland,' then? Curtis? Mac?"

"I sure am." Curt Lind was behind me, with Slim strapped on and ready to go. He made a face. "I just wish they'd waited until after the gig to paint the place. Even all that food isn't drowning out the paint smell."

Mac was doing his usual pre-show limbering up. "I'm with Curt. What were they thinking? Damned paint fumes are a headache looking for a place to happen, or rather, looking for someone to happen to."

"Dude, paint smells like ass." Domitra had already grabbed a skewer of something from the buffet. "You should get one of these. Jerk chicken. Smells a lot better. Tastes a lot better, too. Bree knows her shit."

"...*something for everyone. A killer show, food provided by Noshing But The Best Catering, open bar, and a test of the 707's new sound system. A special hello to Patrick Ormand and his guests, here to celebrate the opening of Ormand Investigations, in San Francisco. These days, Patrick is Blacklight's chief security officer, but he's worked with everyone from Interpol to NYPD to San Francisco Homicide in his day. With that background, we're sure the new detective agency will rock...*"

I glanced out into the house. The total headcount, after all the RSVPs had been counted, had come in at four hundred seventy people, and Bree had been so busy the past week, I'd barely seen her. She'd nailed Solange down as her main help, but there was no way in hell she was going to be able to feed that many people with one person helping. So she'd called in some favours, strong-armed some of her usual helpers into kicking in time and effort in exchange for God knows what, and assembled a staff of about a dozen people. For all I knew, she was paying them out of her own pocket.

The upshot was, Solange had got thrown in the deep end. That got Bree the answer she wanted, about whether or not Solange had the right stuff, and the answer was yeah, she did. The girl thrived on pressure, and she soaked up new information like a sponge. Born versus made was getting answered.

I hadn't known much about what was going on at the cooking end. The last two weeks, I'd been pretty buried myself, deep in rehearsal mode at the Bombardiers studio on Freelon Street. We had Mac sitting in, and Curt as well, and that meant tweaking the set list for a second guitar and two lead vocalists, not to mention working the kinks out of 'Americaland.'

We'd ended up working long hours, putting in a couple of ten-hour days. Poor Tony ended up having to play chauffeur, since both Bree and Solange were busy. I wasn't about to get on the back of Curt's motorbike, and Solange was using her truck to ferry Bree's staff and supplies out to the industrial kitchens she uses. Bree and I'd seen so little of each other the past two weeks, I might as well have been on the road.

Last night, though, we'd finally managed to be home at the same time, and we'd sat down and eaten a proper meal together. She was buzzed and wired—she always is, just before a major gig. I helped her get some sleep in the approved marital way, with a good hard bit of slap and tickle. Just before we both conked out, I'd asked how Solange was holding up.

"Born." Bree kissed me once. "Totally born." Then she'd smiled blindingly at me, closed her eyes, and passed out for the next seven hours.

"We have a fantastic lineup tonight. Our own Fog City Geezers, with two very special guests: the one and only Malcolm Sharpe—yes, folks, that's Blacklight's Mac!—and Curtis Lind, of the Bay Area's Grammy-winning Mad At Our Dads…"

"So where's the rest of the minority ownership tonight? Anyone seen the Lindyhops? I haven't heard a peep out of them since Star Woodley misbehaved at the meeting." Tony was peering out into the house; one wall was a solid line of buffet tables, cook staff at every station. They'd changed the usual layout—the small tables and chairs the audience used usually lived along both walls, with a few rows at the back, but not tonight.

"Whoops, sorry." Tony caught a look from Curt. "I keep forgetting, you really are mad at your dad."

Curt grinned, but it faded fast. "They're both here. I saw Star getting some food a while ago. If she's here, my father's here too. You can't have a remora without a shark, right?"

"This is also a celebration for the New Improved 707! No, not yet—but we've just found out that, once the Powers That Be finish checking out our paperwork and confirm that our money sources are as pure as our intentions, we'll be good to go for a major expansion of the club. So, help yourself to some great food, and prepare to the dance the night away. Ladies and gentlemen and everyone in between, the Fog City Geezers!"

Right. Showtime.

It was a brilliant first set. It's nice, playing with pros. You can't pick and choose when you're just starting out. Back in my early days as a session player, I had to do too much work with clueless amateurs, and I promised myself I'd avoid doing that again unless I was desperate for the dosh. Joining Blacklight had meant I'd never had to worry about not having enough money.

It also meant not having to work with one-trick wonders, or amateurs. Everyone onstage at the 707 that night was a solid pro, and I was damned thankful for it. The MS was making pissy little noises at me; my hands had been tingling and my legs had been shaky all day. Any other time, Bree would have been there, bullying me into resting, making sure I ate properly. Not today, though—I'd been on my own since breakfast. Solange had come over to eat with us; with all the set-up involved in a catering gig this size, they were out the door and loading up two minutes after Bree'd turned on the dishwasher.

The Geezers, well, that's my band. I put it all together, I front them, I do most of what passes for singing when we gig. Tonight, though, I was happy to sit back and let Curt take most of the spotlight. When it came down to it, he was the new kid in town, you know? I didn't have to say anything to Mac, either; he got it. The whole first set, he sang harmonies and vamped it up on the harmonica, just digging it, letting Curt handle the lead singing while I let him handle the flashier guitar stuff. Slim, that PRS of his, got quite a workout.

About halfway through the first set, I stepped up to the mic. Bree was right there front of house, near the side of the stage, wearing her chef's gear: black and white checked trousers, white jacket, sensible shoes, hair pulled back in a ponytail. She was looking cranky, and it took me a moment to realise what the problem was: her hips wanted to move to the music, but she wasn't here in her usual capacity as the rocker's wife. She was here professionally, doing a gig herself, and that meant no dancing.

I grinned to myself. She probably had no clue how hot she looked in that gear, but she was going to find out all about it later, when I got her home and got her to trade the sensible shoes for a pair of her Jimmy Choos. For the moment, though, I had a different way in mind to make her night.

I adjusted the mic. "Oi! Everyone having a good time? Everyone getting some nosh, then?"

Hoots, yells, cheers. Bree was watching me, her hands on her hips; Solange had come up next to her, whispering something and grinning. I saw her wave toward Curt.

"Okay. We've got a new song up next, a thing called 'Americaland.' Before we do, though, can we get a round of applause for the catering staff? Because my wife's the hot chick in the chef's outfit, and she put this all together, and believe me, mates, it was hard work."

I blew a kiss out toward the buffet tables. "Ta, love. For the fantastic food and for everything else, too."

I was nearly drowned out by a huge roar of applause, more hoots and cheering. I saw Bree's jaw drop, blew her another kiss, and turned back to the band. Curtis was looking at me, waiting for his cue. "One, two, one two three four...!"

"Americaland" got its first live look at the 707, and it stone fucking killed. No one outside the band family had heard the song before, but by the time we got to the run-out of "this is Americaland", the crowd was chanting along with Curt and Mac. Tony's piano part was a revelation—he found an edge at the low end of the keyboard and synched up with Kris Corcoran's bass, a kind of double thunder to match up with the two guitars. Billy Dumont was back there behind the drum kit, holding it together. Billy's a seriously underrated drummer, if you ask me. He can do the fancy percussion stuff if you need him to, and as a pure rhythm-setter, he nails it every time.

We ratcheted everything up even higher when we closed out the first set. When we'd put the setlist together, we'd gone with "Liplock" as the first set closer. Curt hung back and played rhythm guitar for that, because Mac is the frontman on "Liplock." The audience would have raised Cain if we'd changed that; after *Book of Days*, "Liplock" is associated with Malcolm Sharpe, no matter where in the world you happen to be. It's become one of his signature tunes.

Besides, Curt didn't seem to have got singing about sex and

making it convincing down yet. He didn't seem to fancy singing about it anyway; his voice was better suited toward the cerebral stuff, politics and broken hearts and the emo stuff, you know? But Mac's made "Liplock" his bitch.

Blacklight spent nearly two years on the road touring *Book of Days*, playing twenty-thousand seaters to start off. When the CD redlined at number one and demand for tickets got out of control, we'd done a second world tour, playing stadiums that held a hundred thousand people.

A stadium show has its own kind of power, but there's a trade-off. You lose something, doing these huge gigs: you can't interact with the audience. They're too far away, separated by security staff and a big stage set, and maybe even by the whole Rock God mystique, shite though it is.

Now here we were, playing a private gig for a few hundred people, and they were right there, you know? No barricades, no security except for Dom, unless Patrick was splitting his attention between his party guests and the band; just us, eye to eye with an audience of invited guests, a couple of feet away. And Mac, who'd started out forty years ago with Luke in a small club band called Blackpool Southern, decided he was going to interact in a big way.

"*Mama, pretty mama, honey lock your lips on me.*"

He was sitting on the edge of the stage, dangling his legs, crooning into the wireless mic. There were a handful of women right up front, dancing and rocking out. Not girls—women in their thirties or forties. No idea whose guests they were, but they were dressed for a party, and that meant serious cleavage.

They were all digging it, but one of them in particular, a leggy brunette with big eyes, wasn't looking anywhere but at Mac, and Mac was looking right back at her. There was something familiar about her, but I couldn't sort out what it was.

"*Slide 'em down lower, I'll be yellin' like a banshee…*"

113

Mac slipped offstage and into the front row. He got one arm round the brunette, and pulled her up close, singing straight at her. *"Lock 'em on me low, there's a fire down below, lock me down, honey, take it deep, take it slow…."*

Her mouth was open, total shock. Then she smiled up at him, and I realised who it was I'd been seeing at the back of my head: Maria Genovese, the NYPD Homicide detective who'd been in charge of the investigation when Blacklight's security chief, Phil MacDermott, was killed. Same big dark eyes, same general look. Worst of all, the same smile. This bird was gorgeous.

"Just a little nibble, honey, just a little touch, don't bother sayin' that I want it too much…"

Maria Genovese had been the only woman I'd ever seen actually get under Mac's skin. She was also one of the few women on earth he had no chance in hell of getting next to. Genovese had a long-term sweetie, and the sweetie was called Charlotte. All his charisma, his charm, every tool he's got, were wasted, lost, on Maria Genovese. She was gay.

But here was this lookalike out in the house, and Mac had one arm round her, resting on her hip. Not only wasn't he letting go of her, he was actually waltzing her onstage with him, for a nice hot dance. And she was going for it. They were onstage now, and crikey, the sex was coming off the pair of them in waves.

"Lock me up, lock me down…"

He had one hand on her bum, pulling her up close, groin to groin, letting her ease back, pulling her up close again. They were doing the bump.

"You got me in a liplock…"

I looked out and found Dom with no trouble at all. She was just offstage, not looking as relaxed as she had when she'd been gorging on Bree's jerk chicken satay. But she didn't look too worried, either.

I glanced at the rest of the band. Curt wasn't watching Mac;

he was concentrating on playing. Kris and Billy, who didn't know about the woman I'd nicknamed the Gorgeous Detective and Bree'd called Detective Lollabrigida, were loving it, feeding off the energy, grinning at each other.

Tony wasn't grinning. He'd toured with us, been there, seen it all go down, watched Mac get his heart broken. We met each other's eye for a few seconds, and yeah, he was thinking the same thing I was. I just hoped Mac was in it for a quick hit of hot sex, over and out. The last thing he needed was a pale substitute for the woman he'd wanted and couldn't have; not fair to either of them.

"Lock it up, lock it down, you got me in a liplock…"

I ran the guitar out, and we hit the last notes. Mac and the brunette were still staring at each other. I stepped up to the mic.

"We're going to take a short break. See everyone in about twenty minutes, all right?"

We stayed out front. There was no reason to hit the band room, not at a private party. Anyway, all the food was out front, and so was Bree. She was handing a few strangers empty plates, pointing out what was in each chafing dish. A few tables down, Solange and one of Bree's regular helpers were doing the same for Heather Speirs and Carla, as well as a group of people I'd never seen before. Across the room, Andy Valdon had snared a table; he was waving at Folkie Lind, who was just coming down the stairs from the gallery, where the office was.

I made my way over to my wife, and gave her a fast kiss. She really did look hot in that chef's gear…

"Hey, JP—the band sounds great." I hadn't seen Patrick come up next to us. "Hi, Bree. Did I say thanks for all this? It's great, even if the paint smell makes it feel as if we're in an episode of *This Old House*."

"Glad you're enjoying it."

I took the plate Bree was holding out, and got a mouthful of food. I had the feeling my plan to jump on my wife later might need to be postponed a day or two. The MS was really making noise at me, arms and legs tingling, and I was hot in all the wrong ways right now. Bree shot me a worried look, but there was sod all she could do to help; we were both working at the moment. "Ta, love. I wish they'd redone the air conditioning in here, but there wasn't time. And yeah, with you on the pong, Patrick. Next time we do this, we're waiting for the damned paint to dry. I can't take the stink."

"It really is strong. When did they finish painting? Yesterday?" Mac had come up, leading the brunette by the hand. Close up, she reminded me of Maria Genovese even more. "Bree, angel, is there anything purely veggie in any of those pans? This is Anabellita, and she's a vegetarian. We need -"

He stopped, wrinkling his nose. A moment later, I caught it myself: the paint smell was suddenly much stronger, strong enough to make my eyes water. "Bree, I think one of your chafing dishes is burning—what in hell is that?"

Beepbeepbeep.

Shit. I must have forgotten to flip the amp to standby; Little Queenie had got herself into some kind of feedback loop, and a damned piercing one, too. I turned towards the stage, but Bree got hold of my arm, and held it hard. She was trying not to cough.

"John, oh my God." Bree was pointing up with her free hand, and her nails were digging into my forearm. Smoke was pouring off the upstairs gallery, down towards the club's ground floor. I saw a long tongue of flame, red-white and hot, jut out into the air right above our heads. It spread to the wooden railings; over the beeping of the fire alarm and the pandemonium out on the floor, I heard the freshly-painted wood begin to crackle. "We have to get everyone out—the club's on fire!"

Chapter Seven

It's a funny thing, being scared shitless—the way it takes different people, I mean.

I already know how fast Bree gets it together in a crisis. Back when I had my first heart attack, stepping offstage after a Blacklight gig in Boston, she'd been on the phone with 911 three seconds later. She'd been the one to tell the paramedics my history with heroin so that they didn't fuck up on my meds, the one to calm the rest of the band down, the one to hold it together. Mac said later I probably would have died if she hadn't had it so together. He's probably right.

I wasn't really surprised that Patrick Ormand was just about as calm as my wife was, either, not once the shit hit the fan. He's got ice water where his blood ought to be. And, right, that's one of the things that narks me most about him, but there are times it's useful. Having the building burning down around us? Yeah, definitely one of those times.

"*The front doors and fire exits on the south side of the building are open. Everyone please proceed out into the parking lot—there's no need to panic. Just leave your belongings and use the front doors. The fire department's on their way.*"

I looked up and saw Jeff Kintera onstage. He'd had the sense to grab a mic, and he was putting it to good use. He was being so damned calm and together, you'd have thought he was telling people to get out into the parking lot because someone was giving away free ice cream.

I made a mental note to myself, to double whatever we were paying him, but I didn't have time to think about it, because I was surrounded by the rest of the band and we were being pushed, not towards the front with five hundred other people, but down the corridor that led to the backstage exit. The last look I got over my shoulder, the entire gallery was a mass of flame and Patrick, standing near the front exits with Carla, was shooing people out in a steady stream, making sure no one lost it enough to start a stampede.

Something heavy crashed down from the upper level, a chunk of the gallery or maybe the roof; it hit the middle of the auditorium, and I saw a huge flare of colour and heat, as the sparks from the burning wood found the catering supplies. There was a deafening crack of noise, and all the air seemed to be sucked out the building for a moment. The tables, where Bree and Solange had been standing not ten minutes earlier, exploded. They went up all together, like a Guy Fawkes display.

"Move." It was Tony, with his hand in the small of my back. The passageway was hot as Lucifer's sauna, and I was beginning to choke. Everything was filled with smoke, and not only couldn't I breathe properly, I couldn't see, either. "You can't do anything, just go. Backstage door—it's open. Shit, JP, will you fucking hustle!"

If this all sounds calm, yeah, well, think again. That whole thing about reacting to being scared shitless, that applies to me, too. I've been in plenty of crises in my time, but the thing is, I'd usually been the one causing the crisis: heart attack, drug overdose, MS meltdown, the lot. Even when Patrick Ormand had completely fucked up and let us get shot at on the red carpet at Cannes a few years back, all my panicking was done face down, at the bottom of a pile; Patrick had covered Bree, and she'd covered me. This was my first time in a crisis where I was just one of the crowd, and I was flipping my shit, losing it, freaking the hell out.

I couldn't see behind me. I couldn't see Bree.

The noise—Christ. Not likely to forget it, you know? It's signed a lease in my nightmares, moved in a plasma TV, taken up residence. It never occurred to me before, that fire has a voice. It does, though: you can almost hear words, hear it chewing and digesting its way through walls and furniture and maybe people, and the thing is, it sounds *angry*, seriously pissed off. There's nothing about the sound of fire that doesn't sound like a disturbed hornet's nest.

"Tony?" I was coughing hard enough to make things hurt. "Is Bree behind you?"

No answer—he just kept pushing. He's bigger than I am, and quite a lot stronger, and he wasn't taking no for an answer. At that point, I was scared half off my nut. Where in hell was my wife?

Part of my mind, the part that wasn't in meltdown panic mode, was trying to sort out the noise of the other five hundred people. The crowd was reasonably calm, all things considered—either that, or they'd pretty much all got safely out of doors. I trusted Patrick and Carla to get people out and make sure no one started a real panic; they were the two most competent people in the building, hands down. Only Domitra came close.

Once the rational side of my brain sorted that out, I got back to stumbling along in the smoke, trying to breath and feeling the tickybox keeping my heartbeat from going nonlinear with being frantic about my wife. I couldn't see anything through all that smoke, and I didn't have any room to worry about what might be happening at the other end of the 707.

That walk through the backstage passage took about three minutes longer than forever. Really, it probably only took about two minutes—from the inside backstage door to the outside one wasn't that far. But I'd reached the point of thinking *right, okay, I've died and I'm in some version of Hell where I'll have to spend the rest of bleedin' eternity fighting my way down this corridor with Tony pushing me in the back and I can't find Bree and no one's answering any questions oh fuck Little Queenie I left the guitar onstage Bree's going to kill me her wedding present I have to go back where's Bree oh Christ…*

Right about then, I got hit in the face with a blast of nice normal air; it was heated air, but it was clean, and I got both lungs full, doubling over and coughing. We were out in the parking lot at the back of the 707, just across from the little warehouse where Paul Morgenstern had kept his Bambi trailer and a couple of million dollars worth of stolen art, and where a roadie named Rosario had pissed off the wrong person and got himself killed. I rubbed the water out of my eyes, caught the reek of ash on my hands, and looked around.

Tony, Kris, Billy…the band was there. Billy was being led away by a paramedic. I heard the bloke say something about oxygen, and yeah, Billy needed it, if the colour of his face was any clue. Mac and Dom were there; Mac looked seriously shaken, something that doesn't happen often. Curt was there, holding on to Solange for dear life—she was crying, and her face was filthy. Katia was there, in meltdown hysterics. Tony went straight for his wife, got hold of her, and held on. He had a couple of burns on his face. They looked painful.

"Solange!" I didn't think I was being particularly loud, but everyone shut up completely, even Katia. "For God's sake, where's Bree?"

"I don't know." Solange had streaks of soot in her hair. One wispy bit had come loose, and it was charred at the end, where something, maybe a spark, had caught it and set it on fire. Her eyes were swollen, I don't whether it was from smoke or crying or both. "The last I saw her, she was behind us. I thought she was coming out behind Curt, but she didn't. I don't know where she went—I couldn't see."

Her voice was all over the place. There was black smoke pouring out the backstage door. "I don't know," she told me. Out of nowhere, she sagged at the knees, and Curt caught her. "I think she's still inside."

I went past them fast, past Tony, past Mac and Dom. I remember that I heard voices, Mac, Curt, voices behind me saying things like *Johnny wait no you can't go in there are you fucking nuts get the fire people it's their job Domitra what in hell are you doing?* I remember that I stopped a few feet shy of the door, and took a good long breath. I remember thinking there probably wasn't much breathable air left in there.

"Stay low to the ground." It was Dom, at my back, ignoring Mac; he was yelling, but my head was elsewhere, trying to figure out how to do this. She'd already dropped into a crouch; like I said, she's competent. "Heat rises—the good shit's down low, the real air. You get a better chance that way. I'm right behind you. Go."

"John! Wait!"

I turned, hard and fast, straight into Dom, knocking her over. Bree was there, out in the parking lot. She'd come round from the front; Patrick and Carla were with her. She was holding Little Queenie wrapped in both arms.

I got across the lot somehow. About five feet away, I stopped.

Like I said, it's funny how differently people react to being scared shitless. Right that moment, I was furious, absolutely murderous. I was honestly afraid that, if I touched her, I was going to beat her to a pulp.

She'd risked dying, risked leaving me alone, to rescue the damned guitar. Knowing why she'd done it—and yeah, I knew—didn't make me any less angry.

"John?" Oh Christ, she'd read it, in my face. "Don't be mad. I couldn't let her burn. Don't be mad. Don't. Please?"

Ah, sod it. The rage could wait.

I got hold of her, and she was warm and shaking under my hands, and I think it was at that point I started sobbing like a damned baby and couldn't stop. Someone, I think it was Mac, came over and prised Little Queenie away from her. I was damned glad about that, because the guitar was between us and the peghead was pressing against my chest, right up against the tickybox, and it hurt like hell. My teeth were chattering. Ridiculous, that was—the air was hot, blasts of heat coming out of the 707. We might as well have been standing just outside a glassblower's furnace.

"You scared the shit out of me." I heard myself, babbling like an idiot. "I thought you were gone. I thought you'd got caught inside. I can't believe you went back for the fucking guitar, it's just a piece of wood, you could have been killed, are you out of your mind -"

Her teeth were chattering, too. "I had to. I'm sorry. I couldn't not. I—you don't understand. Later. Not now. I can't—I don't want -"

There was a crowd out in the back lot, now. They might have been spillover from the party guests who'd come out the front doors, or maybe they were locals, people who lived around Francisco Boulevard. There were sirens blipping and wailing everywhere, police shooing everyone to a safe distance, three big fire trucks, men with axes and hoses and all that fire-fighting gear, hitting the building with everything they had to get things under control.

"I do understand. Shut up." I held on for dear life. "I know why you went back. Tell me later. Just—don't talk, not now. Oh Christ, what the fuck do you want? Sod off, will you?"

"Excuse me." It was a San Rafael cop. He'd probably heard enough people in shock to where he wasn't going to hold me being rude against me. "We need everyone to vacate this area."

Half the guests seemed to have crammed themselves into the overflow lot of the car dealership across the street. We headed over; I was hanging on to Bree's hand a bit too tightly, but right then I wasn't planning on letting go of her. She didn't seem to mind.

We stood there, five hundred people, and watched the 707 burn, pretty much to the foundations.

It was a spectacular fire, if you like fires. I don't, much. I also don't know a lot about them, but for some reason, I got the feeling that this one was hotter and faster than your basic house fire. I remembered the smell of paint; maybe that had helped things get out of control faster than usual. And of course, there were the chafing dishes, and all the fuel downstairs. Those had gone up big and loud, but that was after the fire had caught, well after, in fact. I remembered looking back as the sparks caught the buffet tables; the flames had been mostly white, rather than red, and wasn't white supposed to mean that the fire was about as hot as fire could get?

I had one arm round Bree, and was hanging on. There were four bright yellow fire engines surrounding as much of the 707 as they could, covering the club on three sides, and we were getting cooled off by a fine mist from the water they were hitting the 707 with. I saw a few paramedic ambulances out there, as well. People were being checked out, given whatever treatment the medics decided they needed for smoke inhalation or minor burns, and sent off again. No one seemed to be badly hurt, and no one was panicking.

With my wife right there and safe, I was beginning to calm down myself, at least enough to take inventory of the people I knew. The band were all out, safe and accounted for; Katia was still weepy, but Tony had it under control. He was probably going to have a couple of scars if he didn't head over to the ambulances and get something put on those burns. Kris Corcoran's wife Sandra looked to have stayed calm pretty much the entire time, but Sandra's like that. She's not one to get her knickers in a twist, and her being calm kept Kris calm.

Curtis and Solange seemed fine as well, and thank God for it, because if anything had happened to Solange...yeah, well, it hadn't, and I wasn't going to have to break bad news to Luke. Mac had managed to find the Genovese lookalike, or possibly she'd managed to find him—what was her name? Anabellita, right. She had a big sooty smear at the top of her cleavage; it looked like an arrow, pointing straight down to the good parts, not that Mac needed a roadmap. They were watching the fire-fighters. Just to Mac's left, Domitra was watching Mac, and right behind her were all three of the Bombardiers' road and sound crew.

"Carla and Patrick are okay." Bree must have been doing that marital mind-reading thing we have going sometimes. "And I saw Jeff Kintera out in front. He'd sucked down some smoke, but the paramedics were giving him oxygen."

"Good."

Who else? Heather Speirs had been there; I remembered seeing Solange explaining some of the food to her, early on. Andy Valdon was there, as well.

The ground shook suddenly, and I jumped. A huge section of the roof had caved in. When it hit the ground, a shower of fire and hot sparks went straight up. There was just enough of a breeze to keep the lighter pieces of burning wood high in the air. I wondered whether they were going to be able to save anything at all, whether the damned thing was going to spread to other buildings.

"Looks like they've got it under control." Curt and Solange had come up next to us. Curt's voice was normal, but his face wasn't. He was tight as Bree's shoulders get sometimes. His glasses were dirty. "Four-alarmer, also known in Marin as One Honkin' Big Ass Fire. So much for the new sound system. What a waste of a pair of perfectly good line arrays."

"Oh, baby, I'm sorry. I'm so sorry." Solange sounded soft, and miserable. I wondered what she was talking about. It wasn't as if she'd torched the place, you know?

He shrugged, and looked down at her. "It's just a guitar, Solange. I can buy another one."

Oh, bloody hell—the PRS, his new axe, Slim. It had been on-stage, sitting in its stand, not two feet away from the guitar Bree'd risked her neck to rescue.

Curt had got hold of Solange's hand, and was swinging it back and forth. For all that she was the one who was sorry about something, he was the one doing the consoling. "As long as you're safe," he told her, "I could give a shit about anything else. Hell, I'd burn every guitar I've got to keep you warm."

Bree leaned against me suddenly, and I heard her sigh. She's too tall to rest her head on my shoulder, the way birds always seem to do in books and movies and all that. I could smell the smoke in her hair.

I tightened my arm, got the other one round her, and jerked her into a full hug.

"I love you." I was whispering. No one's business but ours, yeah? Thing is, I needed to say it right then. It wasn't going to wait. "And if you ever pull a stunt like that again, I'll bloody cripple you. Yeah, I know why you did it, and you can tell me all about what I already know later, but listen to me, because I'm only saying this once: Fuck the guitar. You can always get Bruno Baines to make me another guitar, but there's only ever been one you. You're not replaceable, Bree. Got it? We clear now?"

Of course she wasn't answering that. I knew why she'd gone back for Little Queenie; a couple of years back, I might not have known, but I did now. In Bree's head, Queenie was the first real gift she had any right to give me. For her, it sealed the fact that we'd finally got married, that she had some standing, that she was actually my wife. The guitar was as much a symbol to her, of us as a real couple, as her wedding ring was.

She stayed where she was, letting me hold her, not letting me see her face. My legs were shaking, but I ignored them.

Curt was right, the fire was definitely under control; there was still smoke, but it looked different. It smelled different as well, mostly white and billowing up like steam, rather than the scary black flame-shot stuff that had been choking everyone. At least there was no asbestos in there—we'd had that checked, as part of the City's first inspection.

I was watching the doings, and Bree had her back to the club. So she didn't see two fire-fighters coming out of what used to be the front doors with a stretcher between them. They were walking as fast as they could, but they were being careful.

There was a body bag on the stretcher.

I must have jerked, or tensed up, because something clued Bree in that something was going on behind her. "John...?"

"Shit. Someone's dead—they've brought out a body."

I let go of her. She had one hand up, covering her mouth; her eyes looked huge. I took a long breath. "Stay here, Bree, will you? Let me go find out. Stay with Curt and Solange. I'll be right back."

"I'm coming with you." Curt jerked his head at Solange. "What he said. Just—stay here, okay?"

I was already headed across the street. Curt caught me up a moment later. The cop who'd shooed us off to a safe distance was there, talking to someone, a smallish bloke who was covered in ashes and grime and was waving his arms around like a nutter. Whoever it was, he was flipping out.

I got up a bit closer, caught a better look at him, and stopped. Curt ran into me, saw who it was, and said something unintelligible. He got round me, and broke into a run.

The ashy bloke waving his arms about was Folkie Lind.

I finally got my legs back, and moved as fast as I could. Curt was staring down at the body bag, looking like he might be sick any moment; he'd taken his glasses off and his eyes looked naked, somehow. And Curt's dad looked like someone had kicked him in the pit of the stomach, good and hard. Something had knocked all the air out of him, anyway.

"Curt...?" I got up next to them. Something about being that close to the body bag was freaking me out. I don't know why—intuition, maybe—but I already knew who was inside. "What the hell...who...do they know..."

"It's Star." Folkie was swaying on his feet. "It's Star."

Adrenaline is very weird stuff, you know? I've heard all the stories, about someone getting a fright and doing something they physically shouldn't be able to do, like picking up an SUV or climbing a tree when they've got two broken legs, that sort of thing.

But I never stopped to consider that it might be having an effect on me, or on Bree. Looking back, I feel like an idiot for not sussing it out at the time, that both of us were stressed and running on adrenaline. I didn't realise how knackered I was; I didn't realise how close to the edge both of us were, either.

So we ended up in a snarling little fight. And yeah, I'm blaming the adrenaline. That's my story, and I'm sticking to it.

We had a lot to be thankful for. All things considered, the final numbers could have been a lot worse: there were four hundred and seventy people in the building when the fire broke out, and when the smoke cleared, I found out there'd been no critical injuries, three significant but treatable ones, a few dozen minor injuries that were mostly either smoke inhalation or small burns, and one fatality.

I got the information from Patrick. A few years back, when he'd been the homicide bloke for SFPD, he'd gone head to head with the San Rafael cops over the murder of one of the Bombardiers' roadies. That happened about thirty feet away from the 707's parking lot, on the actual property back when Paul Morgenstern still owned the place, and of course that was San Rafael's jurisdiction, not San Francisco's. I remember it a lot more clearly than I really want to; that stretch of time was right before Bree went in for cancer surgery. Every memory I've got from that week or two is coloured by the fact that I'd been scared shitless for my old lady.

One thing I do remember, though—sitting in this same damned parking lot, waiting for the locals and the City coppers to stop pissing to mark their turf, and get on with asking us questions. I'd got the impression that the local coppers weren't too pleased about having their case pulled out from under them by some slick bugger from the city. It was ironic, because it turned out it really had been Patrick's case to handle—Rosario's murder had been linked up to the murder of the Bombardiers' lead singer, and that happened in the Bombardiers' rehearsal studio in San Francisco—but that hadn't made the local cops any happier about it.

The night of the fire, we probably could have left well before we did. The fact that we didn't, that was Bree's doing. She's got this conscience, and it goes hand in glove with this nonstop need to blame herself for shit that's no fault of hers. She's a nurturer, as well, so you put those all together and we ended up with my wife digging her heels in and announcing that she wasn't going anywhere until every person on the catering staff was accounted for, rides home and all.

I got pissy. She was standing there with her hands on her hips, giving me a good hard glare, and I didn't much like that. I mean, bloody hell, she was right, and I felt the same way, so why was she glaring at me as if she thought I was Jack the Ripper? Crikey, I was the one who'd just had to wake Luke up, with an early morning phone call; it was just past six in the morning in the UK, and he was at home, down at Draycote. I was the one who'd had to give him the heads-up about the fire, because the last thing he needed was to turn on the BBC World News and seeing some throwaway news crawl about it. He knew about the party. Solange had been giving her dad daily updates in email about the gig, what she was learning about cookery and catering, how she was liking the pressure.

Solange, Mac, me, Bree, Tony, Carla: nearly half the people Luke was closest to in the world had been at the 707 tonight. He hadn't given me any shit about waking him—he was too grateful to know about it without finding out in some way that would have taken ten years off his life. But that hadn't made making the call easy or enjoyable, you know?

I'd just stashed the phone in my pocket when Bree made her little announcement, and I gave my wife back look for look. I wasn't best pleased with her just then, and I was far too knackered to make more than a piss-poor job of hiding it. Truth was, I didn't much fancy trying to hide it, either. The idea that I was likely to put my own comfort ahead of making sure our people were safe was pretty damned insulting.

"Jesus, Bree!" I wasn't raising my voice, but it had some serious snap to it. "Are you fucking joking? You think I'm that heartless? I'm not going anywhere until we make damned sure there are no more bodies in there, so I'm buggered if I know why you're playing Sunset Boulevard drama queen. Don't you stand there and glare at me like I was Bluebeard, or something. You really think I'm that big a self-absorbed shit, I'm surprised you wanted to marry me."

I heard her suck in air. "I wasn't -"

"No." I heard my own voice, about as exhausted and edgy as it ever gets. "Not now. Not the time for it. Just muffle it. You want to talk about this later, let me know. But not now."

She'd gone white, pretty much to the hairline. Over her shoulder, I saw Patrick, talking to one of the fire department people. Patrick lifted a hand, and waved. Nice clear signal: *come over here.*

Sod it. I wasn't up for fighting with anyone just then, especially Bree. There'd been too many shocks tonight, and we were both pretty trashed; we could talk it out later.

"I'm off to get an update," I told her, and went. I didn't look back.

Not a good moment, I know. But we both needed a couple of minutes to breathe and wind it down. Besides, wanting to talk to Patrick, that hadn't just been an excuse. I wanted to know where we stood.

One of the things that always gets up my nose about Patrick is, he never seems to get any older, or look tired or stressed out. Not sure how he does it—I have my suspicions about him signing a contract in goat's blood—but moments like that, when I feel as old as Methuselah and my whole body feels like an Aunt Sally left out in the rain, it leaves me liking him even less than usual. And I don't much like him to start with. Yeah, I know, he used to be a homicide cop, and he's had plenty of time to get used to being awake and functional at all hours of the day or night, but it still narks me.

"Hey, JP." Typical Ormand. We'd just come through hell, and

he was as perky as a nipple in a blizzard. "I was about to come over there. This is Jan Gelman, with San Rafael Fire. There's some good news, both on the injury front and on the fire itself. The bad news is that we have one fatality. I'm also afraid the club's going to need a ground-up rebuild. Jan tells me it took out three of the four walls, and of course the roof's gone."

"Lovely." I'd already guessed the club was trashed beyond repair; hard to miss, really. I was just glad I wasn't the one responsible for dealing with the insurance people and the bank. "Ta. You said something about good news. Want to share? Because it's been a bad couple of hours and I could use some right about now, you know?"

"Well, good is a relative term. But all things considered, we got off light for a fire of this magnitude. The EMTs tell us everyone's been treated. And Jan, here, tells me they have the fire almost completely contained. Jan, this is JP Kinkaid."

I shook her hand. Nice motherly-looking woman, except for the huge coat and the oversized boots and the smell of smoke coming off her. What was really surreal was that there was a wisp of lace poking out at the collar of the fireman's gear. "Nice to meet you. Contained? Really? I was watching some of those small pieces of burning wood up in the air a couple of minutes ago, and I was worrying they might land on some of the local roofs. I've got no clue whether our insurance would cover that."

"Oh, you mean the spark shower when the back wall caved in?" She nodded toward the club, what was left of it, anyway. "That wasn't a couple of minutes ago—that was about half an hour ago. Time does some very peculiar things when you're caught in an emergency, doesn't it?"

I wasn't sure I believed her—half an hour?—but whatever. "So it seems. Has anyone got a clue how it started? Because we played an entire first set, and there was no smoke, none at all. There was a stink of paint, yeah, but no smoke, not until the set break. One minute we were playing, the next minute I felt my eyes watering, I looked up, and the whole damned upstairs gallery had gone up. And it moved really fast, or at least it seemed to. So why -"

"It started because someone started it." She was looking back at the ruins of the 707, a tiny woman in some bloke's firefighting suit. Her voice was dead calm, and very sure. "Don't quote me, it's not official yet, but this was arson."

"Someone torched the place?" I felt something wanting to move in the pit of my stomach. "You sure about that?"

"About as sure as we can get from a first look."

She turned back and met my eye. Right then, the whole motherly thing went west for good—my mum's eyes hadn't been anything like laser beams.

"As I say, don't quote me, please. A full report needs to happen first, and there's a lot of data that still has to be collected, but this was classic arson patterning. We would have suspected it just on the first look—the fire seems to have started in an upstairs office. The speed, the spread pattern, the obvious high temperatures, how fast it seems to have hit flashpoint, everything about it points to the use of an accelerant. We're treating this fire as suspicious until we're proved wrong. We'll do a full-scale investigation, of course. We'll be working with the police, and we've got forensics experts here already—they'll be on the ground as soon as we certify it safe. So don't quote me on it yet, but I'm sure. I'd stake my reputation on it. This was a set fire."

I just stood and stared at her. There was nothing in that idea that I could wrap my head around.

Patrick caught my eye. The dirty-ice eyes were in full predator mode, and this time, I was damned glad of it. "Nasty, isn't it? You realise that, if the initial indicators turn out to be accurate, this was a premeditated murder attempt. The most common reason for arson—financial reasons—wouldn't apply here. The circum-

132

stances don't add up. I don't think I'm talking out of school to tell you that all indications point to what happened here tonight being a first degree homicide."

"Jesus." I swallowed hard. "Yeah, I get it, ta."

I don't know why that should have hit so hard. Maybe it was the idea that anyone who wasn't actually working for Adolph Hitler or Pol Pot could be capable of setting fire to a building with nearly five hundred people in it. What sort of sick twitch would be willing to risk killing off hundreds of people they didn't even know, just to make sure they got the one they wanted? Crikey, what sort of evil fuck would even consider watching another human being burn? You'd need a monster. Had we actually invited a monster to the party? I couldn't wrap my head around it.

I looked over Patrick's shoulder, across the parking lot. Some of the fire department people were hosing down different areas around the base of the club—hot spots, or something, or at least those particular spots seemed to be sending up bigger gushers of smoke than anywhere around them.

My brain kept wanting to back away from what Patrick had said. Problem was, I was standing right in the middle of it, and that didn't leave me much in the way of backing-out room—denial just wasn't happening. There was the club, and a parking lot full of people, and the reek of smoke and wet wood. I could see what he'd meant: If someone wanted to torch the 707 to collect insurance or whatever, why do it when the place was full? Why not sprinkle whatever they'd used as an accelerant all over the walls and toss a match at three in the morning, when the place was empty? What kind of right bastard would pull something like this?

I turned my back on the club, and looked out and around. I just suddenly needed to see the people I cared about. Yeah, I know, pathetic and stupid, really—after all, I'd already done the headcount, I already knew everyone was safe, I'd already rung

Luke and let him flip out at me. But it was a cold moment and I wasn't ready for just how hard it slammed me.

Star Woodley had been carried out of the building in a body bag. It could have been Solange, or Tony, or Carla. The fact that any one of them could have died and just been collateral damage for whoever the fucker was who'd set the fire, that just made it worse.

A voice somewhere in my head suddenly chimed in: *Never mind the rest of it—it could have been Bree. It nearly was Bree.*

I'd watched her tick off her checklist as she and Solange loaded out this morning, stacking four full cases of chafing dish fuel into the back of Solange's truck. They'd stashed a case each under the first two tables, nearest the stage.

Out of nowhere, there was a picture in my head: Bree, standing right next to the first of those tables. My wife's a pro, and this was her gig; she'd booked it and set it up. Her responsibility meant that she stayed at her station, answering questions, dishing out food, directing traffic. One spark from the gallery right above her head, and she'd have been burnt alive. Christ, I'd seen the tables go up...

Patrick had one hand under my elbow. "JP? I think you should sit down—you're swaying on your feet. Hang on, here comes Bree."

"Yeah, good, okay." I don't much fancy being touched by anyone who's not Bree, usually, but the hold he had on my arm was light, and impersonal, and anyway, I was thankful for it. My stomach had gone into a sort of tight gurgling meltdown. "Bree, love, have you got the car keys? I need to sit."

"I'm here. The Jag's behind us."

She slipped her hand under my elbow, gave Patrick a look, and watched him step away. She was probably still furious with me, but that was going to have to wait. That's one constant, about us as a couple: I come first with Bree, and I always have done. She

134

might be ready to bash my head in with Little Queenie right about now, but I was unsteady and shaky and until I was better and able to cope, that was all that mattered to her.

An hour ago, just an hour, I'd been munching away and thinking how hot she looked in her chef's gear. And upstairs, right above our heads, someone had been slipping into the office or one of the store rooms, dousing the place with something that would burn hot and fast, tossing a match...

"John!"

"Sorry."

I barely managed to get the word out before I doubled over. She went down with me, down on her knees, hanging on as I retched up everything I'd eaten and drunk that day. She held on to me the whole time, her hands nice and cool, rock steady.

It took me a couple of minutes to get it together. Sometime between hitting the deck and me finally being sure there was nothing left in my stomach to get rid of, the MS had kicked in. Talking at all hurt like a bitch, as well. I don't have a sick-up often, and I'm always surprised at how raw my throat feels afterwards. "Wow. Need to sit. Legs are gone."

She got me into the passenger seat, helping me swing my legs in, making sure I was settled in, that there was a bottle of Volvic water in the cup holder, within reach. She wasn't exactly nattering away herself; still narked at me. I reached a hand out and got hold of her, and jerked her down to me, face to face and eye to eye.

"Bree. Listen. Your crew." My throat felt really nasty, but I pushed it anyway. It was important. "Make sure everyone's fixed up. As long as it takes, whatever. I'm fine with it."

"I know." She'd gone very pale. Apologising doesn't come any easier to her than it does to me. "I'm sorry, John. I was stressed as hell and worried about everyone, but that's just a reason, it's not an excuse. Of course I know you wouldn't have it any other way. And it's done—most of my people drove themselves up, and Solange is driving the others home in Duke. We can head home any time."

"Good, because I've hit the wall." I closed my eyes a moment. Exhaustion had kicked in hard, or maybe just the crash from all the adrenaline. Either way, my legs were limp as jelly, basically. I don't think I could have stood up right then. "I love you. Always have, always will. You know that, yeah?"

She ducked her head, not meeting my eye for a moment. When she looked up, the smile she gave me was one I've only ever seen from her a few times over all these years together. She didn't say anything, but then, she didn't have to, not with that smile. It answered every question I could ever ask.

She straightened up. "I'll be right back. I told Carla I'd check in with her before we went."

I watched her in the side mirror. She crossed the road, becoming too small for my peace of mind—yeah, I know, stupid that is, but the truth is, my comfort zone right then had shrunk to pretty much sod-all. I had this bizarre feeling that if I closed my eyes for even a moment, she might disappear, and I wasn't having that.

So I kept my eye on the mirror, and watched her talking to Carla. I saw Mac and Domitra join them, then Tony and Katia, then Billy, and Solange, and Patrick. Patrick wasn't alone; he had Jan Gelman with him, and someone who looked like he might be a cop. There were a few of the local police cruisers out there, and I couldn't be sure, but the one closest to the Jag seemed to have someone sitting in the back seat.

Four minutes, five. Bree was still over there, talking, listening. So was everyone else. Right round the five-minute point, I began trying to get my legs working, because whatever was happening over there, it was something I should probably know about. Besides, it was keeping Bree away from me.

And then there she was, crossing back over, hurrying. She got the driver's side door open, and slid in next to me.

"Sorry—that took longer than I thought it would." She got the car started. Her hands were shaking. "We've got a problem, John. Or, well, it's not ours. But it's a problem."

I turned my head to stare at her. She had her eyes on the road, edging the car out of the lot. As we slid out onto Francisco Boulevard, we passed the police car I'd noticed, the one with the passenger in the back. He lifted his head, and then one hand, resting it against the glass.

It was Norfolk Lind.

Chapter Eight

For Immediate Release, from the desk of Carla Fanucci:
On behalf of the ownership of the 707 Club, and the entire Black-
light family, we wish to express our profound sorrow over the fire that
destroyed the building and cost the life of one of the ownership team.

The cause of the fire is under investigation. As soon as surviving
ownership receives the green light, plans will go forward, to rebuild
and expand...

A few years ago, back when Patrick Ormand was still a New York homicide copper and my first wife was still alive, a sleaze by the name of Perry Dillon got himself bashed across the throat in my dressing room, backstage at Madison Square Garden. Patrick's gig had been to sniff out whoever it was who'd nailed Dillon—using one of my guitar stands as the weapon, in fact—and bust them. For about two endless weeks, his first choice for an orange jumpsuit had been Bree.

There's nothing about that situation I remember without wanting to kick something. I'd had to get proactive, trying to get Bree off safe, and me right along with her, and having a heart attack in the middle of all that, it was a damned nightmare. Besides, the way Patrick handled it left me with a really sour taste at the back of my throat. Even though I'd been the one to suggest him as Blacklight's head of security, the memory of him looking at Bree, as if she was some kind of wounded animal and he was waiting for her to get weak enough to make him ripping her throat out easy, well, it still colours the way I look at him, and it probably always will. Not the sort thing you forget about, and anyway once he decided she was cool, I got it in my head that he liked her too damned much. Once that little notion got into my skull, it wasn't leaving anytime soon.

Still, when my cell went off just before ten the morning after the fire, hearing Patrick Ormand at the other end shouldn't have sent all the old defences up. After all, these days, he works for me.

"This is JP Kinkaid." I was still groggy as hell. The older I get, and the more goes wrong with me physically, the harder it gets to unglue the eyelids in the morning. I was busy knuckling them with one hand, and hanging on to the cell with the other.

"JP? Sorry, did I wake you? This is Patrick Ormand."

"No problem." The sound of his voice was all it took to wake me, but I wasn't about to tell him that. Bree's side of the bed was empty; she must have got up awhile ago, and let me sleep in. "Probably time I got out of bed, anyway. Half a mo, all right? Be right with you."

I dropped the cell on the bed and headed off to the loo. Morning meds with a painkiller topper, because my whole body was giving me fits—the MS was right at the edge. I followed that with a cold wet towel across my face, trying to wake up any sensation that wasn't a dull roar. And all through that, I was aware of the usual pissy hit of satisfaction at making Patrick Ormand wait until I was good and ready to talk with him.

That morning, though, making him wait wasn't entirely about spite—I took all the time I needed because I actually did need it. What the hell, we pay him a retainer, you know? He could damned well hang on.

I threw some clothes on, grabbed the phone, and headed for the stairs. I could smell coffee, and something cooking. Simon had come upstairs, and was weaving around my ankles.

"Okay," I told Patrick. I thought I sounded a bit slurry. No surprise, not with what the trigeminal neuralgia was doing to the nerves in my jaw. "I'm actually awake now. Sorry to hold you up, but it's a bad morning for the MS. What's going on, then?"

"I wanted to give you guys a heads-up." Funny thing—his voice hadn't actually changed, but it sounded different, tighter or something. "I've been talking to the guy in charge in San Rafael. You might want to give Blacklight Corporate a call, and see about getting a lawyer for Bree."

That stopped me in place, suddenly enough so that I nearly fell over the cat. That would have been just lovely, yeah? Going arse over teapot down the stairs, breaking my neck before I'd had my coffee, or kissed my wife good morning, or found out what the fuck Patrick Ormand was on about?

"JP?"

I was grateful for the tickybox, right then; my heart seemed to have suddenly decided to slamdance. "Yeah, still here. What did you just say? Why in hell would Bree need a lawyer?"

"Well…" He was choosing his words, nice and careful. "I don't know if Bree told you this last night—you were in pretty rough shape—but the San Rafael investigators brought Norfolk Lind in to answer some questions. He apparently had some story about Bree getting into a violent argument with Esther Woodley, at

140

dinner at your place, or something. Lind claimed you and Bree threw her out—sorry, did you say something, JP?"

"No." I'd swallowed what wanted out, and now my stomach was roaring up at me again. "Go on, mate, will you?"

"I told the cop in charge that sounded ridiculous to me. I've been a guest at your table plenty of times, including a few when I was pretty sure you really didn't want me there." He sounded completely matter-of-fact. "But neither of you was ever rude to me. And frankly, I can't even imagine Bree throwing someone out of her house. Lucifer could show up with an army of scaly slimy things, and Bree would probably get them seated and give them all a glass of champagne, and something good to eat. But Lind was pretty flat about it. And he said Bree and Esther Woodley had some kind of history, bad blood or something -"

"Hang on." I still wasn't moving, but I was thinking, hard and fast. "Patrick, listen, are you at your new digs? Can I ring you back, in a few minutes? I need to talk to Bree before I do anything else."

If I'd surprised him, I couldn't tell from his voice. "Sure. Same cell-phone number. I've got a landline in the office, but it's been ringing off the hook since about eight this morning—all my guests from last night have been checking in. None of them seem to know whether or not they ought to be thanking me for the lovely party. Anyway, I have the answering machine on, with a nice little *thanks for coming, sorry the building burned down* message I recorded. But I've got my cell on, so call me on that."

He rang off.

I stood there, taking long deep breaths. There was a memory, sitting there like a headache: Patrick Ormand, NYPD homicide lieutenant, telling us that Bree and I ought to get different lawyers. The memory was a good few years ago, but I remembered everything: the smell of the cop shop, the styrofoam cups of half-drunk coffee all over the place, my own feeling that I had to keep

Bree out of Patrick's hands, and Patrick himself, his voice, talking to Bree. *Some friendly advice: I'd make sure you told your lawyer everything, if I were you.*

"John? Is everything okay?"

I'd been so buried in the memory, I hadn't heard her open the door to the ground floor. I came out of it, looking down. She'd stuck her head inside, and was staring up at me.

I went downstairs. No point in hiding it—she'd known without me saying a word that I was worried, and besides, this wasn't going to keep. Bree being Bree, though, she wouldn't let me tell her anything at all until she'd got my breakfast sorted out. Once I'd got a few bites down, she settled in opposite me.

"Okay." She looked at me over the top of her coffee. "Mac called, and Solange checked in. So did Tony. Everyone's been calling my cell—I guess they had enough brains to know that if they didn't let you sleep, I'd mangle them. You look freaked. What's happening, John? Please talk to me."

I was careful about it, picking my words. It was tricky—I didn't want to make too big a deal out of it, but the bottom line was that, if Patrick was right, Norfolk Lind had gone out of his way to put Bree at the top of the list of suspects.

She didn't interrupt me. Bree's a rotten listener, usually; she interrupts everyone except me. Problem is, I didn't realise how freaked she was until she set her cup down, and coffee splashed all over the table, and on her hands. That got my attention, all right. I was up and around to her before the coffee that was left in her cup stopped sloshing about. She looked as if she had no blood anywhere from the neck up, and her hands were clenched hard and tight. My legs were shaking, barely holding me up, and she hadn't noticed. Jesus, she was about to keel over, herself.

"Bree? Baby, what -"

"They think I killed Star?" She'd begun to shake, and so had her voice. "They actually think I set fire to the 707? Norfolk Lind is telling the police that?"

I'd got one arm round her, and I was holding on. I was thankful to be sitting; there was no way I was letting her see how bad the MS was then. "I didn't say that, and neither did Patrick. What he said was that getting a lawyer to talk for you when the cops start asking about what happened at the ownership dinner was probably a good move. Crikey, Bree, breathe, will you? It's okay, I promise."

"No, it's not okay."

She started to cry. Serious tears, as well; whatever was going on here, she was just wracked with it, trying to control herself. That nearly had me flipping my own shit. For one thing, I wanted to hunt Folkie Lind down and choke the life out of him, and for another, there was no way she'd done anything wrong. She'd been down at her catering station the entire first set. There had to be any number of people who'd be able to vouch for that. What in hell was she crying about...?

Yeah, so, I'm dim. All these years together, you'd think I'd have sussed it. This was Bree, after all, the girl whose own mother sometimes called her Bree of Arc. Some days, I swear, she'll walk over hot coals for a shot at martyring herself for shit she's got nothing to do with, and no control over, anyway. So it took me a minute, but I suddenly got it, and the old bulb lit up. I tilted her chin down, and got us eye to eye.

"Bree. Oi! Bree, stop a second, will you? Is this in aid of you feeling guilty because Star's dead? Because if it is, stop. I mean it. Esther Woodley was a mean cow. She fucked you over, and you don't owe her memory any roses. Yeah, I nailed it—I can see that. Tell St. Bree to sod off, all right? Please?"

She was quiet. She had her teeth in her lower lip, and her eyes were muddy with tears, but she was listening, and what's more, she was hearing me. I rubbed her arm, light and steady.

143

"I don't want you doing this to yourself. You blame yourself for every damned thing, and you know what, it makes me crazy and it makes you ill. You blamed yourself for Cilla. You blamed yourself for my heart stuff. Christ, you'd probably be blaming yourself for the Hindenburg going down, if you could find a way to do it. I really hate it, Bree. You didn't do a damned thing to Star Woodley—she's the one who put the knife in, every time. She's the one who insulted Solange and Curt under our roof. She's the one who abused our hospitality and snuck upstairs and went through our stuff. You aren't guilty of anything. So the whole burning at the stake thing, it's just not on, all right? Get that through your head, and no arguing with me, either, okay?"

"Okay." She'd gone sniffly. "Can I get up, please? I need a tissue and a sponge for the table."

I reached behind me, and snagged a roll of paper towels. It was a near thing, and it scared me; I nearly dropped the damned thing. *Right.* I took a breath and got the roll on the table. At least my jaw was easing up, and I could talk properly.

"Here you go, love, have a lovely honk. I'm not letting you up yet, though, because I have an idea and I want to run it past you. I'll call Corporate, and see about a lawyer—no, don't get spooked, I don't want one to protect you. I don't see any way you're going to need protection. I want one so that the San Rafael cops will have someone to annoy. But what would you say to getting our pet detective to investigate this mess?"

She blinked at me. "Wait a minute. Are you suggesting we ask Patrick Ormand to find out what happened last night?"

"Why not? He's a detective, yeah? This is his gig. And I may not get any warm and fuzzies off the bloke, but he's damned good at his job."

I heard my own voice suddenly tail off, and stop. My turn to stop talking because my brain had gone elsewhere, and Bree knew why, too; she could always tell when I was remembering

Bulldog Moody, my mentor and my idol. Bulldog was the man whose work had got me wanting to play guitar in the first place.

Not a pretty memory, that one. A young writer named Ches Kobel had found out things about Bulldog that didn't match up with what Bulldog had told me about his life. And Ches had died.

My feelings about Bulldog—yeah, it was complicated. Thing is, I was supposed to be inducting Bulldog into the Hall of Fame. I was writing the speech, I had less than a week to do it and I'd had no idea, then, whether it was gospel or shite. That mattered, you know? I loved Bulldog and I didn't fancy standing up there at the ceremony and reading a lie. Besides, Ches Kobel had been our guest. He'd sat at Bree's table, eaten her cooking. We'd liked that kid. So I'd asked Patrick to find out the truth...

"It's okay." Bree's voice was very soft. "Come back, John."

I jumped, and met her eye. She had a rueful little smile on her face. Bree doesn't smile much, so when she does, it has a meaning or a mood behind it. It's not always obvious, but this time, I could read her loud and clear: I'd been bitching her out for blaming herself for things she'd had no control over, and here I was, doing it to myself. I don't do irony very well.

"Right." I kissed her fingers, and reached for my cell. "Bree, look. You know, if we do hire Patrick, he's going to ask you about Star. You won't be able to hide anything, not if he's working for you. You okay with that? Because if you've got any problem with it, now's the time to say so."

She sighed. "No. Go ahead and call him."

I lifted one eyebrow at her. "You sure, love?"

"God, yes, I'm sure. I want to know what happened last night, John. I want to know what kind of maniac would pull something like that. I'll answer his questions. I'll even tell him about what happened at the clinic that night. Do it. Make the call."

Patrick answered it on the second ring. "JP?"

145

"Yeah, it's me, and Bree as well. Hang on, let me put this on the speaker—okay, we're on. Let's keep it simple, yeah? How's your availability look for taking on a job? We want to hire you to find out what really happened at the 707 last night, and why."

Having gone through the movie, and decided that we were going to be brave and honest and open and hire Patrick on our behalf, it was a bit of letdown to have him tell us he'd already been asked to do the same thing by Blacklight Corporate.

Of course, we should have known—it made sense, really. Carla'd got him on it right away, and if I'd had half a brain cell working properly, I'd have known that was going to happen. The math was dead simple: Corporate was already paying him a retainer, and that meant he got to earn it whenever Blacklight needed him, full stop. There was nothing in his contract about that $150K we shelled out every year only applying to band tours, or to him acting as security. Blacklight was not only his boss, it was his first priority; he'd agreed to that when he signed on.

"But—does that mean you can't check it out for us too?"

I jerked my head up. Something in Bree's voice had been shaky, and she looked as if she was about to break down and cry. I made a move toward her, but she shook her head at me, and I sat back down again. We've got signals we use, looks and gestures and whatnot, things that evolved over our years together. I knew this one: *I need space to cope.*

"I didn't say that, Bree." Patrick sounded cheerful, the bugger. "It's not about any conflict of interest—I'm pretty sure Andy and Carla would be fine with me sharing. I'm just wondering if you really need to pay me twice for the same information."

I heard Bree take a good long breath. I'd have bet Patrick heard it, as well. "It's—not that simple, Patrick. It might not turn out to be the same information. There are things I would tell you that I wouldn't really want anyone else to know about—except

John, of course, but he already knows everything. Would you be okay with hearing some stuff from me—in confidence, I mean—and not talking to Carla or anyone else about it? And would we have to sign something, or pay you a retainer, or what?"

Absolute silence, a good thirty seconds of it. Quite a feat, that is, depriving Patrick Ormand of speech—we'd only managed it a few times over the years. I pictured him sitting there in an office I hadn't seen yet, looking gobsmacked at the idea of Bree wanting to spill her secrets to him, and not knowing how to handle it.

The idea would have been funny as hell under almost any other circs. As it was, I wasn't laughing, and I wasn't keeping quiet, either. Right now, there was a good chance he was wondering if maybe she'd done something wrong, and there was no way in hell I was having that. Besides, it concerned me as well—I was the person she'd nicked the damned drugs for in the first place, yeah?

I cleared my throat—dry as a bone, suddenly. "Look, Patrick, Bree hasn't said it yet, but I will: what she has to tell you, it's not illegal, or anything like that. Just, personal stuff from a good long time ago. Okay, maybe it was illegal when it happened, but it's old news."

She opened her mouth, started to say something, but I held up a palm, and she was quiet. My turn for a signal. If we were dishing, might as well get it over.

"It's about the circs around my drug bust, back when the earth was still cooling—June 1979. Actually, you probably know a lot of this. You looked at the files during the Perry Dillon mess. You know, back when you were thinking about getting both of us fitted for orange prison jumpsuits? I remember you hinting you knew all about it, anyway."

"I remember." Nice and neutral. "Are you saying Esther Woodley was somehow involved in that? Because, sure, it's been a few years since that investigation, but I don't remember ever seeing the woman's name before."

"No, her name wouldn't have been in there."

It was a good thing Patrick couldn't see Bree, just then. Her voice was steady, but her face was lint-coloured and her hands were folded on the table, hard and tight. Her throat sounded even scratchier than mine.

"She wasn't really involved. That wasn't her style, being out front where she might have to actually step up and take responsibility for anything she did. No damned way. No, Star's style was Little Miss I Know Everyone. She liked to play organiser, everyone's helpful little friend, the backstage behind-the-scenes arranger. Then, now, it makes no difference. She didn't change." Her voice was suddenly raw, bitter. "Thirty goddamned years and she hadn't changed."

She broke off. I could see the muscles in her throat working. She wasn't telling Patrick anything at all just yet—she was too busy trying not to cry.

Right. Enough. This was on me.

"Okay. Patrick? You need to take notes, or something? No? Good. This is tricky for Bree, so I'll tell it. Here's the deal: June 1979, me and Cilla got strung out on snowball—that's cocaine and heroin mixed."

"I know what snowball is." Still neutral. "I used to work narcotics in Miami, remember? They call it speedball, back east. Go on."

"I'm planning to, mate. No, Bree, I'm telling this! Anyway, Cilla left me in Seattle, and I headed back here to do some sessions with the Bombardiers. Didn't realise I'd got addicted—didn't realise I was jonesing. I'd met Bree backstage at the Cow Palace, couple of weeks earlier, and must have remembered her being with the Mission Bells clinic, because apparently I rang her up there, and asked for her by name."

"That's a very peculiar way to put it." I was betting he had one eyebrow of his own up, at least. "'Apparently'? You mean, you don't remember?"

"I remember sod-all." Oh, bugger. Something had just occurred to me, something that probably should have occurred to me before I opened my mouth. Yeah, putting my foot in it, good and proper. "Look, hang on, I've got a question. What we want to tell you, I've just realised, it's an admission to a crime. Thing is, it's a very old crime."

I stopped. I had no clue how to phrase what I wanted to know. Fortunately, Patrick was on it. I never said the bloke was dim, you know? Just annoying.

"If you're talking about Bree's bust, don't worry about it. For one thing, from what I remember, that was a juvenile record. It would have been expunged when she reached legal age. And I'm not a cop anymore, so I'm not ethically or legally obligated to report any of this to anyone—well, not unless I have hard evidence of the commission of a crime. And you telling me all about it doesn't constitute evidence. That's hearsay."

I had one brow up, looking at Bree, another one of those marital signals: *Should I keep on, then?* She nodded: *Do it.*

"Right." Keep it simple, I thought, nice and simple and clear. Funny, how hard this was—if anyone had told me back in New York that I'd end up using Patrick Ormand as a confessional booth, I'd have hurt myself, laughing. I wasn't laughing now. I reached across the table, and got one of Bree's hands in mine.

"Okay. Here's what happened. I rang up the clinic with the horrors. I got poor Bree on the phone, she heard me losing it, and lost it herself. Her mum wasn't about, I told her there were bugs crawling on me and that I was dying without a hit. She got hold of a sample of her mum's stash, the stuff Miranda used to help treat the local junkies with. Bree brought it to me—I was at the Saturn Hotel, local rocker hangout back in the day. She didn't know what she was bringing me, Patrick. We clear about that? She was seventeen, and all she knew was that I'd asked for help. She thought I was dying."

"Yep. Clear." Back to being neutral, the tricky bugger. He was being tactful, okay, but that didn't make me like him any better. I knew just what he was thinking: *yeah, when has she ever not leaped to help you?* "Go on, JP. I know this isn't easy. I seem to remember from the case files that you were deported? How did SFPD get involved?"

"They got involved because he OD'd." Bree's hand was chilly under mine. Her voice was tight, barely under control. She sounded as if she was forcing the words through a hole too small for them: distorted. "They got involved because I brought him an envelope with about three grams of pharmaceutical quality snowball in it. It was enough for twenty people—my mother would have diluted it, easing them off onto methadone or one of the more holistic approaches. I was a fucking idiot. I didn't have a clue."

"Bree -"

It was no use—she'd started and she wasn't stopping.

"John snorted most of it, and his heart stopped. And that rancid bitch Esther Woodley was in the clinic, watching me tear the place apart and breaking into my mother's drug stash. They got involved because she called them after I left, and told them what I'd done. I didn't even know she was there."

"She didn't say anything to you?" All of a sudden, I liked him again. He'd got it straight away, why that phone call of Star Woodley's had been such a shit thing to do. "She didn't try to stop you? That's pretty hard to forgive. Why did she let you do it, Bree? Do you know?"

"Of course I do. She didn't stop me because she was jealous, mean, totally fucked up. She hated that I got to go be staff at shows. She resented that I was trusted. She would have done anything to get me out of there, and I gave her the chance when I flipped out and broke into my mother's locker. I was scared half out of my mind that John would die if I didn't get him something, and instead I damaged his heart and nearly killed him." Her voice broke. "Why couldn't she at least have tried to stop me?"

"It's okay, love." I got round to her side of the table, and wrapped her up. I didn't give a damn about Patrick listening in. It didn't matter. "It's history. Old news. Can you stop feeling guilty about not liking the woman?"

She shook her head. Of course Patrick couldn't see that, her saying no, she couldn't, not yet. He was doing the tactful thing again, riding it out, waiting.

"Patrick, look, I think we need to ring you back in a bit, yeah? That work for you?"

"Sure." Patience on a bleedin' monument, Patrick Ormand was. "But do me a favour, and confirm something for me before you hang up, will you? Do you want to hire me? Separately and apart from Blacklight Corporate? The thing is, they're actually going to be interested in certain aspects of this that you won't care about, and I do need to know."

He paused, just a fraction of a second. "And I want to be really clear about this, upfront. I'm going to want as much information from both of you about what's been happening around this woman recently as you've got. All right?"

I looked at Bree. It was her call; I'd support any choice she made, but she had to make one. The answer was right there, in her face.

"Yeah," I told him. "We're in. I'll ring you back."

There are days when I really do miss obvious stuff, things one of our cats would have no trouble seeing. I'd barely clicked off the phone before Bree lost it. I had just enough sense to shut up and let her let it out. When I finally sorted out what she was saying, I felt my heart do a little samba.

"...she could have stopped me. I damaged you. The heart attack, all of it, my fault." She had her hands knotted hard, and her face was desolate. "I nearly killed you—I *did* kill you. Your

151

heart stopped. My fault. How could she let me do that, out of spite? She knew what I was doing, she knew what I took, she knew how dangerous it was. She knew!"

There was no point in saying anything, not yet. Yeah, I wanted to tell her that was bullshit, but it had to wait, along with something else I had every intention of pointing out to her: She needed to let it go. Thirty years corked up and drowning in a keg of toxic self-regret is a long time, and I hadn't known about Star Woodley's part in what happened that night until a few weeks ago myself. Typical Bree, carrying the weight herself, but I was damned if I was going to encourage her to do it anymore.

I was so damned busy thinking about what she'd been doing, I almost missed the meaning behind what she'd actually just said. When it finally filtered through, I went stiff.

"Bree, stop. Wait a bit, okay? Am I getting this? You're blaming yourself for nearly doing me in by trying to rescue me, and you're blaming Star Woodley for letting you nearly do me in by trying to rescue me, and on top of all that, you're blaming yourself for blaming Star Woodley for letting you nearly do me in by trying to rescue me?" I shook my head. "Bloody hell, it sounds like a comedy bit, doesn't it? Not very funny, though. Bree, for fuck's sake, tell me you haven't been marinating in this rubbish since 1979? Please? Because that's nuts."

She lifted her face, streaked with tears, absolutely wretched. "It's not nuts. Or maybe it is. But it's how I feel. And now she's dead, and it's a horrible awful way to die, and I'm not sorry, John. I still hate her and I'm glad she's dead and I bet it happened because she pissed someone off or got in their way just to show she could or manipulated someone. I bet that whatever happened, she brought it on herself, and I'm not sorry she's dead. Oh Jesus God on a pogo stick, I *suck!*"

All those gestures and signals we use with each other, they're old habits, you know? There's one I used to use quite a lot with

152

Bree, mostly when she was doing her obsessing thing and I needed to snap her out of it by playing the age card, waving my vast experience of being eleven years older than she is: I'd chuck her under the chin with the knuckle of my bent index finger. Usually, it would piss her off enough to get her to stop flipping her shit—it was pretty damned condescending, and I knew it. I hadn't used that one in a while, but I used it now.

"Knock it off, Bree." I knuckled her under the chin. "That's a load of bollocks, is what that is. You didn't start the fire. Nothing to blame yourself for, not on that one—and yeah, it wouldn't be my choice of a way to die, but I'm betting you nailed it: she pissed someone off. Maybe the cosmic shitload she spent half her life piling up finally earned her a payback. Who knows? I don't. But I want you to listen to me, Bree. Both ears, please, before we ring Patrick back. You listening?"

She nodded. Her face was a mess.

"Okay." I picked my words. I needed to say it right, because I didn't much fancy having to say it twice. "Ever since Wembley, you've been blaming yourself for my heart attack. Ever since the quack in London told you my heart got damaged because of the snowball OD, you've been wearing this invisible hair shirt. I've asked you not to, and I know you've been trying. But I want to say something, and I want you to believe it. Drop the defences, love, and just—just hear me, all right?"

Another nod. She was listening, really listening. Good. It was time she heard me say it; I should have said it long ago.

"You know something, Bree? Offer me a time machine, ask me if I want to go back and change what happened, you know what I'd say? Wouldn't have to think about it. If Star had stopped you, done the right thing, instead of playing her bullshit power game, you wouldn't have come to the Saturn. Even if I hadn't gone out and hit a street dealer and killed myself with whatever they cut their blow with, I'd still be married to Cilla, or I'd be dead. Worse

153

than that, though? We'd never have seen each other again. Never, Bree. You realise that?"

She was quiet, watching me. I suddenly wondered if she was breathing; her entire body seemed to be waiting to exhale.

"You really think I'd trade you for a healthy heart?" I shook my head at her. "Not a chance. You can't be that dim."

She started to shake. I got hold of her, letting her cry it out. The whole time, I was thinking, *thank God Star Woodley didn't stop her. Thank God for that.*

"Let it go, love." I had my lips up to her ear. "Just let it go. There's nothing in the world I'd trade the past thirty years for, health or heart or anything else. Why would I? I've got everything I want. Now let's tell Patrick to swing by here and pick up a cheque, sign whatever needs signing, and get him started on finding out what the hell really happened."

Chapter Nine

For Immediate Release, from the desk of Carla Fanucci, recipient list 707 owners and concerned parties only:

Extremely confidential: As some of you already know, the results of the official San Rafael investigation into the 707 fire have been concluded, and the report of the findings is in the process of being prepared. As the designated liaison, we expect to have the report within seventy-two hours, with the insurance company's response to follow shortly. Once we're in possession of the facts, a meeting of the ownership will be needed, to reach a consensus and map our strategies for the 707's future.

On a sadder note, Esther Woodley's memorial service will be held this Thursday in Marin County, California. Andy Valdon will be in attendance as our representative. We have also arranged for a floral arrangement. If you wish to be removed from this list, or wish to at-

tend the service, please email Andy...

I don't much fancy lying to my wife. When it came to the question of Star Woodley's memorial service, though, I'd have lied to her without thinking twice, if I'd had to. There was no way I was letting her near that. Turned out I didn't have to, because as soon as we'd both seen the email, I'd put my foot down good and hard and told her I wasn't having her near the damned service. I was ready to go to the mat over it, but she agreed with me—turned out the idea of going anywhere near made her sick at her stomach. So that was one bit of stress taken care of.

The first thing I'd done, once I got it through Bree's head that yeah, I understood what was upsetting her and I respected it, was to get the call in to Carla, asking for a lawyer hook-up for Bree. Carla'd gone stonewall, which meant she was freaked and horrified, but I told her no, not to worry, this wasn't an instant replay of the Dillon murder. Bree wasn't a serious suspect and she wasn't in any real danger this time—we just wanted a lawyer to buffer us from the official questions. Carla'd promised a name and number in both our emails within the hour. Once we'd done that, we'd rung Patrick back, and let him know we wanted to hire him, individually, separate from Blacklight.

That conversation was surreal. It wasn't the first time I'd asked Patrick to check into the history behind something for me, but this time, it wasn't just my stuff in there, it was Bree's. There were other issues, as well, something we'd forgot about until Patrick showed up with two copies of a contract for services hired in hand and a pen for us to sign with.

Bree got us settled in at the kitchen table, and plugged in the electric kettle. I got the feeling she wasn't looking forward to giving Patrick or anyone else the details of how she'd ripped Star a new one, the night of the ownership meeting. Granted that she hadn't done a damned thing wrong, I could tell she was still squirming over how hard and deep she'd reacted to pretty much everything Star'd done that night. Bree doesn't fancy having to admit she's human enough to be mean, not even to herself.

"Does anyone want a cup of coffee?"

"I'd love one, thanks." If Patrick has sussed that Bree was edgy—and that I was pretty tense, as well—he wasn't showing it. Nice and relaxed. "Before we get started, I need to ask—are you retaining me as husband and wife? Or is this just on Bree's behalf?"

"Both. Why?" I got that out fast. It would have been just like Bree to try and protect me from unpleasantness, but I wasn't giving her a shot at keeping my name off that particular guest list. I shot her a glare, to make sure she got it.

"Just that, now, either one of you can give me a dollar."

I blinked at him. Bree was quicker than me, though. She headed over to the counter where we keep our loose change jar, fished out four quarters, and stacked them up neatly on the table, in front of him.

"Here. Don't spend it all in one place. So, what? We're now officially your client?"

"Yep. Of course, once we actually get going it'll cost you more than a buck, but for right now, this is the retainer, or it will be, once we all sign the paperwork."

He grinned at both of us, and I felt myself loosen up a bit. That was likely just what he was trying to do. "If you want the truth, I don't think it actually does much in terms of legal confidentiality," he told us. "I'm not a lawyer, so the privilege thing isn't enforceable, but part of what I'm offering is the fact that I treat each confidence as if we had full privilege under the law. You'll have to take my word on that. Just don't kill anyone, though. My brand-new shiny contract doesn't actually stretch far enough to cover me becoming an accessory to any criminal activity."

"Right, I think we can guarantee we won't be offing anyone

soon. So, the agreement's symbolic? Works for me, mate. If we didn't trust you, we wouldn't have told you a damned thing."

"I know." All of a sudden, he was serious. "Okay. I've got my one-page standard retainer agreement, two copies. If you'll read it over and sign both copies, I'll do the same, and you keep one and I'll keep one. If you have any questions about it, stop reading and ask me. I want to make sure we're all on the same page. Then we can get started."

We read the agreement, me and Bree together, both of us with our glasses pushed up tight to read the small print. Nothing tricky in there, just good straightforward stuff. At least, that's what I thought.

"Patrick—John, wait a minute, okay? I have a question, before we sign this."

That got my attention. I glanced at Bree; she was making lip-chewing faces. Patrick lifted both eyebrows, just waiting.

"It's—damn. The problem is, I don't know how much of what happened in 1979 is going to be relevant. Probably none of it. But what happens if I give you a fact about someone who isn't covered by this agreement? Do you have to share it with anyone, or is it protected as confidential?"

Oh, bloody hell.

I'd been worrying about my own part in what happened with Bree's drug theft, and about Bree's part in that whole miserable mess. But there'd been two other people involved in that incident.

Star Woodley was dead, and Bree wouldn't be worrying about her anyway. Miranda wasn't dead, though. And if she wasn't covered, that made a huge difference.

Bree's mum is one of the city's most respected and influential surgeons, and she has been, for a good long time. She's also one of the most useful people out there in the community. Her big thing is using her medical and political clobber to get her hands

158

dirty, working with the street people who'd have sod-all in the way of medical care without her. We hadn't stopped to think about it affecting her, either of us. Thirty years ago, she'd taken the blame for Bree; that cost Miranda her medical license for a two-year suspension and got her booted off the board of the clinic, as well. I wasn't up for anything resembling a replay.

"Yeah, Bree's right." I started to get up. "Hang on a mo, Patrick—me and the missus need a huddle."

He looked from me to Bree over the rim of his cup. "I think I can answer it without the huddle. Are you talking about Dr. Godwin? Because unless she's involved in whatever happened at the 707 that led to Star Woodley dying, there's no reason for her name to even be mentioned outside any conversations the three of us may have. It's irrelevant—it doesn't arise."

"Since she wasn't on the guest list, I'd say that answers it." I nodded at my wife. "We good to go, love? Okay."

We signed both copies. He handed us one, and tucked the other away.

"Welcome aboard—nice to have you as clients. I'll do my absolute best for you. And JP, since you're also part of the majority ownership, you get the best of both worlds: you get all my updates on the corporate end of the investigation, but they don't hear anything about whatever I find out specifically for you. Now, with that in mind, I have a couple of questions. Remember, I'm working for you on this one; this is on your behalf. This isn't New York, I'm not a cop anymore, and I don't suspect you of anything. If you aren't comfortable with a particular question, no problem, just say so and we'll move on to the next one. Okay?"

That was a nice little speech, and it came at a good time. He'd probably sussed Bree was freaked, and that made it easier for her, for both of us.

Bree reached for my hand. "Okay. What do you want to know?"

159

It had been a long time since we'd been grilled by Patrick Ormand in a capacity where he had the right to ask us questions,
and we had any obligation to answer. I'd forgotten how good he
is at getting information without actually asking what he wants
to know; it's as if he's got one ear on the interstices, the spaces
between the questions and the answers, as if he's hearing information and answers in the silences, the pauses, the things we
weren't saying.

And it turned out that, for the moment at least, Bree wasn't
going to have to dish about the night of the ownership meeting
at our place. Patrick wasn't interested; he was after something
with a lot more dust on it.

The first few questions seemed harmless enough. He asked
about Star back in the day, nothing major: had Bree ever come
across her outside Mission Bells, or had any idea about what
Star's life had been like? Who had she known? Had Bree known
any of her friends? I was watching Bree, the way her shoulders
had tensed up. They stayed tense, but she answered him without
making a big deal of it, and she answered him honestly.

No, she hadn't had anything to do with Star outside the clinic,
and hadn't much wanted to. She hadn't liked the girl, hadn't
liked the games she played, the way she tried to move people
about like puppets or chess pieces. She really hadn't liked the fact
that Star hadn't seemed able to say anything nice about anyone
unless she wanted something, even back then.

"So that was always an aspect of her personality?" Patrick was
listening, taking it in, sorting it out. He hadn't gone into that
scary click-machine mode he's got, where you can see the gears
and cogs doing their thing, but that was probably because he
hadn't got enough gen yet. "Your take on her—the way she was
back then—is really useful, Bree. I should tell you, Carla put me
on notice to start asking questions before you guys ever left the
707 parking lot. I've been busy since last night."

160

I don't know why that surprised me. This was Carla we were talking about, you know? She's probably the most capable human being on earth. She has Blacklight's interests front and centre, twenty-four seven. The moment she realised the fire was sussy, she'd have got that ball rolling.

"Part of the problem is that almost everyone else I've spoken to so far has talked about her over the past fifteen years or so." Patrick still hadn't pulled out anything to write on, or write with, either; the note-taking was still in his head. "I got some names and numbers from Jeff Kintera, and of course Norfolk Lind had a shortlist. Everyone vaguely remembers her being around, but no one seems to have known her well. Lind is the most obvious source, but the problem there is that he's been mostly unavailable. So I'm trying to get a picture of who she was, because how she got to be the person she was when she died is just as important as why she died. That's dependent on as much information as I can get. So far, everything I have about her back then comes from one source: her mother."

Something about that one fact—that Esther Woodley had been someone's kid—suddenly brought the entire thing into full miserable focus. I looked at Bree, and saw a kind of horror and awareness in her face. The same thing had just occurred to her: neither of us had stopped to think that Star might have had parents still alive. This wasn't just an objectionable adult who'd somehow got herself burnt to death. She was someone's kid, and that someone was still alive, and had just lost their child.

The look on Bree's face must have tipped Patrick off. "Don't look so horrified, either of you. Anna Woodley is in her eighties and she hadn't spoken to her daughter in twenty years. Mom's a fundamentalist type, and she strongly disapproved of her daughter's lifestyle. Actually, I got the impression she disapproved of her daughter, period. She told me her faith required her to leave judgement to the Lord, but I got the feeling her heart wasn't in it. I'm pretty sure I heard something about a serpent's tooth, just before I hung up. Bree, how long had it been since you'd seen her, before that encounter at the 707?"

"Whatever the difference between summer of 1979 and last month is." She looked absolutely miserable. "Shit. Okay. I don't know if this is useful, but—once or twice, back when John first put the Geezers together and they began playing local gigs, I thought I saw her, out in the crowd. I wasn't sure then, though. And I can't swear to it now. I didn't exactly go out of my way to see if it was her, Patrick. She was out in the audience and I stayed behind the backstage rope, and I didn't have to deal with her. Assuming it was her, I mean. I hadn't seen her since that night at the clinic—but the more I think about it, the more I think it was her."

I was waiting for Patrick to get to me, ask me what I knew about Star. That was going to be iffy—for some reason, I was balking at having to admit to Patrick Ormand that I hadn't known Star Woodley existed until that night in the 707 band room. I had a moment of being very narked with Bree, for keeping it secret all this time. What, she couldn't have trusted me…?

It only took a moment to realise how stupid I was being. Of course she hadn't told me; even thinking about it to herself had made her want to crawl into a hole somewhere. Besides, tell me about it when, and why? I hadn't known about any of it until Patrick himself had found out and forced her to tell me, when Perry Dillon got killed in my dressing room. She'd carried that load on her own for a good long time because she'd got used to keeping secrets from me, and pissing and moaning about it now wasn't just pointless, it was stupid, and cruel as well.

"No problem, Bree. Don't sweat it." He sounded very gentle, and just for once, I didn't mind. I caught his eye and we shared a look: *thanks, mate.* "If you don't know, you don't know. One more thing, and then I'm going to head back to the office and see if I

162

can finally get some face time with Norfolk Lind. Your mother was on the board of the Mission Bells. Presumably, she okayed the volunteers?"

I'll tell you what, I've never once underestimated Patrick Ormand's brains. They're quite good, all things considered. Where I get narked is how twisty he gets, how ruthless he is about what he does with the good brains. But that idea, that Miranda might have some gen, that was brilliant. From the looks of it, Bree was appreciating the idea as well.

"I'm pretty sure she did." She reached for her cell. "You think she might remember something about Star? Do you have her number? She might be on duty at the hospital today, but -"

"No, that's okay." He got up, and stretched. It looked like the Q&A was done for the moment. "Carla gave me a full list of numbers and emails, and I'm pretty sure Dr. Godwin's information is in there."

We walked him to the door. Just as we got there, I remembered something I wanted to know.

"Oi. Hang on a minute, will you? There was something I meant to ask you, nothing to do with Star Woodley. That woman, the one you introduced me to, who told me it was arson -"

"You mean Jan Gelman?" Patrick was standing in the open doorway, one foot positioned like a soccer goalie, just in case one of the cats was mad enough to make a dash for the street. "What about her?"

I was remembering the icepick-sharp look, the way her voice had gone calm and cold as a judge. "Not sure. Who is she, exactly? What was she doing there in the first place? Is she one of the firefighters? She had on the gear, but it didn't look like hers—she was lost in it. Who is she?"

The hall was clear of cats, and Patrick shifted. "Jan? She's not a firefighter, she's a forensics expert, Inspector rank. She runs San Rafael's arson squad—her specialty is arson fatalities. She used to be a homicide cop. We got friendly during the Fabiano investigation. She was actually at the party, as one of my guests, which is probably why she knew she was looking at an arson homicide so soon—she got to see the fire in realtime. Thanks for the coffee and the information. I'll check in with you guys later."

We ended up having a sort of extended family dinner that night: the two of us, Miranda, Mac and Dom, Curt and Solange. The way the evening played out, I'm amazed Bree'd ever consider having anyone over again in her life. It was no fun at all.

It started out reasonably painless. Patrick hadn't been gone five minutes, and we were just finishing the washing up, when my cell phone starting playing "Remember Me." I tossed the dishcloth on the counter and headed for the phone, trying to cut the ringtone off before it could make Bree too nuts.

"Johnny? Listen, question for you. Can we buy you and Bree dinner? I don't know about you, but I'm just a skosh unsettled. Besides, I can't help feeling a quiet little talk about this whole mess before all hell breaks loose would be a smart move on our part."

"Works for me. Hang on, though, let me ask Bree." She was watching me, and I put my hand over the phone. "Mac. He and Dom want to buy us dinner and talk things over. You up for that?"

"No." She sighed, a good long intake of air. "God, that sounded rude. What I meant was, no, I'm not up for going out to a restaurant. Dinner, yes, but not if we have to go out."

I grinned at Bree, and uncovered the phone. "Mac? Dinner's fine, but we're both knackered. Bree's not up for leaving the house and I'm not up for watching her having to cook for people. Tell you what, why not come over and we'll send out for something, all right?"

I rang off. Of course Bree wanted to argue that one, but I dug my heels in. She was looking dragged down and tired, and the last thing I wanted was her getting sick. It flips me out when she's down for the count; it reminds me she's mortal, and I'm damned if I want any reminders, ta ever so.

Of course, I know my wife, and letting her know that is probably the worst way to get her to do what I want. That leaves me two choices: either come the heavy husband and put my foot down, or play fragile myself, make her concentrate on worrying about me instead. There was a good long time where I'd have done the fragile thing; it's a lot less work than arguing, you know? But I've stopped taking that road, especially since Wembley. For one thing, it's not fair to her, and for another thing, I always seem to actually end up feeling sicker when I do that. Might be karma, or something.

For some reason, I'm not sure why, this kind of not-quite-row always seems to lead us upstairs and into bed. It's probably something to do with how fierce she gets; Bree being fierce is always an on-button for me. We'd got into a mild back and forth about it, and damned if I wasn't getting turned on, aches, pains and all. She was just trying to convince me that boiling water for pasta and pulling some bolognese out of the freezer for a quick heating-up didn't qualify as cooking, and her own eyes were going the nice traffic-signal green that meant sex in the immediate future because she was heating up as well, when her phone went.

"Hello? Solange, hey honey, what's—what?" She listened for a minute; I could hear Solange's voice, clacking through the phone. "Sure, you guys can come for dinner, so long as you don't have any problem with sharing the table with your godfather and his bodyguard. They'll be over around six. No, that's okay, no help needed, not today, because I'm not cooking. Your uncle is threatening me with bad things if I even think about slaving over a hot stove, so it looks like we're sending out for something, maybe Mexican. Sure, you can put Duke in the driveway if there's no street parking. We'll see you later."

Good, she'd given up on the cooking thing. Of course, I suddenly realised, maybe she was really feeling off. I brought that up, but she said no. I said right, convince me, and she put her hands on her hips; her eyes were nice and green and I was just about to suggest a nice snog to pass the time, when her phone went again. Gordon *Bennett*, it was turning into some kind of bad sitcom thing…

"Hey, Mom. Is everything okay?" Her eyes were still bright green, and they were still aimed at me. "No, I'm fine, just kind of busy. What's up?"

I put one brow up, waiting. Miranda's voice wasn't nearly as audible through the phone as Solange's had been; she's a lot more controlled.

"Tonight…? Damn. No, no, it's just that a few people are already coming by—no, you know everyone, I think. What –"

I watched her face change. So did her voice. "Wait a minute. Who called you? No, I thought Patrick Ormand was going to, but not—look, just come over, okay? We're sending out for something, John won't let me cook tonight—of course I'm aware that he's a very good husband—what? Oh. Six or thereabouts. Mom, I have to go. Just come, okay? See you later."

She clicked the phone off, looked at it for a moment, and headed into the kitchen proper. I had about ten seconds of wondering what she was up to before she opened a drawer, dropped the phone into it, and slammed the drawer shut.

"No more calls, please." She came back to me, and I mean all the way back: full body contact, one hand snaking between my thighs. "We have a winner."

So we actually did get that hour upstairs, and thank God for it, because it was just what we both needed. Tickybox, MS, diabetes, whatever, it doesn't seem to matter: Bree's never lost that fantastic trick of hers, kicking everything and everyone all the way to the curb when it's just us and the bedroom. So yeah, maybe we've slowed down a bit since Wembley, but when we're there, it's brilliant. Just what the doctor ordered.

We dozed for an hour, or at least Bree did. I'd given her a nice little workout, with just enough fun at my end to leave me relaxed. I never did get into REM sleep, though. The brain was too busy for that.

It seemed pretty obvious that they'd decided the 707 fire was arson before they'd even got the damned thing under control. Jan Gelman being a party guest, she'd have seen the flames shooting out from the gallery, and seen them white-hot. Okay, right. I got that; the fact that the idea of someone doing something that fucked up was beyond me didn't change the odds of that being what had actually happened, you know? Jan Gelman was the expert, not me, and she'd been sure.

What I couldn't figure out was why they were concentrating on Folkie Lind. Yeah, he'd been the one closest to Star, but there had to be more to it than just that—by itself, as a reason, it wouldn't fly. Shit, he wasn't stupid. If he wanted to off Star, with or without a good reason, he could have done it in any number of ways that didn't involve the risk of turning nearly five hundred people into a smouldering pile of formerly human toaster pastries.

I couldn't see an answer for that one, not yet. And of course, any shot at a real nap went south about then, because my brain went straight from the question of why they suspected Folkie to the question of why they thought Bree needed a lawyer, with a short break for picturing beating Curt's daddy to a puddle of mush for setting the dogs on my wife to get his own sorry arse out of lockup...

So the nap, which might have got the MS to back all the way down, wasn't on. By the time Bree woke up, I was cranky and achy and doing my best to hide it. Fortunately, the one time Bree's least likely to notice anything is after a nice slap and tickle, so we got downstairs to tidy up for guests without me triggering her alarm buttons. By the time the doorbell rang and I let my mother in law in, I'd managed to push things far enough away from the front of my mind to be able to cope.

"Hello, John."

She waited for me to stand back and invite her in; that's a ritual, going back thirty years, but tonight she was edgy. Unusual, for Miranda—it takes a lot to knock her off balance. I felt my nerves tighten up. "Am I the first one here? Good. Can I get a fast word with you two, before anyone else gets here?"

I followed her down the hall. Bree was just hanging up her cell; she was in charge of ordering dinner, a nice pile of burritos and tacos and enchiladas and whatnot, from our favourite Mexican local. She looked up at her mum, smiling, but whatever it was she saw on Miranda's face, the smile went fast.

"Mom? What's wrong?" She started forward. "Let me get you a glass of something. Sit. Mom? What's going on?"

"Is it that obvious?" Miranda sat. "Sorry, Bree. I didn't want to alarm you, but getting yanked out of a pre-surgery consult by a call from some woman who says she's investigating an arson homicide is a little off-putting."

"Oh, bloody hell, Jan Gelman rang you?" I grabbed the glass of juice Bree'd poured, and handed it over. "I knew Patrick was going to get on to you—he's looking into it for Blacklight and for us, as well. But Jan Gelman ringing up, yeah, that would have made me jump. I've got to say, that's quite surprising, really. What was she after, Miranda?"

"I wish I knew." She caught my eyebrow going straight up, and went slightly pink. "Honestly, I'm probably overreacting. She seemed straightforward enough. She said she'd been given my name as part of a list of people to call for information about Esther, she was going down the list, she knew I was busy but would I mind answering a couple of fast questions? She did her best to downplay it—but you know, when my secretary took the call, she told this woman that I was in the middle of a consult— I've got a patient with a medulloblastoma. Whatever this woman told my secretary was enough to get her to pull me out of what I was doing. And that worries me."

"What did she want to know? Specifically, I mean?"

That got my attention off Miranda and back to Bree. Her shoulders were as tight as I'd ever seen them. What the hell?

"Nothing too worrying, not really." Miranda'd noticed, as well. She doesn't miss much, not when it comes to Bree. "That's what I don't understand—there was nothing in what she asked me to have warranted my secretary dragging me out of a consult with a patient about a brain tumor. She asked me how well I'd known Esther back in the late seventies. I told her I remembered Esther, of course, but that I hadn't had any interaction with her since an incident at the clinic, back in 1979. She wanted to know if I knew of anyone who might have had any reason to call Esther an enemy."

"What did you tell her?" Bree's voice was as tight as her shoulders.

"I told her no, of course." Miranda met Bree's stare, steady even blue to fierce muddy green. "That's the plain truth, Bree. I certainly have reasons to remember Esther Woodley. I didn't like the girl at the time, either, but I simply can't see it being relevant—disliking a college student thirty years ago hardly qualifies as enmity today. If this arson investigator is looking for possible motives for Esther's death that far back, I think she's well off base. You know, I'm not a clinical psychiatrist, but to be willing to set fire to a building full of people because you want to kill one particular person there? That argues someone with a reason very much in the here and now, not someone with a cold grudge."

She stopped a moment, waiting for one of us to say something. Neither of us did. "Immediacy," she added, and drained her glass.

"That's the word I was looking for. Also, someone ruthless, or just insane."

"Or desperate." I don't know where the words came from, or the idea, but there they were. There was a picture in my head, as well, too clear for comfort: the office upstairs at the 707, a pair of hands manipulating a tin of something, splashing whatever was inside about, reaching for a lighter or a match...

Both women were looking at me. "I'm thinking someone needed her gone, as of right then," I told them. "So yeah, immediacy works. Hang on, there's the bell. Showtime."

Turned out everyone else had come together in Solange's truck, and the food showed up about ten minutes later, so the timing worked out nicely. We didn't talk about the fire at all, not during dinner. That wasn't what Bree would call supper table conversation. We talked about music, food, medicine—not a word about the 707.

After dinner, though, that was different. Bree was rinsing plates, I was loading them into the dishwasher, Mac had a dish-cloth and was hand-drying our pricey stemware before handing them on to Curt to put away, and Solange was setting out cups for after-dinner coffee and tea. It was right about then that Domitra, doing some scary leg stretches in the doorway of Bree's office alcove, brought it up.

"So did anyone else get a phone call from Patrick's pet arson expert?" She tilted all the way sideways, straightened all the way up, and dipped the other way. I was getting dizzy just watching her. "Or was it just us?"

There was a loud crash, and everyone jumped. Curt had dropped one of Bree's cherished Baccarat wineglasses. It hit the hardwood floor and went up like a small landmine on impact, spraying shards and crystal powder in every direction.

"Farrowen! Oh no you don't, you tricky bugger!" I got up fast, grabbing the Siamese. Last thing we needed was one of the cats

170

getting a crystal splinter lodged in a paw, or something. The two boys were at the front of the house, so I tossed Farrowen in with them—she's far too aristocratic to struggle, but was doing that pissy Siamese *wow-wow* thing with her voice—and pulled the door shut.

Back in the kitchen, Solange was sweeping up. Bree was reassuring Curt; he looked absolutely miserable.

"...no, honestly Curt, it's fine. The pattern's available from half a dozen different places. Besides, it's just a wineglass, not the Holy Grail or something. I'll have them send me a new one, so can you stop apologising?"

"Okay. I just—oh, damn!"

His voice broke. I just stood there, feeling thoroughly useless, blinking like an idiot, and everyone else looked too unnerved to do much of anything.

"Oh, baby." Solange was there, one arm round his waist. I felt my heart go a bit soft on me; how many times in the past thirty years had Bree been there when I needed her, doing that, using just that tone of voice? "Come on, Curt. You need to sit. Lean on me, it's okay..."

Everyone was quiet, waiting. He got settled. His face was very red, and there was a vein thumping away over one eye. Right, I thought, high blood pressure. No salt. Right.

"Um—Curt?" Bree had eased herself into a seat across the table. She looked really tired, suddenly. "Look, I don't want to pry, but here's the thing. If you're worried about Jan Gelman or anyone else thinking you torched the 707 and killed Star Woodley, get in line."

Curt took his glasses off, and rubbed his eyes. He looked about ten years old without the specs on, you know? Completely defenceless. Bree shook her head at him.

"Seriously, take a number. I've already got a list of lawyers I'm supposed to choose from—no, John, don't look at me like that.

We can pretend we want a lawyer to give the cops someone to talk to, but we both know they think I'm involved. Curt's father made a point of telling them all about me throwing Star out of our house, and it won't take them long to find out that my not-love for the woman goes back to before Curt was born. They already called my mother."

Curt had his voice back. "My father did that? Jesus. I'm sorry, Bree. I'm not surprised, but I'm sorry."

"Why aren't you surprised?"

We all turned. Domitra had her hands on her hips, looking nice and focused, and just about as intense as Jan Gelman had looked, telling me and Patrick that the fire was arson.

"Dom, angel, thank you for asking." Mac blew his bodyguard a kiss. It was a nice light gesture, pure Mac, but he didn't look amused, and his charm was about as banked down as it ever gets. "I'd like to know more about your parental unit myself, young Curtis. In Luke's opinion, your dad's unpredictable, is borderline-nutter on the subject of his reputation as a local producer, and has a hair-trigger temper. But Luke also says that that, at bottom, he's probably a decent bloke, just selfish as hell and not particularly aware of anything outside his own immediate thing. Now, your sweetie's dad is as sharp as they're made, generally, but I get the feeling your opinion doesn't match Luke's. So I think we've reached a point where you need to clue us in. What in hell is the story with your father, Curt?"

"The story?" He looked straight at Mac; the rest of us could have been invisible. If Mac's charm was banked down, Curt's was missing entirely. "He let my mother die. In a way, he actually killed her. Good enough for you?"

I heard someone, possibly Miranda, let out a held breath. Solange's mouth was a thin line. She probably knew the story already, whatever it turned out to be.

"Dude, sounds harsh. So what happened?" It was Dom, still

completely matter of fact, no sentiment or softness anywhere; she just wanted to know. It was probably the best way to get Curt to dish. "Some kind of accident, car crash or something? He get careless?"

Curt's hands were balled up, hard and tight. "There was nothing accidental about it. They'd been separated for about three months. My mother was fed up with being left at home with two kids while my father spent months at a time not giving a damn about anything but producing shows. She was fed up trying to get him to act like he was part of a family. He was the one with the money—my mean little prick of a grandfather trained his boys how to use it to hurt people who dared offend them. So my father took her name off the medical insurance. He left me and my sister on, but he took my mother off. He didn't tell her, either. She found out the hard way."

I could guess what was coming. So could Bree; she reached out and got hold of my hand.

"She was ill." Miranda's voice was very quiet, and she wasn't asking. It was a statement.

"She had Hodgkin's lymphoma, late stage three. She was ravaged with it." If his voice had got any tighter, it would have snapped in half. "Turned out they both knew that, when she left. Turned out he knew that when he removed her name from the insurance and left her with no way to pay for treatment. He wouldn't even pay for basic maintenance or childcare or anything else until the court forced him to. He fought her every step of the way: pricey lawyers, the whole nine yards. The court finally pinned his ears back, but by that time, it was too late."

"So you remember it?" Miranda sounded very gentle.

"Yes, I remember it. Why wouldn't I? I was seven, my sister Ashley was eleven. We both remember it just fine. Ashley lives in Florida—she hasn't spoken to him since she got married. Me, I'm stuck with him."

"Dude sounds like an asshole deluxe, yo. So, she died? And you had to go live with him? That must have pissed you off. Having to hang out with him, that had to suck."

Thank Christ for Domitra. None of us knew what to say— what could you say, really? But Dom's got no sentiment and no problem saying whatever she thinks needs to be said. Trust me, I know; once, a few years back, I'd been at the receiving end of that. She'd called me passive-aggressive and spoiled, and said she couldn't make up her mind whether I was a dick or just a dimwit. She'd pretty much saved my relationship with Bree, being that up-front, and maybe my life as well.

Curt was looking up at Mac. "Luke's wrong, and he's right too. My father's a user. My father wants what he wants, and he'll walk right over anyone who gets in his way. Nice enough guy? Sorry, man. I'm not the one to ask. My father's a mean asshole in my book, and he's a user."

"You said that twice." Dom was still stretching. She had one leg up behind her, in a pose that would have made perfect sense if she'd been on the ice at the Olympics. "User, how?"

"User, as in he uses people. Look at him and Star, if you don't believe me. She spent fifteen years handling all the shitwork he couldn't be bothered with, travel bookings and venue security and stuff like making sure the bands had food in the dressing room. You think he ever said thank you?" He snorted. "Yeah, right. I know she was pretty creepy and, okay, she got something out of that relationship. So what? Why does Star being a dysfunctional freak excuse him? She spent half her time keeping the peace between him and Paul Morgenstern, back when my father was trying to buy the 707 the first time, and I don't think my father even noticed. If it doesn't fit his personal requirement to see himself as King Norfolk the First of Bay Area Rock and Roll, he doesn't give a damn or even see it. But you know what? That's exactly why I don't buy into him killing Star. He's a user, she was useful. End of story."

I opened my mouth to say something, but didn't get a chance; Bree's phone, sitting on the butcher's block table, began to buzz. She flipped it open, and peered at the caller ID.

"Huh. No name, just a number." She sounded puzzled. "Hello? Yes, this is Bree Godwin. Who is this? How can I help you?"

I was watching her. For some reason, the tickybox had kicked into overdrive, and I had no idea why. Bree was silent, listening, not saying anything. Everyone else in the room seemed to have caught my nerves. When she finally did say something, the nerves didn't exactly loosen up.

"No. No, I'm afraid I haven't arranged for an attorney to represent me yet, Inspector Gelman."

I was on my feet, heading across the room. Bree looked across at me, the phone up against her ear, her eyes wide. "But yes, I'll be doing that first thing in the morning. And as soon as I do, my lawyer will call you back. And now, if you'll excuse me, I have a house full of people. Yes. Yes, goodbye."

She clicked the phone off. Her face was the colour of ash.

"Bree?" I'd forgot anyone else was in the room. "What the hell...?"

She swallowed, good and hard. "They've identified the accelerant. It was chafing dish fuel. She wants to ask me some questions, and she thinks I should bring my lawyer."

Chapter Ten

We ended up having breakfast with the lawyer Carla'd come up with for Bree. She turned out to be a woman called Lenore Tannenbaum, and no joke, she was one of the scariest people I've ever met in my life.

The conversation Mac had mentioned wanting got bumped off the top spot on the priorities list. Bree was trying to not flip out, and she was failing miserably. She's opened up a lot since we got married, but she's still private by design, you know? Melting down in front of our friends, that doesn't appeal to her any more now than it ever would have.

But she was flipping her shit, and as far as I could tell, there was really only one way to deal with it. I got my arm round her waist and turned her around.

"Right. Dom, could you move over, please? We need to get

into Bree's email, and her computer's behind you."

Dom moved. The kitchen had gone completely quiet; Solange was busy rubbing the back of Curt's neck, Mac had slid into a seat next to Miranda, and no one was saying a damned thing.

Bree popped her email open. Carla'd promised us she'd have a name and number for us, and of course, she'd come through. She always does. I saw the name—*Lenore Tannenbaum*—with two numbers, office and cell, both San Francisco area codes. The office number had a full business name above it—*Tannenbaum and Culpepper, Attorneys at Law*—and an address practically right round the corner, on Fillmore Street. Right. Unless I was reading it wrong, or unless the firm was hip deep in people called Tannenbaum, this woman was a partner, maybe a founder of the firm.

The weird thing was, I knew the name. Lenore Tannenbaum, Tannenbaum and Culpepper: both names were familiar, but my brain wasn't letting me in on why. I was pretty sure I'd never actually come across anyone with that name, not one on one, anyway. But I knew that name. Maybe she was high profile, one of those people who get their name in the news. Carla was likely to come up with someone who had visibility.

I put my lips up against Bree's ear; no one heard her but me. "Let's ring her. Get her on the phone now, yeah? Set this up, as soon as she can make it. See if she wants coffee in the morning. That way, we can talk to this Gelman chick, give her whatever gen she wants, and move the hell on. I'm not having this rubbish cost you any sleep. Okay?"

"Okay." She had a pen in one hand, writing down the info. Her hand was nice and steady. Good. "Where did I put my phone?"

We left everyone in the kitchen, and I followed Bree out into the hall. By the time the doors swung shut behind me, she was already punching in numbers.

I only got her end of the conversation—she wasn't putting the speaker on, not with guests in the house. I got the other end of the conversation as a series of short sharp rattles in between what Bree was saying, or trying to say.

"Is this Lenore Tannenbaum? Oh, good. Hi. My name's Bree Kinkaid, and I'm sorry to be calling after work hours, but— excuse me? Oh, I got your number from Carla Fanucci, my husband's PR manager—what? No, I was calling because—sorry? Oh, yes, the arson investigator did call me, and she—hold on, could you say that again? Well, as soon as possible would be— wait, I didn't quite—yes, tomorrow morning would be great, if you're available…"

It went on another minute or two, this lawyer bird breaking in every half-sentence to rattle off something or other, or ask a question, or whatever. My wife's not easy to interrupt, not unless it's me doing the interrupting, but this woman was managing it. Right around the fourth interruption, I started making bets with myself, about how long it would take before Bree started getting shirty over it, because as soon as it did, she'd try and get some control over it, maybe by grabbing some home court advantage. She doesn't much fancy feeling pushed off her balance. My guess was, it would be sometime before the eighth or ninth interruption, maybe sooner. She was starting to sound frazzled and irritated.

"…what? No, I wasn't intending to call her back until I have a lawyer. Okay, listen, here's the thing. We live about five minutes from your office—yes, Pacific Heights. My husband has multiple sclerosis and I'm diabetic and I'm afraid neither of us moves too fast in the mornings, so why don't you plan on coming here for a conversation and some coffee? 2828 Clay—we're between Scott and Divisadero. Half past nine? Actually, ten would be better, and if you're allergic to cats, you might want to take some allergy meds before you get here, because we've got three. Anyway, look,

I've got a house full of dinner guests, and I need to get back to them. See you in the morning."

She rang off, took a deep breath and let the snap out that she'd obviously been holding back on, herself. I'd been right about her getting irritated. "Jesus, lady! How about letting the prospective client finish a fucking sentence, already! What's so funny, John? Why are you laughing?"

"Just won a bet with myself, that's all." Perfect. Seventh interruption; I'd nailed it. She was still looking ruffled and pissy. I reached out and tilted her chin down.

"Okay, look. Here's me, being the heavy husband. She's coming over in the morning? Good. Let's go let everyone know it's being handled, and then put it out of your head until tomorrow. No, I mean it, Bree. Not having you make yourself nuts over it. If you can deal with this lawyer, we'll sign her up, give her some dosh and let her cope. If not, we'll find you another one."

Everyone split fairly early. Maybe everyone's reasons for wanting to come over, whatever everyone had to say, had got taken care of already; Miranda'd said her piece, Curt had lost it and Solange was busy trying to chill him out, Mac had got his question about Folkie Lind answered, and I didn't think Dom gave a shit about any of it, not beyond basic curiosity. It's not as if it affected her, or Mac, you know?

Our doorbell rang right at ten the next morning. That was definitely a point in this lawyer's plus column; my feeling is that if I'm paying a professional to show up and get stuff done, the professional having the sense to realise that neither of us appreciates having our time taken for granted is a good start.

Bree was setting out cups, waiting for the kettle to boil. She'd managed to put some muffin batter together, beautiful lumpy batter loaded with blueberries; I'd already snagged one off the cooling rack, and damned near burned the roof of my mouth off, on molten fruit.

179

"Is that the bell? John...?"

"Yeah, I'll get it."

I don't know what I was expecting. Probably someone who looked like the brunette bird from *Dynasty*, back in the eighties: shoulder pads and dark glasses and stilettos and maybe botox. You know, sort of tucked up high powered tight as a drumhead? Joan Collins, that was it: high-powered lady lawyer with eighties hair and an attitude. She'd have to have some serious cheek, to keep interrupting a potential rich client. I'd got that picture in my head, and it didn't want to go anywhere, especially since the bell rang again before I could get all the way down the hall.

"Crikey, I'm coming, hold your bleedin' horses." Lovely. Now she had me talking to myself, like a nutter. A lawyer who looked like Joan Collins and who was also apparently short on manners or patience. Not a good omen, you know?

"Right," I muttered, and opened the door.

"Good morning." She was looking up at me, and I do mean up. "You must be John Kinkaid. I'm Lenore Tannenbaum. Am I late?"

Yeah, well, so much for eighties nighttime telly. I'd got the stiletto part right, but even in those, she didn't quite reach my shoulder. And the stilettos were the only thing I'd got right. Her hair was iron grey, a nice fluffy bun at the back of her neck, and not a shoulder pad in sight. She didn't look like Joan Collins, not at all. She looked like Joan Collins' kindly old grandma, playing the part of a librarian in a black and white movie...

She cleared her throat, and I jumped. *Shit*. Here I'd been mentally calling her on bad manners for not letting Bree finish a sentence or giving me time to get to the front door, and I'd been so gobsmacked, I'd left her standing on the doorstep.

"Sorry," I told her, and let her in. "No, not late at all. My wife's in the kitchen. I hope you like blueberry muffins."

All things considered, it went off quite well. Tannenbaum had managed to nark Bree with the nonstop interruptions, but apparently she saved the habit for the phone, because she didn't interrupt that morning, not until she had to. She just let Bree talk.

Bree shook hands with her and introduced herself. I saw the tiny double-take, caught her eye, and bit back a grin. We hadn't actually discussed what we thought we'd be dealing with, but it was pretty obvious that it wasn't what we'd got.

Bree got the lawyer settled into a chair, and poured her a cup of coffee. She'd moved the muffins to a plate on the table, and I saw Tannenbaum eyeing them over the edge of her coffee cup. The kitchen still smelled of them.

"Here, have a muffin, they're brilliant." I pushed the plate toward her. "I'd join you, but I've already had one. They're made fresh this morning—Bree's a cook."

"Oh, thanks!" She took a bite. "This is good. You know, I think Patrick told me Mrs. Kinkaid was a professional chef."

Bree was watching Tannenbaum across the table. "Please call me Bree. Are you talking about Patrick Ormand? I didn't realise you knew him."

"I will—call you Bree, I mean. And I'm Lenore." She smiled at us, very sweet, and I had second thoughts about her looking like a librarian. Harmless? Bollocks to that. "Oh, yes, I met him back in 2005, when he was still SFPD Homicide. It wasn't exactly love at first sight—I was counsel for the defence on the Vinny Fabiano case. I had him on the witness stand for the best part of an hour, trying to take him apart. He told me later he had nightmares about it for weeks."

That answered the nagging question of why her name was so familiar. *Lenore Tannenbaum, Tannenbaum and Culpepper.* Right—I knew where I'd seen those names before. "Hang on a minute. You were Paul Morgenstern's lawyer, yeah? I remember I had to do a deposition or something – "

"Yes, that was me. I was Paul's attorney." She'd put that muffin away at really high speed, considering she didn't look to weigh a hundred pounds. She wasn't skinny or underfed, just really tiny. "I tried to get you and the members of the victim's band—the Bombardiers, wasn't it?—into our conference room. We got them in there, but I seem to recall we sent one of our people here to get yours done. You were ill at the time, or at least that's what our people were told. Coming here is a little out of my usual comfort zone. I generally prefer to have my clients come to me."

Yeah, well, so it looked like I'd been right about the whole nighttime telly thing in the first place. Maybe she looked like someone's sweet old gran, maybe a ten-year-old kid could have picked her up with one hand, but she had the attitude. And there was that smile. She had the shark thing down to an art form.

She also had brass bollocks, bringing that deposition up with a straight face. I remembered it as a major pain in the arse, an entire afternoon locked in our dining room with a bunch of suits, answering question after question about every fucking detail that might have had anything to do with Vinny Fabiano and his roadie cousin Rosario getting killed. I'd been sick as a dog, the MS kicking hard, Bree'd been seething and helpless, but even if I'd been feeling fine, it wouldn't have gone down as a nice way to spend an afternoon.

I don't pull out the celebrity privilege thing too often. For that little do, though, I'd have done whatever it took to make sure they had to come to me, sick or not. Tony and the rest of the Bombardiers hadn't been so lucky. I remembered how narked they'd been—Damon Gelb, the soundman who'd had the bad luck to find Vinny with his head bashed in on the floor of the band's Freelon Street studio, told us later that he'd been asked to describe it about eight times. He couldn't imagine what they'd been after. Whatever it was, he hadn't enjoyed it; finding Vinny dead on the floor had been bad enough the first time.

"...would certainly not want you answering any questions from anyone at all unless I was there."

Damn. I'd done it again, let my head go walkabout and missed something. There's not much advantage in the home court thing, if I was going to keep messing up that way. Besides, it had got me in trouble before, too many times. Whatever I'd missed, it was major, because Bree'd obviously made up her mind.

"So, you'll be there with me? Great. That's really what I want. It's not that I can't hold my own with the cops—ask Patrick about that, if you don't believe me. It's just that I don't want to, not about this."

Tannenbaum was watching her. I took a good look at those eyes, what they seemed to be doing in the way of dissecting and taking mental notes, and revised my opinion of her scariness factor up another few notches. Patrick Ormand at his worst hadn't managed to do what that look was doing to the base of my spine, which was twisting it up into a dirty great knot.

"I can see that. Let me be frank, before we go any further: It's clear that you have some deep issues about this entire thing, and before I agree to represent you, I'm going to want to know why. I'm not asking you whether you played any part in the fire; my decision to represent a client has nothing to do with guilt or innocence, presumed or otherwise. But I don't take on a client who wants to hamstring me by not giving me the basics."

I could have cheerfully thumped her. Who did this bird think she was, anyway? I was grinding my teeth, trying not to mess it up for Bree: *Right, we're the ones with the chequebook, counsellor, and we get the final say here, so deal with it, and don't talk to my wife as if you were doing her a favour, because the boot's on the other leg.*

But it wasn't my call, it was Bree's. And Bree was pale, but she was nodding, as well. If she was as narked by Tannenbaum assuming we had no say in who was going to represent us to the cops as I was, she wasn't saying so, at least not yet. When she did

183

say something, finally, her voice was steady, nice and calm: trying for Zen.

"Okay. I don't much like myself for it, but it's the truth: I hated Star Woodley's guts. She did something really ugly to me a long time ago, something that's still having repercussions today. She nearly cost my mother her livelihood, she nearly cost me jail time, and she nearly cost John his life."

"She sounds like a prize, but wait a moment. Just stop." Tannenbaum—I couldn't wrap my head around that nice matey little *call me Lenore* thing, not yet—held a hand up. "You haven't retained me, Bree. Unless and until you do, nothing you tell me is covered by client-lawyer privilege. Are you asking me to represent you?"

Bree got up, and headed into her office alcove. She came back out holding her chequebook.

"How much do you want? I just want to get this crap with Jan Gelman over with. I'm in the middle of something, working on something I mean, and I just want this whole thing off my plate. And by the way, I didn't kill Star Woodley. Just so you know."

I had to admire Tannenbaum's technique, you know? It was brilliant. And this was Bree's choice; I'd have backed her either way, of course, but truth is, my own bristles about Lenore Tannenbaum and her high-handed assumptions to one side, I thought Bree was making the right call. Bottom line was, if this woman had actually managed to reduce Patrick Ormand to a squirming mess on the witness stand, she was what we wanted. I was just sorry I hadn't been in the courtroom to watch her do it.

Meantime, Bree was giving Tannenbaum the gen. "Esther was one of the new minority owners of the 707 Club. She had some kind of partnership with Norfolk Lind, a production company called Lindyhop. I don't know much about that, but Andy Valdon, in Blacklight's office, probably knows all the details by heart—you could ask him. John's band, Blacklight, has the majority stake. Anyway, we hosted an ownership meeting here, a buffet meal, business afterward. Star snuck upstairs after dinner and let herself into our bedroom. I found her in our master bathroom, going through our medicine chest, probably looking to see what drugs we use." Her voice was suddenly bitter. "She was always so very interested in what drugs other people were doing. So very, very interested. Bitch."

I got across the room, good and fast. "Oi! It's okay, baby. Just breathe."

"I am breathing." She was still locked up in a stare with her new legal rep. "I booted her out, or actually, John did. And that was the last time I ever saw her. If Jan Gelman thinks I set fire to the club to take out Star Woodley, she must be doing some pretty major drugs herself, because she's hallucinating. I didn't even see Star at the show that night."

"Good. This is all information the investigators are going to take a good hard look at, if we're looking at an arson homicide. From where I'm sitting, going by what you've just given me as your possible motive, there's nothing there. But I have the feeling there's more you want to share with me."

She must have seen Bree's face tighten up, because she lifted one hand. "No, don't tell me yet. We can talk about that before I agree to let you sit down with the San Rafael police or anyone else. Let's arrange to get some paperwork signed tomorrow morning, and I'll let Inspector Gelman know we're ready to come up and have a chat."

The way things turned out, Bree and her scary new attorney did the interview at Jan Gelman's San Rafael office without me.

I wasn't precisely chuffed, and I might have started a row over it, if I'd thought for one minute that not having me there had been the lawyer's bright idea, not my wife's. But Bree made it nice and clear: she thought she could get a better handle on what Lenore Tannenbaum was good for if they did it one on one, and she wasn't having to concentrate on me. So yeah, I wasn't happy about it, but she was right, and I stayed home.

Bree was driving, another way of keeping the home court advantage; she extends that whole comfort zone thing to her car. She headed out early—she and Tannenbaum wanted to set aside time to go over the different scenarios Jan Gelman might hit them with before they walked into her office.

"John..." She bit her lip. She looked as worried as she sounded. So much for not concentrating on me when I wasn't there. "Babe, are you sure you're okay with this? You look a little shaky. Maybe I should stay home. I can reschedule -"

I got one arm around her waist. "Bree, love, will you stop? I'm fine—nothing's off at all right now. And yeah, I was a bit narked about you not wanting me along, but not after I thought about it. She's your mouthpiece, not mine. Go do your thing. Oh, good, I've made you laugh. What's funny, Bree?"

"You and the word 'mouthpiece.' James Cagney and Tony Soprano by way of South London." She looked at her watch. "Crap, I need to go. If I'm running too late to make it back for lunch, I'll try and call, okay? If I don't, just dig in. There's plenty of stuff in the fridge. If I'm not back by about half past one, grab something. And remember to eat."

She kissed me once, good and hard. For a nice hopeful moment, I thought she was about to do what she's done just before I've gone onstage with Blacklight, every gig since 2005: reach one hand between my thighs, grab, and give me a good hard squeeze to remember her by, while I'm busy doing something that isn't her. Not that morning, though.

Now that I wasn't booked to trot up to San Rafael, I actually had a few things I wanted to get done. Most of it needed to happen downstairs in the studio, but there was one particular item I wanted to sort out before I did anything else. I'd been pushing a notion about in my head since the morning "Americaland" had come together in the basement. It had got pushed all the way to the back of the queue by the mess at the 707, but now it was front and centre, demanding that I pay some attention to it. There was no point in doing anything about it until I ran it past Tony first, and I rang him.

I've known Tony thirty years, hung with him stoned and straight, toured with him for the best part of two years. I've got a pretty good take on his headspace, and I could tell: the lad was bored. I wondered if he'd been driving Katia half off her nut, being underfoot all day. She'd been trying to open her own travel agency for the past few months. They had no money issues, not now, but she was probably jonesing to get her old man out from under her feet.

"JP? Hey, man, what's up? You doing anything interesting? How's Bree holding up? Katia told me that creepy woman with the fire department wanted to talk to her."

"Oi, mate. Yeah, Bree's off to San Rafael with her lawyer. I'm betting you remember her—her name's Lenore Tannenbaum. She was Paul Morgenstern's lawyer, a few years ago. The woman who wanted all those depositions—know who I mean?"

I held the phone away from my ear for a few moments, grinning. Tony remembered Lenore Tannenbaum, all right.

"Tony, okay, right, look, take a breath, okay? The woman's good at her job, and that means she's good for Bree. I don't give a damn about anything else. Besides, she nearly managed to make Patrick Ormand cry on the witness stand—that's got to be worth a few points in the plus column. Look, mate, I want to talk to you about something. Nothing to do with this 707 thing, just an idea I've been playing with. You busy right now? Want to swing by for a while? Bree left a mass of food in the fridge, if you fancy having lunch."

"Hell yes." He'd stopped sounding restless. "You sound all Man

187

of Mystery and shit. Give me half an hour to take a shower and get dressed, and I'm there."

I rang off. With about an hour to kill before Tony got here, heading downstairs wasn't on; I always lose track of time down there. Besides, I can't hear the doorbell in the studio. The room's essentially soundproofed, and that's only partly so that I'm not distracted while I'm working. Pacific Heights has some serious noise ordinances.

Luckily, I always keep at least one guitar in the front room. I'd barely grabbed the Martin off its stand, tuned it, and settled back in my rocking chair for some nice slide practice, when the doorbell went.

Piss-poor timing, that was. I'd found my way into a hard-edged little run on the Martin, the slide grabbing and biting; there was a riff in there, something I could get my teeth into, and I wanted to explore it. It was too soon for Tony to have got here, even if he'd decided to pass on the shower. I wasn't expecting anything in the way of deliveries and I didn't think Bree was, either. Right—best to ignore it, and maybe they'd just go away.

The doorbell went again. They weren't leaving. *Right.* Just sign whatever the petition was, sign for whatever the package was, get rid of them, and get some more work done. I set the Martin back in its stand and headed for the front door.

Norfolk Lind, looking like he'd just spent a few days in a back-alley dumpster somewhere, was standing on the doorstep.

"Bloody hell." For a few seconds, that was pretty much all I could get out. "What the fuck are you doing here?"

He was squinting at me. San Francisco was having one of its nice bright sunny days, and he didn't look to be coping very well, because his eyes were watery. "Um—hi. Can I come in? I wanted to talk to you, sort of."

"You must be joking." The cheek of the bloke was a complete mindfuck, you know? I was having a serious wrestle with myself, because my hands wanted to ball up into fists, and once I let them, they'd have got used on the little wanker, I was that furious. "Can you come in? You've got brass bollocks, even showing your face here. You want to talk to me? The only thing I fancy talking to you about is whether you've got the medical insurance you're going to want once I chuck you down my steps. Right now, my wife's up in San Rafael with a pricey lawyer, so that the local coppers can put in the boot about what happened to your nasty little chewtoy. Bree getting grilled, that's on you, mate. That's your doing. You tried getting yourself out of lockup by throwing my wife into it instead. I don't know where you get your cheek, but right now, I could break your fucking neck and laugh while I was doing it."

I'd half-expected him to do the nutter thing he'd done with Luke, losing it and going for me. If I'm being honest here, I was half-hoping he would, because I was pissed off enough on Bree's behalf to have crippled him if he'd tried anything.

He didn't, though. He took all the steam out of me instead.

"I know. I'm sorry." Nice and simple, no theatrics, no attitude, no patented Folkie Lind craziness. His shoulders had slumped and his eyes were still watering. "I was scared shitless and I said the first thing that came into my head, but it was a totally assholic thing to do, and I shouldn't have done it. That was one reason I decided to come by. I was sort of hoping I could apologise to your wife, but I guess she's not here."

Brilliant. I couldn't just shut the door in his face—for one thing, I wanted whatever information he had, something I could hand over to Bree's lawyer. Besides, he looked like a coconut shy with a few too many road shows under its belt: beat-up and defeated, you know? And he'd apologised.

He was standing there, still waiting, still looking small and wasted and bedraggled, still keeping quiet, not pushing, just watching me. I came to a fast decision.

"Okay." I stood aside, and waved him in. "You've got fifteen minutes to speak your piece, and then you're out. I've got a bandmate coming over. And believe me, mate, if anything goes wrong in San Rafael, you don't want to be here when I hear about it."

For someone who wanted to talk to me badly enough to risk getting turfed off the front steps, he didn't seem to be in any big hurry to get started. He followed me in to the front room, just looking around. He didn't look to be in any better shape under the lights than he'd looked outside: he hadn't shaved in a day or so, and his eyes were bloodshot, and still watering. I got the feeling he hadn't slept much since the fire.

It suddenly came into my head: what if he and Star had a thing going? Was he missing waking up and finding her there? I couldn't imagine it—she'd had this weird asexual vibe about her—but, well, sex is a funny old thing, and you never really know what's going on with people, not where the old slap and tickle's concerned. And if he'd lost his sweetie as well as his business partner or number one groupie or bath slave or whatever the hell she'd been in his reality, it was small wonder he looked so lost and fried.

"I really like your house." He was still standing in the middle of the room, looking around. He sounded wistful. "I didn't get to say so when I was here before—first there was Curt, and then Star misbehaved. But it's a way cool house. It feels like people live here, like it's a home. It's been a long time since I lived in a place like that."

"Why not? It's not like you can't afford it—Curt told us you had plenty of money."

I've got no clue where that came from; it just popped out. He turned and looked at me, and I realised, I'd tensed up, expecting him to go ballistic, the way he'd done at Luke. No way in the world I was ever going to relax around Norfolk Lind.

190

Besides, if what Curt had told us about his mum was fact, Folkie was a murderer. And I wasn't thinking about Star, either.

The dosh we have to pay for healthcare isn't something I have to keep in the front of my head. I've got enough in my pocket to cover a neighbourhood or two for the next few years if I fancied it. Anyway, I come from the UK, where it comes out of your taxes and it's all laid on.

But I've had thirty years of watching my elegant mother-in-law get her hands dirty, finding ways of getting medical care for junkies and street people who haven't got tuppence to rub together, and that's clued me in. Bree's the one who writes the annual cheque to the Mission Bells Clinic, but it's one of the biggest numbers we put on a charitable donation every year. Christ, I'd almost died a couple of times. I've seen the bills. I know what it costs.

If someone's critical and they can't afford medical care, they've got no choices, you know? They die. My bottom line was, if Norfolk Lind had done what Curt claimed he'd done, if he'd taken cancer treatments and the money to pay for them out of his ex's reach, out of spite—Christ, if he'd done it for any reason at all—then he'd killed her.

And yeah, it really was that simple. There's not much grey there, not between those particular bits of black and white.

"You want to ask me something. Don't you?"

My face must have given it away. He was just standing there, waiting for me. He was the one who'd wanted to talk, but right then, he'd been sharp enough to know that keeping his gob shut and letting me draw first blood might be the smart way to go. Home field, you know?

"Yeah, I do." We locked up, eye to eye. Mine are dark brown, hard to read, and I know it. I take advantage of that when I have to. "Curt told us you took his mum's medical care away when she was dying. You really do that? Because I like that kid, and I'd

191

hate to think he came from anyone who could be such a shit."

"It's not that simple. Curt likes to think everything's black and white, but it isn't."

"Sorry, mate, that's pants. You're dead or you're not."

"Whatever." He shrugged, and I thought about breaking his neck. "You can believe what you want. Curt loved Eileen. He remembers her being sick, he remembers us fighting, he remembers her dying. So it's my fault, and that's what he and his sister are always going to believe. He was seven years old and that's the way he remembers it. What's your excuse? You've been through a messed-up marriage. But you didn't have to deal with lawyers. Your first wife offed herself. She died without any blame to you. I guess maybe it's just easy for you to talk."

I had my mouth zipped down hard. There was stuff he didn't know, and it was none of his damned business.

Yeah, Cilla had taken herself out, gone the suicide route by way of enough street smack to take down an elephant, never mind the ravaged underweight junkie I'd loved enough to marry, once. That much, he'd got right.

He was wrong about the blame, though. We'd been estranged for years, finished as a couple even before the night Bree'd come to the Saturn Hotel with drugs she'd stolen from her mum. That same night, Esther Woodley had taken her chance at getting rid of the boss's daughter, and turned her in to the cops.

But I'd been too lazy to bother with a divorce. No reason to bother, no reason to think about it all, you know? Twenty five years, and I did nothing. Cilla got money every month. She had our London house. She was thousands of miles away, not part of my life, and the girl I lived with was absolutely brilliant at hiding how much I was damaging her by letting things coast.

No blame to me? That was bullshit. I'd let Cilla down, and I'd hurt Bree doing it. Christ, Bree'd been there for Cilla when Cilla needed someone, and I hadn't been. But there was no way in hell

I was sharing that with Norfolk Lind. It was none of his damned business.

"Right. You don't think it's black and white, then you tell me what the grey zone is. Because from where I'm sitting, mate, there isn't any. But you know what, I don't actually go round looking for reasons to think people are bastards. If Curt has it wrong, what really happened?"

"Eileen left me. She took the kids with her." It was mind-blowing, how disinterested he sounded. "Curt thinks I knew she was sick, but he's wrong—Eileen must have told him I knew. Maybe she even believed it. But I didn't know shit. That's why she left me in the first place, for Christ's sake. I'd been out producing shows pretty much nonstop, and I got back and she was gone, boom, emptied out the house and elsewhere. I never saw her face to face again. Everything was done through our lawyers. I signed what he told me to sign, and I guess she did the same thing. My lawyer happened to be a lot meaner than hers. By the time we got to the point where I actually had to walk into a courtroom, she wasn't there—she was in hospice care, stage four, too far gone. By that time, I knew she had cancer, but I didn't know that bastard lawyer had eighty-sixed her coverage until after the whole mess was final. He'd left the kids covered."

I opened my mouth, and shut it again. He was telling the truth. I may be dim about some things, but I could have been ten times as thick as I was and I wouldn't have missed it. He was telling the truth.

"So, what, you've been walking round with this for fifteen years? You just signed shit and never looked at it, and your kid doesn't know that? Crikey, mate, Curt called his band Mad At Our Dads. You don't think maybe it's time you got off your bum and sorted that out? Why don't you tell him, tell his sister? Too lazy, or do you just not give enough of a rat's arse?"

"I've tried about a hundred times. All it does it make things worse." There was that shrug in his voice again. "He doesn't want to hear it and he doesn't want to believe it. I think it probably fucks with the way he remembers his mom. And I don't want to trigger a stroke or something—he's got my high blood pressure. Look, that's not what I came to talk about. I want to tell you something, see if you have any ideas about it."

I heard a rumble out in the street; Tony's Land Rover needs a good tune-up. "Talk away, but make it fast, because my company's just got here and I'm turfing you out when the doorbell goes."

"It's about the 707 ownership." Outside, Tony was locking the truck; I could hear the double *bleep* of the alarm. "About Lindy-hop. Your guy Andy has the financial statements, but they don't say where the actual money came from, at least I don't think they do."

"What do you mean, you don't think so?"

"Well, it's just that I never really read them over, or anything. Star handled all the money stuff for Lindyhop. I just signed on the dotted line, where she told me to."

I stood there, gawking at him. This was the hot shit producer bloke, who'd nearly lunged across the table for Luke's throat because he thought his rep as King Local Rock Producer was being insulted, and he didn't even read what he signed before he signed it? And he made a habit of it, as well; hadn't he said the same thing about his divorce papers?

There were footsteps outside; Tony had arrived. I finally found my voice. "Are you telling me the money you put up for the 707 wasn't yours? Where in hell did it come from, then?"

"That's just it. I don't know. Star got it from somewhere. And I think someone should find out. I can't shake this feeling that it might be important. Anyway, thanks for listening."

He followed me out into the hall. I opened the door, and saw Tony's eyebrows go all the way up.

"Come in, will you? No, Folkie, you stay where you are. Tony, I want to talk about signing the Geezers up on Fluorescent Records, cutting a CD, but that's going to have to wait."

Chapter Eleven

Bree got back late afternoon in a mad rush, trying to get home in time to fix us some supper. I'm pretty sure she wasn't expecting to find the house full of people in the middle of an emergency meeting; most of the ownership of the 707, and our pet detective as well, were gathered round the dining room table, trying to sort out where in hell Lindyhop's purchase money had come from. We were so deep into it, I didn't even hear her come in. Tony'd parked the Range Rover out on the street, and she'd come up through the basement.

"Hey, Bree." Patrick noticed her before I did, and got up; nice southern gent manners, or something. I don't remember him climbing up and down out of his chair back when he was still a cop and Bree was a suspect, but he probably had. "Is anyone blocking the garage? Does someone need to move their car? Are we in your way?"

She was in the doorway to the dining room, looking harassed. "No, not at all. Hi, everyone. John? Can I borrow you for a minute?"

"Right—excuse us, yeah? Back in a few."

We headed out into the hall, letting the door close behind us. "Sorry about the horde, love, but we've got a situation. Folkie Lind dropped by with a small bomb this morning, and this lot's here trying to sort it out. Actually, two bombs, but one of those is Curt's problem, not ours. Everything all right, then? You didn't ring, so I thought we were okay for time. You'd have rung me if things went wrong, Bree, wouldn't you?"

"Of course I would. And yes, it went fine." Something that might have been a smile moved across her face. "I think I picked the right lawyer. Lenore is scary as hell when she's got her *don't fuck with my client* face on. Mostly Gelman wanted to know about the chafing dish fuel: where I had the supplies stashed, how long had they been there, would it have been possible for someone to help themselves to a can or maybe even a few cans without me or the rest of the catering staff noticing, had I seen anyone trying to do anything like that. She seemed to be concentrating on the accelerant, how accessible it was, once I told her how I'd stashed it."

"What, she didn't even ask about you not liking Star? I thought that was the whole point."

"Oh, she tried. Lenore just never let her get past the first five words. Scary, scary lawyer lady, worth whatever she charges me. I don't think I'm done with Gelman yet—there was a definite 'I'll be back' vibe going on—but today, it was all about the arson, not about the murder. I'll give you the details later." She leaned over suddenly, and kissed me, tongue tip to tongue tip. "Hey. Mmmm. Nice. Did you remember to take your afternoon meds?"

"Yeah, I did, and I had some lunch, as well." I got one hand round behind her, and rubbed. "And no, before you start fussing,

197

I'll tell you straight up, I'm not having you cooking for everyone. Mac's already declined pizza—he says he's got a date, I'm betting with that Maria Genovese lookalike. Dom just rolled her eyes, so there's two people taken care of. Tony's off soon, as well—he told Katia he'd be back for dinner. I didn't mean to saddle you with a house full of people, Bree. Truth is, I lost track of time. Turns out, our Curt's dad is as thick as a sack of potatoes."

"Oh, I don't know." Her mouth thinned out for a moment. "I don't think throwing me to the sharks to get his own sorry ass out of the hot seat qualifies him as thick."

"Yeah, he came by to apologise to you for that. But you're wrong about him not being dim, love—the bloke's a total wet when it comes to business. You're not going to believe this, but Lindyhop's share, the dosh they put into the 707 deal? It wasn't their money, or even Lind's money—Star got it from a third party. And not only didn't he think to mention that fact on the financial disclosures before he signed them, he hasn't got a clue where she got it in the first place."

Her jaw had gone slack. "Wait a minute. I thought Carla and Andy were handling all this. You mean, Carla didn't verify this stuff? She didn't know the money wasn't their own?"

"Not a clue. First she heard of it was me ringing her up about an hour ago. She's—not happy. Andy didn't sound as if he were planning on doing any cartwheels, either."

"Holy shit." Bree looked as boggled as she sounded. "Wow. Carla actually slipped up on something. I wonder if they're snow-boarding in hell? John, just how much money are we talking about, here? I know Lindyhop is a minority shareholder, but I haven't been in on any of this."

"A hundred thousand dollars." Her jaw had dropped again, and I didn't blame her. "Mind-boggling, isn't it? And yeah, Star got it from somewhere or someone—it definitely wasn't their dosh. Either that, or she pulled it out of her arse. Thing is, she doesn't seem to have left any records lying about where anyone can find them. And it's not as if we can ask her."

"That's nuts." Bree had a very odd look in her eye. "I'll bet anything you like that wherever she got it, the source was shady. Anything you like."

I grinned at her. "I don't gamble, and if I did, I wouldn't bet against a sure thing. Problem is, Folkie did what it turns out he always does: signed where she told him to sign, and no questions asked. Seems the bloke makes a habit of doing that. I can't imagine why he's not living in a cardboard box under the highway, if he's that trusting. You'd think he'd know better. That whole thing, signing stuff without reading it first, that turns out to be why Curt's mad at his dad."

"Uh-oh. I don't suppose you want to fill me in on that one, do you...?"

I shook my head at her. "Later, all right? Right now, let's finish up and get people out of the house. Tony needs to head out and Mac's got a limo picking him up any minute. I'll give you all the gen after everyone's gone."

We got back into the dining room just as Mac was ringing off his cell. He got up, and stretched.

"My ride's here. Dom, angel, go enjoy yourself somewhere for a few hours. That's precisely what I'm going to do." He looked at my wife. "Bree, sorry to wave and run, but the lovely Anabellita awaits, and so does my posh chariot. Before I go, though, one thing: I want to make sure we're on the same page here. Johnny and I are the reps for Blacklight's majority stake in this, but I know it bores Johnny half to death, and I've got no intention of getting burned over it. Patrick, I'm confirming what Carla just told you: go as deep as you have to, peel skin if that's what it takes, but find out where Esther Woodley got that hundred thousand. And keep us in the loop. Sorry if that's an issue for you, Lind, but that's the way it has to be. We have a corporate interest

to protect." His glance flicked over towards Bree. "Not just corporate, either. We've got family to protect, as well."

Patrick nodded, but he was watching Folkie Lind. And Lind
was nodding, as well.

"No, it's cool. I'm not arguing about it. Hell, I was the one
who brought it up, remember? It's just that peeling skin off me
won't get you answers, because I really don't know where she got
it. Star always handled the money for Lindyhop. She had twenty
years worth of contacts, and I probably don't know even half of
them. She liked making deals and stuff. I'd rather produce
shows—that's what I'm good at, not deals."

"What about Lindyhop's records?" Oh, bloody hell. Patrick
had his predator on, teeth and all. "I want access to those."

Folkie shrugged. He didn't seem worried. "Sure, help yourself.
Well, help yourself to the ones that survived."

There was a moment of complete silence. We were all looking
at him. I don't know what the others were thinking, but I was
wondering if he'd gone and trashed all his recordkeeping.

"Survived?" Tony was staring at him. "What's that supposed to
mean? Survived what?"

The look Folkie Lind gave him, you'd have thought Tony was
five years old, and stupid with it. "The fire. What else?"

"Hang on." My legs had gone shaky with standing, but I wasn't
sitting, not yet. This was news to me, and from the looks of it,
everyone else was as surprised as I was. "Lindyhop's records went
up with the 707? What were they doing there? I've got one of
your company business cards—it shows a street address in Terra
Linda. You've got an office. We've been going over this for hours,
and you didn't say anything about it before. What the hell...?"

"I didn't? Huh. Sorry, I thought I did. It's probably not important anyway, but Star brought everything to do with Lindyhop's
707 dealings up to the office at the 707. You know, the tiny one
upstairs? It was just a small carton of stuff. She told me she asked

Jeff Kintera if she could store them there, and he told her yes."

Dom was up and moving. She doesn't do sitting still for long periods very well. "And you didn't ask her why? Dude, you born without curiosity, or just without brains? They let you out without a keeper? What's up with that?"

Next to me, I heard Bree swallow a noise at the back of her throat. Having been on the receiving end of one of Dom's reactions, I could have told her this one was pretty mild by comparison, but yeah, it was still funny. Dom doesn't do tact, or at least, if she does, she hasn't ever while I was around. In any event, the comment seemed to have got under Folkie's skin.

"I didn't ask her because I didn't have time. I was on my way up to talk to the Mystic in Petaluma about a show next month, and she was heading to San Rafael. And I didn't get to ask her about it afterwards, because she was dead, damn it!"

"Stop. Hold on." Crikey, there it was, the full hunt mode; something about this conversation had flipped Patrick Ormand's inner homicide cop switch to the on position, because out of nowhere there he was, smelling blood in the water. "Are you saying this all happened on the day of the party?"

Folkie was staring at Patrick as if he'd just watched a puppy turn into a cobra. All of a sudden, there was caution in his voice. "That's what I said, yes. I got into the office around eleven and she was just getting off the phone with Jeff Kintera and we talked for a couple of minutes. I went off to get my email and when I stuck my head in before I left, she was just taping up a cardboard box. I asked her what was up and she told me she wanted to organise the 707 financials, so she was going to head up to the 707 and do it up there."

"And...?" Patrick was on to something; you couldn't miss it. I remembered that look, back when he was hunting Bree: the way his jawline tightened, the way his entire face smoothed out, the way those dirty-ice eyes got cold and hot at the same time. He had Norfolk Lind's full attention. Yeah, cobra was the word, all right. Folkie's eyes were locked up in that staredown, and nothing short of someone getting between them was breaking that lock until Patrick wanted it that way.

"There is no 'and,' man." If Patrick's headspace was obvious, the fact that Folkie was telling the truth was just as clear. Whatever it was Patrick had caught a scent of, Folkie was clueless. "I never saw her alive again."

Even with all the upset, I managed to get my business with Tony done, just by walking him out to the truck.

Everyone except Patrick had gone, and it was nearly dark. It was no surprise that Tony went for it; the idea of getting a Geezers CD out on Fluorescent Records was a no-brainer. Blacklight's had its own record label since before I even joined the band. That was something Chris Fallow, best manager that ever lived, had got for the band, freedom from Decca and control not only of our own catalogue, but freedom to choose who we wanted for worldwide distribution, as well. The Bombardiers weren't as lucky; they've had nothing but grief from their own record label, but they're contracted for two more CDs. They're stuck.

The CD idea should probably have come to me years ago. Thinking about it, that seed had probably been planted the day of the meeting at the 707, when Luke mentioned that Fluorescent had signed Bergen Sandoval. That meant we were likely looking to sign some new blood, and, well, right, so the Geezers weren't new, but we were different and we were here and besides, I own a chunk of the bleedin' label, so why not put it to use? Hell, if we'd signed a mean tricky shit like Bergen, why not the Geezers?

"So, what? Get us in the studio and lay down some tracks?" Tony was nodding. "Hell yes. Might be fun to get a couple of guest singers to sit in, too."

I grinned at him; Tony's head was in the same place mine was, apparently. "Curt for 'Americaland', maybe Mac for 'Liplock'? That what you mean? Yeah, with you on that—I'm playing with ideas. I'll email everyone tomorrow, and see if there's anything I need to clear with our management first. I'm betting it's cool, though."

"Yeah, me too. What's the point of owning the record label if you can't record whoever you want? I've been seriously thinking about asking the Bombardiers if they want me to buy us out of our contract. Shit, at this point, owing our soul to the company store seems major stupid."

"Pretty much, yeah." I lifted an eyebrow at him. "Now I think about it, I'm surprised you haven't done that already."

"What, and give them another excuse to call me Bankcuso and Moneybags and shit like that?"

Okay, so, maybe I'm dim after all, but I heard something in Tony's voice that surprised me. It sounded almost like bitterness, but that's nuts, because Tony doesn't do bitter. He's just not that kind of bloke, his head doesn't work that way, and he had to know that however much his mates in the Bombardiers take the piss off him, they're still his mates. Anyway, I couldn't think of anything he had to be bitter about, not with enough money in the bank to never have to worry about it again.

It wasn't just the money, either. He was finally getting some of the industry attention he'd deserved all along, and I was damned glad to see it happen. People he'd always wanted to play with but who couldn't be arsed to consider him before the *Book of Days* tour were ringing him up, asking if he'd sit in with them. A nice safe future and respect, those things just don't add up to bitter, not in my head, anyway.

Maybe he sussed that I was surprised, because he changed the subject. Just as well, because I didn't have the first clue how to ask him about it. "So," he asked me, "what do you think of Folkie Lind's bullshit? Do you believe him?"

203

"What, about Star taking the Lindyhop records over to the 707? Or about him not ever bothering to ask her where she kept getting their dosh from?"

Tony shook his head. "Both, I guess. I just can't figure out how he gets his pants on or his shoes tied if he's that big a dumbass. I guess maybe if you're born into money, you don't pay attention to it the same way normal people do. I can hardly wait to get Katia's take on this one. My wife doesn't have a lot of time for the clue-impaired. You'll probably be able to hear her calling Folkie names all the way from Potrero Hill."

He opened the Range Rover's door. "Speaking of which, I need to get home—I'm already late, and Katia's pretty stressed. Give me a call or email me or something and let me know what's up with recording for Fluorescent, okay?"

He headed off down the hill. The fog was beginning to come in—I could hear the horns, out at Ocean Beach—but I wasn't quite ready to head back indoors, not yet. Something he'd said had got me uneasy; problem was, I couldn't place what it was.

I teased at it for a bit, trying to sort out what had tweaked me. Was it the bit about believing Lind, when he said Star'd taken the Lindyhop financials up to the 707...?

"John? Is everything all right?"

I hadn't heard the front door open. Bree was in the doorway, looking worried. "Patrick's getting ready to head out, but he said he wanted a word with us together first."

I headed for the house; it was getting chilly, and she had her arms wrapped round herself. "Sorry, love. Just trying to sort out something."

Patrick was in the kitchen, playing with Simon. It's something I always remember about him, whenever he's done something that's left me wanting to bash him: all three of our cats adore the bloke, and have from the first. Not too many people I can say that about, you know? Wolfling and Simon aren't particularly discriminating, but Farrowen's got the Siamese pickiness down to an art form.

Right then, he was busy scratching Simon under the chin, and our not very bright youngest cat was rattling the crockery. Simon's got a purr like the engine of Curt Lind's motorbike.

"Hey, JP. Hope I didn't interrupt you, but I have a couple of ideas I want to go check out, and I didn't want to go without talking to you and Bree alone first."

"Right." I headed for the mugs; Bree was plugging in the electric kettle. "Bree, there's enough for three cups, yeah? Okay. So, what's going on, Patrick? This a progress report?"

"Actually, I was hoping to ask you a couple of things. Assuming Bree isn't fed up with answering questions, I mean—I know Jan Gelman can get pretty intense."

He wasn't in shark mode, not just then—too busy fending off Farrowen, who'd jumped up on the table, caught the look and a small warning *don't even think about it kitty* noise from my wife, and jumped down on the bench to curl up next to Patrick instead. So he was getting purrs in stereo, and that makes it tricky, trying to be a pissy asshole when cats are cuddled up against you.

"It wasn't that bad." Bree got cups on the table, and slid in next to me. Damn—she was chilly up against me. I watch for that these days, with her diabetes. "Carla hooked me up with a really good lawyer. You've met her—Lenore Tannenbaum."

I thought I saw something ripple across Patrick's face, just for a moment. That doesn't happen often, you know? He's the original poker face.

"I've dealt with her, yes. That was back when I was with SFPD." Was that something in his voice, as well? "I can imagine Jan didn't get one word out if Tannenbaum didn't decide to allow it. She's—let's just say she's a pro, and leave it at that."

I was openly grinning now. "Yeah, she told us she'd got you up on the stand, during Paul Morgenstern's trial. She tried dragging me in for a deposition during that little mess, but I was sick as a dog and they had to come to me. She sent her minions or flunkies or groupies or whatever the hell they are -"

"Associates." Patrick took a mouthful of tea. "You got lucky. Trust me, JP, you got off light. Counsellor Tannenbaum is a bloodbeast. She's never happier than when she's got shreds of someone else's skin dangling from between her teeth."

Takes one to know one, I thought, but I didn't say it out loud. "Yeah, well, the Bombardiers weren't so lucky. You should hear Tony on the subject. But she's got Bree's back, and that's all I care about. What did you want to ask us about, Patrick?"

"The 707." Patrick was watching me, those dirty-ice eyes of his about as easy to read as a blank wall. "You played there quite a few times before, didn't you? Have I got that right?"

I blinked at him. Not what I was expecting, that line of questions. "Not really—just a couple of times recently. Once we get this mess sorted out and get the place rebuilt, I'm planning on booking the Geezers in there a lot, but mostly, we've played here in the City: the Fillmore, Great American, Slim's a couple of times."

"No, I don't mean recently. I meant, back in the days when Paul Morgenstern owned it."

That threw me completely. I couldn't suss why he'd want to know that; after all, Paul hadn't owned the place for five years at least, and he wasn't going to own it again. He'd been one of the major Bay Area producers, someone with a hand on most of the local switches and his fingers in every pie, but this was one pie his fingers were out of for the long haul. Not much you can do to keep your hand in when you're doing fourteen to twenty for second degree murder, grand larceny, money laundering, collusion and a few other things. Hell, Lenore Tannenbaum was probably the only reason he wasn't sitting on Death Row at San Quentin. The law gets quite twitchy about anything that looks like it might be funding terrorist activities, these days.

Point is, though, Patrick was asking about ancient history. I shook my head at him.

"The answer's still no, mate. Sorry. I sat in for a couple of benefit gigs back in the day, but I honestly barely knew Paul. Like I told you, I kept the Geezers mostly in the City for the local shows, and Paul was all about the North Bay. The bloke you want to talk to is Billy Dumont, the Bombardiers drummer. He handles most of their local bookings and they used to play there quite a lot, just because they like doing local gigs and most of the venues for their size audience don't exist anymore."

"Why not?" Still watching me, still unreadable. But I got it, suddenly: he had something in his head, all right. Every word I said was information, and he was going to use it. Next to me, Bree listened, and took small sips of her tea.

"Not economically viable, that's why. The cost of producing a show these days is nuts. You're talking about modern audiences, and they're sophisticated, you know? They want the full rig: special effects, top of the line sound, interactive, the lot. And that costs a metric fuckload of dosh. One show during the *Book of Days* tour probably cost about a quarter million, and that's the arena stuff. You get into playing the stadium circuit, double it. If you're playing clubs, you don't have to supply the gear, because the smaller venues have their own PA, their own lighting rig. You just bring your axe and your band, and bob's your uncle: plug in and play. Since there's no big outlay, you don't have to charge high ticket prices."

Patrick was tapping on the table. I've noticed that about him; there are some little tricky habits he doesn't know he's got. That tap thing? He does it when he's focusing. You could practically see the wheels in his head turning. "So basically, it costs more to stage a show for a name band at a medium-sized venue than the band could reasonably expect to recoup? Have I got that right?"

"That's it. That's the beauty of being a big enough act to do stadium tours, if we fancy it." I grinned at him. "How much did we pay you as bonus money, for taking over security on the *Book of Days* tour? Right round two million, or something? Drop in the bucket, Patrick. Petty cash, basically. Hard to wrap your head around those numbers—why do you think I let Bree handle the money?"

Next to me, Bree had been quiet, listening to the conversation. She finally spoke up.

"Patrick, I'm curious. Why do you want to know about the 707 back in the day? Because that is what you want to know, isn't it? Why would it matter now?"

I thought, for just a moment, that he wasn't going to answer her. He was a copper for a good long time, was Patrick Ormand, and they don't answer questions, they ask them. But he's not a cop anymore, he's an investigator, and he was working for us on this one.

"You may remember me asking you about Esther Woodley, whether or not you had any idea of what she'd been doing over the last twenty years." He was taking his time, being careful about how he put it. "I'd already begun the hunt for that information, before Norfolk Lind dropped his little bombshell tonight. It was a lot easier than I thought it would be—Carla has a way of unlocking doors that would otherwise be off limits to most people."

We were quiet, waiting. I had Bree's hand under the table, rubbing it; it was warming up, but not nearly fast enough for my liking. Patrick gave us a moment, and then went on.

"Carla got me access to the Lindyhop phone records. They have an office phone, but it seems to be attached to an answering machine—they use it for messages, and not much else. All their real business is done on their cell phones. I have the request in to Lind, to get a look at her cell phone records. But I also got a piece of information from Jan Gelman, just before I came up here. It seems the San Rafael investigation already got their hands on Lindyhop's credit card records for the past six months. She was willing to share an interesting tidbit."

He stopped. There was that look of his, the one I like the least: barracuda, sniffing blood in the water.

"Right." If I wasn't following, neither was Bree. She looked as confused as I felt. "You going to tell me Star Woodley financed Lindyhop's 707 share off her MasterCard?"

"No. But there are seven separate instances of expenses incurred on Star Woodley's Lindyhop American Express card over the past four months—lunch, tanks of gas, things like that—in the same town in Lassen County: Herlong. Her presence there needs some explanation, all things considered, especially since they're all on the same day of the week, and all pretty much within the same block of hours."

"Still not getting it, mate. Why shouldn't she go to Lassen County? Up near Reno, isn't it? Lots to do in Reno. What's so weird about the town? And if she was doing stuff up there, stands to reason she'd be doing it during a specific time—it's a good long drive."

"Herlong Prison is where Paul Morgenstern is incarcerated." Patrick got up, set Farrowen carefully back on the bench, and nodded at us. "Every visit was on a Tuesday, every meal was within half an hour of the end of visiting hours, all at the same diner, the one nearest the prison. I won't know for sure until I go up and pull a few strings with the boys in charge, but right now, it looks as if Star Woodley kept Morgenstern on her active contacts list. I'll be talking to some people and taking a day trip. I'll keep you posted."

Chapter Twelve

What with the MS and the heart issues and just the basic fact that I'm up near sixty, morning isn't the easiest time of day for me. It never has been, not with a touring rocker's schedule; that gets you used to late nights, and long lie-ins the morning after. These days, though, the first half-hour is a complete bitch, what with trying to sort myself out physically, seeing what hurts, what's likely to keep hurting, getting my meds together, all that rubbish.

It's bad enough as it is, you know? But what really frosts it for me is having the morning start off with a ringing telephone. I've never yet been woken up that way and had it turn out well, no matter if it's me or Bree getting a hand on the phone first. Usually it's Bree—one habit she's never got rid of is trying to get the phone before it can wake me up. That one's probably hard-wired, or something, and she's usually quite good at it.

There's not much even Bree can do about it when both phones go off at once, though, and that's what happened that morning: "Remember Me" in one ear and "Sympathy for the Devil", Bree's ringtone of the moment, in the other. Bad omens in stereo.

We were short on sleep anyway. We'd stayed up late, having one of those late-night conversations that always seem to happen in bed, while I'm waiting for the heart to slow down after a good long snog. I was just beginning to drowse off after the tickybox finally steadied the heartbeat down off the accelerated samba the sex had left it stuck in. Bree, though, she was wide awake, and sharp enough to remember something I'd said hours ago. She snuggled up next to me, and planted a light kiss at the back of my neck.

"John?"

"Mmmm?"

"What were you talking about before? I mean, when you said Folkie Lind makes a habit of signing stuff blind?"

Yeah, well. So much for sleep.

I rolled over. Since I know Bree well enough to know she wasn't about to smile, thank me for the gen after I told her, and fall asleep as soon as I'd finished talking, I might as well suck it up and make myself comfy, yeah? Of course, I'd called it; once I'd finished telling her about it, sleep wasn't on, not until she calmed down.

"Let me get this straight." She was propped up on one elbow, her hair swinging. "His ex dumped him for not paying enough attention to the fact that he had a wife and kids, and he responded by not paying attention to what his divorce lawyer was telling him to sign, and he accidentally signed away her chemo? Are you fucking kidding me? You're joking, right?"

"No joke." I swallowed a yawn. "Not much for irony, but yeah, I see it. Pretty hard to miss. You can see why I said you were

211

wrong about him being smart, yeah? He hasn't got any sense at all, just a sort of low cunning. Tell you the truth, though, I can't help thinking there's something nice about him not wanting to tell Curt, not messing with how Curt remembers his mum."

"I see what you mean. Kind of sweet, actually, especially since it wouldn't make Curt like him any better. At least he's smart enough to get that much."

She settled back down, and I closed my eyes. Good. Time for a bit of kip...

"You know, I can't help wondering if he could really be half as flaky as this makes him out to be. I mean, he's good at what he does, isn't he? I checked him out online, and he's put on hundreds of shows over the years. He's even got his own wiki entry. So how could he possibly have pulled that off if he was out to lunch half the time? I don't get it, John. And don't even think about telling me that he's been fronting for Esther Woodley all this time, that she was the capable one or the power behind the throne or anything. Just—don't."

I opened my eyes and eased over onto my right side; the left side was pissing and moaning at me. There was moonlight on the wall, and I could hear Farrowen's distinctive little Siamese *wow-wow* noise. She was probably lamenting about being shut downstairs. "Wasn't about to, love, believe me. But the gigs, how he got it done? He handled the small stuff, mostly. I mean, we're not talking about Bill Graham or Chet Helms here, Bree. We're not even talking about Paul Morgenstern. I doubt Folkie Lind ever put on anything major, nothing more than a few thousand people in the house. He doesn't do festivals or even the bigger local shows—it's clubs and small venues, mostly."

I swallowed another yawn. Bree was still propped up, waiting for more or thinking it over, maybe both. The heart had settled back down to normal, but the MS was being stroppy, and I wanted some sleep. I was feeling light-headed, as well, my mind

212

going off into that drifty, child's balloon space, where things all seem very clear at the moment, but half the time they don't really make any sense in the morning. My eyelids felt about as heavy as the tickybox, pinned inside just under my collarbone.

"Maybe that's why he tried getting the 707 away from Paul Morgenstern, or at least why he wanted the majority share when Paul finally sold the place," I told her, and smothered another yawn. "Nice venue he could call his own little kingdom, that would have suited him down to the ground."

All of a sudden the bed creaked; she'd sat up all the way. My eyes had pretty much gone into sleep mode, but she didn't answer me. She was quiet so long, it got my attention off sleep and back on her.

"Bree? You all right?"

"What you said, just now." She was speaking slowly, sorting it out. "About Folkie Lind trying to get the 707 away from Paul. Someone else was talking about that recently, but I can't remember who, or when. And I've got this feeling, John. I think it's important. I promise I'll stop bugging you and let you go to sleep, but help me out here. Do you remember who it was? Or do you know the details?"

I closed my eyes again. It wasn't about sleep, not anymore— she'd got my brain back out of kip mode and into think mode, even though the body was still ready to pass out. I kept the eyes closed, trying to get the memory up and clear. It only took a few seconds, and there it was.

"It was Curt," I told her. "When he was telling us about his dad doing his mum out of her meds money. He said his dad's a user, and that's why he doesn't believe Folkie killed Star, because Folkie's a user and Star was useful. Remember?"

"Yes! That's it. He said - " She punched the mattress, and that made me jump. I couldn't remember seeing her this intense about anything that wasn't food or me, not for a long time.

"Fuck! I can't remember what he said. It was something about his father trying to buy the 707 the first time, something to do with Star—goddamnit, I can't remember!"

"Oi! Calm down, love, will you? Give me a minute, let me see if I can remember."

I could hear Curt's voice in my head, reacting to Domitra's dispassionate little question about what was up, between the two Linds. What had he said, exactly?

"Got it. Curt said Star'd spent half her time keeping the peace between Folkie and Paul, back when Folkie was trying to buy the 707 the first time. He said he thought Folkie couldn't even be arsed to notice that Star was playing Henry Kissinger, or whatever."

"When?"

"Bree, it's about two in the morning and my brain's not really up to coping. Be a bit more specific, lady, would you please? When what? What are you on about?"

"What you just said, about him trying to buy the 707 the first time. What first time? When did that happen? Was that before Paul went to jail, or after, or was it years ago, or what?"

"That's a damned good question." It was, too. "Haven't got a clue, though. The 707 wasn't a big part of my world until recently, you know? I was sort of vaguely aware there was a local promoter with a company called Lindyhop, but that's basically it, Bree. And I didn't know Star Woodley existed."

"I wish I didn't either." She shivered suddenly, and lay back down, pulling the duvet up around herself. "Damn, it got chilly in here. You know, John, I remember what Curt said, but I don't know when that was. I don't pay attention to the 707 either—I mean, it could have been twenty years ago or twenty minutes before Paul got sentenced."

I settled back down next to her, and got some cover over myself as well. She was right, the room was chilly, or maybe it just felt that way because I was knackered. "We can get Patrick on it in the morning, yeah? Or we could give Carla a chance to spackle the crack in her Super Woman shield, and let her get us the details."

"Okay." She sounded drowsy, suddenly, as drowsy as I felt. I wondered if she'd remembered to take her night meds. She leaned forward and kissed the back of my shoulder. "Let's do that. God, I'm zonked out tired—Jesus, it's after three! Good-night, baby. Sorry I kept you awake."

When both phones went off five hours later, I was miles down in REM sleep. But the fact that it was both phones managed to get just far enough through the bizarre little dream I was hav-ing—something about Curt and Luke doing some sort of amateur juggling act with flaming guitars, very Jimi Hendrix at Monterey by way of an acid flashback—to make me realise that Bree wasn't going to be able to get them both. I could hear her scrabbling away for her own phone, and "Sympathy for the Devil" getting cut off, but "Remember Me" was still ringing away, about a foot from my head.

"Shit!" Bree had her cell in hand, and was out of bed and heading for the door. Pure habit, that is. I sat up and reached for mine, trying to stop the song; problem is, I didn't stop to brace myself for the first hit of morning MS stuff, and it nailed me. The entire left shoulder and arm were basically in flames. It was bad enough to surprise a noise of pain out of me, and that's some-thing I try to never let happen, not if Bree's there to hear it. There's sod-all she can do about it, and she flips her shit if she thinks I'm in pain.

"Hello?" She was talking into her phone, but her eyes were on me, and she saw just how bad it was. The look of complete help-lessness on her face—yeah, well, that's all I need to say about it. She wasn't going anywhere, not until she was convinced I wasn't going to need any help getting out of bed and off to the loo, and

215

help was just what I was going to need. The pain was everywhere, little sharp razor cuts running along the nerves on my left side. Under the duvet, my left leg was spasming, and the duvet was shaking. There was no hiding that from my wife.

She headed for the bed, talking the entire time. "This is Bree—oh, Lenore. What? Of course I sound half-awake, it's kind of early to be—what? Yes, we were up late last night, and John tends to sleep in anyway. What time is—what? I don't know, I can probably come over today, but it's going to depend on how John feels. What's the—what? No, I don't know what time. I don't even know what time it is now—Jesus wept, will you please stop interrupting me! Look, I'm sorry, I can't talk to you right now, Lenore. I need to go help John. The phone woke him up and it's a bad morning. I'll get back to you."

She tossed her phone on the bed. I'd got mine in hand, stopping the song; she was having a bad enough morning, without having to listen to "Remember Me." It took me a minute of fumbling to get the phone actually open and connected. If the MS didn't ease off, today was going to be a stone fucking drag.

"This is JP." Crikey, my voice sounded as rough as the rest of me felt. This was going to be grim. Of course, anyone who rings me at eight in the morning isn't really angling for warm and fuzzy, yeah? Sod being chirpy in the morning, anyway. "Hello? Who's this?"

"It's Carla." Carla sounded pretty ragged herself. "Sorry if I woke you, but I need to give you a heads-up: when Jan Gelman calls you and says can you come up to her office because she wants to have a friendly little chat about the money sources for the 707 buyout, tell her she has to talk to me. Don't talk to her, not about that. Okay? If she wants anything at all about the financials, ours or anyone else's, she has to go through our legal channels, and that information goes through me. She's already tried back-dooring Mac, and I need to keep a handle on it from here. So just tell her to call my office, okay?"

216

"What – " I stopped. Shit. Lovely, just brilliant. The jaw was locking up on me; trigeminal neuralgia. "Carla, bad morning. MS is hell right now. I need meds. I'll ring you back."

"Bathroom. Extra painkillers." Bree was right there, one hand under my arm, taking the cell away from me and tossing it on the bed with the other. Thank god for it, because I was seriously shaky. No idea what had triggered this little lot—with multiple sclerosis, you don't even need a trigger, not really—but I could have done quite nicely without this.

It took awhile, Bree getting my meds together and helping me back to bed and settled in. Even if I'd fancied ringing Carla back, it wasn't happening. Bree'd gone into her fierce flat protective mode, and heaven help anyone who tried getting round her to get at me until I was better able to cope. After thirty years together, I'm not nearly dim enough to argue with her when she gets into that headspace, and I don't fancy arguing anyway. Her taking care of me when I need it, that keeps me alive, or at least ambulatory.

The MS is a funny old thing, though: my head's never sharper than when my body's playing Judas on me. While I was lying as still as possible, trying to relax as many myelin-depleted nerve endings as I could, Bree headed down to the kitchen to make some coffee and feed the cats, and my brain was clicking into gear, sharp as a tack.

I kept coming back to what Curt had let drop, about how his dad had tried to get the 707 out from under Paul Morgenstern. What I'd told Bree was true: I knew sod-all about that. I didn't know what had gone down. I didn't know when, either.

But I remembered what Curt had said, his choice of words. He'd said Star had kept the peace. And that had to mean that Folkie trying to buy it hadn't made Paul happy. Paul hadn't wanted to sell.

So Star had known Paul Morgenstern, known him well enough

to play negotiator and peacemaker between Paul and the bloke she herself claimed was her business partner. She'd had a finger in that pie long since, from the sound of it. And not to speak ill of the dead and all that rubbish, but nothing I knew about Star left me believing that she'd been visiting Paul Morgenstern in Herlong Prison to bring him brownies and clean socks. Curt might call his dad a user, but Star Woodley had been world-class at it. She liked power, and secrets, and control. The way she'd handled Bree's drug theft proved that, no room for doubt.

I shifted both legs, bit back noise, and held still again. But the brain kept clicking away.

Dodgy financials, that was much more Mac's thing than mine. A hundred thousand dollars that hadn't come from Lindyhop's own funds, and that was another question, one nobody seemed to be asking: why would Star have needed to go anywhere except the company chequebook for Lindyhop's share of the purchase price? Why hadn't she just used their own funds in the first place? If Lindyhop wasn't solvent, didn't have it, they could have borrowed against assets, surely? I knew that much—Curt came from a shitload of money.

No answer for that one, not yet. But one thing looked to be obvious: whatever Star had been up to with Paul Morgenstern, she'd probably got either power or money out of it.

Had she got Lindyhop's hundred thousand from Paul? My first thought was that this was the obvious answer. Problem was, that didn't hold up. It didn't make any sense, and I just couldn't see it. Paul had been left basically skint after he'd finished paying off his lawyers. Grand larceny, second-degree murder, trafficking, money laundering, abetting terrorism: that had been quite the roster of charges his legal team had to defend against.

Hell, Mac had bought Paul's PRS waterfall and some of the art Paul actually owned, the stuff that hadn't been stolen and hidden in plain sight. That had cost him over a hundred thousand dollars, and it barely made a dent in Paul's legal fees. Lenore Tannenbaum didn't come cheap, and she'd been the lead on a whole team of pricey lawyers defending Paul Morgenstern. They'd all have built swimming pools off the fees they'd collected.

But if Star hadn't got that dosh from Paul, where had she got it? And why had she needed it in the first place? And if it hadn't been for money, what in sweet hell had she been up to, with all those visits to Paul?

The bedroom door clicked open, Bree getting one hip on it and closing it again, before any of the cats got ideas about coming in and jumping on the bed. They're opportunists, our cats are. She had her hands full, carrying a tray with coffee for her, warm tea for me, cool enough for me to be able to get down without making the jaw do anything. She got down next to me, not touching me, leaving me plenty of room, not wanting to risk making it worse. One of the cruellest things about this damned disease is the way it takes away wanting to be touched. Touching Bree is one of two things I live for, you know? That, and music. And the damned disease takes both things away from me.

"You know what I want?"

I turned toward her. The painkillers were taking their time about kicking in. I wasn't talking, but I didn't need to. I've got that one-eyebrow-up thing down, and she knows what it means.

"I want to turn the damned phones off." She sounded tired, really tired. That upset me—it's another sign that she wasn't invincible, getting tired just like anyone else. "I want to turn them off and stick them in a drawer. Just for today, I want to not have to talk to lawyers who don't let me finish sentences, or to detectives who like wounded things, or Carla or Solange or Mac or Patrick Ormand or to anyone. I want to just lock the door and turn off the phone and pretend there's no outside world. And I don't want to have to think about Star Woodley or Paul Morgenstern or the 707 Club, or anything else. I'm sick and tired of the world right now. I want it to fuck off and leave us alone, just for a day."

I got one hand up, and let it rest on her thigh. Maybe the painkillers were doing their thing after all. "Do it. Sod the world. They can wait."

"Really?" She set her cup down on her own nightstand, and turned back to me. "Can we?"

"Yeah." I nodded, winced, and tried again. The words came out a bit slurry, but they came out, and that was the important thing. "Anyone wants us today, sod it. They can leave a message. Turn the phones off and come back to bed, love. Rest of today, we're not at home."

The problem with the real world is that, most of the time, it won't cooperate. You can you put your foot down, tell it *look, mate, this is the way it's going to be and it's no good getting shirty about it because I'm having it my way this time*, and it laughs in your face and tells you to fuck off, basically. It's got this annoying habit of dumping you straight into a bad case of Sod's Law.

That day, I didn't have much of a choice. That relapse was a corker, all the way on the wrong side of the ledger; the painkillers kicked on, quietened things down to nearly bearable, and then wore off completely, long before it was safe for me to take another hit. I don't know whether the high tolerance to drug dosages comes from having been a junkie for awhile, but whatever it was, it basically took me down that day. Just because it takes a high dose of drugs to do the job properly, that doesn't make it safe for me to overdo, especially not with the heart issue. The tickybox complicates things even more.

So, even if I'd wanted to sit there answering my email with one hand and using the cell phone with the other, it wasn't on. I'd been right about the day being a stone drag if the pain didn't ease off, but I was surprised, and disturbed, about just how hard the relapse was hanging on. Usually, pain meds and sleep are enough to at least take the edge off, and once the edge is gone, I usually get at least a bit of normalcy back, with a reasonably short time.

Not that day. I spent all of it in bed, except for Bree running me a hot bath, loading it up with her mineral salts, and settling me in. We've got a jacuzzi tub, but the jets stayed off that day. My skin, all of it, wasn't even dealing with basic air too well. Pressure from water or anything else simply wasn't on.

Bree spent the day with me; she probably wouldn't have left me alone at all if I hadn't made her take breaks, and that was unacceptable. Yeah, well, so I was fucked up in terms of being able to cope, but she's got diabetes and I may be a spoiled selfish sod, but I'm not about to forget that she needs to keep her blood sugar balanced. So I shooed her off downstairs for some lunch, and told her not to even think about coming back up until she'd fed herself properly.

"Coming the heavy husband." It hurt to talk, and it hurt worse to smile, but I managed both. "No arguing. Off you go."

Left alone, I tried to doze. I don't want to go on too much about the MS, I know it makes rotten listening if you haven't got it yourself, but the thing is, it was beginning to sink in that maybe the way me and Bree'd been handling the disease for the past twelve years was going to need serious rethinking. I've managed to keep it in the relapsing-remitting phase, but I was starting to wonder—and Christ, not a pleasant notion, not at all—if maybe it wasn't moving into progressive.

If it was, I was likely looking at the beginning of the end as a functional musician. If the way the body was reacting today was anything to go by, there was no way in hell I'd be able to play, not if this shite was going to be the norm in future. If this was the future, I was done.

I closed my eyes. The room was doing the frug around me, the ceiling moving in circles. I thought, *right, this is new, vertigo's a whole new damned side effect, give me a damned break please,* and then realised that I was probably in the middle of what they called a panic attack. I'd never had one before, so I couldn't be sure, but it felt like panic. I'd come out in a cold sweat all over my body, I couldn't seem to get enough air into my lungs, and just under my left collarbone, the tickybox had suddenly kicked into a low overdrive. Not good.

I flexed my fingers, hard and tight, and bit back noise. It hurt like hell, but I did it, and that was the point: some control over what my body was getting up to. That stopped the panic where it was, and I took a page out of Bree's book; she does yoga, breathing exercises, *in, out, inhale, exhale.* I don't do yoga, myself, but I've watched her do it for years, and I've got a handle on the breathing thing. It worked, too—got the heart quieted down, as well.

The thing is, about the MS? I didn't really want to know. I mean, right, suppose I had made the jump from relapsing-remitting to progressive, what was I supposed to do about it? Fuck-all, basically, except throw some new meds at the new flavour and hope they worked. The doctors haven't even sorted out what causes the damned disease in the first place. All they could do was find a way to decide whether I was getting worse permanently, or just going through a rough patch for some other reason. Even that much was going to be dodgy, because the tickybox and MRI equipment don't play well together. I didn't have the first clue how my neuro could even confirm it, one way or the other.

The bottom line was, either way, there was a huge noisy row coming up in my not too distant future, because if and when I pointed any of this out to my wife, she was going to flip her shit. Bree's a doctor's daughter, with some serious control issues and a huge investment in my health. Me not wanting to know, that wasn't going to fly with her, and I'd have bet the house on her mum backing her up. Miranda probably puts her nose into other peoples' business less than any other mother-in-law in the world, but she's also a surgeon. And since she was the physical reason I hadn't died at Wembley, I couldn't actually tell her to save her breath to cool her soup, you know?

At the back of everything, of course, was the memory of my old friend Jack Featherstone. I really didn't want to look at that; that took a lot more courage than I seemed to be able to pull up, right then.

I'd seen him just a few days before he'd died of complications from a rampaging out of control case of progressive MS. He'd been one of my best friends, one of the first people to hook me up to the scene in London, one of the great session bassists out there. By the time I got to say goodbye, the MS had taken him to pieces, ravaged him, shown him no mercy at all. By the time he died, he was in a chair fulltime, barely able to talk, nothing working anymore.

I pushed the memory away, as hard and fast as I could. I wasn't there, not yet.

In, out, inhale, exhale. The pain seemed to actually be backing down, just enough to let me pull my mind off the MS and back onto what in hell Lenore Tannenbaum had been thinking, ringing Bree up at the hour they used to reserve for hanging people. I let myself indulge in an inner grin; whatever it was she'd wanted, she was going to have to stable that damned high horse of hers, and wait for it. Yeah, I know. Petty of me, but she really needed a nice little clue, that just demanding something didn't mean you got it...

I dozed, a nice little nap. It must have been deeper than I thought I'd get under the circs, because I slept until Bree got back upstairs.

I opened my eyes, and focussed on her. It took a second for the sleep haze to fade off, but when it did, I took a second look, and managed to pull myself nearly upright. The look on her face got all my attention.

"Bree! What is it?"

She opened her mouth, and closed it again. Scary, because my wife's not usually at a loss for words. Right that moment, she looked—I don't know, not so much gobsmacked as completely confounded, as if she'd seen a little green man with three heads dancing in the back garden, and wasn't sure how to parse it.

"Bree...?" I was struggling to get out of bed; the nap had helped, I could move without yelling, but I wasn't going out for the Olympic sprinting team anytime soon. "Baby, what the hell's going on? I've been snoring. What...?"

"Lenore Tannenbaum just came by." She swallowed, good and hard. "I don't have a lawyer anymore. She's just dropped me as a client—she wouldn't tell me why, she just gave me back the retainer I paid her. She says she can't represent me after all."

Chapter Thirteen

It was right around then that my brain, which had been dancing around the different issues that had to do with the 707 Club, finally started gathering the strands together, and damned if there wasn't something in there that might be a pattern.

Not that I recognised it straight off, though; I was too busy being insulted on Bree's behalf. Where in hell this Tannenbaum cow got the nerve to wake us up at some insane hour of the morning, not be willing to wait for a return call, and then ring our doorbell and upset my wife, I couldn't even guess.

"She did what, now?" I flexed a foot, and it let me do it without a lot of pain. Good job, too, because I was getting out of bed, and the MS could sod off if it didn't like me doing that. The more I thought about Tannenbaum, the angrier I got, and the look on Bree's face wasn't helping me calm down any, either. "You told her you'd ring her back. She took your retainer. You telling me she had the cheek to come over here, ring our bell, and dump you as a client? Who the fuck does this bird think she is?"

Bree still had that lost look on her face. "I think she thinks she's my former lawyer, is what I think. What's really bugging me is that she wouldn't tell me why. I mean, what? She doesn't like my money or my blueberry muffins? Or does she think I set the fire? Because I didn't, John. I really didn't."

Oh, crikey. That hadn't occurred to me, believe it or not, I was too pissy on Bree's behalf, but that got my attention. And maybe her face was puzzled, but her voice had gone shaky.

I got out of bed, fast as I could do it, and got both arms around her. Her voice wasn't the only thing that was shaking.

"I already know that, love, believe me, and so does anyone with half a brain. But I'm not having you upset. Let's get this sorted out, right now. Where's your cell?"

She nodded toward the bed. "In the nightstand drawer. Are you going to call her?"

"Damned right I am."

She'd turned both phones off, and it took a few seconds for hers to come back on. I fumbled with it, trying to remember how to do what. Used to be we both had basic cells, but she upgraded to this fancy all-purpose Blackberry, bells and whistles and internet access from anywhere, plays videos, the lot. I'd thought about getting one for myself—she's got really attached to hers, how useful it is, especially on the road. But all the extras put me off, rather. I like a tool to do what I bought it for; guitars are musical instruments, not food processors or whatever, and a cell phone, in my head, is something with a keypad and a speaker that lets you exchange voices with the person or people at the other end. Besides, anything that isn't music, I tend to be slow about new tech. I'm not a geek about anything but music gear. Bree's the computer geek in our family.

226

I found her phone book, and scanned down the list. Nice and easy; Bree alphabetises everything by the way it's actually spelled. I was about to click on Lenore Tannenbaum's name, punch up her number, when a thought popped into my head.

Bree must have seen me hesitate. "Can't you find her number? It's under T, down near the bottom. Or you could just click the Recent Incoming Call log."

"Yeah, got it. Hang on a minute, though. There's another call I want to make first."

I scrolled back up the list, and found what I wanted. He answered the phone on the second ring.

"Ormand Investigations. Hey, Bree, is that you? Is everything okay?"

"Oi, Patrick. It's JP. Not sure how you define 'okay,' but Bree's worried and I'm pissed off enough to commit a felony or two. Lenore Tannenbaum came by and dropped Bree as a client, no explanation given. Now my wife's worried that Tannenbaum thinks she's an arsonist, and that's why she's been dumped, but I've got a different notion in my head. I want to get your take on it, all right?"

"Bree's not an arsonist." He sounded friendly, right up near the edge of amusement: indulgent. "And I doubt Lenore Tannenbaum's stupid enough to think that—she's a very smart woman. Whatever her reason, I'm sure it isn't that. Bree really doesn't need to worry about that. How can I help you, JP?"

"You can answer a question for me. Is Tannenbaum still Paul Morgenstern's lawyer? I mean, does she still represent him, even though he's in prison for the long haul? And if you don't know, how do we find out? Should I get Carla on it?"

Bree's head jerked up. Patrick was quiet for a minute. I gave him time, letting him sort it out. When he finally spoke up, there was a note in his voice I don't think I'd ever heard there before, not while he was talking to me: admiration.

227

"I don't know, JP. That's a damned good idea, and a very interesting one. It would certainly explain a few things, wouldn't it, if she's still repping Morgenstern? You're thinking she dropped Bree as a client because she realised this whole 707 thing would be an ethical conflict of interest? Is that right?"

"Yeah, that's it." I looked up at Bree; she was watching me, chewing her lower lip. "Patrick, hang on, will you? I want to put this on speaker, but it's Bree's phone, not mine, and I don't know my way round all the shortcuts. Bree, love, could you sort this out, please? Nothing secret about the conversation, I just don't know how your gear works."

She took the phone and used her thumbs on the appropriate buttons. "Patrick? Are you still there?"

"Hey, Bree." Tinny, but perfectly audible. "JP tells me you're worried about Lenore Tannenbaum's reasons for giving you back your retainer. Don't be. I know for a fact you're not on Jan Gelman's suspect list."

She closed her eyes for a moment. "You may know that. I don't. Gelman told us they'd formally identified the accelerant as chafing dish fuel. She asked me all these questions, about where I stashed it, why so much, could other people have taken it, did I keep an eye on it, stuff like that. She sounded as if she thought I'd done it, Patrick. But I didn't set that fire."

Out of nowhere, his voice was firm; it was Patrick Ormand, the cop in charge. Just like the old days, yeah? Except that this time, he wasn't sniffing for Bree's blood.

"Bree, listen to me. Tracking down the accelerant source would have been the first thing on Jan's list. She had me in her office this morning, and she had plenty of questions for me, too. I'm working for you and JP. You're my clients. So I think that, under those circumstances, I'm going to tell you some of what I was asked, and what my responses were to those particular questions. Okay?"

Bree blinked. "Okay. What kind of questions, Patrick?"

"She wanted to know, very specifically, about the placement of people during the first set. I'm a trained cop, Bree. I notice that kind of thing automatically, on duty or off, and she knows that, believe me."

I was beginning to see where he was going. "Yeah, we believe you. So?"

"So I was able to situate a sizeable list of people for her, and that included Bree. Jan has my signed statement for everything I answered, and one of those items is the fact that, so far as I remembered, you never left your station at the head catering table, not from the time I got there until after the fire broke out. You're about as clear as you're going to get, until they arrest whoever actually did set that fire."

I could have kissed the bloke, right through the phone. "So you put Bree in the clear? Patrick, mate, you rock."

He laughed. "Why? For telling the truth in a police inquiry? She wasn't only asking about Bree, you know. She wanted to know about nearly everyone who has anything to do with the club ownership."

"I wonder if Tannenbaum knows Bree's clear?"

"I don't know, JP. But it wouldn't matter. Tannenbaum wouldn't drop Bree as a client just because she thought Bree was guilty. Lawyers don't work that way. Her job is to defend people, guilty or innocent." He thought for a moment. "And get as rich as possible doing it."

I headed over to Bree's rocking chair, and sat. Bree came and sat on the floor next to me, the phone in her hand. Patrick was still talking, and what he was saying made sense.

"And now that we've got that out in the open, let's look at the field of other reasons why she'd drop a wealthy client out of the blue. That's not your basic lawyer behaviour. I like JP's idea, about there being a possible conflict of interest. You do realise, if you're right about that, there must be something going on, to do with Paul Morgenstern? That moves finding out what Esther Woodley was doing during those Herlong visits to the top of my priority list. I'll rattle some chains tomorrow morning, first thing—there are a few favours I can call in on this one."

"Thank you, Patrick."

I glanced down at Bree. She looked and sounded a lot calmer. Right that moment, none of my usual Ormand hackles were up. He'd managed to do just what I'd hoped he could do: set her mind at ease. I made a mental note, to send him a bonus when this was done with.

"Yeah, what Bree said. Cheers, mate. Brilliant job. I just want to make sure we're on the same page here. I was going to ring Tannenbaum and tear some long bloody strips off her, once we were done here. But I'm guessing I should probably hold off on that, yeah? Let you do your thing?"

"Yes, please, JP. That would be best." He paused, a good long one this time. I swear, I could hear the gears working, meshing up clear through the Blackberry. I might have to reconsider getting one of those for myself, after all. "I have the feeling that, once we get the reasons for all those visits to Herlong, we'll know why Lenore Tannenbaum felt she couldn't represent Bree. I'll get on it first thing in the morning."

I kept my promise, about not ringing Lenore Tannenbaum. But the conversation with Patrick reminded me that I'd told Carla I'd get back to her, and being narked had left me with enough energy to get it done. That meant changing phones, since Bree hasn't got Carla programmed into hers. And of course, I pulled mine out of the nightstand drawer and powering it up, there was the red message light, blinking away.

Bree was heading for the door, but she stopped, and looked back at me. "Are you hungry? I was thinking I'd get dinner started—something not too chewy, maybe soup or pasta."

I held up my free hand. "Half a mo, love, all right? Be right with you—I've got a message. And yeah, soup, pasta, whatever you fancy cooking. I'm actually hungry, and it all sounds good – "

I broke off. Not only had my voicemail kicked in, Bree's phone had begun playing the opening drum and piano riffs from "Sympathy for the Devil." Since her Blackberry's set to vibrate as well as ring, the damned thing began hopping about on the bed, almost in rhythm. I went back to my own messages.

(beep) Thank you for calling. You have two unheard messages. First message, sent today at eleven fourteen a.m. To listen to your messages, press star...

"JP? Carla. Listen, I don't think Jan Gelman's going to call you after all. I got her on the phone with Andy, and we've agreed to pool our information. Of course we'll both cherry-pick, but it means she has no reason to ask you anything. Sorry if I got you up too early—hope you're feeling better by the time you get this."
(beep)

Right. So much for that—there was the rest of the day's worry, done with. I was about to click for my second message—Solange had rung me, for some reason—when Bree yelped. She doesn't do high-pitched noises very often; she just hasn't got the upper register to handle it.

I turned around, hard and fast. She was grinning like an idiot, and actually bouncing in place. Right about then, what she was saying filtered the rest of the way through my head and I realised, she was talking to Solange herself.

"...told your father yet? Because Luke's going to lose it, in a good way, I mean. Hell, I forgot to ask, did you say yes? Was it romantic? Oh god, sweetie, I'm so excited for you both!"

I was grinning, ear to ear. That sentence, that look on her face, that bounce? Only one thing I could think of Solange's news being.

Bree glanced up and caught the look on my face. "Solange,

231

hang on. I want to put this on the speaker, okay? John's listening in and all he's getting is me."

She got the speaker going, a lot faster than I'd have been able to do it. And there was Solange, half an octave higher than her usual voice, which is nice and light and clear to begin with. She wasn't quite at "peel the paint off the walls" levels, but it was close.

"...of course I said yes! I was waiting to ring Dad, because it's the middle of the night at home, but I couldn't wait, I had to tell someone or else I was going to explode and anyway you live here, oh lord that sounded so rude I'm sorry I didn't mean it that way oh damn Aunt Bree you know what I mean..."

"Oi! Solange, hang on, yeah? Take a breath. You're going to hyperventilate." I was grinning like an idiot. "Am I getting this right? Curt pop the question, then?"

The girl was seriously blissed. "Over dinner at La Ginestra in Mill Valley. Uncle John, it was *amazing!* I mean, he went all traditional at me: ring in a glass of champagne, waiter wheeling over a cart with an absolute mass of roses under a silver cover, down on one knee next to the table, the lot. I made a complete ass of myself, and burst out bawling. The entire restaurant cheered—I think half the people eating there tonight know him."

"The boy's got nice manners. I'm betting your dad's going to be pleased. He likes Curt." I glanced at Bree; she was misty-eyed, and I didn't blame her. It was a nice mental image Solange had just painted for us. "Your aunt and I are pretty pleased, as well. Any idea when you're going to get it done, or is it too soon to say?"

"Soon." All of a sudden, she wasn't sounding as Cloud Nine; Solange has a good hard-headed practical streak. "Because Mad At Our Dads is going on tour next month, and I can't go, remember? School starts about three days after they leave town. So we want to get married and have at least a tiny honeymoon before we both go to work. Right now, I swear I'm tempted to just

232

ask you two to be witnesses, get Mac and Dom as backup, and head off to City Hall. Just—get it done."

I had one eyebrow all the way up. "Right. Solange, look. You know Luke's going to back you up, no matter what, but the entire family's going to want a big damned do. And even if your dad backs you up, he's going to feel hurt, if you do it that way. You ready for the fallout?"

Out of nowhere, she sounded uncertain, and much too young to marry anyone. "No. No, I'm not. And really, it's not the way I want to do it—I want Dad there, next to me. That's the way it's supposed to be. But working with Bree, I've got an idea now about just how much planning that kind of do really takes, and we don't have that kind of time."

"Are you worrying about the actual wedding?" Bree had her caterer's voice on. "Or about the reception? Because I really don't see the problem. Why not have the best of both worlds, sweetie? It would be different if you were poor, but let's face it, you're not, either of you."

"Do you mean -" Solange stopped. I could practically hear her trying to sort Bree out, over the phone. "What do you mean, Aunt Bree? Best of both worlds, how?"

Bree was practically tripping over her own words, her brain was moving so fast. She had that focused look, the one that always turns me on. "Get your dad and Karen and Suzanne out here, if she's available. Your uncle and me, Mac and Dom—a nice quiet little civil ceremony downtown. And then when Curt's back in off the road and you can synch up with a break from school, you and I can put our heads together and throw one of the biggest damned bashes anyone's seen in years. Hell, you can do one here and one at Draycote—let the locals cater that one. Have it outdoors, and we can all stand around and flip off the *paparazzi* in the helicopters—John? What's so funny?"

"Nothing. Bree's got a point, Solange. Get your dad on the phone, wake him up if you want to, he won't mind. Let him know."

Bree had got hold of my hand, and was swinging it. That put a funny old tickle at the back of my throat, because she isn't really much for initiating that kind of contact—she never has been. If she's offering comfort, or help, that's one thing. But that spontaneous touch deal, that's the sort of thing she leaves up to me. "John's right, you need to call him. Well, maybe not right about waking him up—Karen doesn't sleep well and she needs all the sleep she can get. But first thing in the morning, definitely. You guys can figure it out from there. Get Carla in on it, get the list, a nice personal note from the immediate family to everyone, letting them know the circumstances, something like that."

"And promise them a whacking big feed-up somewhere down the road? Aunt Bree, that's brilliant! I'll do it, of course, once I check with Curt. I should probably get off the line, and ring him. They're just finishing up rehearsing, down at the Plant. He went off to work awfully blissed."

"Solange, listen." Out of nowhere, Bree sounded very gentle. "I don't want to pry, and I know this is none of my business. But I don't know Curt very well, and something occurs to me. You've got a huge family, the whole band, all of us, at your back. Is Curt going to be okay with that?"

I know I've said it before—about eight thousand times, maybe nine thousand—but I'll say it again: there are times my wife takes my breath away. It would never have occurred to me, asking Solange about that. But of course, it could be an issue: Curt had a sister somewhere halfway across the country, and he had his dad, and so far as he knew, his dad killed his mum. Getting married is tricky enough. Being married is even trickier, without having dodgy little emo issues like being jealous of your wife having a happy family adding to it.

But Bree had thought of it, and from the sound of it, she'd got Solange considering the question. "Wow. I honestly don't know. I think he is, but—oh, damn! Aunt Bree, I don't know how he's going to—damn it!"

"Ask him." There was an odd little twist to Bree's voice. "Be upfront. Hiding stuff, especially early on, will mess you up down the road. Trust me on this, Solange, okay? I know what I'm talking about. No one knows more about how to screw things up by building walls around the hard issues than I do. You just end up breaking your own heart, and hurting everyone around you. It's not worth it. Just—ask him, okay?"

I swallowed, good and hard. I still had her hand, and I lifted it to my lips, and put my lips against it, just for a moment. She met my eye, not smiling, but her face was soft, remote somehow, and I knew she was remembering. That's my old lady—she's got heart, but spine as well. Remembering, letting yourself remember and cop to what you did wrong, enough to learn from it? That takes courage.

"I will. I promise." Solange hesitated; she isn't much with the emo stuff, either. "Aunt Bree? I just want you and Uncle John to know—well, thanks for being here for me. I really love you both. Goodnight."

Chapter Fourteen

Worry's a very weird thing. Sometimes you don't even realise how worried you are. Then, out of nowhere, you find yourself doing something so bizarre that you all you can do is scratch your head and ask yourself, *what in hell was that in aid of, mate? What were you thinking?*

That conversation with Solange, her good news, had pushed my worrying about Lenore Tannenbaum dumping Bree as her client to the back burner for the rest of the evening. I was feeling better physically, just well enough to go downstairs, nice and slow, and watch Bree put together a scratch meal. We talked about Solange and Curt, about probable reactions from the band family, stuff like that. Neither of us mentioned Star Woodley or the 707 or Lenore Tannenbaum.

But pushing something back isn't getting rid of it, and I was still worried. I must have been, because I can't think of anything else that could have got me to agree to a road trip with Patrick Ormand, heading for Lassen County. And oh, right—can't leave out the whole prison visit part of the deal.

What really nailed me was the fact that the damned phone woke me again, the next morning. It was just past nine, not what Bree calls "asscrack of dawn" early, but still much too early to want to cope. Even if I did mornings well, two days running of being woken up by way of the cell phone was enough to leave me nice and pissy. I actually managed to grab the phone before Bree could; I was just awake enough to have a butchers at the caller ID before I answered.

"Carla? What in hell?"

"Sorry, JP." She sounded as if she'd been awake for six hours, probably with a full workout in there somewhere. Behind me, Bree was muttering under her breath. "I know it's early, but this won't wait. I'm arranging a plane out of SFO for Patrick Ormand, up to Reno, and he seems to think you might want to go up with him. I need to know, so I can get a car rental that works for both of you, not just him."

I swung my legs out of bed, and flexed both ankles. Good—nothing too painful. Bree was sitting up in bed glaring, whether at me or the phone I couldn't tell you.

"Right," I told Carla. "Why in the name of sweet bleedin' Jesus would I want to go to Reno with Patrick Ormand? What sort of drugs is the bloke on?"

Bree had just got out of bed herself, heading for the loo to get my meds and water, but that stopped her in her tracks. She turned and stared at me. I must have still been half asleep to have not sorted out what was going on. But I hadn't, yet.

"Not Reno." Carla sounded patient. Not easy, considering she had a time deadline on something and I was holding her up by asking stupid questions. "Herlong. The plane goes to Reno—

that's the nearest airport. Patrick's going up to talk to Paul Morgenstern. I need to know if you're going or not, because we have to dovetail it around Herlong's visiting hours. Today's Friday, and that means no visitors get processed after seven pm. Anyway, I need to confirm you on Paul's Approved Visitor list, and that'll take calling in some serious favours, because you can't usually do that without all kinds of official requests. Did you want to go? The plane will be on the tarmac at two."

"Crikey. Carla, hang on, will you please?" Bree had headed straight for the bathroom, but instead of her coming back out with my pills and water, I heard the shower start up. That was a dead giveaway; Bree's two cups of coffee, black no sugar, are second on her morning list, after she brings me my meds. She only showers first if she thinks she might have to hit the ground running, and if she'd forgot my meds, it meant she was already in full-on *oh shit must wake up now* mode.

Meanwhile, I was bending, stretching, checking the nerve endings, listening to the tickybox, clearing the cobwebs off the brain. Bree's not the only one with a morning routine. "Patrick told you I might want to go along for this little road movie?" I asked Carla. "He happen to say why he'd think that?"

"Just that you were worried about Bree, I didn't get why. He seemed sure you'd want to be there when he talked to Paul, JP. If you don't, no problem, but I need to know, stat. If you're passing, I'll rent him a small fast car, but if you're going, I'll get something more comfortable. It's not a long drive from Reno, maybe sixty miles, but it's high desert—Lassen County. Do you want to go? I'm not trying to nag, but I've got to get things arranged."

So, yeah, worry's weird. I can't think of any other reason for me to have told Carla, *right, I'm in, no I don't need a hire car, I'll get Bree to drive me, where's she taking me, General Aviation terminal on the north side, right, we'll get there by one, Patrick's covered for a ride, good, right.* And I wasn't even surprised to hear myself agree to it.

I fully expected a huge row with Bree over me going. I mean, okay, the trip was one thing, but the idea that I planned on strolling into a federal prison ought to have sent all her *are you fucking kidding me* buttons beeping away at top volume. It was just the kind of thing to bring out the Valkyrie in my wife. At the very least, I expected the heavy artillery: hands on hips, a shitload of *oh I don't think so* and whatnot, and her calling me *little man*, which always makes me want to thump her.

So I braced myself, took a good long breath, and headed into the loo to get my own meds. She was just getting out of the shower, wrapping her hair in a towel, while I was filling a paper cup and taking the usual battery of pills.

"So." She was watching me. "What was that about you going to Reno with Patrick? Was I having some kind of, I don't know, audio hallucination, or something?"

I was keeping a wary eye on her shoulders. If they hunched up too tight, the row was on. "No, that's right. He's off to talk to Paul Morgenstern. I'm not sure about the details, but he thought I'd want to be there. And he's right, Bree. I do. For one thing, he can answer my question, about why Tannenbaum dropped you. It's not a pleasure trip, or anything like that."

"Sounds like a buddy movie or something." Her shoulders were staying right were they were. Good; I might get out of this one without having to deal with a meltdown. "So you told Carla yes? You're going?"

I kept my voice nice and even. "Yeah, I am. Makes sense, really. The plane leaves from General Aviation at SFO at around two. I told Carla you'd drive me, but I can ring her back and get a pickup, if you'd rather not."

She was quiet, watching me. I was holding my breath. No row? I couldn't sort it out. Why wasn't she flipping her shit?

"Stop looking so twitchy, John, will you please? And for heaven's sake, you can breathe now." She sounded almost amused. "I won't say I'm sitting here waving pompoms at the idea of you walking into a place where they use barbed wire and guns to keep people from leaving, but I get why you want to go. And of course I'll drive you to the airport. Are you spending the night up there? Do you need me to pack you an overni—hey!"

I'd reached out and hooked her to me. She was nice and warm, and completely stark. Good; either the diabetes was behaving or she was turned on, or both. If she wasn't turned on, she was about to be, whether she knew it or not. I got my free hand up, and yanked the towel away from her hair.

"No bag. Not spending the night anywhere near a prison. Seriously, love, thanks for not giving me hell over wanting to go. I can't explain it, but I have the feeling I ought to be there. What's the time? Not ten yet? Oi! Where do you think you're off to, lady...?"

Patrick was waiting for me at the airport. It's a funny thing; he'd been at the receiving end of Carla's efficiency a few times before, and of course, he'd done a major tour with Blacklight, with our own chartered luxury jet. Hell, back when he was looking into the Perry Dillon murder and Bree was his number one candidate for a prison jumpsuit, Bree'd had him flown from New York to Boston in a hired helicopter.

So he wasn't new to how we do things, but I don't think he'd expected Carla to hire a private Gulfstream to fly us to Reno. He might have predicted the limo she'd sent for him, and maybe even guessed at it taking him straight to the plane, but the plane itself? He definitely wasn't expecting that.

"Hey, JP—glad you decided to come. Hi, Bree."

"Seemed like the move." I leaned in the window of the Jag. "I'll ring you when we're leaving Reno, love, all right?"

We got ourselves settled and belted in, and got our choice of liquid from the cabin attendant. It was right around that point Patrick seemed to get that we were the only passengers.

"Wow. This is very—luxurious." The engine was powering up, nice and smooth. "Did Carla hire the jet just for us? Or is this Blacklight's?"

"Probably hired. I don't think we own one of these." I thought about telling him Carla was still so narked at being caught out over Lindyhop's financial bullshit that she'd have spent her last tour bonus if that's what took to get that issue fixed, but I know Patrick. He didn't need me telling him, he already knew.

The Gulfstream taxied out and got airborne. We had a nice mellow flight, with just about an hour in the air coming up and then another hour on the road. At least, that's what Bree'd come up with, when she mapped the trip out on her computer, before we'd headed out. Down below, the Bay Area highways were already backing up with Friday afternoon getaway traffic.

Patrick accepted a plate of fresh fruit and warm bread from the cabin attendant. I waved her away; Bree'd fed me before we left the house. Patrick peered out the window.

"That traffic looks nasty. It's nice to be up here, not down there. JP, we have about an hour in the air, and I want to go over some things. Have you visited a federal prison before?"

I raised an eyebrow at him. Stupid question, really, and he had to know it. "Not that I remember, no. Why?"

He told me, for pretty much the rest of the flight. Turned out the question wasn't so much stupid as it was rhetorical, because what I didn't know about walking through the gates of a medium security federal prison to visit an inmate made me damned glad Paul Morgenstern wasn't doing his time in maximum security digs instead. Medium security was twisty enough.

"Okay." We'd buckled in for the approach to Reno airport, and the attendant had cleared away our glasses and done the cross-check, and strapped herself in for landing. "No coats or jackets. No wearing khaki, bright colours or anything they don't think is suitable? That sounds weird to me, but whatever. They'll want

ID, check, got plenty of that. My meds won't be a problem, but we leave the cell phones in their coat check room, because they don't let anything with a camera function inside. No money inside, either. Obviously nothing that could be grabbed and used as a weapon by an inmate who's suddenly gone allergic to small spaces. I doing all right so far?"

He nodded, and I went on, ticking it off on my fingers. "We park, we sign in, you do the talking. We give them all the shit they won't let us bring in, do the metal detector thing, probably get frisked. You're still doing all the talking, by the way. We sit down with Paul, assuming he agrees to it. That reminds me, all the paperwork's been done up front, yeah? No surprises? Because if there's any sort of cock-up, Carla's going to be seriously pissed off at spending all this dosh on a plane and whatever she's got for you to drive us around in."

The plane eased down; I saw the peaks of mountains, real ones, disappearing and reappearing as we banked. "We're both cleared," he told me. "I don't know how she did it, and I don't really care. It usually takes weeks to get a clearance, but we're both cleared. That's confirmed. Paul's agreed to our names being added to his Approved Visitors list. That makes it a sure thing he's going to see us. Herlong inmates are only allowed twenty names on that list, and they can't just shuffle them on and off, so this is a commitment on his part. We're good to go, there. Just follow my lead, and let me do the initial talking. If Paul doesn't give me the answers to your questions as part of my questioning, you'll have plenty of time to ask him yourself. But let me get the ball rolling for both of us."

A few years ago, when Patrick had still been a homicide cop with SFPD, we'd got him to take a week off to come to the South of France and find out who'd killed a barmy film director called Sir Cedric Parmeley. The entire band had been in the middle of that particular shitstorm, and Carla had pulled out all the stops to get Patrick what he needed, including a collection of Norwegian sharpshooters. One of the shiniest stops she'd pulled out was his car rental: she'd got him a bright red Ferrari. I'd been very cross with her about that, for personal reasons.

I'm not sure what Patrick expected Carla to have waiting for him in Reno, but if he was disappointed at what he got—an SUV—he didn't show it. It didn't hurt that he'd got his hands on some kind of official credentials that got us through the rental line at light speed, and with a lot more deference than I'd have thought a humble private detective had coming.

I waited until we were out of the rental lot and onto Highway 395 before I brought it up, but one of my eyebrows had been up around my hairline pretty much since we'd picked up the truck. "Nice quick little in-and-out you pulled off back there," I told him. "I didn't know a detective license carried that much of a punch with it."

He grinned sideways at me, a real grin, not the famous Ormand Shark Attack toothy thing he does. "It doesn't. The punch is Carla's doing. She called Pirmin Bochsler at Interpol and got a few pieces of auxiliary credentialing as fire insurance. We probably won't need it at Herlong, at least I hope not, but I won't pretend I don't like having the extra backup."

He kept his eyes on the road. So did I, for a while; this was the first time I'd ever been in this part of the world, and for someone who gets the Bay Area from the passenger seat on a regular basis, the scenery was as dull as it gets. It was brown, scrubby, nothing I'd normally bother looking at twice. High desert isn't much to look at, apparently, at least not from ground level.

It was a nice bright afternoon, and the traffic was dead opposite what had been going on in the Bay Area. Maybe people only used this road if they were headed toward the prison. I found myself wondering where that rest stop was, where Star Woodley had filled her tank and had a meal those times she'd visited Paul.

243

There were very few places along 395. I made a mental note to ask Patrick if he planned to stop on the way back, ask the proprietors if they recognised a description...

"Almost there." Patrick had turned the car onto a narrow road, paved and well-maintained, but still, definitely not part of the main highway system. "That's the prison up ahead."

He parked the SUV, and killed the engine. It was not quite a quarter of five; Friday visiting hours run from five to eight.

It was time to empty the pockets of anything the Herlong staff might consider contraband, make sure I had all the ID they could want, try to wrap my head around strolling into what had to be the least inviting example of real estate I'd ever seen in my life, and maybe figure out just what I could possibly ask Paul Morgenstern that Patrick couldn't have asked instead.

"JP?" He was out of the truck, waiting for me. "Ready?"

Right. Showtime.

I don't really want to talk too much about the prison itself. The bottom line is, it's a prison; it's not supposed to be cheery. Just as well, since there's nothing cheery about a big pile of concrete buildings with windows too small for even a bloke my size to squeeze through. Depressing as hell, especially since they'd finished off with a fence topped with razor wire. Not what you'd call curb appeal, you know?

We didn't get near the housing areas, which was fine with me. I'd have bet there were no lace curtains or comfy chairs, and it probably didn't smell like Bree's kitchen in there, either. I'm pretty sure there was no bread baking, and no coffee brewing.

Herlong wasn't supposed to do anything but remind the people calling it home for the next however long that they'd seriously fucked up somewhere along the line. This was the government's way of letting them know it.

I hadn't thought about what was involved in physically walking into a prison. I don't know if Herlong is even typical, the way it's built, but it has a sort of outbuilding you have to go through before they ever let you near the main buildings, on the wrong side of all that razor wire, where the inmates hang out.

Before I even climbed out of the SUV, I'd come to a decision about how to cope: I was going to follow Patrick about like a puppy, and let him deal with the formalities. That was a no-brainer. Me trying to stroll in and take charge of anything at all was doomed from the start, basically. I'm a foreign national, I've got long hair, and one pass over my ID would probably give them all the gen on me having been popped for hard drugs and being with an underage girl, not to mention having been deported thirty years ago. No point in pushing it. Let Patrick cope.

Whatever strings Carla had pulled were well beyond basic strings and all the way into rope territory, or maybe wire cables. They must have been, for the wheels to have been greased this smooth at this short a notice. When we walked in, the uniformed bloke at the front desk looked up and asked if he could help us. At least, that's what he said, but his voice was more on the *hold still until I say move, and you'd best have your papers in order* level.

That changed in a hurry. Patrick gave him our names, and handed over both our IDs, and out of nowhere, the bloke did a double-take and got very polite, very fast. Next thing I knew, we were being escorted down the hall to a sunny office to meet the warden, another one of those nice middle-aged women who looked motherly right up until she smiled at you. I seemed to have been hip-deep in those recently.

"Mr. Ormand? A pleasure." She was shaking hands with Patrick, and talking to him, but her eyes were straight at me. "I understand you came up from the Bay Area. I hope you had a pleasant flight. And is this Mr. Kinkaid...?"

I had a bad moment, there. Considering we were in a place surrounded by razor wire and full of convicted felons, and that she had the right to call a full lockdown or shove someone into solitary for a week, having her staring at me was off-putting, to say the least.

Luckily, it only took a few moments to realise that she was looking curious, rather than dangerous. Anyway, my mum raised me to always offer a hand when I was visiting someone else's house, especially the hostess, and I couldn't see why that wouldn't include Herlong Correctional Institution. The Big House is still a house, you know?

So I held out a hand, and watched her go a nice bright shade of pink as she took it. "Right. I'm JP Kinkaid—very nice to meet you."

"I know—I mean, I know now, who you are." She was gushing. "I just couldn't believe it was the same JP Kinkaid. I have every Blacklight album, and I even managed to get to one of the shows you did in Seattle, for *Book of Days*. My mother lives up there. It was a fabulous show, just fabulous."

Once I got that she wasn't mentally measuring me up for a custom cell, that she was just being a fan, dealing with the situation got quite a lot easier. There's a basic shorthand you learn to use with fans you're up close and personal with, at least with the ones who aren't handing you a sharpie and asking you to autograph their private parts.

Besides, I'd be lying if I said there wasn't some satisfaction in being the one causing the double-take and the eyebrow-lift, rather than Patrick and the fancy cred Carla'd got for him. Yeah, I know, petty. But true.

I was just about to get into the fan chat thing—*glad you enjoyed it, was that the first or second show, were you there when Heart sat in with us*—when I glanced over at Patrick, and saw him looking at his watch, just before he slipped it off his wrist. Right—we were here on official business, at least he was. Time to get on with it.

We went through the moves: handing over our stuff, passing through the metal detector, getting frisked, signing off on a checklist of all the stuff we were leaving outside the prison. It was unsettling, a reminder that the blokes inside weren't going anywhere, that we couldn't bring anything in that might even give them ideas, much less anything they could use.

I don't know whether this is the way it's usually done, but we were walked through by the warden—she actually escorted us inside. She seemed very concerned about making us feel at home, whatever the hell "at home" in that context means. You'd have thought she was a realtor trying to sell us a condo or something, pointing out all the amenities and mod cons. I couldn't imagine why she thought we'd care that the vee-shaped white bunkers were the housing cellblocks, or that the hulking complex off to one side was actually a work program facility where the prisoners refurbished tanks for the US Army, but whatever. It was civilised of her to try putting us at ease. Or, rather, putting me at ease; Patrick was probably used to this kind of thing.

We were actually through the main gate and onto the prison grounds when she seemed to remember something. She turned and looked at Patrick over her shoulder.

"By the way," she told him, "I'm not sure you're aware that you're not Paul's only visitors this evening."

I was bringing up the rear, sticking to my plan to let Patrick handle it. He stopped so suddenly, I nearly ran into his back. I couldn't see his face, or see if anything showed in those dirty-ice eyes of his, but I got a stellar view of his shoulders. He went as tight as Bree gets, and his back jerked before he got control of it, and relaxed everything. From right behind him, I could see the effort it took.

"No, I wasn't aware of that." It was amazing, how normal his voice sounded. The bloke's got glacial runoff where his blood ought to be. "I'm surprised no one let me know. Is that usual?

Last-minute additions to the visitor pool? We were hoping for a one-on-one conversation."

"Oh, no, definitely not usual." We'd come to the end of the outdoor path. She sounded a bit defensive. "And we would have let you know earlier, had we known. Paul didn't make the request until earlier today. But when an inmate asks that his legal representation be present for a third party visit, we allow that. In fact, we can't not allow it—it's a basic prisoner's right in this country."

If I'd been doing the driving, I'd have been tempted to say *ah, sod it*, shake hands with the warden, get my watch and cell phone, and climb straight back into the rental. A threesome with Lenore Tannenbaum sounded like an hour's worth of pure hell. Of course, it did mean I didn't have to ask Paul who his lawyer was. That little question had just been answered.

"I understand that." Patrick was still sounding smooth, but his hands were giving him away—they were twitchy, the fingers wanting something to tap. I've noticed that about him from the first: he's got restless fingers. He wasn't as calm or as smooth as he sounded, not by half. "And of course he has the right to have his lawyer with him. I won't pretend to be happy about it, though. I know the lawyer in question and she has a talent for making things harder than they need to be."

The warden led us indoors, into about as miserable a place as I've ever had to hang out. Nodding to the staff who were waiting for us, she looked back at Patrick, and I swear, I thought I saw amusement in her face. It might have been sympathy, or just comprehension. You don't get the sort of job she'd got by being dim, you know?

"Yes, I understand." She sounded just as smooth as he did. "I'm acquainted with Counsellor Tannenbaum. But again, no other options were open to us. We only limit visits if the inmate has given us reason to restrict his privileges, and Paul doesn't fall into that category. He's a model inmate, and a very hard worker—in fact, he's spent the day at the tank facility. Besides, those limits wouldn't include his lawyer."

I missed whatever Patrick had to say to that, because my attention was elsewhere. Herlong Prison's visiting area was a whole new experience, and it didn't strike me as something I wanted to be careless about.

Visiting hours were just starting off, and the place was still pretty empty of visitors. But a lot of inmates were obviously expecting people to show up, because there were quite a few of them sitting and waiting.

There were also a scary number of prison guards in the main visiting room. Really off-putting, that was. Patrick had warned me we'd probably have every word overheard by the staff, but that was before we'd found out Tannenbaum was coming; turns out that lawyer visits are in small private rooms, and the attorney-client privilege thing means the whole thing's private, no eavesdropping allowed.

I had a moment of feeling sorry for the inmates. I mean, crikey, you're away from your family for however many years, they get to visit on the fly maybe once a week if they don't live too far away, and when you finally do get to see them, there's some bloke with his ear turned your way, and making damned sure you know it. I tried to imagine what it would be like, living in a tiny box and only getting to talk to Bree once a week for seven years with some beefy prison official listening in and me having no right to tell him to sod off, but I couldn't wrap my head around it.

And yeah, I know, these blokes pulled some scary shit to have fetched up at Herlong in the first place, but I could easily have done some time myself, for possession of narcotics. So could Bree have. All it would have taken was Patrick deciding to prosecute her as an accessory for the Perry Dillon murder...

This time, wandering down Memory Lane, I actually did bump

into Patrick. The warden had stopped at a door with a clear glass top. There was another guard, in front of it.

"We'd scheduled you to be out here originally, but we changed that when Paul's attorney was added to the list. And of course, the circumstances of this entire visit are a little unusual—we don't usually get requests from Interpol."

That was another question answered, how Carla'd got me and Patrick both on that approved list with zero notice: she'd gone straight for the Higher Authority thing, and got Pirmin in on it. My brain went to a happy place for a moment, imagining the look on Tannenbaum's face when she tried to object to anything Patrick might ask, and getting told, *yeah, well, suck it up sweetheart*, because Patrick was authorised by Interpol...

"JP? Is something the matter?"

"No, nothing at all. We ready, then? Cool."

The warden had already murmured something, and gone on her way. The guard stepped aside—he didn't seem to be carrying a gun, and I'd already noticed none of the guards seem to have them—and opened the door.

Last time I'd seen Paul Morgenstern, we'd been sitting on the deck of his Sausalito house, admiring the sunset. The irony of the situation had been nuts: we'd been there because Paul had thrown a memorial for the bloke it turned out he'd actually killed. That was the same party where Mac had sussed out that the art on Paul's wall, including a famous painting by Goya, was not only real, it was mostly stolen. To put the tin cupola on the day, Bree'd just come out of cancer surgery and Patrick had still been a homicide cop, digging little pits and waiting for someone to fall into them. Not exactly a family scrapbook sort of day, you know?

That had been a few years ago. Back then, Paul had been your basic record producer and club owner—a bit podgy, too many late hours, not enough exercise. And I know that prison's supposed to change a bloke: prison pallor, bad food, all that rubbish. What I'd never heard was that being in lock-up for years on end was supposed to make a bloke look better.

"Hey, JP Kinkaid!" He got up and offered me his hand. "How are you doing, man? I heard about the heart attack you had—glad it didn't take you out. Congratulations on *Book of Days*, by the way, great album. How's your wife?"

I shook his hand and said something conventional, God knows what. I was absolutely gobsmacked. Unless my memory was doing some unacceptably bizarre things, the effect of about five years in prison on Paul Morgenstern had been pretty much what you might expect from the Fountain of Youth.

Paul had said his hellos to Patrick, and sat back down. I noticed the guard, the bloke who'd been on the other side of the glass-topped door when we'd got here, had come inside. It was pretty obvious he wasn't going anywhere just yet.

Paul was still talking. "...seriously, JP, there wasn't one cut off that CD that didn't leave me wishing I'd produced it. Absolutely kickass. I heard the tour was a monster, too. Hey, why are you guys standing around? Take some chairs. The warden told you my lawyer's coming for this, right?"

Patrick was already settling into a chair. He didn't even glance at the guard. "Thanks. Yes, we were told, just now. I gather we're waiting until Counsellor Tannenbaum gets here?"

Paul got up and stretched. "Sorry, Friday's one of my early days at the tank refurb facility. I didn't get my workout this morning and I'm a little stiff. Yep, we're waiting for Lenore. I think I can help you guys out, but she needs to be here."

Both of Patrick's eyebrows were up. Paul jerked his head at the guard, not trying to hide it. "There's stuff I'm pretty sure I want to talk to you about, but it's confidential, and I'm not saying a word until she okays it. Don't worry, she said she'd be here by half past five—speak of the devil! Perfect timing."

I hadn't heard the door opening behind me. Not hearing, that scared the shit out of me. Bloody hell, we were sitting in a prison, yeah? Not the ideal place to not pay attention to who might be coming up behind you. I felt the tickybox ramp up, took a deep breath, and waited for it come back down, trying for Zen.

"Hello, Paul. I see everyone's here. I'm not late, am I? Oh, good." She was holding the door open with one hand. The guard went past her; he had absolutely the blankest expression I've ever seen on a human face, and I couldn't help wondering if he'd come up against her before. Then the door swung shut behind him, and I saw him take up a position outside.

"Well, now." She pulled out the chair next to Paul's, and got herself settled. Her eyes were aimed straight at Patrick. "Let's get started."

Chapter Fifteen

I've never thought Patrick Ormand was dim. I've known from the start that he's got a photographic memory: eidetic, I think the word is. In all the times I've either come up against him or got him to help me sort something out, I've never seen him reach for a pencil. I've never known him to forget a fact, either.

That memory of his was going to come in useful tonight, because it was all he had. Any prison policy that turfs you out for wearing bright colours, and flips its shit over a watch or a cell phone, is going to get shirty about things with sharp points. No pencils or pens allowed, and no recording devices, either. Memory was pretty much it.

The atmosphere in that visitors' room changed the moment Lenore and Patrick went eye to eye. I might not have noticed it straight off, if I hadn't already known the history between them.

As it was, I couldn't miss it. I don't gamble, but if I did, I'd have had no clue where to lay my money. He's a shark, she's a barracuda: he's bigger, but she's got sharper teeth and she's faster. I've got no idea which one is the meaner.

"How are you, Patrick? I haven't seen you since we had you on the stand during Paul's trial."

Oh, crikey. Between the cheerful tone of voice and the smile, my stomach thought about wanting to crawl behind my spine. Maybe I ought to chuck worrying about why she'd dumped Bree as a client, and just be thankful she'd done it, instead.

If she'd hit any nerves, Patrick wasn't showing it. The bloke's a master duellist when he needs to be. "I'm fine, thanks. I recently opened my own detective agency—getting the license was a lot easier than I expected. Having worked with Interpol probably didn't hurt."

She was watching him, not saying anything. Paul and I weren't meeting each other's eye; I wasn't sure if that was deliberate, or just instinctive.

Patrick was smiling back at her, finally, and my stomach did another dance, taking the tickybox along with it. That grin was the worst of Patrick Ormand, the one he saves for when there's blood out there, and he's jonesing for a taste. "I have to say, I was surprised Paul felt he needed to have his attorney present for this. It does save me a question, though. One of the main things I wanted to ask was whether he was still being represented by Tannenbaum and Culpepper."

The surroundings, the whole reality of sitting inside a federal prison, were definitely messing with my head. They must have been, because there's no way her teeth could actually have got sharper or pointer between smiles, but they looked that way to me. "Well then," she told him, "that's a timesaver, isn't it? Let's get down to business, shall we? Visiting hours here are finite and not arguable, and Paul will have to be back in his housing at eight-twenty if he wants dinner tonight. Anyway, I have a ten o'clock flight back to the Bay Area."

"Oh, I doubt if this will take that long." Patrick was looking at Paul now, rather than at Lenore. He'd got complete control of himself: voice, face, the lot. "I have a shortlist of things I wanted to ask, but I gather Paul already knows what he wants to tell us. Why don't we do it that way? Paul can tell me whatever it is he thinks we ought to know, and I can decide whether his statement pre-empts my questions. And if you decide at any time that he's saying something he shouldn't, you can stop him. Will that work for both of you?"

She nodded, and I got the feeling they understood each other perfectly. "Paul? Are you all right with that, or would you prefer a straight Q&A?"

Paul was doing a little eye-locking of his own; he and Patrick were hooked up. I was beginning to feel like someone in the cheap seats of someone else's show: passive, just watching. For the moment, that was fine. "I'm cool this way. This is all off the record anyway, right? No recording equipment? The bottom line is, we're talking about a hundred grand of my money, and I'm damned if that asshole Lind is going to walk with it. He's sure as hell not going to walk with my club, either."

It was a good thing I'd decided to let Patrick do all the talking, because my jaw was too busy dropping to be good for anything else just then. It wasn't the only thing dropping, either; so did the penny, with a clang you could probably have heard halfway back to Reno.

Meanwhile, Paul was still talking. "...all clean money, totally legit. I can account for every cent. This is my royalty money. I never even see it. It goes into straight its own bank account. There's a paper trail on every dime of it. I haven't touched it since I set up my power of attorney, until this whole thing with the 707 changing hands came up."

He stopped to take a decent breath. His voice had sped up and jumped; this was something that mattered to him, bigtime. And I somehow didn't think it was about the money, either.

Patrick was keeping one wary eye on Lenore. "If I can interrupt for a moment, Paul, I just want to make sure I have this right. Basically, you're saying you have a verifiably legitimate income stream, handled and administered by a designated third party, through a power of attorney?"

"That's right." Lenore opened her mouth, but Paul glared her down. For some reason, he'd gone red. "And don't tell me to shut up about it, Lenore. There's nothing illegal about it, damn it! The way I set the power of attorney up, I can't touch a red cent of it until I get out of prison—I locked that part of the paperwork so tight, it's wearing stainless steel panties. I figured I was going to get out of here at some point, right? Those royalties are going to be pretty much all I've got, and I earned them. That money's clean, and it's mine."

"Okay." Patrick had shifted gears. I couldn't tell if the others saw it, but it was right there, that subtle change that hits him when he's gone into cop mode, or at least into the space where he's hunting something down. Everything, even the one word, was a giveaway: he'd gone somehow leaner, somehow more taut, physically and verbally.

"You mentioned not allowing Norfolk Lind to walk away with your money or your club. That seems to indicate that you found a legal way to use part of those royalties as a way to keep at least some percentage of the ownership of the 707, by fronting it to Lindyhop Productions. If your attorney okays it, I'd like to know how much money we're talking about—not just the one hundred thousand, but the account total."

"Sorry, I don't think I'm okaying that." Lenore had gone just as scary-professional as Patrick; the air in the room had gone so parky, I could feel the chill. "You're asking for information well

256

out of your purview, Mr. Ormand."

He raised an eyebrow at her; that "Mr. Ormand" had been pretty damned formal. "I don't see how. The auditors are going to find that information out for themselves, Counsellor. This is more than just a question of money—there's an arson homicide under investigation. Paul has just stated that he can provide a complete accounting for the legal provenance of his royalty account. So what's the problem?"

He paused just a moment; I got the feeling he was hunting for exactly the right words. I know Patrick well enough to get that when he's doing that, whatever he's going to say will probably have an extra meaning or two attached to it. And whatever it was, Lenore Tannenbaum seemed to get it, at least from the way she was watching him.

"I'm not in a position to make any promises, obviously." Yeah, he was picking every syllable, all right. "But providing Jan Gelman with information that might help her nail this thing down might be useful when Paul's next parole hearing comes up, especially if Paul's part in it was clean."

He turned his attention to Paul. "Jan Gelman's the arson investigator for San Rafael Fire and Police. As I say, I can't promise anything. If I could, this conversation would be going down a very different road. But it's your call."

Paul looked at his lawyer, and she looked right back at him. I got the feeling this was what they'd wanted to hear, because she gave a tiny nod. Paul turned back to Patrick.

"I don't have the exact figures, not the current ones. But I had a big bump in the last two royalty streams—three CDs I produced came out, and they're all doing well. Plus, I co-wrote five of the songs. The last time I got numbers, it was about a hundred and seventy thousand. That was before the hundred thousand I authorised to Star Woodley, for the 707 deal."

I was beginning to get twitchy. I got why Patrick was being

careful, but the clock was ticking and they were playing this dainty little game of *bullshit, bullshit, who's got the bullshit.* I wasn't in on the game, and I wasn't enjoying being passive, not anymore. I wanted to know what the hell was going on, and Patrick was taking his sweet time getting down to it.

"You authorised a hundred thousand dollars to be released to Star Woodley. Was there a proviso that those funds would be to retain your interest in the 707?"

Paul snorted, a nice rude noise. "Oh come on, man, don't make like you're that naive. Of course it wasn't. How could I demand a proviso? I've got my sorry ass parked in a cell for another three years minimum, unless the parole board decides I'm no longer a threat to law-abiding citizens or wealthy art collectors or whoever the fuck they think they're protecting. I'm not allowed to own a share in anything right now, remember? The last thing I needed was some asshole from Homeland Security faking up papers that 'proved' I'd stolen my own royalties. The money was for Star to put down as Lindyhop's share. She and I had an entirely different agreement, though. And just because that bastard Folkie Lind decided to kill her, that doesn't mean the deal is off. I provided that money, and either I get it back or I get a share worth that much in the 707."

He swivelled around in his chair, until he was looking at me. "You're the majority shareholder—Blacklight, I mean. I just want to let you know, I'm willing to fight this one out, with whatever I've got and whatever it takes. I never thought you guys wanted a piece of my club, and maybe I should have prepared for that. But you're a good guy, and Blacklight's a class bunch of people. I've worked with Mac Sharpe, and he's straight up. I have no problem being a junior shareholder to Blacklight. So you tell me this much: do you really want Folkie Lind as a partner, knowing he bought his way in with borrowed money and killed off his assistant to hide the loan?"

"That's a definitive accusation, Paul." Patrick's voice—crikey, yeah, no nice memories attached to that tone. For a bad moment, the years rolled back and I was sitting in NYPD Homicide Lieutenant Ormand's office in Manhattan, completely helpless and wondering if I'd done enough to keep Bree out of prison. "Do you have anything substantive to back up that statement?"

Paul snorted, about as rude a noise as I'd heard in a while. "Give me a fucking break, will you? You're not stupid, so don't play stupid, okay? If I had hard evidence, you really think I'd be wasting time talking to you? I'd have handed it to my esteemed counsel over there, and let her use it to bargain my ass the hell on out of here."

"No, I'm not stupid." Patrick needed to play poker. He'd have made a million without breaking a sweat. "If you don't have anything evidentiary to back up that accusation, what do you have? Because without evidence, it's an opinion and nothing more, and your opinion is worthless to both of us. What else have you got?"

"Do the damned math, *detective*." Something was twisting its way through Paul's voice, something vicious and violent, and my nerves were reacting, good and hard. This wasn't the urbane generous friend of the local music scene, this was a prisoner in a federal detention centre, someone who'd killed a man. He ticked points off on his fingers. "What burned? The club, the only witness to where the money actually came from, and all the paperwork. Who gains? Figure it out, Sherlock. One plus one. This isn't rocket science. No one else got anything out of it, and that little asshole Lind gets everything he wants: my money, my club. Well, I don't think so."

"Paul -"

He didn't even glance at her. "Shut up, Lenore. Don't even think about telling me to zip it. Fuck that. Folkie Lind killed her, and if either of you have half a brain up your ass, you already know it."

Patrick's voice was very quiet, very even. "You say the only person who could prove Lindyhop's share actually came from you was killed in the fire. I'm afraid that's a little unclear. Are you saying you'd assigned the power of attorney over your royalty account to Esther Woodley?"

"Are you nuts? Of course not. I ̶"

Paul stopped. I watched possibly the meanest, smuggest grin I've ever seen spread across his face.

"Well, what do you know about that?" He shook his head, mock-rueful. "Looks like I'm the one who needs a math tutor. One plus one equals proof of ownership. Me trust Star Woodley with that much power? Not a chance. Go talk to Jeff Kintera."

The ride back from Herlong to Reno was one the weirdest road trips I've ever taken. You'd have thought that, considering the nasty little stone Paul had dropped into the middle of the pool, we'd have been rabbiting about it non-stop, all the way back to the Bay Area.

Yeah, well, you'd have thought wrong. Patrick didn't say a word. I stayed quiet, wondering whether he planned to stop for food, maybe ask questions, but no. By the time we were halfway to Reno, Patrick driving the posted limit and obviously having to hold himself back from doing ninety, I'd already sussed he was going to head back and straight to Jeff Kintera. It was annoying; I'd had my own head-on with Lenore Tannenbaum on the way out, and I wanted to talk about it. But Patrick was silent.

I rang Bree from the Reno airport. She must have been surprised at getting me home before nine, but she met me at the gate. She watched Patrick climb into a taxi—he hadn't thought to ring Carla from Reno, and I hadn't bothered reminding him—and turned the Jag north on 101 before she said anything at all.

"So," she asked me, "how was prison? How's Paul doing? And did you find out what you wanted to know?"

I grinned at her. It was dark, and she had her eyes on the road, so she probably didn't see it. I was just so damned glad to be home. "Paul's doing better than he's got any business doing, considering his digs. That place is bleedin' awful—if I had to hang out there, I'd write myself off in about a week. And yeah, I got what I wanted. I got to ask it face to face, matter of fact. Your ex-lawyer decided she wanted to jam with us."

Her head jerked, and so did the Jaguar. "What!"

"Eyes on the road, please, lady. Yeah, Lenore Tannenbaum was there. Patrick wasn't too pleased about that, but it came in useful. We found out where Star got that money from. And Paul dropped a hell of a bombshell."

I gave her a fast recap. She listened, sorting it out in her head, piloting us up the highway and off onto city streets.

"So Paul had a side deal going with Star? And Jeff Kintera was—what? I don't know what to call that, John. The bagman?"

"Damned if I know—go-between, maybe. But yeah, basically, Star was acting for Paul and letting Folkie think she was acting for him." I thought about it for a moment. "That's if Paul's telling the truth. Could be total rubbish, every word. We won't know until someone gets the gen from Jeff Kintera, and maybe finds a way to verify it."

She pulled into the driveway, and waited for the garage doors to roll up. "So that's why Patrick looked like that. He really had that whole bloodthirsty cop thing dialled up to warp eleven, didn't he? I think I'm a little sorry for Jeff Kintera, John. I bet Patrick's on his way to find Jeff even as we speak."

"Yeah, well, better him than me. It's his job, love. Are we having dinner in, or do you want to send out...?"

A nice evening, that was; until we went upstairs for the night, we didn't talk about Herlong, not a word. We just sort of tacitly got there, our usual marital mind-reading thing. We ate the sautéed veggies and warm fresh bread Bree'd done us up for supper, I helped load the dishwasher, and we spent the next couple of hours relaxing in the front room, me with a guitar, playing a nice string of sixties hits: the Monkees song "I'm A Believer", things like that. I even managed to get her singing with me on a couple of tunes. She put some strength into the vocal for "What Becomes of the Broken-hearted." That surprised me; after all, that particular song was a hit when she was still in nappies. But she knew every word.

Later, curled up together under the duvet with the cats locked downstairs for the night, she finally brought it up.

"So what got Lenore Tannenbaum all the way to Herlong, John? What happened? Or shouldn't I ask?"

I was stroking Bree's hair. I love doing that, I love the feel of any part of her under my hands. And in a dark room, I can tell myself she's still a redhead, that my heart attack and the long months of recovery hadn't taken most of the colour out of her hair, and probably a few years off her life as well. Tonight, the tickybox was nice and steady and the MS was well in the background. After a day as stressy as the one I'd just done, I'd have expected all systems to be on standby for meltdown, but everything was mellow. She was waiting for an answer, though, and I was glad I had one to give her.

"As far as I could tell, Paul got her on the phone and demanded her. I didn't say much during that session, Bree—much better leaving the talking to Paul. He was dead set on talking, whether his lawyer wanted him to or not."

I swallowed a yawn. Relaxed as I was, I was also knackered, and no surprise; it had been a very long day. I wasn't done with the recap yet, though, and I knew it. Besides, I was actually looking forward to telling Bree about it.

That two minutes of conversation with Lenore Tannenbaum had been the only part of the meeting where I hadn't felt like a bystander, or a court reporter taking notes, or something. Patrick was done; whatever else he'd planned on asking, whatever else had got trashed just by Paul having his lawyer along, the info about Jeff Kintera had given him what he needed. As far as Patrick was concerned, his day was finished.

So he'd got up to go, shake hands, thanks ever so, time to roll, but I stopped it. *Half a minute*, I'd told him, and turned to Lenore.

We'd locked up, eye to eye. This was between me and her. It was nothing to do with Patrick or with Paul, either.

"I've got a question for you, Counsellor."

She raised her brows, waiting. We were both standing, and I don't often have a height advantage, but I did just then. And yeah, if she was supposed to have the advantage because of where we were, she wasn't getting it from me. I was remembering Bree, looking lost, wondering why she'd been casually jettisoned as Lenore's client without a word of explanation, wondering if this woman actually thought her capable of burning someone to death. I stood there, looking down, getting more narked as I remembered it, and I'm damned if she didn't prompt me.

"A question, you said?"

Ah, sod it. Might as well let it rip.

"Yeah." I'd nearly jumped at the sound of my own voice, black ice and total disgust. "I want to know who the fuck you think you are. I want to know where you get off, taking my wife's money and her trust and her information, and then dumping her as a client without a word. Was it all about this? Conflict of interest, because you sussed out Paul had something on? Mind you, speaking just for myself, I don't actually give a rat's arse. But if that's something that would pass an ethics review board, or whatever handles that kind of thing, no wonder there are so many rude lawyer jokes out there. Don't expect me to recommend you to anyone wanting good legal representation, counsellor. Take someone's money, leave them dangling, fuck you very much? That's how you do business? You really are a piece of work, you know?"

She turned the colour of Bree's best pasta sauce. So, yeah, I'd finally got out of the bystander's chair and into the action, and I got her to blush.

"I'm sorry." She had a hard grip on it, but she knew she was bright red and she didn't like giving away that much control. "I really had no intention of upsetting Mrs. Kinkaid. But ethically, I couldn't continue as her attorney. That was clear after Paul called me—I'm still his attorney of record and his insistence on sharing his information about the 707's funding constituted a clear conflict of interest. But I should have at least explained that much. I just hadn't realised that your wife was so—sensitive."

"Then you're not very bright, are you? Not very observant either." Gordon *Bennett*, the snap felt good; I'd actually made her flinch. I hadn't known just how narked at her I really was. "But yeah, that answers my question. I'll let her know it was you fucking up, not her. Paul, nice to see you. Glad you're looking so fit. Patrick? How do we get our gear back and get out of here...?"

Now, hours later, Bree reached out a hand and laid it against my cheek. Nice warm bedroom, nice quiet night, just the two of us, shutting the world out. Telling her all about it had felt damned good. "Wow. You really bitchslapped her that hard?"

"Damned right I did. I wasn't planning to, Bree—that's just the way it came out. Didn't know I was that pissed off."

She watched me. I twirled a strand of her hair round my finger. "She was telling the truth. She really didn't drop you because she thought you were guilty and she didn't want to be saddled with a whackjob arsonist for a client. She dropped you because the picture with Paul and the 707 was muddled. Are you okay with that, love? Now that you know why?"

She nodded. "I am. Thank you, John. It was just—I can't even wrap my head around someone setting a fire like that. The idea

264

that anyone would think I could do that...but she doesn't, and if Patrick is right, Jan Gelman doesn't either. So I can sleep easier."

"Good. Then give me a proper goodnight kiss, and let's get some kip."

If I'd been asked to lay odds on being woken up by my damned cell phone three days running, I'd have passed on the bet. But that's just what happened: eight in the morning, fathoms deep, and there was "Remember Me" playing in my ear on one side and Bree jerking herself out of bed on the other, snarling something unprintable.

"What the fuck...?" I wasn't bothering with politesse or good manners or whatever. I couldn't even get my eyes focussed to see who I was about to snarl at. "Who...?"

"JP? Oh shit, I woke you again. Sorry. It's Carla. Listen, I have a situation and I need help."

That woke me up. Bree, third day running, had already hit the loo and come out with my pills and some fresh water. "You need what, now? No, wait, right, half a mo, I need my meds. Okay— now, what? You need help from me? You serious?"

"Completely." She didn't sound rattled, but she didn't sound happy, either. "Actually, it's a big favour, and I really ought to be asking Bree. Let me explain..."

She did. Bree nodded towards the bedroom door—*can I get some coffee started or should I stay?* I patted the bed—*stay, I think I need you here*—and she sat back down, waiting as I listened to Carla lay out what was going on and what she wanted from us. By the time she was done, I got why she wanted it. I told Carla to hang on, and hit the mute button.

"Carla's begging a favour. Emergency off-the-record meeting of the 707 braintrust, so that Jeff Kintera can explain what in hell he's been up to for the past five years. Patrick wants to get the whole thing out on the table, and he wants home court advantage."

"So he wants to do it here?" Just for a moment, she looked exhausted. "Damn. No, it's okay, I can see why. When does she want to do it? Please tell me she hasn't already taken it for granted we'd say yes and told everyone to be here by nine, because if she has, I'm going to miss the meeting. I'm going to be LA, looking for a place to buy a gun."

I grinned. "Almost sorry I had the mute on for that one, love. But no, she said whatever time's good for us, so long as it's today and earlier is better. What works? You want to call this a lunchtime thing, or take it later...?"

We ended up telling Carla to get everyone round our place at three. That way, Bree didn't have to feed them anything beyond coffee and a tray of snacks. Not that she minded, but I did; I was getting pretty damned tired of everyone using 2828 Clay Street as their personal hospitality suite. And I made sure Carla did all the phone work, getting people here.

The lineup at our dining room table was slightly different from the last meeting Bree'd hosted. Heather Speirs sent her regrets, she was in Oregon, and could we send her the minutes? Andy Valdon wasn't there either. Katia actually came without Tony, mumbling something about a headache; she was in a peculiar mood, and I hoped they hadn't had a row. And of course, there was no Star Woodley insulting the other guests, sneaking off to rummage through other peoples' medicine cupboards, not letting her eyes settle on anything.

Jeff Kintera got there first, and he was nervous. I didn't know whether he knew that Paul had dished, or if he even knew why he'd been asked. But he was edgy, cautious, as if he thought he was about to get the sack from his job, or something.

And Bree, for a change, wasn't much help; she wasn't doing her usual "all my guests are kings and queens and I must pamper and cosset them" thing, not that day. She welcomed him in and steered him toward the dining room, made sure he got himself a

266

cup of coffee, and headed back into the kitchen. I noticed she had one of her notebooks open on the kitchen counter, so maybe she'd been trying to get work done on her mysterious project while she was making sandwiches.

By the time everyone else arrived, though, she'd finished up whatever it was and settled herself at the table. Patrick had had a quiet word with Bree, got her approval for what he wanted to do, and seated himself directly across the table from Jeff. The rest of us sat back and waited. By this time, I really was wondering if anyone but me, Bree and Patrick knew what was going on.

"Thanks for coming, everyone." Patrick wasn't wasting time. His eyes were aimed straight at Jeff, and Jeff was stonefaced. "We asked for this meeting because JP and I spent yesterday afternoon in Lassen County, talking with Paul Morgenstern and his lawyer at Herlong Prison. He gave us a vital piece of information regarding the recent funding of Lindyhop's share of the 707. That was with his lawyer's approval."

I was watching Jeff's face, and so was Bree, next to me. So I caught the look of panic when Patrick mentioned Lenore, and I saw Jeff clamp down good and hard. If he hadn't known before why he'd been asked to an ownership meeting, he did now.

"You went to see Paul Morgenstern? What the hell would you want to visit that dickhead for? He doesn't have a damned thing to do with the 707 anymore."

Shit. Folkie Lind not only hadn't known, he still didn't. I remembered the first meeting, thinking Lind was going to lose it and go for Luke, and I caught Dom's eye. She nodded; she'd already sussed that Folkie wanted watching. I let my breath out and under the table, Bree squeezed my hand.

Patrick wasn't breaking the eye lock with Jeff. "Actually, he does. That hundred thousand dollars raised by Esther Woodley for Lindyhop's ownership participation was a loan from a legitimate funding source owned solely by Paul Morgenstern. The legality of the funds has been verified. Star Woodley wasn't representing Lindyhop, Mr Lind. She was given the money, and accepted it, on behalf of a continuing ownership stake for Paul Morgenstern."

"But he's in jail!" Folkie was on his feet, a pulse slamming away over one eye. His face a really unhealthy colour. "That motherfucker can't own a damned thing! You just sit there saying Star backstabbed me, and expect me to believe -"

"Dude. Sit the hell down and chill. I said, *sit down.*"

I jumped a mile. I hadn't seen Dom move, but there she was, with one hand on Folkie's arm. It didn't look as if she was doing a damned thing, but Lind made a noise and sat, hard and fast. He sat there, rubbing the arm and looking stunned. Patrick gave it a moment, and picked up right where he'd left off. He didn't sound like a detective, suddenly. He sounded like a cop.

"Based on what Morgenstern told us, I spent this morning fact-checking. He told us that he'd handed a discretionary power of attorney over his royalty accounts to you, Mr. Kintera. Is that accurate? I'd like your confirmation, please."

You could have cut the quiet in our dining room with one of Bree's pricey chef's knives, it was that dense. We were all watching Jeff Kintera, except Dom—she seemed to be hoping Folkie Lind would get up to something and give her an excuse for a workout. But Lind wasn't moving. He was staring at Jeff Kintera, just like the rest of us.

"That's right." Oh, bloody hell, another damned poker player. "It's an unpaid position, as a favour to my boss. There's nothing remotely illegal about it."

"In that case, you shouldn't mind answering a few questions about it." Patrick had taken note of that choice of words, *my boss.* "Did you in fact provide Esther Woodley with Lindyhop's purchase money for the 707?"

"Yes, I did." No hesitation at all. He'd gone very formal, suddenly. "At Mr. Morgenstern's instruction. It's not a loan, it's a grant with specific terms attached to it. It stipulates that the ownership share reverts entirely to Mr. Morgenstern within ninety days of his release from prison, whenever that happens. I have the paperwork, signed and notarised."

"Bullshit." Lind was up, fists balled up, shouting at the top his voice. "That's total bullshit! You're a goddamned liar! Star wouldn't do that. There's no way Star would do that to me!"

"I'm sorry." Jeff looked away from Patrick, finally, and it hit me: he wasn't offering up convention. He knew he'd just handed Folkie Lind a gut punch and he really was sorry for the bloke. "I have all the documentation. I'd be happy to show it to you, once the auditors are done with it."

"Why?" Lind was whispering. Bree had my hand under the table, and she was holding on for dear life. She'd seen it too: Gut punch wasn't nearly strong enough a word for what I could see on his face. Not sure there's a word to cover that level of betrayal. "Why would she do that to me? Twenty years we worked together, and she turned around and did that? I don't understand."

"She liked power." Bree sounded sad, almost remote, but she still had my hand. I felt one fingertip rub against my wedding ring. "She liked secrets. I'm sorry she hurt you, sorry she stabbed you in the back, but I'm not surprised. She was—I don't know. Missing a piece, something human. She just never could do anything because it was the right thing to do. It had to add to her somehow. It had to feed into her whole 'do they know who I am, do they know what I can do' thing. She was willing to let me go to jail for it. I'm sorry, Folkie. It's what she was."

He opened his mouth. I've got no idea what he was going to say or do, because Patrick's cell phone, tucked safely into his pocket, suddenly went off.

"Excuse me—I have to take this," he said, and flipped the phone open. "Patrick Ormand."

I heard a voice, small and tinny. Patrick listened for about two solid minutes, keeping quiet, taking it in. When the tinny quack finally stopped, he finally spoke up.

"Okay. Thanks, Jan. Yes, I'll let everyone here know. You'll be calling the appropriate people? Good. Thanks for letting me know."

He clicked the phone off, and looked around the table. No one was saying anything. I was holding Bree's hand, and she was holding her breath.

"That was Jan Gelman in San Rafael. They've completed the investigation into the 707 fire."

He stopped, looking around the room. I wondered what he was waiting for: just effect, maybe, or some remnant of having been a homicide cop. Old habits die hard, but when he got that no one was going to prompt him, he dished.

"Esther Woodley's death has been ruled misadventure."

For the better part of a minute, no one said a word. We were all too busy gawking at him. Mac was the first person to get his voice back.

"Misadventure? What in hell? Are you saying that fire wasn't deliberately set? Because, bollocks to that, Patrick. That damned thing went too fast and burned too hot not to have had some help."

Patrick was already reaching for his jacket. "No, I'm not saying that, and neither was Jan. What she said was that, from how fast the fire hit flashpoint, they've concluded that it was intended to be a small contained blaze that got out of hand, and took who-ever set it unawares."

"Oh, for fuck's sake!"

I jerked my head around. Folkie Lind looked like he was about to have a stroke, and his voice sounded like someone was feeding it through a phase shifter, it was so high up his normal register. The words were pouring out. I had the feeling he'd be saying them to himself, for a long time to come.

"That's what she was doing up there, wasn't it? She was trying to burn the papers, trying to hide it. That stupid bitch! I saw her upstairs, did I tell you that? I went up to use the owner's john and she was just heading into the upstairs office. She couldn't shut the door behind her fast enough. Stupid, stupid, stupid!"

Patrick shrugged his jacket on. "Is that what you were doing up there? I saw you come down. Jan Gelman asked me who'd been doing what, and where, within a few minutes of the first alarm. I was able to situate some key people for her, but I didn't see Esther Woodley, and I wondered why. That was just a few minutes before the flames hit the upstairs railings."

Mac was shaking his head. I couldn't tell whether he was more gobsmacked or disgusted by the incompetence. "So the arson was supposed to be—what? A small fire in a trash bin, or something? What did she do, shove her copies of the paperwork into a pile, sneak a tin of Bree's chafing dish fuel upstairs, and douse the lot with it? What in hell happened, Patrick? What sent the fire out of control? Are you seriously saying the club burned because Star Woodley was clumsy?"

"There's no way to know, not now. But it's a reasonable assumption, Mac—clumsiness, incompetence, maybe pure bad luck. I doubt she realised the smell of paint was anything more than just a smell—she probably didn't know the fumes were highly flammable. It must have hit flashpoint very fast, and Mr. Lind just told us she had the door shut. Enclosed space, volatile mixture of accelerants—it would have engulfed her before she could do a damned thing to stop it. She probably never knew what hit her."

Epilogue

For immediate release, from the desk of Carla Fanucci:

On behalf of Luke and Karen Hedley, and the entire Blacklight family, we're delighted to confirm that Solange Hedley and Curtis Lind, founder and frontman for Grammy winners Mad At Our Dads, were married in a private civil ceremony in San Francisco.

The bride wore a vintage Zandra Rhodes dress that belonged her late mother. A reception is planned for early next year, when the groom's band will have finished their upcoming festival circuit tour, and the bride will be on break from her classes at the San Francisco Chefs Academy. A second reception will be held in the UK. No firm date has been set for either party. Details and photos of the ceremony will follow as we receive them.

In other news, Fluorescent Records has announced the signing of the Fog City Geezers to an open-ended recording contract. In an un-

usual move, Geezers founder and frontman JP Kinkaid has chosen to record a live show for the band's first CD release. A West Coast tour, starting in Northern California and finishing in Southern California, is scheduled for October and November.

In closing, I have an update on the progress of the rebuilding of the 707 Club. The work is proceeding on schedule for a January reopening. The new club will boast a significantly expanded FOH capacity and a state of the art PA....

I don't know much about weddings, but I've heard brides are supposed to look nervous or wistful or jubilant, or whatever. I couldn't have told you what Solange was thinking or feeling that day—I was too unnerved. She looked so completely like her mum that 2828 Clay Street felt haunted: Viv had never even seen our house, but that day, it was *deja vu* for Luke's lost love.

It had got to him, I could tell. The last time he'd seen that Zandra Rhodes number on anyone, he'd been slipping a ring on Viv's left hand. Solange had asked Luke to please send Viv's wedding dress; she had a lot of her mum's gear in her own closet.

Of course he'd done it. He'd actually packed it and brought it on the plane with him. But there must have been a lump at the back of his throat, because he wasn't talking much.

Mac wasn't immune to it, either. Leaving Dom out of it, Viv had probably been the closest he'd ever had to a pure female friend. He had his own face in order—Mac knows how to do a public mask—but not perfect control. He was seeing ghosts.

Bree might have been the calmest of the lot of us, except for Domitra. That was surprising, considering she'd had less than a week to pull this together; I'd have expected her to have gone her usual melt-down perfectionist route. Besides, there was press outside, and her feelings about the *paparazzi* aren't what you'd call warm and fuzzy, you know? No hope of invisibility there, not with half Blacklight wandering up the front steps dressed like a flock of penguins, and the next generation of rock royalty making it official in our front room. But she was nice and mellow.

"Curt, that's a nice tux." She'd stopped in the hallway with a tray of champagne flutes. "Very elegant."

"Thanks." Curt reached out and got Solange's hand, and lifted it to his lips. "You know what? It just occurred to me, I'm possibly the luckiest human male on the face of the planet right now. Wow. I know, I know, *non sequitur*. But it's true."

I lifted an eyebrow at Bree—*not as lucky as I am, mate*—and she smiled and ducked her head; she'd caught at my thought. I found myself wondering if Curt and Solange would develop that marital mindreading trick. I'd have bet Luke and Karen already had it, and in a weird way—after all, they're not a married couple—I know Mac and Dom do.

Karen wasn't calm at all. She was a bit emotional, wanting to cling to Luke's hand. Maybe she was missing Suzanne, who was hitting the stage with Bergen Sandoval in Toronto, and had rung up to squeal at her stepsister. Or maybe Karen just got weepy at weddings. After all, it's not as if Solange is her kid.

Solange had been hanging in the front room pretty much since she and her parents had got here. She kept glancing towards the door. I couldn't imagine what she was waiting for; I'd thought at first she was afraid the judge Patrick had got to perform the ceremony wasn't going to show, but he'd shown up half an hour ago, and Solange was still jerking her head towards the door, waiting for something. Bree's interchange with Curt got the bride's attention back where the groom obviously thought it belonged, which was on him.

"Doesn't he look hot?" She gave his tux the once-over. "Maybe someday he'll look really distinguished in his, the way you all look in yours."

She looked around at us, dad and godfather and uncles. I always think of weddings as excuses for the women to get all done up, break out the diamonds and the fancy gear and all that, but we seemed to have broken the rule on that one. The women had dressed down for this do, letting Solange shine, but the blokes, nearly all of us, were in tuxes.

Things had been busy since Patrick had handed down the official verdict on the 707 fire. I'd got the Geezers signed to the Fluorescent deal, and poor Bree'd had to cope with yet another meeting round her dining room table, as we thrashed out what we wanted for the first CD. Carla'd got the okay from Curt's label for him sit in with us in Seattle, so that we could record a live version of "Americaland"; Mad At Our Dads was playing Vancouver the night before Seattle. Damned lucky, too, because we all felt the CD wasn't going to be complete without that cut. It had "massive airplay, big hit" written all over it.

We'd come to a consensus about how to sort out the 707 ownership mess. Since the money had legitimately come from Paul, Folkie Lind was going to have to either come up with his own stake money and pay Paul back what Star had taken, or else find the money and accept Paul as a fellow minority shareholder when Paul got out of prison. It was a sensible solution, but unless both Folkie and Paul went for it, it was nothing but talk. We hadn't had a chance to talk to either of them about it, not yet. Too much happening, you know?

Jeff Kintera keeping his job had looked to be another muddy issue, but that one sorted itself out. Mac pointed out that the only thing Jeff was guilty of was loyalty, and why should that get him the sack, when he hadn't done a damned thing wrong? Tony had backed him up, and the more I thought about it, the more I realised they were dead right. After all, Jeff had been hired by Paul, kept on by Paul, trusted by Paul, and treated right by Paul. Loyalty wasn't a crime. Hell, it wasn't even a fault.

So Jeff stayed on as club manager. Folkie Lind might have disagreed with that decision, but he wasn't getting a vote, not until we sorted out whether he actually had a stake in the club or not.

Business took a back seat when Solange rang up to ask us for a huge thumping favour: she and Curt had set a date, her dad and Karen were flying in for it, and please would we let them have the ceremony at 2828 Clay? Because, she told us, our house was where she'd come to feel most at home, and City Hall would be an absolute circus and anyway they had a six guest limit and she and Curt wanted a few more than that, and...

Of course Bree had made a few happy noises, grabbed the reins, and run with it. She'd had just enough sense through the euphoria of watching our band baby get married to get Carla in on it. Carla had done the math and the guest list work with both Solange's guests and the rest of Mad At Our Dads, which meant all Bree had to do was cook and do her gracious hostess number. Patrick was there as both guest and security, which had to feel weird; he'd come up with a retired judge to act as officiant.

I checked my watch. The email invites had listed the ceremony at half past three, and it was twenty-five past. We'd opened up the front of the house by pushing the pocket doors into the walls, and turned the front room-parlour-dining room into one very good-sized party area. The judge was setting himself up with his back to the big bay windows, and the guests were making their way in that general direction. I was doing a quick head-count, and about to join Bree in the front room, when the doorbell rang. I couldn't imagine who it was; everyone on the guest list except Suzanne was present and accounted for.

"Uncle John?" Solange had slipped out into the hall. "I'm expecting one more person. Can we let him in?"

You're probably thinking I'm dim, and yeah, I probably should have known. If I'd remembered Bree's advice to Solange about hiding things and family and checking with Curt, finding Folkie Lind on the doorstep one more time shouldn't have come as much of a surprise, you know? But it did. He was dressed for the

276

occasion, too. That put me off, since I'd never seen the bloke in anything that wasn't casual. I was still gathering my wits while Solange was edging past me and letting him in.

"I'm glad you made it—we're about to begin."

She sounded pleasant enough, but I suddenly realised something: I'd never heard her call her about to be father-in-law anything at all, not "Folkie" or "Mr. Lind" or anything else, and she still wasn't. I had no clue how she thought of him. For all I know, she had him pegged in her head as "Grumpy" or "that ass."

"Thank you for inviting me. That was very kind."

There was something different about him, beyond the formal gear; something in his attitude was different, but I couldn't place what it was. He nodded at me, and slipped to the back of the room, and I headed off towards Bree, standing behind Luke's shoulder, with Tony and Katia at her other side.

"*Friends, loved ones, family of Solange Vivienne Hedley and Curtis James Lind, we are together here today…*"

The ceremony was simple, and quick. I'd have had no problem coping with whatever they'd wanted to do, writing their own vows and all that, but they surprised me. There were no long cringe-making lectures about the meaning of love, no extras, no frills, just a few lines, a promise exchanged between them, and bob's your uncle, show over, time to hit the catering. The judge pronounced and Curt leaned over to kiss his wife; his glasses slid down on his nose, and I saw Solange's left hand, now sporting a plain platinum band, go up to touch his hair. The gesture was so intimate and so tender, I felt like a damned peeping tom for a moment.

"Wow." Bree's eyes were damp, and she was keeping her voice down. "How cool was that? They just sort of knew, didn't they?"

I slipped an arm round her waist. The guests had headed for the buffet. I wasn't up for talking, myself, but it wasn't just sentiment—I was keeping one eye on Folkie Lind.

He'd been hanging at the back during the ceremony. It was

277

obvious to me that Curt either hadn't known his dad would be there, or didn't much care. I found myself hoping Solange hadn't got Folkie out there without a word to Curt. That sort of surprise is a piss-poor way to start things off.

But if there was any tension, it wasn't showing itself. Curt was shaking hands with people and looking like a bloke who can't believe his luck, and Folkie was watching me. Not that I was aware of it, until Bree laid a hand on my arm. I glanced up and there was Folkie, heading straight for me.

He stopped in front of me. It was very weird—he hadn't done anything at all to get anyone's notice, but the place went quiet. He knew it, too, because he pitched his voice to carry.

"I just wanted to come by and congratulate my son and his wife." He wasn't looking behind him, or anywhere but straight at me. "But I also wanted to tell you that I've been thinking it over, and I decided something. I'm out of the 707 deal. I don't want any part of it. Paul Morgenstern can have his share—hell, he went to enough trouble bribing Star to stab me in the back with that money, might as well give him what he wants. I never want to see that damned club again."

I opened my mouth to say something, God knows what, but he'd already turned his back. It wasn't a snub; he was looking for his son. There was something in his voice that hadn't been there a minute ago.

"Congratulations, you two. I hope you're very happy. Here's a piece of advice, and take it or not, Curt, it's totally up to you: try being a little more there for your wife than I was for your mother. Take care of yourselves. Take care of each other."

He turned on his heel. Before I could get a word out, he was out the door, down the front stairs, and gone.

The day after the wedding, Mac and Luke headed back to the UK with Dom and Karen in tow, and we finally got the house to ourselves. It felt like the first time in weeks Bree and I'd been alone together, and I'll be buggered if she didn't feed me breakfast, give me a fast kiss, mutter something about an appointment, and head for the car.

I'd probably have been more narked about that, if I hadn't actually wanted to do something without her home anyway. I waited until I heard the Jag's engine fade out, and then I got my cell phone out of my pocket. I was trying to remember how to change the settings.

Most people I know change their phone settings constantly, but I'd had mine set the same way for the best part of six months, and it took some serious fumbling with the options tree before I got to where I wanted. By the time I got there, I was muttering under my breath: *recorded announcement, no, screen saver, oh bloody hell where is it....*

Ringtones. Right. I scrolled down the list: quite a few Blacklight tunes in there. I had a bad moment, trying to remember if I'd ever downloaded the one I wanted, and yeah, there it was, right down at the bottom. I hit the play button, making sure it worked.

One good deep breath, a single click, and I had a new ringtone. I'd had "Remember Me" on there a good long time, but I was about to hit the stage and the road again, and it was time for a change.

When Bree got back a couple of hours later, I was down in the studio. The MS was laying all the way back, and the tickybox was doing its thing. It seemed to be one of those days, when I felt well enough to almost forget that I was sick. With the Geezers gearing up for even a short tour, I wanted my fingers ready to rock and roll, you know? It had been a few years since we'd left the Bay Area, and that first tour, we'd done purely covers, no original material. That was going to change, as well. I refused to believe the magic in the air when we'd written "Americaland" was a one-shot deal. There were more songs going to happen...

"John…?"

I'd been bent over the neck of one of my chambered Pauls, playing more with a tone than with a riff, and I hadn't heard the studio door open. Bree had put her head round the door, and I looked up, and went nice and stiff.

"John?" She was nervous as hell. "Do you like it?"

Her hair wasn't quite the same as it had been, before the long months after Wembley; there's nothing in a bottle anywhere that was going to put the rich dark auburn back there, not the way it used to be. She'd gone for a deep brown with a lot of red in it instead, and had it trimmed and styled. It had gone from halfway down her back to just below her shoulders.

"Please say something." Shit. I'd gawked a bit too long, and her shoulders had bouldered up. "Oh God, I knew it, you hate it, I thought you wanted me to…"

"Oi! Bree!" I was up on my feet, setting the Paul down, gathering her in, getting my hands in her hair. She looked—I don't know. Younger, less tired, maybe less beaten down. Not sure why a bit of colour in her hair would have that effect, but it did. "Hate it? You joking? You look bloody wonderful."

She let her breath out. "Really? You aren't just being nice? Because I wanted to get this done for awhile, but I wasn't sure you'd be okay with it. And it couldn't wait anymore."

That got my attention. "Okay, why couldn't it wait? You want to go red for the Geezers tour? Why are you looking so guilty, Bree?"

"Well…." She had the oddest look on her face. "You know I've been working on something for a while -"

"Your little notebooks? Yeah, I noticed. Come on, love, just dish. What's going on?"

"I wrote a book."

I let go of her. Wasn't planning to, mind you—I just needed a good look at her face. "A book?"

"A cookbook." All of a sudden, she was focused and fierce. "I'd wanted to put one together just for myself, recipes I can use cooking for us. But then Solange talked about wanting to open a specialised restaurant, remember? And when she broke down because of Curt, and cooking without salt—it got me thinking. I'm not the only one out there cooking for a family where the members have different health issues, John. There's a need. Solange was right about it being too common. And the older generation, our generation—there are a lot of us, and the health issues get broader and more complex."

"True." Crikey, she was turning me on, being so fierce. "So you wrote a cookbook to deal with it? That's what all those little notebooks were in aid of?"

"A cookbook, and a proposal. Solange helped me research some of the recipes. And good lord, John, I learned a *lot*. At least neither of us has any anaphylactic allergies. Anyway, Carla found me a really good agent who handles books like that. I gave him the proposal and we had a few conversations about it, and, well…"

Both my eyebrows were as high as they would go. "And…?"

"He has two publishers who want it. He said something about an auction." She tossed her head. She was just trying to pop the vertebrae in her neck, but her hair must have been a bit lighter than it was before the trim, because it was moving quite a lot, and a strand of it brushed against me, soft and silky and with colour in. I got one hand behind her, resting there, rubbing…

"I'm just hoping they aren't interested because they think I'll go on talk shows and be some rocker's wife author wannabe." Her own eyes were going greener and greener; I wasn't the only one turned on around here. "Not going to happen."

"Good." I had her by the hand. Studio lights off, door closed, set the house alarm, up the stairs. "Right. Upstairs?"

"Yes, please!"

Books, music, family, health: for half an hour, none of it mattered. It was just me and Bree in the bedroom, me taking her places, tasting her sweet and salty, running my fingers through her hair, her doing what she's done from that first time together: kicking the world to the curb. Outside, the fog started its evening movement, rolling in off the Golden Gate, muffling the city. Maybe later, if we were up for it, we'd drive down to the Beach and have a nice walk along the Great Highway, watching the stars poke through the marine layer, and the waves rolling in…

"Mmmmm." Her eyes were still a bit out of focus, but she was coming back. I'd stayed where I was, letting her take my weight; she had her arms wrapped around me, but they felt relaxed. "John, how would you feel about a walk later? Maybe down by the beach?"

I looked down at my wife. There was plenty of light in the room, and she tilted her head against the pillow, seeing me smile. "John? Did I say something funny…?"

"A bit, yeah." I kissed her. "You must have read my mind."

JP Kinkaid

Photo by Nic Grabien

Deborah Grabien can claim a long personal acquaintance with the fleshpots—and quiet little towns—of Europe. She has lived and worked and hung out, from London to Geneva to Paris to Florence, with a few stops in between.

But home is where the heart is. Since her first look at the Bay Area, as a teenager during the peak of the City's Haight-Ashbury years, she's always come home to San Francisco, and in 1981, after spending some years in Europe, she came back to Northern California to stay.

Deborah was involved in the Bay Area music scene from the end of the Haight-Ashbury heyday until the mid-1970s. Her friends have been trying to get her to write about those years—fictionalised, of course!—and, now that she's comfortable with it, she's doing just that. After publishing four novels between 1989 and 1993, she took a decade away from writing, to really learn how to cook. That done, she picked up where she'd left off, seeing the publication of eleven novels between 2003 and 2010.

Deborah and her husband, San Francisco bassist Nicholas Grabien, share a passion for rescuing cats and finding them homes, and are both active members of local feral cat rescue organisations. Deborah has a grown daughter, Joanna, who lives in LA.

These days, in between cat rescues and cookery, Deborah can generally be found listening to music, playing music on one of eleven guitars, hanging out with her musician friends, or writing fiction that deals with music, insofar as multiple sclerosis—she was diagnosed in 2002—will allow.

Visit her website at www.deborahgrabien.com

CPSIA information can be obtained at www.ICGtesting.com
Printed in the USA
BVOW03s1328230414

351463BV00002B/200/P